PRAISE FOR AT]

The Seer's Daughter

"...the perfect culmination of paranormal mystery with steamy and sensual romance and just enough suspense and intrigue to guarantee a chilling, goose bump-invoking, story line... *The Seer's Daughter* would be a brilliant option for adaption to screen—there's a television series/movie in here for absolute certain."
—*AusRom Today*

"...as chilling as it is sexy... This is much more than a romance. The paranormal aspects along with the secondary characters really make the story. The descriptions, language, emotions, dialogue... are all cleverly written to keep you engaged and the pages turning, while the suspense will make sure you read this story with all the lights on."
—5-star Top Pick, *The Romance Reviews*

"If you are looking for a book to give you goose bumps and keep you watching over your shoulder, then I can recommend this one! ... I got dragged away from this book late in the evening by my husband, as I had an exceedingly early start the next day. This didn't stop me from thinking about the book and what I had read for well over an hour after the lights went out, as well as dreaming about it!"
—Archaeolibrarian, 5 stars, Amazon review

"I love paranormal books, especially when there's romance thrown in, and this... will send a chill up your spine, raise the hairs on your neck, and make you tremble with emotions. What a rush! One of my most favorite reads this year! ... It's almost like Stephen King meets Christina Dodd... I loved it; can't wait for book two!"—5 stars, Amazon review

"...a perfect blend of paranormal fiction and romantic suspense that had me completely captivated to the very last page... flawlessly delivered."
—Faridah, 5 stars, *Readers Favorite*

"One of the best ghost/demon stories I have read in a while! It had romance, witches, demons, AND ghosts! Absolutely loved it!"—5 stars, Amazon review

The Alchemist's Son

"...go the hell out and buy both of these books now because they are freaking FANTASTIC. I am not exaggerating when I say this is some of the

best romantic suspense I have ever read, paranormal or otherwise; I literally couldn't put down *The Alchemist's Son* until I got to the final, thrilling climax."
—5 stars, Amazon review

"I could not put the book down. It has so many twists and turns that keep you turning one page after another."—5 stars, Amazon review

"This book is as good as the first, with twists and turns! You get the good ol' creepy feels! You may be wanting to look behind you, or not go in your attic or basement anytime soon! I wish this author could write as fast as I can read; I would never put her books down!"—5 stars, Amazon review

"Kept me on the edge of my seat. Several scenes I was holding my breath reading what was happening next...."—5 stars, Amazon review

"If you love paranormal, romance, suspense and spine-tingling books, you'll love this!"—5 stars, Amazon review

"This book had my hair standing on end and gave me chills from start to finish. Once again I could not put it down, and loved how, no matter how hard I tried, I just couldn't guess ahead what was going to happen next."
—5 stars, Amazon review

Desperate

"What can I say other than I absolutely loved this book from the start, and the prologue really set the pace for a fast-paced plot with lots of suspense and the right touch of romance. The plot was strong and progressed well and I loved the flirty banter between Eric and Ivy, which added to the growing relationship between the pair and provided a few good sex scenes illustrating their intense chemistry... the author has done an amazing job of penning this novel and I can't wait to read more of their work in the future."
—*The Romance Studio* (TRS), 4 stars

"Suspense and steamy romance line the pages of this fast-paced thriller, with action and drama from start to finish.... If Athena Daniels keeps it up with writing like this, I have no doubts that she will establish her place amongst the most well-known authors of erotic literature.... If you're a fan of romantic thrillers, I would definitely recommend giving this one a read."
—Official Review, *Online Book Club*, 4 out of 4 stars

ALSO BY ATHENA DANIELS

Desperate Series

Desperate (Book One)

Beyond the Grave Series

The Seer's Daughter (Book One)

The Alchemist's Son (Book Two)

Girl Unseen (Book Three)

THE ALCHEMIST'S SON

BEYOND THE GRAVE
BOOK 2

ATHENA DANIELS

Sunset Coast Publishing

*For everyone who believes love survives
beyond the grave.*

ACKNOWLEDGMENTS

My deepest gratitude and thanks once again, to Dana Delamar, my editor, my mentor. Thank you for your advice, guidance, patience, and countless hours you have put into the story to turn it into what it is today. You have made this journey far less scary and so much fun!

Thanks and appreciation to Leah Frost and Laura Dawn, my fabulous beta-readers, for pulling through on crazy-short notice and for your insightful feedback and catches.

Love, always and forever, to my sister Leah for so many things, but most of all, for believing in me.

Unconditional love to my family: my husband, Ali, and my boys. Thank you for your support, understanding, and encouragement.

And last, but not least, I would like to thank my online friends and each and every one of my readers. Your encouragement and enthusiasm for the series has allowed me to continue to write. For this, I will be eternally grateful.

Chapter One

Monday
Six Days Before the Blood Moon

Cryton, South Australia

S top!" Sage Matthews demanded, bounding down the narrow staircase at the back of Beyond the Grave, her late grandmother's shop. "What the hell do you think you're doing?"

Sage confronted two burly men hefting her grandmother's boxes into their arms. The front door had been propped open with a beer carton, and Sage could see through the shop-front windows that a large moving van was parked outside, ramp extended from an open rear door.

"You Sage Matthews?" Burly Guy One set down his box, wiped his palms down the front of his pants, and faced her. His heavily lined face said he was around fifty. Somehow, the toothpick stuck in the corner of his mouth managed to stay in place when he spoke.

"I am," Sage replied. "And you have to stop what you're doing right now." She pushed past Burly Guy One to stand directly in front of Burly Guy Two, who was still attempting to remove the box he was carrying. The carton that Sage had just unsealed this morning was full of Nan's diaries. Diaries Sage desperately needed.

Sage's grandmother, Celeste Matthews, had been killed in a brutally ritualistic manner, and Sage had been looking for a specific journal that Nan had been keeping before her murder. The notebook, Sage believed, contained detailed notes about her grandmother's discovery of an ancient prophecy, a prophecy that directly involved Sage.

"We were told everything would be packed up." Burly Guy One said from behind her, annoyance peppering his tone. "If we have to wait around for you to finish packing, it will be extra. *Bloody women*," he added beneath his breath.

As though oblivious to the conversation around him, or perhaps deliberately ignoring it, Burly Guy Two stepped around Sage and carried the box that contained the only written account of her grandmother's final days toward the door.

Furious, Sage placed herself between him and the door. "I told you to stop."

Burly Guy Two, with his flannel shirt stretched tight over his beer belly, was a country man, a man's man. He frowned, peering down at her from over the top of the box, clearly not pleased with what he no doubt considered an irrational woman who had not done the job she should have.

"Don't have time to stop," Burly Guy One said, stepping toward her. "Got exactly one hour to finish up here, so we can be at our next job on time. Because of what happened with Roger here last week," Burly Guy One said, indicating his partner, "we're both bloody well on probation. If I lose my job, my wife will shoot me. So out of the way, lady."

Ugh! "I cancelled the job." Sage ignored the uncomfortable twist in her stomach at the lie. "Look, uh, what's your name?"

"Bob."

"Look, Bob," Sage said in her best I'm-being-reasonable tone, "I'll phone through to your office and clear everything up right now. Just put the boxes down."

It was enough to make Bob hesitate. Roger, not so much. He shuffled his feet and glared at her.

With everything that had happened since Sage's return to her hometown for her grandmother's funeral, cancelling the movers she'd booked when she'd arrived had been the last thing on her mind.

Originally, Sage had intended to stay in town just long enough to attend the funeral and make sure Nan's belongings were safely in storage. Then she'd discovered Nan's murder had been part of a satanic ritual. Celeste's life, and quite literally her eyes, had been taken by Luke "Lucky" Keyton, a local lad who had turned serial killer when he'd become possessed by a malevolent spirit entity. A demon.

And as if that weren't disturbing enough, when Sage had delved into the final days of Nan's life, retracing her last steps, Sage had discovered a shocking truth about herself, and who she really was.

Sage Matthews was the seer's daughter, a white witch destined to fight a master demon and keep the forces of Hell from reaching the earthly realm.

Go figure!

According to an ancient prophecy, the fight was destined to happen in six days:

"Every hundred years, at midnight on the night of the blood moon, the veil between

this world and a far darker one will be at its thinnest, unsealing a doorway that should never be opened, allowing the unspeakable to come through and unleash hell on earth."

This Sunday night, Sage would be coming face to face with the demon.

The idea should have terrified her—and it did—but when Sage had learned that the demon had been responsible for the deaths of her beloved grandmother and her mother years before that, her fear had quickly transmuted into anger.

Sage was livid.

And more determined than ever to learn everything about the prophecy and her role in it.

The answers lay in the pages of an ancient grimoire, a book of spells and rituals that Nan's best friend, Ada Slatterley, had given her very life trying to protect.

Sage was running out of time to prepare for Sunday night's battle with the demon, and a couple chauvinistic moving men were not going to stop her. She pulled her phone from her jeans pocket and dialed the number for the moving company.

At least the phone reception isn't an issue today. Lately, it had been becoming more and more unreliable, no doubt due to the strange disturbance in the electromagnetic field across the town. Unusual static electricity saturated the air and clung like a nefarious smog in the sky above Cryton, interfering with electrical devices and radio reception.

Along with the change in atmospheric conditions, Cryton itself seem infused with an unsettling energy, a sense of impending doom. The air tasted like anger, but the change was in fact something far more menacing.

It was pure unadulterated evil.

Demonic.

But this was just the beginning. According to the prophecy, the changes in town were about to become much worse as the countdown to Sunday's blood moon continued.

Sage prayed she'd be ready in time.

But there was still so much to do. She tapped her nails on the phone. *Come on!*

The line was a bit crackly, but the phone was finally ringing. It looked like her call would go through.

Roger bared his teeth in a silent snarl, stepped around Sage again, and continued to walk toward the door, oddly determined to remove the box of Nan's diaries. Out of nowhere, the hairs rose up on the back of Sage's neck and a thought planted itself in her mind: *Stay away from him.*

Except she couldn't let him walk out the door with those diaries. With the phone between her shoulder and ear, Sage ducked in front of Roger, placed her body in the door frame, and spread her arms, palms flat on either side of the opening.

The static finally cleared from the line and the call connected to the moving company. "Good morning," Sage began. "My name is—"

An odd sound, low and menacing, like something a wounded animal might make, rose up from Roger's chest. He raised his Blundstone boot and kicked Sage's thigh, knocking her leg clean out from under her. While she struggled for balance, Roger transferred the box to one hand, and with the other, pushed her out the door and into a large potted plant, which crashed down on top of her.

Momentarily stunned, and covered in soil, Sage opened her mouth to abuse him when she saw a six-foot-three pissed-off male charging at Roger.

Ethan.

Detective Sergeant Ethan Blade, Homicide Squad, South Australian Police Force, her lover and so much more, had left her sifting through boxes of Nan's things searching for the journal barely ten minutes ago, to walk down the main street to the bakery for much-needed takeaway coffee.

Ethan tossed the coffee onto the sidewalk and lunged at Roger. Before Sage had time to do more than blink, Ethan had Roger face down on the ground, his hands cuffed behind his back. The box of Nan's diaries had spilled, emptying across the concrete.

Anger surged through Sage's veins at how carelessly Nan's precious diaries had been treated, but then Sage caught sight of Ethan, and momentarily lost her train of thought. Ethan was something else when he was like this, all furious alpha male in full protective mode. His almost black hair was mussed and collar length, more through not having time for a cut, than by design or fashion. Either way, it worked. From his stormy dark eyes, all the way down his finely honed body, Ethan was the sexiest man she'd ever laid eyes on.

And he's all mine.

A concept that still blew her mind.

Ethan cast a speaking glance at Bob, who held up both hands in a *Do I look stupid? I'm not going to fuck with you* manner.

Seemingly assured that that was indeed the case, Ethan was at her side in a heartbeat, picking up bits of broken terracotta pot. The power, the sheer energy, that radiated off him was nothing short of intoxicating. Sage took a breath and inhaled a mixture of heated virile male in the prime of his life and the worn leather of the jacket Ethan wore to hide his gun. A heady and delicious combination.

"Angel, look at me."

Her pulse fluttered at the way his pet name for her rolled languidly off his tongue. He'd coined the endearment based on the angel she wore constantly around her neck, an amulet of protection given to her by her mother before her death when Sage was just three years old.

"I'm okay." Sage picked herself up and started shaking soil off her clothes.

"You fell quite hard." Ethan had been a bit... overprotective of her since last Wednesday night. But she supposed he had just cause. Having your girlfriend get abducted by a serial killer and then coming face to face with a malevolent spirit hell-bent on killing you was bound to bring out a man's more... dominant qualities.

Sage's thigh throbbed from the kick with the steel-capped boot, her shirt had been ripped in a couple of places, and she was covered in dirt, but aside from some scrapes and bruises, she'd be fine. Just as well; she didn't have time to be out of action. "Really, I'm okay."

Ethan's intense gaze raked over her body one final time, as though he were cataloguing her scratches in order to calculate just how severe his retribution would be.

"Care to tell me what the fuck is going on?" Ethan demanded, moving toward Bob and flashing his badge.

"Easy mate, uh, Detective Sergeant, sir," Bob said. "We're just doing our job."

"Angel?" Ethan turned to her. "Were they just doing their job?"

"Perhaps a little too well." Sage briefly explained the encounter to Ethan.

"So why the fuck didn't you leave when Sage asked you to?" Ethan demanded of Bob. "Seems to me it would have saved you a whole lot of trouble. And pain."

Bob raised his hands in surrender, then clapped them to his head and winced, as though in severe pain.

"No one lays a hand on Sage," Ethan said, glaring at first Bob, then at Roger, lying still on the ground. "But me."

Ethan clenched and unclenched his fists a few times before pulling out his radio and barking through a couple of codes. A 212 and a 415, and then he gave the address of the shop. Bob edged his way toward the door.

"Why didn't you leave?" Ethan asked again, his voice low, yet forceful. Bob had justified himself to Sage earlier by saying he was on probation and scared of losing his job, but now he appeared strangely dazed. And very eager to leave.

"The question is not that hard," Ethan said, clipping his radio back onto his belt. Bob froze, flinching. "Why the fuck didn't you leave when Sage asked you to?"

"I—" Bob's shoulders sagged and he released a breath. "Something... I don't know what came over me." Bob glanced at Roger, lying on his stomach with his hands cuffed behind his back. He hadn't moved since being cuffed. "And I've never seen Roger lose his temper. And especially not at a pretty sheila, no matter how frustrating she might be. I... I can't explain it."

A patrol car skidded to a stop in front of the shop. As the moving men were loaded into the squad car, Sage heard pieces of the conversation between the local police officers. *Another assault... six more arrests last night... people acting strangely... unprovoked violence... something not right in this town...*

Yes, Sage agreed. There was definitely something not right in this town. And it had been that way for quite a while.

Leaving Ethan to do his police thing, Sage packed Nan's spilled diaries back into the box, carefully straightening the pages that had been bent. She then crossed the pavement and picked up the empty takeaway cups, looking at their spilled contents with regret. The scent of coffee would have to be enough to recharge her.

As Sage reached the porch of the shop, she paused at the empty wooden chair where her cat, Liquorice, usually slept on top of a crocheted blanket her nan had made. With a stab of pain, Sage wondered for the umpteenth time since last Wednesday where her little friend was. More than a pet, Liquorice was her companion, and they had a certain... connection that had rekindled and deepened since her return to Cryton.

Where are you, little buddy? Sage called out with her mind, hoping he could hear her, as she'd recently discovered he often could.

Sage hadn't seen him since she'd been abducted by Lucky. She pictured Liquorice, with his silky charcoal black fur and the white tip on his tail, and felt a sharp tug in her stomach. She hoped that wherever he was, he was safe. And would come back soon.

Sage walked back inside the shop, threw the empty cups in the bin, and stilled. The temperature seemed to have dropped several degrees in a single second, and she caught a sudden movement out of the corner of her eye. She whipped her head around. Nothing. As usual. The tiny hairs on the back of her neck were standing on end, and her pulse was racing.

She couldn't see anything, but every fiber in her being told her that she was being watched. By *him*.

He was here. Unseen, but the sudden, unexplained rush of anxiety confirmed his presence. She'd learned to recognize what the demonic entity felt like. It was a heavy coat of darkness, of anger and hatred, that sent a chill running down her spine. A foul odor filled the air, making her gag. Planting her feet, she clasped the angel pendant around her neck and imagined it casting a protective cocoon around her.

She took a deep breath, then jumped when Ethan called out to her from the door. "You pressing charges, Angel?"

She let the amulet slide through her fingers and fall against her skin. "Uh, no."

How could she? She understood better than anyone that Roger wasn't himself just now. It was this town, this house. The dark energy that had moved into Cryton had seeped into the air. You inhaled it into your body, dragged it into your lungs, and it changed you into something you weren't.

Roger was no more responsible for what had happened just now than her friend Mark Collins had been on Wednesday night when he'd attacked Sage. Mark was a paranormal investigator and star of the TV series *Debunking Reality*. He'd been investigating the strange goings-on in the house and had helped her discover that a demon was stalking her.

She'd been shocked when her friend succumbed to the demon's influence and turned on her. But friendship was no match for a malevolent demonic entity who had the power to possess human bodies, if the conditions were right.

Suddenly the unsettling feeling in the room was gone. The temperature returned to normal, and she could *breathe* again. She rolled her shoulders.

Then she sensed something else. Sage whirled around, sure someone was in the room with her. Had come up from behind and was now standing right next to her. She wasn't scared, not like she was when *he* was around. But the feeling was so strong, it was unnerving. She looked around, but no one was with her.

Then she saw it. A notebook on the otherwise empty bottom shelf.

It hadn't been there before. She'd cleared all the shelves during her packing. Perhaps it had landed there when the box had fallen. And yet… it appeared to have been neatly placed on the shelf. Sage crossed the room and picked up the notebook. Opening the cover, she flicked through the pages. *This is it!*

Sage finally had Nan's journal.

She just hoped it contained the answers she needed. She had six days to prepare for the demon's attempt to breach the portal, and she was going to need every scrap of help she could find. If she failed, the world as she knew it would be no more.

Chapter Two

The steam from the shower in Ethan's hotel room fogged the mirrors as he washed the dirt off Sage's body. The masculine scent of his soap—sandalwood and rich spices—washed over her. His solid, muscular frame dwarfed the cubicle, his elbows occasionally thumping against the glass as he massaged her back, then tenderly washed her hair.

At Ethan's insistence, they'd eaten a brief takeaway breakfast at the local bakery and come back to his hotel room for a quick shower and to get some clean clothes. Ethan had a meeting with his special-operations unit, Taipan, and aside from intending to devour Nan's journal from start to finish, Sage's list of things to do started with a short visit to her nan's closest friends, Joyce, Pat, and Mona. Sadly, only three of Nan's circle of friends were left.

Although there certainly had been several ritual murders other than those of Nan and Ada, it did appear as though the grannies had been specifically targeted. Was it because they'd had the grimoire?

From what Sage had already guessed, and from reading the parts of Nan's journal she'd been able to flick through so far, Sage had ascertained that the women had been just as involved as Nan in deciphering the prophecy and preparing for what needed to be done. Nan made numerous references to sitting down with the "girls" and deciphering what they could. They were as close friends as you could get, their bond forged through a lifetime. "As mad as hatters and as thick as thieves" was how Nan had often described them. They'd always been there for each other.

Sage hoped they were going to be here for her now.

"It was strange, though," Sage said, impatiently pulling away from Ethan's touch, anxious to get out of the shower and get back to the journal. "How that mover, Roger, seemed intent on taking that particular box, even when I told him not to. And then to just lash out and attack me like that..."

"Those boxes contained Celeste's diaries, didn't they?"

"Yes. Of all the boxes he could have picked up, he seemed set on taking that one."

Ethan didn't say anything more. He didn't have to. It was no coincidence that Roger was trying to take what would hurt Sage the most. The demon had a way of looking into your heart and into your soul. He could see what would cut you to the bone, and he seemed especially jealous of love.

Sage reached for the handle to the shower door.

"Relax for a minute, will you? You won't do yourself any favors if your health suffers again."

Ah! Now she understood Ethan's determination to do what she considered wasting time eating and taking a shower. Sure, she was covered in soil, and Ethan wanted to clean her cuts and scrapes to avoid infection, but it ran deeper than that.

He was still worried about what had happened to her physically *after* Wednesday night. The night she'd summoned forth and channeled through her body the energy that had fought off the demon and saved Ethan's life.

She'd felt fine at first. They'd come back to Ethan's hotel room the next morning, where they'd made love with a passionate desperation unrivalled by anything she'd ever experienced. Despite what still loomed ahead of them, she'd never felt better. The battle with the demon had finally erased any doubts Ethan had left regarding what they were dealing with. He'd accepted the supernatural. Something her black-and-white, just-the-facts detective had stubbornly fought.

Sage had been euphoric; she had the man of her dreams, the love of her life, and they were taking on this prophecy *together*.

And then... something had come over her in the early hours of Friday morning. As though the energy she'd summoned inside her—through her—and used to fight the demon had drained away. Left her body ruined. She'd barely had the strength left to swallow.

Worried for her, Ethan had taken her to the hospital in Tellmer. The white walls had been unbearable, as had the lights they'd insisted on shining in her eyes. Sage had demanded Ethan take her away. She'd known that whatever her condition was, it couldn't be treated by conventional medicine.

The doctors had determined she was suffering a severe migraine attack, coupled with symptoms of shock after her abduction. They'd given her painkillers and told her to go home and rest. Though there was nothing simple about the migraines she was having, Sage found the tablets took the edge off.

And she didn't have time to be sick. Her strength had returned. In full. Actually, more than in full. Whatever condition caused her debilitating migraines, it also had a flip side. When she wasn't in pain, she felt strong, powerful. As though her internal batteries had become supercharged. Though another attack had come on after the run-in with the movers this morning, it had already passed. She was getting better at this healing thing. Sage took a deep breath as the rush of energy came on. Ethan pulled her close, her back to his front, and pressed his cheek to hers. She felt his smile.

"You're looking better, Angel." Relief was evident in his tone. "Although you can definitely carry off the Goth look, I much prefer you with a little color in your cheeks."

"And here I was planning to make vampire glam my new thing."

He released her, chuckling softly as he finished finger-combing conditioner through her hair, and she savored the moment. No man had treated her with so much love and care before. She started to turn to kiss him.

"Hold still," he murmured and she froze at his abrupt change in tone. She felt his fingers parting her hair.

"What?" Her heart began to jump in her chest. "Ethan, what is it?"

He cursed and smacked the wall.

She whipped around. Ethan's gentle smile was gone, and his eyes had narrowed to winter-cold slits.

"Ethan?" The water continued to spray down on them, but it was no longer relaxing, its gentle rain now an irritating downpour.

"He cut your hair." Ethan spoke through clenched teeth. "That goddamn son of a bitch took a section of your hair."

Ethan turned the taps off with such force, she'd never be able to turn them on again. Water ran in rivulets down his naked body and she grabbed a towel and draped it over his shoulder after they stepped out. Head bowed, he clutched the fabric as he reined in his temper. She laid a hand on his shoulder. According to his partner, Detective Senior Constable Nate Ryder, Ethan was calm and calculating, cool, even to the point of cold, under pressure.

Except when it came to her.

"I'm going to kill Luke Keyton," he said, lifting his head and meeting her eyes in the mirror. The words weren't a threat. They were a statement of fact.

"Not before I've finished with him." Sage met his gaze. "I need him alive for Sunday." Sage needed the demon for the ritual, and as long as Lucky was possessed by said demon, it would make her job much easier to get the demon to the portal.

Ethan began rubbing the towel over himself. In spite of everything, the sight of his naked body sent a wave of heated desire through her. He was magnificent, from his messy towel-dried hair to his sexy bare feet to the mighty fine rear view.

"What would he want with my hair?" Sage asked, forcibly dragging her mind back to the issue at hand.

Despite the variety of tools designed for torture that she'd seen on Lucky's workbench in his cabin, Sage was unnerved by the thought he'd kept her hair. Hair somehow felt so *intimate*.

She didn't remember him cutting it, so she could only presume he'd done it sometime between when he'd shoved the chloroform-covered rag in her mouth and when she'd woken up on that dank cabin floor.

"Did he cut the hair of any of the other victims?" Sage knew that Lucky had removed the victims' eyeballs, then covered the sockets with round pieces of black cloth. He'd drained their bodies of blood and left a satanic brand on the palms of their right hands. But she'd never heard that hair had been removed.

"Not that was noticed," Ethan said. "I will find out for sure though." He placed his hands on her shoulders, his eyes narrowing with intensity. "I'll be dead before I let him anywhere near you again."

"I know." She held his gaze for a moment, then broke the contact. What if the demon killed Ethan this time? How could she possibly live without him? She kept her eyes averted from his and pretended to concentrate on wrapping her towel around herself, tying it in a knot between her breasts.

"Let me look at you." Ethan tugged off the towel and pored over every inch of her skin, checking for cuts and abrasions. "Stay there."

He was back in no time with a small medical kit, and on his knees, proceeded to tend to her. Although she'd barely been injured, taking care of her made him feel better, and Sage would be lying if she said she wasn't enjoying his attention. And the way his hands felt on her damp skin. Her nipples tightened into hard peaks and a rush of heat pooled between her thighs.

"I can't believe this, but I can barely find any of the injuries I saw earlier." His voice was deeper and a bit rougher. "And the bruise on your thigh is already fading, not darkening the way it would normally. I can't believe how fast you heal now."

"Then you can stop worrying about me." Unable to resist, she sifted her fingers through his messy locks of damp hair.

Ethan stood and rubbed his palms down Sage's arms. "You're getting cold." His eyes were narrowed, intense, his lids heavy.

"Cold is not how I'd describe myself right now."

Pain flickered across his face. "You've been hurt."

"I'm not hurt. I'm fine. Really."

"I'm not an animal. No matter how much I desire you, no matter what effect you have on my common sense, I do have some degree of control. Which I won't have if you stay naked."

Mother of all things holy, she didn't want him to have any control. She wanted him to do every single one of the things she read in his eyes. But they didn't have time. Ethan had a meeting, and she had... something urgent to do. They had places they should be. It was just hard to think of exactly what right now.

With a sigh of regret and a slight tremor in his usually steady hands, Ethan slipped his soft gray T-shirt over her head. The worn fabric glided over her peaked nipples and heated skin, stimulating her already aroused senses. She hugged the material tight against her, closed her eyes and inhaled, letting Ethan's masculine scent fill her lungs.

When she opened her eyes, she was hit with Ethan's dark stormy ones. He was completely still, focused, barely taking a single breath.

Even if she had a choice of her full wardrobe back in Adelaide, she would have chosen to put this on. If it meant Ethan would look at her the way he was.

11

"Jesus, Sage," he breathed. "I'm only a man."

She thought of all the seductive lingerie she had in her drawer at home, bought for various sexual encounters over the years. The barely there bras, the lacey scraps of the matching panties. The bustiers, the corsets, the six-inch heels, the garters, the thigh-high stockings. The naughty nurse uniform... Not one piece of lingerie could have made her feel sexier than the look Ethan gave her as he raked his gaze down her body.

"Eth—" Sage's voice was barely a whisper. "We have to go."

As he closed the distance between them, she instinctively stepped backward, feeling her back touch the towel rail, his erection hard against her firm stomach.

"Go where?" Ethan placed his hands on the wall to either side of her. She was surrounded, caged by a hard, muscular body. His heat, the intensity with which he looked at her, was overwhelming.

"Uh... places." For the life of her she couldn't remember where she had to be. Or why. "We don't have time," Sage argued weakly, ignoring the part of her that screamed in protest.

His lips caressed the column of her neck, and goose bumps skittered across her skin.

"We're making the time," he murmured, his voice deep, smooth whisky in a smoky jazz bar. Her neck and her mouth dried, and her body responded to the command in his voice, her muscles tightening with anticipation.

"But..."

"Are you too sore?"

"No. But we—"

"Then I'll show you why you'll make the time."

In one swift move, he grabbed the hem of his T-shirt and whipped it up over her head. He crushed his lips to hers before she could argue further, pulling her naked body flush against his much larger, harder one. His strong, capable hands circled her waist before he scooped her into his arms. She fell against him, her hardened nipples pressing into the warm skin of his chest as he carried her to the bed and dropped her onto the mattress.

Sage bounced, then shimmied herself up the bed, but he was faster. Catching her by the ankles, he yanked her down so that she was directly beneath him.

"You don't seriously think you can get away."

"Would it matter if I did?" Sage's voice was a throaty whisper.

"Nope."

Ethan gave her a look that sent her feminine awareness into a frenzy. He kissed a maddeningly sensuous trail down her neck, across her collarbone, and by the time he drew her nipple into his heated mouth, she was gone.

They'd had incredible chemistry from the beginning, but something had changed since the night they'd fought the demon. They could barely keep their hands off each other, the craving for a physical connection almost overwhelming.

Was this merely love, or something more?

The energy flooding Sage's body blotted out further thought. All she wanted, all she needed, was Ethan.

———————◆———————

Ethan leaned back against the desk and watched Sage toss on her clothes and dash around his hotel room, gathering her phone and notebook. He would never tell her how worried he'd been these last seventy-two hours. She'd been dangerously weak and had slept fitfully, almost constantly, woken only by intermittent nightmares as her subconscious dealt with unimaginable horrors.

Throughout those first two days, he'd barely slept at all, afraid that if he took his eyes off her for even a second, she'd slip away. He'd never been as scared in his life, or as powerless. He didn't understand what had happened to her on Wednesday night and had even less idea what to do to help her. So he'd held her tight and placed his face close to hers on the pillow. He'd discovered his cheek was the most sensitive at picking up her shallow puffs of breath.

At a particularly low point, and acting on an instinct he didn't understand, he'd picked up the grimoire. If he hadn't known better, he would have sworn the damn thing had been trying to get his attention, calling to him, but he'd ignored it because, well, that notion was just stupid. Irrational. The ancient book with the yellowed pages was just an inanimate object.

But when he'd picked it up, he'd be damned if it didn't feel as though the thing were purring in his hands like some kind of cat.

Lack of sleep, he'd chalked it up to. He was not unfamiliar with the varied and irrational psychological effects of sleep deprivation. The longer he'd held Sage's grimoire in his hands, the more his mind had cleared. He'd run his fingers over the old and surprisingly well-preserved leather cover, tracing the symbol embossed on the front. That symbol intrigued and fascinated him. He could have sworn it matched the one on a pendant he'd found in his father's belongings. He'd need a trip back to his apartment in Adelaide to be a hundred-percent certain.

It fascinated him, this strange book that Sage had been guarding with her life, and he'd begun flicking through the pages. Of course he'd been curious as to what information it contained; he was a detective. Despite being forced to concede that they were in fact dealing with the paranormal, in the form of a demonic entity and an ancient prophecy, he couldn't quite bring himself to believe that chanting verses from a spell book would prove much value. The book's appeal to him was only for the potential clues it might hold to help solve this problem.

Because he sure as hell didn't have any fucking idea.

He'd begun reading the grimoire with high hopes. Something, anything, no matter how small, might be a vital piece he was looking for. A lead. A tiny thread that would unravel this whole damn case.

The grimoire's first half was composed of numerous spells: summoning protection, crystal cleansing and purification, calling upon angels and guides, and strengthening something called a third eye. A *third* eye? Really?

He wasn't familiar with all the terminology, but he got the gist. At first, he'd concluded that the grimoire was indeed a crock of shit. At best, a placebo for the person using it; at worst, a weapon to instill fear in someone who believed in its power.

But, strangely and importantly significant, however, was the section that described the serial killer's signature perfectly, right down to the satanic brand on the right hand, and the black circles of cloth that covered the eyes.

Eyes are the mirror of the soul someone had scribbled in the margin beside an arrow pointing to the eerie black holes. And souls were what the demon sought, what he fed on, and what made him stronger.

When Sage had begun writhing on the bed, he'd set the book aside. It had fallen open. He'd closed it again, had moved away, and with a thump, it had opened again. To the exact same page.

Ethan had stopped believing in coincidences years ago, so he'd read the page aloud. The Latin words had been soothing, rhythmic. Sage's breathing had become less labored, the tension around her eyes had eased.

Of course, it could have just been the sound of his voice, but on some level, he'd known it was the words. A spiritual lullaby, he'd decided it was. He'd felt its healing power. Ethan himself had felt oddly calm, and as he'd read, he'd pictured the magical words healing and strengthening her vital organs.

Not that he believed in magic. Well, he hadn't until recently, that was. If there were such things as evil spirits and demons, then it surely followed there were other things he didn't understand either.

Either way, it didn't matter. The more he'd read the passage to her, the faster Sage had recovered.

And today… today she was looking better. Much better. The migraines still worried him, but at least her energy levels appeared to have returned to normal. Whatever had happened that night had changed her. Altered her in ways he was still unsure of.

The experience had changed him too.

"I… I don't quite feel like myself at the moment," Sage said, picking up her belongings and putting them in her bag.

"In what way?"

"My body, my mind, it all feels different," she said. He scrutinized her. Was it his imagination, or did her eyes appear greener? Her complexion, a lovely peaches and cream, seemed somehow luminous. Was it possible she was more vivid, more *alive*, than she'd been before?

Or was he just more in love with her?

"I'm scared," she blurted, her eyes seeking his, and his gut twisted. "I'm going to give this my best shot. But… what if I don't figure out what happened Wednesday? What if can't do it again when it really counts?"

Her words echoed his own insecurity. The constant, nagging dark shadow in the recesses of his own mind.

What if I can't save her?

"Forget I said that," she said abruptly, closing her eyes and taking a deep breath. Ethan could almost see her spine turn to steel in front of him. His heart squeezed.

"*We* can do this." Ethan crossed the room, bridging the space between them. "You're not alone, Angel. I need you to remember that. You have me, and if that's not enough, you have my team, Taipan. Every resource available to me: the department, my personal security guys, and everything that comes with that. Know there isn't any length I won't go to, to give you what you need. Nothing I wouldn't do for you. I'd move mountains, rearrange the stars if they weren't to your liking."

Her eyes shone bright. "Now that you mention it, I've always thought the Southern Cross should be moved more to the east..." She grinned and something shifted inside his chest.

"Consider it done."

"I love you." The simple truth of those words was reflected clearly on her face, the depth he found in her eyes. Her love felled him to his knees, had him worshipping at her feet.

"I love you too, Angel." His voice was a husky rasp, barely recognizable. "We'll get through this." Because they had to.

"I know." Her voice hardened. "That son of a bitch killed too many people I love not to pay. And pay dearly."

Touching her temples, she squeezed her eyes shut, then paced away from him. After a moment, she cupped her hands over her ears, then shook her head.

Was it another migraine? "Angel?"

"I wish they'd service the air-conditioning. It's irritating."

"The air-conditioning?" Ethan listened, but couldn't hear a thing.

"It's misfiring or something. That sporadic twang, like a break in a record. Can't you hear that?" Sage frowned.

"No, Angel," he said softly. "I can barely hear the air-con at all, let alone hear the fault in it."

Sage rubbed her ears. "The ceiling light is humming. It sounds like the buzzing of a bee. The hard drive on your laptop is whirring, making the desk vibrate. I can hear the drone of the bedside lamp, and someone close by is having a shower. There's a hammering of the pipes as the water rushes through."

It shouldn't be possible, but then so many things that had seemed impossible days ago had been proved to be not only possible, but cold, hard fact. "You're worrying me." Ethan ran his hands up and down her bare arms.

"I'll be okay." Sage looked up at him, her mouth firm, her eyes uncertain.

"Craig is waiting out front. Keep him with you at all times today."

Craig was more than a security detail. Outside of Taipan, he was the best protection money could buy. After today, she'd not spend a second out of Ethan's or his team's sight, but he needed everyone in Taipan present when he spoke with them this morning.

Ethan glanced at the time. "I wish you'd reconsider coming with me." Walking out the door was going to be one of the hardest things he'd ever done.

"I can't," Sage said, no fight, only certainty in her tone. He didn't like it, but he understood. After losing a few days, she was eager to move forward and prepare for Sunday. He was just as keen to talk over with Taipan the best way to keep her safe for the duration. This was unlike any other case; there was no precedent, no procedure to fall back on. That was the detail that irritated him the most. The unknown factor.

He was going in cold. In addition, his team would be forced to take him at his word. There was no proof. No evidence to back up his claims of what they were dealing with.

God knows he'd taken long enough to believe it himself. His gut tightened painfully at how badly he'd treated Sage. Christ, he couldn't believe she would even talk to him, let alone allow him to love her.

He'd been an asshole, plain and simple. He'd hurt her significantly by not believing her. He'd let her down.

He wouldn't do it again.

His phone vibrated on the desk, and he picked it up to read the text.

"That was Nate. I have to go." Ethan's fingers flew across the screen of his phone as he replied.

He looked up from the phone at Sage. "Craig answers to me, not the SA police. His sole responsibility is to keep you safe. Make it easy on him," Ethan added after a pause. "Keep your phone on you at all times."

She grinned. "Yes, Dad."

Ignoring her teasing, Ethan slipped into his leather jacket and checked that his weapons and handcuffs were secure. "I'll call you when I'm finished. I may be several hours though, depending."

She took his hands in hers and unclenched his fists. He inhaled deeply, then slowly released his breath.

"Relax." She kissed the crease between his brows. "I'll be perfectly fine."

"You can't know that."

"No, I can't," she conceded. "But I can promise to do my best to stay safe."

That would have to be enough. "I can't do my job properly if I'm worrying about you. Stay close to Craig."

His phone vibrated with another incoming text. "I really have to go."

"You've mentioned that," she said with a small smile. His chest tightened. He opened the door, and kissed her one more time. Hard. Possessive.

Mine.

As they stepped outside, an uncomfortable tingling started between Ethan's shoulder blades, and he instinctively reached for his weapon. With every sense he possessed on high alert, he scanned the area in front of the hotel room, the car park, and beyond to the surrounding trees. He couldn't see anyone, but someone was watching them.

Who? Or more likely, *what?*

Ethan hoped it was Keyton. A serial killer he knew how to handle. But as the light summer's breeze dropped away and a wintery chill washed over him, Ethan knew that wasn't the case. He'd felt this way Wednesday night at the cabin.

It was the demon.

Adrenaline raced through his system, looking for an outlet. How did you direct your fury at something you couldn't see? Something real, but without a solid bodily mass?

How do I fight that? How do I protect Sage?

As Craig walked from his vehicle over to them, Ethan sent up a prayer to keep Sage safe.

His prayer ran far deeper than his love for Sage. If what he'd read in the grimoire about the prophecy was correct, and he'd come to believe it was, it wasn't only his life that depended on Sage's ability to beat this entity, but that of every single soul on earth.

Chapter Three

Luke Keyton, or "Lucky" as he was known, fingered the silky blonde strands of hair in his pocket and watched Sage Matthews kiss the detective goodbye. When he caught a glimpse of her tongue entering the bastard's mouth, Lucky's pants tightened painfully. He wanted her tongue in his mouth. Hell, he wanted a lot more than just Sage's kiss. He wanted her life. *Literally.*

A trail of saliva trickled out the side of his mouth and down his chin. Absently, he wiped it away with a dirty sleeve. He pulled a roll-your-own from his pocket and sucked gently as he lit it. Closing his eyes, he savored that first draw; no other inhale for the rest of the cigarette would be the same as the first.

Just like killing. No other death gave as great a thrill as the first. No matter how you tried to spice it up.

Except for *hers.*

He knew she'd be different. When he was finally allowed to have her, she'd give him that virgin thrill of his first victim: his father.

He wanted her. *Now.*

"Be patient." Virgil spoke directly into his mind. He was holding Lucky back; the timing had to be right. He couldn't afford to make any more mistakes. Lucky had messed up last time, and his little plaything had escaped.

For now, Lucky would watch… plan… *anticipate.*

There was much to do before Sunday night's blood moon. There had to be seven sacrificial deaths given to the demon. He'd already offered up four, and the bond between him and the demon had grown deeper with each ritual he'd performed. The dark power that rose and welled inside him was intoxicating. Addictive. As if he were feeding an insatiable beast.

Lucky had intended to immediately kill Sage Wednesday night, but when he caught her, he'd become excited. The thrill too tempting. He'd thought to take his time, draw out his pleasure.

After all, he'd only get to kill her once.

He bitterly regretted her escape from the cabin; the thought of watching her take her last breath left him physically aching.

Her fear when he'd so briefly had her had been delicious on the tip of his tongue. Lucky licked his lips; he could still taste her.

He'd have her again.

Soon.

She had to be killed before the blood moon. Her death signified the demon's victory. With her out of the way, there was nothing that could stop Him from fully entering their reality.

Sucking hard on his cigarette, Lucky studied the goon standing watch on the other side of the road, hiding in the darkness of the trees. The fool stood out like a nun in a brothel. To Lucky anyway. The countless hours the thug had spent honing those muscles were a complete waste of time. Not to mention the weapon his hand rested on. The gun was as useless as an ashtray on a motorbike. And a human body was inconsequential. Nothing more than the vessel that contained the only thing of real value.

The soul.

Lucky looked inside the goon, peering into that secret self, the repository of all that a human truly was. He was a good man. Mostly. He had a dark side he kept hidden from his wife and boss. Private thoughts that scared him, but those very thoughts had drawn him into his line of work. His noble profession distracted him from what was going on inside his own mind. The fight being waged daily between dark and light. A fight that Lucky could use to his advantage. It was remarkably easy to sway that balance, to manipulate his prey, and Lucky's gift was finding the right enticement.

The goon whipped his head around and his eyes scanned right over the place Lucky was standing. The goon would be experiencing a tingle between his shoulder blades right now, the hairs on the back of his neck standing on end. His heart would be beating faster, and a fine sweat would bead on his forehead. He'd know something was *off*. His most primal instinct—survival—had been triggered, but he wouldn't know why.

The goon could sense him but couldn't see him.

Lucky had shrouded himself in darkness. The thing that triggered the goon's sixth sense was the same thing that made Lucky invisible to the naked eye. The goon knew something felt... *wrong*, but without fail, his logical mind would kick in and override his instincts. Because his eye, his physical apparatus, couldn't see the danger, the goon would convince himself he had nothing to fear. He'd roll his shoulders, stretch his neck, and force himself to shake it off.

And that would be his mistake.

An error in judgment that would cost him his life.

Sage's detective should already be dead. Lucky's plan, on Wednesday night, had been to kill him in front of her. As well as serving a higher purpose, it would have made her angry, would have brought out that delicious dark side.

Love was her weakness. A weakness she shared with the majority of the human race.

Fools.

On the blood moon, *He* would get his victory. The darkness would finally get the chance to show the world how it should be. There were far too many rules with love. Too many conditions and restrictions. *Don't do this. Don't do that.*

Darkness was freedom. A freeing from any and all consequences. *That* was how life was supposed to be.

Lucky flicked his spent butt on the ground, where it flamed on some dry sticks and gum leaves, but he didn't bother stamping it out. Fires were a human concern. His focus was on Sage, who was leaving the hotel with another goon. The hulking, bald-headed goon ushered her into his vehicle using his physical body for protection. Lucky spat on the ground.

They just don't get it.

As the hulk drove Sage away, Lucky let her go. He'd been hoping for a chance to get her alone. He'd have to keep watch. There'd be another chance. Lucky was big enough to admit he'd been caught off guard Wednesday night. Surprised when she'd tapped into her power. He'd underestimated her that night. He hadn't realized she knew what she had inside her; she'd spent her whole life trying to deny it. He also hadn't fully understood the strength of her love for the detective.

Worse, he'd underestimated the detective.

But how was Lucky supposed to have known who he was? He'd never truly looked at the detective before, except as a nuisance between him and Sage.

Lucky had become aware of something in the detective's soul that night. Something to which the detective himself was oblivious. Sage likely thought Lucky had spared the detective.

As if! Compassion and love were for the weak.

Lucky hadn't killed the detective because he *couldn't.* Not then anyway. Instead, he'd thrown him as hard as he could at the wall, even though he'd known Sage might heal the man. Pieces had begun to fall into place for Lucky, as *He* revealed how much of a threat the detective truly was.

The taste was bitter in Lucky's mouth, but he had to consider that even in human form, Sage was his equal. The light to his darkness. There was a very real chance she could destroy him and the darkness he could summon, just as he'd planned to snuff out the light she could draw upon.

And now the stakes had been raised.

With the arrival of the alchemist's son, they were playing for not just the next hundred years, but for *forever.* He couldn't allow her and the detective to win.

Hands thrust deep in his pockets, Lucky eased back into the shadows. He licked his lips, and recognized the taste on his tongue.

It was time to hunt the next sacrifice. Number five of seven.

To please the demon. Add to his strength.

Lucky planned on heading into the battle on Sunday with as much power as possible.

Chapter Four

Gravel crunched loudly beneath the tires of Craig's navy blue 4WD Land Rover as he pulled into the driveway of Joyce Booth's house. The trip had been a silent one. Craig was not one for small talk.

"Stay here." Craig stepped outside the vehicle and assessed the surroundings. He wore black cargo pants and a black T-shirt with Security emblazoned across his broad back in large white block letters. He ran a hand over his smooth bald head and spoke into an undetectable communication device as he walked his surveillance.

After a while, Sage grew restless and alighted from the vehicle, slinging her bag over her shoulder. He crossed to her immediately, scowling behind his jet-black sunglasses.

"I told you to stay here."

"I did. I just didn't stay inside the car."

He towered over her, and she craned her neck to look up at him as she spoke.

"You're going inside now?" he asked.

Sage replied that she was. She'd never had her own personal security before and wasn't sure how intrusive he intended to be. It was with a measure of relief that she discovered he was planning on waiting for her outside the house after he'd finished doing whatever a bodyguard did to ensure the place was secure.

Sage pictured Lucky, with his thin lanky frame, and couldn't imagine him wanting to go through Craig to get to her. As restrictive as it felt, Craig's presence did make her feel safer and allowed her to set thoughts of Lucky aside so she could concentrate on the job at hand.

Grimoire stowed safely in her bag, Sage inhaled the fragrance of the geraniums that lined the stone path leading to the front door. Bending down, she ran her fingers across a broad leaf of the geranium plant in a stone pot at the front door. She picked off some expired flower buds and traced her fingers along the plant's central stem. When she'd first touched it, the plant had looked in serious need of some TLC, but strangely, it was already looking remarkably better. The leaves were greener, fuller. Sage had always had a certain… way with plants, but now her ability seemed far stronger than it had been before. Wednesday night had apparently changed her in many ways.

She knocked at the door. No response.

"Hello?" Sage called out loudly through the rusty wire screen. The rickety timber door frame had once been coated in white paint, but the paint had now cracked and was peeling away in little curls.

The hundred-plus-year-old house was a typical style for houses in the country, with its wide front porch and wraparound veranda. Situated on a large one-acre block, it nestled amongst gum trees that provided much-needed shade from the harsh Australian sun. Leaves and twigs were falling to the ground, nipped off by the beaks of the pink and gray cockatoos that were sitting in the tree.

A large white cockatoo with a big yellow crest landed on a low-hanging branch and looked directly into her eyes, surprising her.

Hello, she greeted it. Other people might have spoken directly to the bird, but Sage recently had realized that animals heard her just as clearly, if not more so, if she used her mind.

The sulphur-crested cockatoo flew over to the wooden balustrade, using its large white wings to slow its descent.

The demon can now take many shapes. Be careful who you trust.

A shiver ran the length of her spine as the warning was delivered directly into her mind.

Before Sage could ask anything further, the bird took off with a flap of wings as though suddenly spooked by something. The hairs on the back of her neck prickled and she rubbed her arms as she scanned the area around her. Sage glanced over at Craig, who was leaning against the vehicle, not reacting to anything untoward at all.

Sage rolled her shoulders and took a calming breath. She had always known she had a deep connection to nature. Believed everyone shared it. She hadn't realized though that her connection to the natural world was far more profound than she'd ever dreamed.

But today, everything seemed magnified. Her senses were in a heightened state. She was sure if she concentrated, she could hear the wildlife to the edge of town. The surge of energy that had run through her body on Wednesday night had changed her. Not just in a sensory way, but in a physical one. Despite the migraine that continued to hover on the fringes of her vision and the chilling warning from the cockatoo, Sage felt as though she could run a marathon.

Joyce eventually appeared at the end of the hallway, and turning on the light, she began her trek across the faded linoleum to the front door. At seventy-nine, Joyce was the baby of what had been Nan's closest circle of friends, and today was dressed in a pale blue collared dress, which she had teamed with a pearl necklace and matching earrings.

"Hello, dear." Joyce greeted her enthusiastically, enveloping Sage in a hug, her bony arms fragile around Sage's neck.

"How are you coping?" Sage eyed her critically.

"Oh, I'll get by. What other choice is there? Come on in. Pat and Mona are out back. We've just made a fresh pot of tea."

A large, white maintenance van pulled into the driveway.

"Now what would Ken be doing here?"

"It's okay," Sage called out to Craig when he pushed off from where he'd been leaning on the vehicle, watching them. "It's Ken Baker from the local maintenance company." Craig nodded, acknowledging he'd heard her, but didn't take his hand off his weapon.

Sage turned to Joyce. "I rang him. I've arranged for Ken to put on some new doors for you. The ones you have barely keep out the flies."

Until now, there had been little need for security in Cryton like there was in the city. When Sage had been growing up, it was rare that they'd locked the front door.

The recent murders of Nan and Ada had changed all that. Through Lucky, the demon had killed Nan, who had discovered and begun researching the prophecy through the grimoire; not long after, Ada had been murdered. Ada had taken custody of the grimoire after Nan's death. Sage suspected that was what had made Ada the demon's next target.

Since Joyce, Mona, and Pat had been helping Nan and Ada, and Sage intended to ask them for help as well, that made them possible targets too.

"I can't afford new doors, dear," Joyce said, her eyes widening in panic. "I had to replace the fridge last year, and I'm saving up for a new washing machine."

"It's been taken care of," Sage said. "Pat and Mona are getting new doors as well, plus new window locks or whatever security is needed. Ethan, Detective Blade, has arranged for extra security patrols. They will just be drive-bys, but that should send a message to anyone watching."

Joyce's faded blue eyes glistened. She put a hand on Sage's arm, her grip surprisingly strong.

"You're a good girl. I hardly sleep a wink these days."

"I know." Sleep was something that would likely elude all of them until this was over. Sage lowered her voice. "Are you seeing... shadows? Hearing noises?"

Joyce visibly shuddered. "We all are. And that old blue cattle dog keeps us awake barking."

"Whose dog?" Sage struggled to recall someone who had a cattle dog this close to town. The only one she knew of belonged to the Joneses about two kilometers away. He was a working dog, kept for herding sheep. He was looked after, but slept outside. Had he been wandering around during the night?

"It's a ghost dog," Joyce said, and an involuntary shiver trickled down Sage's spine.

"Why do you think that?"

"We've seen it." There was a tremor in Joyce's voice when she whispered the words. "Last night—"

Sage put her hand on Joyce's arm to interrupt. "We'll talk about it inside," Sage said, as Ken stepped onto the porch. Ken wiped his hands on his overalls, then extended one to Sage in greeting. He clasped Joyce on the arms, and leaned in for a brief embrace.

"Friendly guy," Ken said, indicating Craig with a glance over his shoulder. Craig was still leaning against the vehicle, arms crossed over his massive chest, facing them.

"You were very quick," Sage said to turn the attention away from Craig. "I phoned you barely an hour ago, and you said it wouldn't be until after five before you could leave the store."

"I forgot it's school holidays, so when Dave-o turned up with his son"—he indicated the lad in the passenger seat—"I had a change of plans. Dougie's sixteen now, can you believe it? He'll turn out just fine once he gets through this teenage rebellion phase he's goin' through. Some good old-fashioned work experience should help with that, so I thought I'd bring him along instead of his old man."

Ken grinned at Dougie Roberts, who scowled back at him through the van window.

"Hey, Dougie, get out here," he called, then to Sage he said, "Nothin' teaches better than hands-on trainin', and Dougie here could use a callus or two on his fingers. He's looking a bit soft, if ya ask me. Skin ain't seen the sun in far too long. And what's with the black nail polish the boys are wearin' these days? *Boys,* mind ya. In my day, nail polish was for girls, and even then it was pink." He looked at Joyce. "How ya holdin' up, Joyce?"

"Well enough," she replied. "Want a cup of tea? Cool drink?"

"Maybe in a bit. Gotta work up the thirst first."

"I'll be seeing you out back then, Sage," Joyce said, turning to go inside.

"Tough old stick," Ken commented as they watched Joyce disappear.

Joyce was holding up remarkably well, considering two of her life-long best friends had been brutally murdered. Tragedy either toughened you or broke you.

Ken gave Sage the once-over. "You're lookin' well. Grown up real pretty."

Ken moved off, walking around to the back of his van, keeping up a constant stream of chatter. Sage ended up following him so that he didn't have to shout.

"Damn shame about Ada and Celeste," Ken said as he filled his arms full of tools. They clanged and clattered when he dropped them on the porch by the front door. He circled back to the van, Sage on his heels.

"Dougie, get your ass out here," Ken demanded, rapping on the window with his knuckles as he headed back to the rear for more supplies.

"What the hell is wrong with people these days?" Ken continued. "The murders have destroyed the morale of the whole town." Ken hefted out a large metal toolbox and gave a few items to a sullen Dougie, who'd finally managed to drag his tall, lanky frame out of the car.

Sage took a drill from Ken and a smaller box containing drill bits and nails and walked to the front door. Since she was in the position of following Ken around anyway, she might as well make herself useful.

"I want all new doors, heavy duty, and all window locks replaced," Sage said, repeating her instructions from this morning. "And if there's anything else you notice in need of repair or upgrade, please do that as well. After what happened to Nan and Ada, I need all their friends to be, and just as importantly, to feel as safe as possible." Living in fear was torture.

"Dougie," Ken growled. "Put that phone back in your goddamn pocket and hold the damn door. And while you're at it, pull those pants up. Your arse is hangin' out."

Dougie took his time finishing whatever he was typing into his smart phone, so Sage held the door while Ken dashed back to the van. After a long moment, Dougie slid his phone in his hip pocket and glared at her with kohl-rimmed eyes.

Sage suppressed a shiver. She had no reason to be frightened by a sullen teenager, but there was something... *off* about his eyes.

"They say you're the Angel of Death," Dougie said.

Sage's blood turned to ice. Not because of his words—people in town had always talked about her—but because of the sound of his voice. It was two-toned, the base note a deep baritone. Of course it could be because his voice was cracking with maturity, but something about that voice seemed familiar...

"Why?" Sage asked, not because she cared, but just so he would talk again.

"Because everything that's happening now is because of you."

Yes, definitely a creepy lower tone in his voice that shouldn't be there.

"You're certainly giving me a lot of credit."

Dougie smiled without humor, drumming his painted black fingernails on the door as he contemplated her. Instinct screamed for her to run, but she planted her feet more firmly on the ground.

"What about you?" Sage asked. "Do you think I'm responsible for everything going on in town at the moment?"

"I know you are," he said in that same chorded voice. "But not in the way *they* all think."

Sage held his gaze, and for a moment she was looking at someone older, someone with intelligence far beyond Dougie's tender years. Others, perhaps, might attribute it to the kohl he'd lined his lids with. Sage knew differently.

"Never been as busy in my life," Ken said, coming back with some wall plugs and a glue gun. "With the bad, comes the good. There's always the flip side of the coin. The whole town has been doin' up their security. Ever since Celeste and Ada were uh, well... ya know. Everyone is worried."

Dougie continued to stare at Sage unnervingly. She angled her body away, giving the impression she was unimpressed with his obvious attempt to intimidate her. Inwardly though, she had to admit he was creeping her the fuck out.

Ken continued to work and chatter, seemingly oblivious to the tension.

At sixty plus, Ken Baker was an outdoors man who, despite his slight paunch from a beer drinking habit, kept himself active and fit. As was the way in country towns, everyone knew everyone else's business, so Ken was always keen for a chat and never short of a yarn. But Ken was talking too much even for Ken. Was he... nervous?

"Is everything okay?" Sage placed her hand on his arm.

Shockingly, an image of something flashed in her mind. Something dark, something that tasted like death. Fire, smoke, and burning flesh. A road, River Terrace. Animals ripping at a human body. A satanic symbol, six, six, six.

Sage withdrew her hand, stumbling slightly as she stepped backward.

Ken froze, then narrowed his eyes at her suspiciously.

"Sorry," Sage apologized. "It's these shoes." She peered down at her sensible sneakers and winced. Why couldn't she have been wearing sandals, or even thongs? She stood up straight and affected an expression of nonchalance, while she gave her stomach a chance to settle. The images disturbed her more than she cared to admit. She'd had certain *impressions* of thoughts from animals before, but this was the first time anything like this had happened with a person. What had she seen? What did it mean?

Dougie smirked. "Told you, old man."

"There's talk in town, ya know," Ken said, turning back to the task of dismantling the old door.

"So, I've been told." Sage glanced at Dougie.

"Ya know I'm not one to gossip," Ken said.

"*Okay...*"

"But people are talkin' just the same. They're sayin' it's no coincidence that strange things are happenin' since ya returned." Ken paused, his drill whining a high-pitched *whir* in reverse to remove an old screw. "Damn thing's rusted solid," he complained. "Gonna have to rip it off and hope for the best." Using his hammer and a large yellow-handled screwdriver, he began banging away at the hinges.

"What do *you* think, Ken?" Sage said, trying to keep her temper in check. "You've known me all my life. Do you believe I'm responsible for the murders? The murder of my own grandmother?"

"Course not." Ken fumbled and dropped his hammer. "Well, not directly, anyway. They think you're responsible for the other things in town. The strange things."

"*What* strange things?"

"People talk, Sage. It's just talk. Ya know what us country folk are like. We gotta look out for our own. And even you'd have to admit it's a bit too much of a coincidence that weird things are happenin' only since you came back. For years, this town was a quiet, peaceful place to live. Then out of the blue, there are three, four murders. And other things too."

"Aside from Ada, the murders happened before I came back," Sage pointed out.

"The young ones are actin' out," Ken continued, as though she hadn't spoken, but she noticed the concern in his gaze as he flicked it toward Dougie.

"We ain't never had crime much before. And now there's break-ins nearly every night, and sheep have been goin' missin'. Plucked right out of the paddock into thin air. And Mrs. Coote's pig too. The one she kept as a pet. And people's been seein' things. Hearin' things. Whispers in the night. They's wonderin' what witchcraft you're stirrin' up. Wonderin' what evil you've brought back from the wicked city into our good town."

She'd been gone for years, but nothing had changed. She was still a freak, a witch, to these people. Sage's hands balled into fists, and she narrowed her eyes at Ken.

Ken wiped his hands on his pants. "Now don't ya go lookin' at me like that. I'm doing ya a favor by lettin' ya know what's bein' said. What with Celeste and her dealin' with that stuff beyond the grave, and then ya had those paranormal investigators turn up and do a show on ya. I've always liked ya, Sage. You and Celeste both. Good people, both of ya. But even you must admit, you've always been more strange than not. Ya can't blame people. It's human nature that people will talk."

"Ken," Sage said, unable to keep the impatience from her voice. "The paranormal investigators weren't doing a show *on* me, they were investigating the unexplained things going on. You realize they are happening *to me* as well as the town, you know."

Dougie snickered, and Sage glared at him. He held her eyes for a moment, then looked away.

Ken continued to work. "Perhaps some of your magic got outta hand. I don't think you'd do it intentionally. No, of course not. An accident. It must have been an accident."

"I don't do magic!" Although, after Wednesday night, Sage was not so sure about that. Something had happened, but it wasn't "magic" in the sense Ken was talking about.

"Oh, don't go tryin' to hide it from me," Ken said. "I knew full well that Celeste was a witch. A white witch though, a good one. She did plenty of good in the town. It only stands to reason that you're a witch too."

Okay, he might have a point there. There *was* something different about her. Again, Wednesday night had proved that without a doubt. It's just that it wasn't what Ken thought it was.

"She's a witch, all right," Dougie said.

Sage gave him another glare, then turned to Ken.

"Ken," Sage said slowly, wanting to stick to the truth as much as possible. "I may be what the town considers to be 'different' to them, but I'm not responsible for anyone's death. Not one single person, especially not Nan or Ada, and certainly not Mrs. Coote's pig. I'm just as concerned about discovering what's going on in town as anyone else."

"Too much of a coincidence." Ken frowned. "The timin' of your return. The trouble in town. I don't think it was deliberate, perhaps ya don't know what ya did, is all I'm sayin'. A spell gone wrong. You're a good girl, but playin' with magic is a dangerous thing."

Sage crossed her arms. She could easily spend the day arguing point by point with him, proving the flaws in the logic of each one of his statements. But she didn't have the time. Plus, he wasn't interested in the truth. Neither was anyone else in town. They'd already reached their conclusions.

Freaky, witchy, Sage was to blame.

"Good afternoon, Ken," Sage said stiffly, her tone cooler than she'd intended because of the smug look Dougie was giving her.

Realizing there was no reason now to be holding the door, she let go and straightened her spine. "Thank you for coming on such short notice. Text me when you've finished with all three houses, and I'll come in and settle the account."

"See ya around, Angel of Death," Dougie said.

Sage leaned close in to him, ignoring the stench of unwashed teenager, and whispered forcefully in his ear. "Stay the fuck away from me and mine."

Dougie's only response was to smile.

"Sage!" Ken stood up straight, his mouth hanging open. "You grandmother didn't raise ya to speak that way. Apologize to Dougie."

Too late, Sage realized that she'd "heard" Dougie's comment in her mind. Ken had no idea what had provoked her.

"I don't think I will," Sage answered Ken but looked at Dougie. "I'm quite sure Nan didn't raise me to do any of the things I'm about to do. But that's not going to stop me from doing them."

----◆----

Just like the last time she'd visited, Sage found Joyce, Pat, and Mona seated on the patio out back sipping tea from dainty rose-decorated china cups. A gold-edged china plate with homemade scones and a pot of jam sat in the center beside the crochet-covered teapot.

On the center of the table, next to the china milk jug, looking grossly out of place, was a revolver.

"What's with the gun?" Sage asked.

Ignoring the question, Patricia pushed a plate in her direction. "Why don't you try Mona's fresh scones?"

Patricia was dressed as immaculately as always, in perfectly pressed cream pants and a floral shirt. She'd been a medical receptionist most of her life and still presented herself as professional and stylish.

"Try them with the jam," she said, pointing to a jar with perfectly manicured fingernails. "Mona won the contest for the best apricot jam in the Barossa Valley last year for the third time in a row. Famous it is."

"Congratulations, Mona," Sage said patiently.

"Go on, and put a nice dollop of cream too."

Of course, there was no way Sage could eat, but she took a scone, ripped it open, and placed it on a delicate gold-rimmed floral china plate.

The three elderly women seated at the table looked like typical grandmothers, but Sage wasn't fooled. Underneath their seemingly fragile veneer, just like Nan had been, these women were tough old birds.

A fact she was counting on, come Sunday.

"The gun?" Sage repeated.

"It's a Smith & Wesson, 631 Lady Smith.32 Magnum," Joyce said. "It has a four-inch barrel and adjustable sights. We just call her Lady Smith. You know, like Lady Diana. Except of course Diana wasn't a gun, she was a princess. Tea?"

Okay... "I'll see to it, thank you." Sage topped up everyone's cups, then poured herself one. "Good to know you know all about your gun, but what's it for?"

"Protection of course, dear," Joyce replied, and behind her round glasses, her watery eyes reflected her fear.

"Protection from whom? Lucky?" Sage's stomach twisted. She hadn't considered how letting Lucky go could affect them.

"Yes, and no," Joyce said.

"Explain?"

"We're preparing ourselves for a repeat of what happened a hundred years ago," Pat explained. "You know, when everyone went mad."

"You've read Mary's diary?" Of course they would have, if they'd been as deeply involved in understanding the prophecy as Nan had been. A hundred years ago, Mary Pullman, a pastor's wife, had embarked on the same journey Sage was on now.

Mary Pullman was the previous seer's daughter. Keeping her actions mostly secret, Mary had kept a detailed diary describing in quite some detail the horrors of human sacrifice and the satanic rituals that had taken place in the main street. Nan had discovered Mary's diary in the attic above the shop.

Sage took a sip of her tea, then added a little sugar.

"There's no way I'm going to be unprotected in the middle of an apocalypse and tossed into a raging fire as a sacrifice," Mona said. "We'll shoot the zombie-fuckers before we let that happen."

Sage almost dropped the teacup. She set it back in its dainty saucer.

"We can all use it, can't we, girls?" Pat said proudly. They all nodded in agreement. "We all took turns pulling the trigger yesterday. Trouble is, our eyesight isn't what it used to be. We were getting better at hitting the target by the end though."

"Sure. If your target was Charlie's wheelie-bin," Pat said.

Sage winced and tried not to imagine these women with failing eyesight with a lethal weapon in their hands. Since Charlie placed his wheelie-bin at the entrance to his property, a long, winding track, Sage guessed the ladies were practicing in the adjacent paddock.

"I've arranged extra security patrols," Sage informed them. Gesturing to the gun, she said, "Can we put this somewhere else? Like in a safe?" She imagined someone being accidentally shot during a second helping of scones and cream. "You do know it's illegal to own an unlicensed gun?"

"I'll hide it," Pat said quickly. "I know just the place."

"It'll be safer at my house," Mona said.

Pat and Mona both reached for it at the same time, and Sage's stomach flipped as they struggled with it. A china cup toppled over, and the gun skidded along the table with the wave of spilt tea. Sage leapt up and snatched the gun before it could land on the ground.

"Is this thing loaded?" Sage asked, when she could breathe again.

"Is it?" Mona asked, turning to Joyce.

"I really can't remember dear," Joyce replied, frowning. "Perhaps."

Oh, dear God. Sage opened the cylinder to make sure it was empty, then slid it carefully into her bag.

"I came here this morning not only to see how you all were, but also to ask for your..." Sage was about to say help, but decided "cooperation" was more appropriate.

"Wednesday night, I came face to face with Lucky, with the demon within him, and I discovered I have certain... powers, just like the prophecy said." Sage briefly described what had happened, how the energy had flowed through her. The effect it had had on the demon.

"I know without a shadow of doubt that I am the seer's daughter."

Mona let out a whoop of delight. She was wearing a red polka-dot dress with full, puffy sleeves. With her wiry gray hair and red-framed glasses, she reminded Sage of a grandmother you'd see in a comedy script. The crazy cat lady. Except Mona didn't have a cat; she had a scruffy little terrier she liked to dress up with pink bows.

"Nan had the gift of sight," Sage continued. "She could communicate with those who've crossed over. She may have had other gifts, but I've never seen or heard anything similar to what happened to me. In working with her on the prophecy, did she happen to mention to you exactly what this energy is, or how I use it?"

"No, dear. But we all knew you were special," Pat said.

Special? Crazy people and wayward children were special too...

"There was nothing? Nothing at all you remember her saying that might help me?"

"Celeste was determined to keep you out of it. She wanted to handle it herself, with us, to keep you safe. It's why she sent you away to the big smoke." Sage had already read in Nan's diaries her account of how she'd encouraged Sage to move to Adelaide. Sage had thought it was to have a career; she'd never for a second believed it was to protect her from an evil entity in town.

"I appreciate what she did, and why she did it, but I am the seer's daughter the prophecy speaks of. She should have prepared me."

"But at the time she encouraged you to leave," Pat said, "we didn't know what the entity was exactly. We knew it was dangerous, of course, and it was after you, but we didn't know about the prophecy or the grimoire until we found Mary's diary. Perhaps if we had, things would have been different."

"And now it's too late," Joyce said. "Where's the gun?"

Sage ignored Joyce's question. "I'm not the same girl I used to be," she said, her voice hardening. "I fully intend to fulfill my role in the prophecy." *And get retribution for Nan and Ada.* She took a sip of tea and wished it were something stronger.

"In Nan's journal," Sage said, "she wrote that you'd all been practicing the verses from the grimoire that need to be chanted on the blood moon. Nan was going to perform the part of the seer's daughter, and you were going to be casting a circle of protection while the ritual was performed. This Sunday, I will be the seer's daughter as I was meant to be, and I'd appreciate it if you would do for me what you would have done for Nan. Are you still prepared to do that?"

"Of course, dear!" Joyce said, and the others agreed with the same enthusiasm.

Some of the tension in Sage's shoulders eased. Far from sounding fearful, they sounded... *excited.*

"I know that with Nan and Ada, you'd been doing everything possible to prepare yourselves for Sunday, but aside from the things I will ask you to do, I want you to take a step back." Sage softened her voice. "Nan and Ada were killed trying to alter the details of the prophecy, to protect me. But you can't alter fate. I'm here now, where I'm supposed to be. Where I'm *destined* to be. And I need you to take a step back and let me do it. I can't do that if I'm worried about your safety."

Christ, now she sounded like Ethan.

"Nan wrote that you'd started to collect the items needed for the ritual, that you had found and collected the grave dirt from Lucky's equivalent a hundred years ago."

"We have, dear," Pat said proudly.

"Where is it?"

"In the circle," Joyce said. "Not the real one, the practice one."

The real circle that Joyce referred to was the portal, a circle of ancient stones situated somewhere in the bush behind Nan's shop. It was where Sage intended to go after this.

"What do you mean by 'practice circle'?"

"We made a replica of the original," Joyce explained. "We'll show you."

"In a moment. I just have a couple of things I need to know first," Sage said. "I've only had a chance to briefly read through Nan's journal, but I didn't see anywhere a mention of the demon's name. Did you come across it?" Having the name of the master demon was crucial to the banishment part of the rite.

Joyce closed her eyes and shook her head. "No."

"It was the last thing we tried before Celeste's death," Pat said. "We think something went wrong that night, during the séance. The protection wasn't strong enough, and he broke through."

"Ada found her body the next morning," Joyce finished softly, her eyes downcast. Sage swallowed past the constriction in her throat.

"That's exactly what I'm worried about. Why I asked you to step back. Promise me you won't do anything like that again. I've got this," Sage said, praying it to be true. If she was right, interfering with the prophecy and opening themselves up to the entity had made them easy targets.

I refuse to let him hurt anyone else.

32

"Thank you for everything you've done so far," Sage said, "and for being such good friends to Nan. I know she loved each one of you."

"We loved her too," Pat said, eyes glistening.

"That's why I know she wants you to be safe. Please don't try to get the demon's name or try to help me, other than learning the verses in the way we've discussed. I need each one of you whole and well come Sunday. The success of the ritual depends on it."

It was their energy, coupled with the power of the words from the grimoire that would be an important factor on the night of the blood moon. Sage was already light on helpers; the picture depicted in the grimoire showed a circle of seven hands. With the death of Nan and Ada, Sage was down to three. She needed to find another four, three, if she included Ethan.

"You don't want to underestimate us," Joyce said pointedly.

"Shall we tell her?" Pat asked in a whisper.

"Maybe," Joyce replied, just as quietly. "But I don't think Celeste ever wanted her to know."

"That was before. Things are different now," Pat argued. "*She* is different now."

"Maybe," Joyce repeated, considering. "Let me think on it."

"I'm right here," Sage reminded them. "Tell me what?" As if she couldn't hear them when they were directly across the table from her. Their hearing might be failing, but Sage's had never been as keen.

There was a pause before Joyce spoke. "What we were doing in the circle. Come."

"Why do you feel the need to lie to me?" Sage asked, hurt.

"She just means that we can help you more than you think on Sunday night," Pat said, taking Sage's arm. "Let's show you the practice circle."

Sage slung her bag over her shoulder. She could tell she wasn't being told the full truth, but she chose not to fight with them, for now. Better she learn what she could and ask the hard questions as they came up. These ladies might be descended from sheepherders, but they weren't going to pull the wool over her eyes.

———— ◆ ————

At a surprisingly brisk pace, Sage followed the women down a cracked concrete pathway lined with fragrant geraniums.

Joyce opened the tin door to the shearing sheds, and they walked through her late husband's workshop. Vises and circular saws sat fixed to the timber bench tops, and the dusty shelves were lined with empty Vegemite jars filled with nails and screws. A half-finished wood project sat untouched, as though Harry would walk back in at any moment and finish it off.

When they stepped out of the workshop, Sage shivered, and, instincts on high alert, looked around. She had that sensation that *he* was watching her, but she saw no dark shadows or other signs of his presence.

They stopped in a clearing in the gum trees behind the pig pens. As Joyce had suggested, there was a large circle of rocks, in the center of which was a pile of dirt.

"Here it is," Joyce said proudly.

Pat knelt beside the pile, her knees cracking as she did. She picked up a green Milo tin, and Sage knew straight away that the tin didn't contain the powdered chocolate drink.

"It's dirt. From the grave of Virgil," Pat said almost reverently.

Sage felt the blood drain from her face. "Who's Virgil?"

"Virgil was the person the master demon possessed a hundred years ago," Joyce said.

"Like Lucky in today's time," Pat explained.

"How do you know it was the right grave?" Sage asked. "How do you know who the master demon had possessed?"

"Celeste found it," Joyce said. "That's how we know it was the right one. And after she died, we thought we'd collect the grave dirt and practice the rite. See what happened."

"Did anything happen?" Sage asked.

"No."

"Well, sort of. I had nightmares that night," Pat said softly. "Woke up with a horrible dark shadow standing by my bed. I haven't slept with the light off since."

"Yes, me too," Joyce added and Mona nodded, her eyes opening wide with memory.

"Seems we all did," Pat clarified. "It was absolutely horrifying. We thought it had something to do with the tin. So we got it out of Joyce's house and put it in the circle out here."

Sage shivered. Did they knew how close they had come to fates matching Nan's and Ada's? She would bet that the dark entity in their rooms was the same one following her. They'd already come to the attention of the demon. Did that make them the entity's next targets?

Sage had an amulet around her neck; what could she do for these women? Stronger locks and security patrols weren't going to be enough. She would have to ask Pia Williams, the psychic medium from Mark Collins's paranormal investigation crew.

Wrapping her arms around the women, Sage pulled them close. Their bones felt so fragile; a fierce rush of protectiveness flooded her.

"You need to take this." Pat thrust the Milo tin of grave dirt into Sage's arms.

"What about our gun?" Joyce asked.

Sage hesitated. She felt guilty taking it from them, but after the little episode she'd witnessed earlier, leaving it with them seemed unwise.

"Look after yourselves," Sage said by way of answer. "I'll go the back way to the circle behind the shop." It was a path along the river she'd taken many times as a child. "The walk will do me good. Give me a chance to think."

She tucked the Milo tin into her bag alongside the grimoire, Mary's diary, and Nan's journal. She'd barely started down the path when Joyce called out to her. Sage walked the few steps back to her.

"I just want to say thank you."

Sage smiled. "You don't need to thank me."

"We're happy you're here taking this on. You're not the same little girl we once knew. You've grown up real strong. Celeste would be proud."

A lump lodged in Sage's throat. "Thank you for saying that." She leaned in and gave Joyce a hug.

It wasn't until she was well along her way that she realized her bag felt a little lighter. The Lady Smith was gone.

A dry laugh escaped her lips and she shook her head in wonder. "Joyce, you sly dog."

The tightness in her chest eased slightly. Nan's friends might be old, but they were far from helpless.

The demon would meet his match come Sunday.

Chapter Five

On the outskirts of Cryton, four matching black Land Rover Discovery 4WDs converged on the twenty-acre property Ethan had just purchased. He unlocked and opened the large metal gate in the exterior fence, its rusty hinges squealing in protest. The homestead had sat vacant for over two years, which made the seller only too happy to unload his late grandfather's property for a reasonable price.

Gravel crunched beneath Ethan's tires when he pulled up in the large round space in front of the main building. He was the proud owner of a run-down old homestead featuring dry dusty soil and the tangy scent of sheep dung.

Six pairs of boots belonging to the members of Taipan tromped toward the front door of the hundred-plus-year-old stone house. With a tin roof and a wide veranda, the main building was sprawling. In the early 1900s, the house had been converted for use as a hospital, and the rooms modified for maximum space. It was perfect for the control center of Ethan's operations in Cryton. There was room enough to house all of Taipan, as well as a large master bedroom for him and Sage.

Ethan drew in a deep lungful of country-fresh air. Unable, unwilling, to leave Sage's side when she had been so frighteningly ill in his hotel room, he'd begun to make plans.

Working from a hotel was no longer a viable option because of security. Too many civilians coming and going in an establishment not under Ethan's absolute control. On a standard case, it didn't matter where Taipan were based. Most communication was carried out from their person or their vehicles.

But this was not a standard case. The type of protection Sage needed was not usual. For the first time in his life, Ethan gave thanks for the generous amount of money he'd amassed over his lifetime, but never given much thought to. That money allowed him to ensure she'd get the best protection possible.

While she'd been ill, he'd fired off an email to his business manager, who'd swiftly located this property. Originally intending to rent, Ethan had acted on impulse and purchased it instead. He didn't need to answer to a landlord over the damage that would occur when they installed their security equipment, and he sure as hell wouldn't have asked for permission.

The twenty acres were already fenced with eight-foot tall dog-proof fencing. And if nothing else, the farm was a sound investment. With its sprawling paddocks and rolling green lawns, in a property market on the rise, it was prime real estate.

But Ethan had thought no further than doing whatever it took to ensure Sage had a safe haven. If he couldn't be with her, he'd at least be able to breathe knowing she had somewhere to be. Surrounded by security. His men.

The property was perfect.

But as he stood on the wooden veranda of his new house, he couldn't shrug off a heavy sense of foreboding. An unexplained sense of dread, like a sinking rock in his gut. The tiny hairs on the back of his neck were raised, and his heart pounded in his chest, adrenaline racing through his veins. He'd experienced less anxiety preparing a drug bust on a heavily occupied biker's warehouse.

A black crow called out from a nearby gum tree, its caw sounding like wicked laughter. A hessian bag folded in half was to his left, and a black and white cattle dog lay on it, eyeing him warily. But when Ethan blinked, the cattle dog was gone. The bag was there, but there was no dog.

Maybe he needed more sleep.

He rolled his shoulders and cracked his neck, then dug the keys out of his pocket and managed to drop them on the mat. Nate Ryder, Ethan's partner and best friend, picked up the keys and handed them to him, a wordless look of concern creasing the corners of his eyes.

His men were watching. Waiting.

Something felt off. But what? Had the others sensed it too?

Hopefully this purchase hadn't been a big mistake. There was a reason people generally visited a property in person before buying. Sure, the place was beautiful enough, with its original architectural features preserved, but pictures in a real estate advert didn't convey the "feel" of a house.

Ethan unlocked the door, then stepped aside to let the men file in. The front door opened into a large central space, with the kitchen to the right. In the center of the main room was an oversized wooden table perfect for his meeting with Taipan. With its original picture rail and rosebud lights on the ceiling, the house certainly was impressive.

Sam whistled in appreciation. "Nice digs." Tall, lean, athletic, and twenty-five years old, Sam Wells was the youngest member of Taipan. His almost abnormal agility had earned him the nickname "Spiderman," which had been given to him the night he'd leapt an inconceivable distance from the roof of a twenty-story building to another to catch their perp while everyone on the ground watched in awe. And horror. Ethan had fully expected to be scraping his body off the pavement, but Sam had thought nothing of the leap.

"It should be suitable," Ethan agreed, casting his eyes around the room.

"Farmer Blade." Nate nudged Ethan.

"Can it, Ryder. You know as well as I do we need a base. This is as good as any."

"Yeah, but not all of us would *buy* the base." Nate grinned.

Ethan shrugged. "It's an investment."

Not that he'd brag about it, but he could have bought this place many times over and not made a dent in his account. In addition to receiving a sizeable inheritance, Ethan had an interest in finance. Although dabbling in the stock market didn't hold the thrill and excitement for him that risking his life going undercover did, his investments had paid off handsomely.

Ethan didn't do police work for the money. He did it because he believed in making a difference. His years on the force had given him a strong sense of justice. His mother had been killed by a criminal retaliating against his chief superintendent father. While he was fit and able, Ethan would do what he could to get killers like Lucky Keyton off the streets to prevent more innocent victims, such as Sage's grandmother and... Sage.

The men spread out, inspecting the space.

The house felt still. *Too still.* Every sound Ethan's team made seemed amplified, their heavy steps on the wooden floor unnaturally loud. He had the sense he was walking into someone's house uninvited.

"Creepy," Jake Brown commented, a shudder causing a visible ripple beneath his tight black T-shirt. "No offense."

Ethan moved to the windows and after a bit of not-so-gentle persuasion, the wooden frames gave way, opening. "Just been empty a while."

Jake frowned. "There's something... I don't know what exactly, but something seems... *wrong* about this town too." He looked across the unkempt paddocks. "It's as pretty a town as I've seen, what with all the heritage shops and leafy gum trees. But you get out of your car and take a breath, and it's like the air curdles in your lungs."

"You scared, Browny?" Sam asked with a grin.

"Fuck you, Wells. If you didn't treat everything like a goddamned joke, you'd know what I'm talking about." Jake's dark hair was cut in the traditional cop cut, his arms and chest heavily tattooed. A solid five-foot ten and built like a tank, with a scar that ran from the top left of his lips down his chin, the result of a knifing during a drug-lab raid, Jake looked like little on earth scared him.

"How old is this place?" Nate asked, ignoring the boys' familiar off-duty banter.

"A hundred and thirty-five years," Ethan replied. "Thereabouts."

"It feels like it," Nate mumbled, sniffing the musty air.

Ethan agreed with Jake's assessment; the house was creepy. Something about this place made him feel unwelcome, even though it was now his. He opened the front door and made sure every window was as wide open as it could get. Fresh country air was bound to make a difference.

Max, Daniel Smith's German Shepherd, snarled at something in the doorway that led off to the bedrooms. Ethan spun around. "Hey, Max. Don't you like my new place?" The dog's teeth were bared and his hackles raised.

A highly trained police dog, Max had been partnered with Daniel for several years. It was unusual for him make noise at all, let alone do so for no apparent reason.

"What is it, bud?" Daniel asked, looking the dog in the eye. Max calmed and sat, but continued to emit a low growl.

"He's been doing that a lot ever since we got here," Daniel commented, standing.

"Here, meaning this property, or here, meaning the town?" Nate asked, glancing at Ethan.

"The town." Daniel was six foot and fit, with closely cropped hair and a neatly trimmed goatee. "It's not like Max. I'm a little concerned. If he keeps it up, I'm going to have him checked out."

"And there's no goddamned phone reception here, either," Sean Wynter added. Sean, along with Jake, appeared the most menacing of the unit. Heavily muscled, with a shaved head, goatee, fair skin, and a body covered in tattoos, Sean easily went undercover in biker stings.

He frowned at his phone. "Well, there is," he amended, "but it's unreliable at best. Why'd you buy a house in this town? If you ask me, you've lost your goddamned mind, Blade."

"Didn't ask," Ethan replied.

"One boring country town is the same as the next, if you ask me," Sam said.

"Didn't ask you either," Ethan said, joining in the banter.

"Radios are playing up too." Sean turned the knob of his handheld on and off a few times. "Nothing but static."

"Mobile reception comes and goes, as does the Internet," Ethan explained. "Be persistent and keep trying. Get used to it. Odd is what you can expect while you're here." Ethan moved through the kitchen, opening doors and cupboards.

Mrs. Coote, the owner of Cryton's second-hand store, aptly named Second Chance, had furnished the house with the basics. Although the place came with some original furniture, such as the dining table, as well as some of the equipment necessary to run the farm, Mrs. Coote had, at no extra charge, arranged cups, plates, cutlery, and other necessities. Ethan would have to remember to send her a gift to show his appreciation.

Opening the fridge door, Ethan saw that she'd stocked it as well. A six pack of beer sat on the bottom shelf and he dragged it out, handing a bottle to each of the boys. *This ought to improve morale.*

As Ethan had predicted, with beers in hand, the six men fell into comfortable conversation, catching up on recent events, both with their cases and their personal lives, occasionally breaking out into full laughter at a clever joke.

The mood turned serious when Ethan stood, took the large worn file from his briefcase, and set it on the table in front of him. That single action changed the energy in the room. Wooden chairs scraped across the floor as the men arranged themselves in a semicircle, Max lowering into at-rest position at Daniel's feet.

The room soon fell silent, and Ethan had their complete attention. An absolute concentrated focus unmatched by anyone who had not undertaken the extensive training these men had.

They'd already read the official reports on the case, so he kept his summary brief. "As you're aware, the serial killer has been identified as Lucas Graham Keyton, known around these parts as Lucky. Average height, slim build, greasy blond hair, twenty-eight years old. Luke's father, William Terrence Keyton, passed away when Luke was fifteen—a tractor accident—and Keyton's mother, Raylene, died six months ago, ruled inconclusive. Officially, I've not linked their deaths with the recent murders; unofficially, I've not ruled it out. Until recently the people around town would not have believed Keyton a serial killer. I've pulled the cases and added them to the current investigation. Again, outside official channels."

"Why weren't the murders officially linked?" Daniel asked.

"Different MO."

Ethan saw the raised eyebrows and intrigued exchanges between his men. He would explain why they were working outside the system after he'd finished delivering the facts of the case.

"Luke Keyton was abused by his father—emotionally, physically, and I haven't ruled out sexually—and during the most recent interview, it's clear he holds, quite understandably, a great deal of residual resentment and anger toward him. His mother, Raylene, was a highly active and respected member of the local church in town. When Keyton went to her, she didn't report the abuse. She'd grown up here, and with no extended family, had nowhere else to go. This town was her life, and with child-abuse claims or worse, incest allegations, her reputation would never have recovered. Of course, it's also possible she didn't believe him. Keyton has always been considered a bit slow, and when I first interviewed him, he certainly seemed a few fries short of a Happy Meal. Either way, Keyton's childhood was less than desirable."

"Poor bastard," Jake muttered.

Ethan agreed. "I wouldn't be surprised to learn that Keyton's first murder had been his father. When no one will help you get justice, you may feel you have to take it into your own hands." *Especially if you're an angry teenage boy.*

"Around the time William Keyton died, the local police department recorded reports of occult activity by a satanic group. Its leader? None other than Luke Keyton. Naturally, his devout Christian mother wasn't pleased. Trouble at home flowed into trouble at school. His first official criminal record began as a juvenile. Theft, animal cruelty, B & E, drug possession, and assault charges all followed from eighteen onward. Keyton became a loner and an outcast." With all that anger and unresolved childhood issues, it was the perfect recipe for the making of a sociopath.

"Keyton smokes a particular brand of roll-your-own cigarettes," Ethan continued, "is unemployed, and in fact has never held a job. He often travels around, seemingly aimlessly. During our first interview, it became apparent that basic concepts like time or knowing the day of the week are irrelevant to him."

Ethan pulled out a separate file. "His killing style is ritualistic. The victims were all stabbed five times, four of the puncture wounds strategically placed in the shape of a cross, with the fatal blow slightly off-center to pierce directly through the heart. The official murder weapon has not been found, although several other knives and weapons were bagged and tagged from the scene. Due to the satanic nature of the ritual, I suggest we look for an athame, or ceremonial blade. It may be double-edged and will have a black handle that may have symbols carved in it. The murder weapon may be hidden in a separate location entirely, or he may have disposed of it." He pulled out a series of photographs and placed them on the table.

"The eyeballs from each of his victims were removed from their sockets, and replaced with circular pieces of black cloth. Removed, Keyton explained, because eyes are the mirror to the soul. Jars of eyes, both animal and human, were found in his playroom." *Where he'd taken Sage...* Ethan pushed the memory aside and continued. "A symbol, three curved lines coming out of a central circle, forming the image six, six, six, was branded into the palms of the right hands. Traces of adhesive were found around the mouths of the victims, but the duct tape had been removed, suggesting that the killer had needed to silence the victims for a period of time, but had later felt the need to remove it, reason unknown. All victims were killed and drained of blood in a separate location from where they were found."

"Daniel and I went over Keyton's cabin after we arrived last night," Sam said. "Sick bastard."

"Is it still secure?" Ethan asked.

"Yes."

"Did you find any hair?"

"As in souvenir type hair?" Daniel asked.

"Yes," Ethan said, forcing his hands to unclench. "A section of Sage's hair is missing."

"Didn't notice any," Sam said, glancing briefly at Daniel for his confirmation. "We did a thorough search too. We know you and Nate have already been through it, but you can never have too many eyes. Everything had been relatively organized. On display. We would have seen sections of hair. Bastard must have it on him."

"Yes, but why?" Ethan asked. "With everything we now know about his ritual, what would he want with her hair?"

"Maybe there's somewhere else he stores his things," Sean suggested.

"We can't rule out that possibility," Nate said. "We've searched his house, his playroom, his van. We need to consider he has another place to hide. There are numerous abandoned houses in the area; we'll have to search each one."

"Heard you had him, then he got away." Jake zeroed his intense gaze on Ethan, the scar across his lip giving him a permanent scowl. "Kinda surprised by that little nugget. Care to share how you let that happen?"

Ethan unclenched his teeth. The facts of Lucky's escape didn't sit well with him either. "Wasn't by choice, that's for fucking sure," he muttered and said no more. For now. Although he knew he'd be having *that* conversation with his team very soon.

"So, Blade," Sam said. "Interesting details you're not caring to share aside, sounds like a routine serial killer case to me. You've identified the perp. Arrested him, let him go. Caught him a second time, let him go again." Sam's lip twitched. "Seems like you just need to catch the fucker and keep him this time."

"I didn't *let* him go, asshole," Ethan said without heat. *The first time anyway.* "He was under arrest and under guard, handcuffed to a fucking hospital bed. Based on the security footage, it looks like he somehow hypnotized the guard into uncuffing him."

"Hypnotized?" Jake shook his head.

"Think that's strange?" Ethan asked. "You haven't heard anything yet."

"Which brings me back to my earlier question," Sam said. "Aside from a slippery serial killer you need help catching and keeping under arrest, what the hell are we doing here?"

It was a question Ethan too had pondered when he'd first been assigned the case. Special Ops was not wasted on cases that could be handled through standard channels.

"What did Ian tell you?" Chief Superintendent Ian Hallow, Taipan's boss.

"Jack shit," Sean grumbled.

"We're coming off the Jones case," Daniel explained. "Shit went down, and the whole operation got blown wide open. Enough done by the book to see the guy locked away for life. Don't expect much heat from the DA on this one. Did you hear we nailed Harvey Fucking Jones himself?"

"Did you?" Ethan asked, impressed.

"Well done, bros." Nate slapped Jake on the back. "Bastard's been dancing around us for years."

"And we didn't even let him go," Sam added with a smirk.

"We were going on a three-day break when we thought we'd see what we could do for you," Daniel said.

"I'm not following." Ethan indicated the file on the table. "I thought you'd at least been given the official brief."

Sam, Jake, Daniel, and Sean exchanged glances. "We came because you sent the email asking us to," Jake said.

"What the hell?" Nate gave Ethan a pointed look.

"Ian asked me what I needed," Ethan said through clenched teeth. "I told him to send Taipan. The entire fucking team."

"He didn't send us so much as a smoke signal," Jake said.

Ethan cursed. Ian had left him and Nate out here alone deliberately. He wanted as few people knowing the real situation as possible.

The betrayal stung. Far more than he'd anticipated. Ethan's gut twisted and he abruptly stood and crossed the room. With his arm on the sill, he stared unseeingly through a window.

Ian had lied to him. Without Ian, what was there to stop the government from coming in and wiping out the whole town again? How long did he have before they took action?

"So why are you here?" Nate asked, still sitting at the table with the team. "Aren't you all on leave?"

"Always wanted to holiday on a farm," Sam joked, seemingly attempting to lighten the mood. Ethan could feel the concerned glances being thrown in his direction, but the team didn't realize how deadly this situation had just become.

"Accommodation looks a bit basic," Sam continued, "but I'll see what the cocktail waitresses are like during happy hour."

"Ian may have refused to assign us to the case," Daniel said. "But we came because you asked us. Yes, officially we're on leave. But your message on Wednesday said it was urgent."

Taipan's bond went deeper than their employment. Although the work they performed was assigned to them by the department, the unit—which didn't officially exist—operated largely as a separate entity.

Ethan pushed off the window and turned to face his team. His mates. He'd give his life for these men and they'd do the same for him.

His other plan, one that had been forming during this case, again came to the forefront of his mind. He intended on going out on his own, starting his own investigation and security firm. Following rules and taking orders had never been his strong point. The only thing that had held him back was losing the bond he'd forged with Taipan.

But if Ian was working against him, it meant he had no support from the department. He was out here on his own without resources and backup anyway. There was a reason Ian had tried to keep the remainder of Taipan away. The only thing that made sense was that the government was planning on moving in.

Ian was deliberately keeping Ethan and Nate separate from Taipan. Ethan couldn't work under those conditions. Taipan was his life. And yet... now Sage was his life.

How the hell do I combine the two?

"You have to leave," Ethan said, walking back to his team and placing his hands on the table. The men shifted restlessly, and a rumble of unease went around the room.

Jake frowned. "Why the fuck would we do that?"

"Because I don't know what the government has planned. For all I know, the goddamn army might converge on Cryton any fucking second, wiping us all out."

Jake made a low noise in the back of his throat. "What the fuck, Blade? What the hell are you talking about?"

"What haven't you told us?" Daniel said, leaning forward. Max let out a low growl.

Ethan hesitated. For the first time ever, he considered not telling his team what was going on. Staying would cost them their careers, if not their lives.

"We can catch one scrawny serial killer by Thursday." Jake stabbed the table with his index finger. "Somebody better start talking fast because from what I can see, we can have this case wrapped up with a nice fucking bow in less than twenty-four." He leaned back, placing hands the size of dinner plates on his solid hips. "Keyton's already been in custody once. Twice. An easy arrest too, by the reports. He's a crayon short of a pack; it's only a matter of time before he slips up. The town's a decent size, but the population is small. The whole area has been cordoned off for some time. Keyton is still around here somewhere, and we've the chopper for eyes in the sky. Keyton can't use his house, the cabin, or his van. We've secured all three. There are only so many places the punk can be hiding."

Jake spread out his hands in front of him. "Come on boys. This is *us* we're talking about. *Taipan*. We'll have the son of a bitch locked up by nightfall."

"Goddamn it." Ethan thrust his hands through his hair. "You think I would have called you if it was as simple as that?"

"Then fucking tell us what's going on," Jake demanded, standing up and invading Ethan's personal space.

Jake had every right to be pissed. They didn't hide shit from each other, and Ethan didn't get to make decisions for his team. Not in this case. They'd make their own. To do so, Ethan needed to give them the facts. No matter how insane they sounded.

"Jesus, Browny," Ethan said, shoving him lightly in the chest. "Don't get your knickers in a twist. Sit the fuck back down or buy some deodorant. I'll fill you in. After that, it'll be your decision what you do next."

———— ◆ ————

For a room filled with six large men, it was deathly quiet when Ethan started speaking again. "Before I jump into what's happening today, I want to update you on a little town history. Share some information I received from Zach, the details of which were confirmed by Ian, albeit unwillingly." Zach was Ethan's off-the-books technology whiz. If it was recorded in digital form, Zach could access it. Just not necessarily by legal means.

Jake leaned forward. "Share."

"My great-grandfather worked a case with Ian's grandfather back in September 1915," Ethan began. "The department was called in to investigate a string of serial killings, much like what we've been called in on, the same month, almost the same day, exactly a hundred years later."

Ethan pulled out some off-the-record photographs Zach had somehow managed to retrieve and placed them on the table.

"When the team arrived on scene, they'd observed that the whole town had succumbed to some type of madness." Ethan indicated the disturbing black and white photographs. Scenes that could be the shorts for an early horror movie.

"No one was acting themselves. They were rioting, running around naked, committing depraved and morbid acts in the streets. Rituals were being performed that were clearly satanic in nature. The team took action when they discovered that young children, babies, were being ritually sacrificed in the main street. Understandably, they couldn't allow the situation to continue. The town had become uncontrollable; it was total anarchy. The department were out of their depth."

"Christ," Sam said. "How'd they deal with something like that back then?"

"Considering the whole town appeared to have become affected within a short space of time, they determined they were dealing with a contagious disease. Something that affected the brain, like mad cow disease or rabies. In an effort to contain the outbreak, they herded every man, woman, and child into the local church and burned it to the ground."

"What the fuck?" Jake demanded, as the others murmured their displeasure.

"It's true," Nate said. "They deemed it a tragic, yet necessary, operation. Then sealed the file."

"Which is how it stayed until now, a hundred years later, when history seems destined to repeat." Ethan took a deep breath. They were going to think what he said next was crazy, but he had to make them believe. Thank God Nate was there to back him up. "But we are not dealing with a virus; we're dealing with something dark, something not of this world."

"What the fuck?" Sam said. "You mean like spirits and ghosts and that shit?"

Ethan nodded. "A demonic entity."

"Come on!" Sam laughed, looking around the table as if everyone else was in on the joke.

"I'm serious."

Sam crossed his arms, staring at Ethan. "You truly believe that woo-woo crap? Sure, people practicing the occult do evil things. Delude themselves into believing they're Satan, commit horrific atrocities. But to believe there really is a... *demon* wandering around?"

"Nate?" Ethan asked, turning to him.

Nate nodded. "There's no denying what we're dealing with is satanic in nature. From what I've personally witnessed, I believe Keyton has been possessed by a demonic entity. Furthermore, I also believe that similar entities have possessed others in town. Just like what happened a hundred years ago."

"I didn't want to believe it myself," Ethan said. "But Keyton was able to do things a normal person can't do. He held me suspended in the air. And Mark Collins, founder of Paranormal Research and Investigations, host of the TV show *Debunking Reality,* was also possessed and held Sage at knifepoint Wednesday night at the cabin. His actions, his mannerisms, were out of character. Subsequent interviews confirmed our suspicions."

"Jesus Christ," Jake mumbled.

"I don't believe in ghosts and stuff," Sam said. "At least, I didn't," he added with a frown. "You're really not shitting us, are you? This isn't some kind of joke?"

"We're not messing around," Nate said. "We know it sounds crazy, but it's all true."

The team sat in silence, and Sam shook his head, running his hands through his hair. After a moment, he looked up at Ethan. "Of course I believe everything you've just told us. It's just—" Sam took a breath. "We've dealt with devil worshippers and cults before, and they are into some real fucked-up shit."

"I'm on the fence," Sean said. "Would have said absolutely no to believing in shit like that before today, but I know you wouldn't bullshit us. So... well, fuck."

"I believe it," Jake said, surprising Ethan. Surprising all of them, judging by the expressions of his team.

"Don't look so bloody shocked." Jake leaned his large frame back in the chair. "Years ago, I went to a psychic with my mum. That woman knew stuff she shouldn't."

"What do you mean she knew stuff she shouldn't?" Nate asked.

"It was at that time... you know, when I lost my wife and the baby," Jake said, eyes downcast. "He was only two months old." He closed his eyes a moment and his hands fisted.

Ethan would be surprised if the horror of that event ever left Jake. How do you get over losing your brand-new family in a split second?

The driver of the other vehicle had been a nineteen-year-old probationary driver high on the drug Ice. Jake had already been on the police force, but the accident was the catalyst that drove him into special ops and then into Taipan. Jake usually led in any drug operations they were assigned.

"The psychic lady said Felicity came through. At first, I was pissed. I mean how fucking insensitive. But she... hell, she told me stuff that only we knew. How I called her Flick, something that happened on our honeymoon. The name we were going to call our boy before we changed our minds the moment we saw him. No one else knew that stuff. I couldn't help but believe. That shit is real."

Nate nodded. "Pia Williams, the psychic medium on Mark Collins's team, knew the serial killer who had Sage was Luke Keyton at the same time, if not before, Blade did. She was also able to 'see' and direct us to the cabin where he'd locked up Sage. As she clearly wasn't involved in the abduction, her abilities are undeniable."

Nate met Ethan's gaze. They were both remembering the things she'd told Ethan about his past, things she couldn't have known if not given to her by an otherworldly source. That night, Ethan had become a believer in the abilities of psychics. *Some.* For every genuine psychic, there were fifty charlatans. But he now knew that genuine ones did exist.

Max sprang up and began barking again at the empty doorway that led down the corridor to the bedrooms.

"Max," Daniel commanded. "Heel."

Max lowered himself to the ground at Daniel's feet, but kept his eyes on the empty hallway and continued growling low in the back of his throat, teeth bared, the hair on his back standing on end.

"You see what I mean?" Daniel asked. "It's like he's reacting to an intruder standing in the doorway, but clearly there's nothing over there."

An icy wave skittered across Ethan's skin even though the afternoon was humid, the air still. There was no draft blowing the curtains in the window. Nothing to explain his sudden chill.

Nate absently rubbed his arms, Jake and Sam shifted in their seats, and Daniel shuddered as he ran a hand soothingly down the dog's black back. Everyone reacted to something they'd sensed on another level at the very same time Max did.

"This is the shit I'm talking about," Ethan said. "We're dealing with something beyond our five senses. If something feels off, it *is* off. There's nothing logical about this case, and we'll likely second-guess every single goddamn thing that happens."

Three loud noises sounded from the rear of the house. *Bang! Bang! Bang!*

"What was that?" Jake rose. Max began barking.

"Is anyone else here?" Jake asked, hand on his weapon.

"No," Ethan replied. The team moved to check out the house and Ethan's computer sounded with the ding of an incoming email. He would have normally left it, but he caught the sender's name out of the corner of his eye.

Craig West. Sage's security detail.

Ethan's pulse quickened even as he reassured himself it was likely just an update on her movements. Standard procedure. He whipped out his phone. There was no text message. No reception either.

Fuck!

Ethan bent over his laptop as he read the heading: *Urgent.*

A vise closed on his stomach. In fifteen minutes, he was due to relieve Craig. He'd planned on meeting up with Sage at Joyce's house. He was going to talk to the ladies, then bring Sage back here.

Craig wouldn't email with "urgent" unless there was a problem. Ethan clicked the message and the first sentence chilled him to the bone.

Subject missing.

For a long moment, Ethan's heart ceased to beat. The team were back in the kitchen; he was distantly aware of them making comments about the place being secure.

Max began to growl again, this time at him. Ethan couldn't blame the dog; a toxic stew of conflicting emotions churned in his belly and must be pouring off him in heavy waves.

Having Sage snatched out from under him by the serial killer was still a fresh wound. The email was throwing salt into it.

Nate began reading over his shoulder.

Sage Matthews entered Joyce Booth's house 10:17 a.m. as advised in previous report Subject's car remains in front of the house, and subject hasn't come back out. At 12:50 p.m., three elderly ladies exited the house, preparing to leave. When I enquired about Sage's whereabouts, they acted strangely and wouldn't answer my questions. They have advised, however, she's not inside the house, claiming she left sometime earlier. To confirm, her car is still out front and has not moved. The subject's phone is ringing out. Request further instruction. Would you like me to gain entry and search the house?

"Fuck." Nate snatched his jacket from the chair, strapped on his gun.

"He's lost her," Ethan bit out, his tone pure ice. "Sage is missing."

Clicks of guns in holsters, the rustle of utility belts, as Taipan scrambled into action behind him.

Ethan fired back an email.

Do NOT enter the house. Ethan couldn't be sure of Craig's method for doing so, and didn't have time to brief him.

Maintain surveillance outside. I'll be with you in five.

"She'll be all right, mate," Nate said, slapping him reassuringly on the shoulder.

Ethan had to believe that.

He couldn't lose Sage a second time.

Chapter Six

Sage took the bush track, which ran from the rear of Joyce's property along the river to behind Nan's shop. It was a track she'd followed numerous times during her childhood and knew every step of the way. Yet as she walked, Sage filled with a nervous energy that grew stronger the closer she drew to town. A heaviness settled within her chest, making her breathing labored.

Soon, the gum trees cleared, and she was at the bank of the Murray River. Nan's house was only five hundred meters farther along.

Dry leaves crunched beneath Sage's feet, and she deliberately took a deep calming breath, inhaling the warm humid air mixed with the fresh eucalyptus scent of the Australian bush. There was no obvious reason for her pulse to be racing. No reason for the level of anxiety she was experiencing.

She stopped short, abruptly remembering. "Damn!" So focused on seeing the circle for the first time, she'd completely forgotten that Craig was positioned in front of Joyce's house. She should have checked in with him. Apprised him of her plans. Ethan was going to have a conniption, especially after the promise she'd made that morning.

She'd head back. But wait… It would take longer to double back, since she was almost at the circle now. It would be a better to ring Ethan and let him know where she was. He could arrange for Craig to meet her at Nan's shop. After she'd seen the circle. The idea of Craig accompanying her to the circle didn't fill her with warm fuzzies.

Satisfied she'd found the solution to keep everyone happy, she continued walking and pulled out her phone.

No reception.

Damn. A brand-new phone tower had gone up just outside Cryton last year; reception should no longer be a problem.

It must be a black spot. Sage picked up the pace and kept walking. She'd more than likely get a few bars again closer to Nan's shop, closer to town.

With every step she took, Sage's unease grew. There was a tingling between her shoulder blades, a prickling of the tiny hairs on the back of her neck.

Sage was being watched.

She felt *his* dark presence like a heavy winter coat. His evil essence hung in the air, and as much as she resisted his pull, she still had to suck the stench into her lungs to breathe. Her heart raced; she could almost see a knife about to be plunged deep into her flesh. Out here, no one would hear her screams.

Head lowered, Sage focused on each footstep as she pushed through her rising panic, fighting her body's commands to run. She refused to be cowed by the demon.

Each step reminded her she'd walked this trail countless times, knew every tall gum, every bush, and every bend in the track. She willed herself to find comfort in the familiar, to focus on the low chirping of crickets and the buzz of cicadas in the background. He was not going to stop her from doing what needed to be done.

And then the insects fell silent.

A chill skittered across her skin and her guts turned to jelly. Her heart began to race and sweat broke out on her forehead. *He* was getting closer.

Breathe.

Her grip tightened on her phone, and a quick glance confirmed there was one bar of reception. She dialed Ethan's number. Just listening to his voice right now would be what she needed.

The number rang once, then the screen went dark and the phone wouldn't turn back on. It behaved as though the battery had died, even though it'd had almost a full charge at Joyce's.

I've got to go back.

She could no longer make her legs keep moving forward. Seeing the circle now held no appeal. She'd come back tomorrow with Ethan.

Something dark moved in the bushes.

Frozen, all she could do was stare. What had she seen? And then she saw it again. A small, black shadowy movement.

There was something familiar about it. Something that had nothing to do with *him*.

Her feet finally obeyed her commands, and she headed toward her last sighting of the shadow. Just beyond where she'd seen the little shadow disappear was the graveyard behind Nan's shop. And just beyond that, the circle.

She was here now. No use turning back. Swallowing her fear, Sage pressed on until she was standing at the rusty metal gate, hidden almost entirely by scrub and bushes, that marked the entrance to the graveyard. The wire and picket fence had fallen down long ago.

Sage stepped over the fallen wire and moved around the ill-defined space. An area had been cleared around each grave, exposing the names of those buried there.

She counted seven graves, all female, but didn't recognize any of the names. Who were these women? And why weren't they buried in the town cemetery only a few kilometers away?

Sage followed a track that ran off to the left. It led away from the others to a single, lone grave. As she grew closer, she saw that the soil had been disturbed. The grave was smaller than the others. *Lance Virgil Keyton* the headstone read.

An icy tremor ran the length of Sage's spine. *Keyton?*

This was the grave Joyce had told her about, the person who had been possessed by the master demon a hundred years ago. *A deceased relative of Lucky Keyton.* Engraved clearly next to his name was the symbol on the front of the grimoire. The same symbol on the amulet around her neck. Her hand automatically rose to the angel, felt its reassuring connection.

Then the bush crackled again, and something black raced toward her.

She stepped backward and stumbled, landing hard on the ground.

Then the black thing was on top of her.

Clawing and... *snuggling* into her neck.

Liquorice!

"Silly cat," Sage said, relief and residual fear coming out as nervous laughter. "Where have you been? You nearly gave me a heart attack." She stroked her shaking hand down his soft black fur and held him tightly, then grabbed her bag and phone and rose to her feet.

Before she left, Sage took one last look at the group of graves. She had no idea who they were, but they must have been significant.

They're witches, Liquorice said, his words forming in Sage's mind.

"Who are?" Sage asked. "The people buried in those graves?"

Yes, Liquorice answered. *They are Mary's witches, her seven for the circle.*

Of course! Mary hadn't acted alone a hundred years ago. The prophecy required seven to cast the circle of protection while the seer's daughter performed the rite. Like Sage, Mary would have needed seven also.

Although... Sage knew Mary hadn't told her pastor husband about the prophecy, or what she needed to do as the seer's daughter. Had she snuck away for secret meetings with the witches?

Curious though. Who had buried the witches here? And why?

Mary put them here. To energize the soil of the circle, Liquorice said. *They belong to the prophecy now.*

A gust of air brushed over her face, bringing her thoughts to the present and reminding her she couldn't stay here any longer. She needed to get back to Ethan before he discovered her missing. As curious as she was to see the circle, she'd better wait until tomorrow.

"Time to go," Sage said, peering into the shadows of the gum trees around her. The temperature dropped several degrees in a second, and Liquorice growled. She was feeling more uncomfortable by the minute.

Nan's shop, Beyond the Grave, was only two hundred meters toward the road. She knew a shortcut, quicker than taking the track. From the main street of town, she'd try to call Ethan. If there was no reception, she'd use the shop phone, provided it was still in service. Ethan would get Craig to give her a lift back to her car, which she'd left outside Joyce's house.

"Come on, Liquorice." She moved forward, but the cat jumped out of her arms. *Follow me,* he said.

"Not tonight," Sage told him firmly. Sage had no intention of letting Liquorice out of her sight, and knowing the hotel's no-animal policy, she began thinking of ways she could smuggle him into Ethan's room undetected.

The wind whipped up, sending wispy tendrils into Sage's eyes and making them water. The leaves rattled loudly above her, the branches bending with the sudden onslaught.

Liquorice took off. Sage grumbled under her breath as she hurried to catch up. *This had better be good.* A few times, Liquorice disappeared out of sight behind bushes, but she managed to keep track of him. Where was he leading her? The circle?

Liquorice took her into the thickening bush.

Without stopping, Sage checked her phone. Still no reception. Glancing at the sky, she guessed she had two hours—at most—before nightfall. A dry branch snapping beneath her sandshoe made her heart race. Liquorice stopped, looked over his shoulder to check she was all right, then continued on.

Breath trapped inside her lungs, Sage continued forward. Gooseflesh broke out across her skin, as fingers of pure ice walked up her spine. Wherever Liquorice was taking her, the demon didn't like it.

Sage rolled her shoulders in an effort to relieve some of the tightness.

Liquorice meowed. *Hurry!* The air was now so thick she struggled get enough oxygen no matter how hard she sucked in her breath. She recognized the sensation all too well. It was the same heavy pressure she felt on her chest during the nights she'd spent in Nan's house. And in the cabin.

He was becoming angry. His fury was an icy gust of vile wind that blew through her body.

There was nothing stopping him from attacking her, like he'd attacked Ethan Wednesday night. She gripped the angel around her neck tighter.

Beneath the silence was an even deeper stillness. Not a single chirp from a cricket, nor a lone tweet from a bird. Not the slightest breath of wind, not a rustle of a leaf, as though even the trees were afraid to move.

Liquorice stopped, hissed, then growled, his hackles standing on end.

Run! her mind screamed. The entity was so close, she thought it touched her.

One hand gripped her pendant, and the other gripped the rough bark of a tall river gum tree for balance as a wave of dizziness washed over her. Her head began to throb, her migraine coming back with a vengeance.

"Let's get out of here," Sage ordered Liquorice.

She turned around to leave, but a mist rolled across the ground, blurring the trail. She felt disoriented. Confused. She could no longer see Liquorice.

Which direction did he go?

She was alone.

But then wasn't.

There was… something light, a glow just past the tree in front of her. Sage walked toward the strange light.

And froze.

She'd stepped into an alternate world.

Something primeval, and not of this time.

A low vibration hummed in her ears, soothed the throb in her head.

She sucked in a breath and she looked at the area in awe. A circle of rocks, each one perhaps a meter high. The circle was complete, each stone angling inward and touching the one alongside it. The circle they formed was large, perhaps eight meters in diameter.

With her mind, Sage followed the angle of the stones to where they pointed upward, and imagined the invisible point where they met in the sky. A pyramid with a circular base. A towering cone. The center of the circle was smooth, perfectly graded, filled with a fine, talcum-like powder.

It was just like the picture she'd seen in the grimoire. Identical.

And pristine.

In contrast to the cemetery, no weeds or bush tangled around the stones. Her first thought was that Nan had cleared here, but she quickly realized nothing grew here in the first place.

This place, this isolated, vibrating circle of rocks, was not of this dimension. It might be physically in this world, but it was not *of here*.

Unsettling to her now though was the abrupt absence of fear. She was safe. Protected. The stones were calling her. She heard their whispers.

And she answered with her own.

She moved forward to the edge of the circle, lowered herself to the ground, and touched one of the rocks with an open palm. A vibration rolled through her body, her skin tingling as though she'd received a low voltage of electricity.

She was strangely calm.

At peace.

A tear rolled down her cheek, but she wasn't sad. She licked her lips and tasted the saltiness on her tongue. She didn't understand what this was, this strange place.

But she knew one thing for sure. Knew it with every cell of her body.

I am meant to be here.

A warmth spread up her arm, energy transferring from the vibrating rock through her hand and into her body. Sage fought against the weight of her lids, struggled to remain alert.

Something was happening to her. She willed her eyes to open, and when she did, she was somewhere else. No, she was here, at the circle. But not tonight. The images flashing behind her eyes were from another point in time. The past perhaps?

No, it was still to come. She was seeing *the future.*

It was night time, late, and a full moon with a reddish hue cast bloodied light across the landscape. She was surrounded by thick bush; gum trees rose high into the night, reaching into the sky with spindly ghost-like arms.

53

She was standing at the edge of the circle and the ancient stones had been... activated? They were glowing, vibrating. The hum was soundless, but it thrummed through her body like heavy metal music at a rock concert. The night was strangely silent, not a single cricket chirped, not a leaf stirred in the trees.

The circle was the only thing alive. Breathing... pulsing... *calling*....

A whooshing began, a rushing in her ears. The aggressive roar of an ocean before you're swallowed by a monster wave. Screams, cries, shrill shrieks, and pained wails mingled in one long haunting song.

But the noise was wholly within her, a disturbing contrast to the night, which was silent and still.

And then, she was no longer alone.

Around the stone circle was a ring of seven people. Hands joined, they chanted a song that belonged in the very distant past. There was power in the words, and she saw an energy, a tangible glow, rise up and around, blurring their dirty and bloodied bodies.

And then she saw Ethan.

Behind him was a raging fire. Savage, and wildly hungry. It was feeding, not on wood, but on human souls. The more it consumed, the hungrier, the more ferocious, it became.

Ethan had his back to the beast, the flames rejoicing as they licked closer.

Run! Sage screamed until her throat was raw. But Ethan couldn't hear her. She tried to run to him, but something was holding her back. Stopping her from moving. She cried out to him, but her ravaged voice could not carry over the roar of the fiery beast. Ethan mustn't have heard her, because he didn't run.

Instead, he remained still, the beast closing in behind him.

Ethan's eyes found hers. Joined like a key in a lock.

And he smiled softly. Calmly.

It was the most gentle smile she'd ever seen. Tender and filled with love. Contentment. He was still, as though he'd finally found peace.

Anguish rose in her throat and choked her. The horror of what was about to unfold stole her voice. Her very soul.

The beast was upon him now.

Ethan must know he was about to die. Yet he didn't move. She thrashed at her restraints, bloodying her wrists.

Oh, Ethan. Why don't you run?

And then she realized.

Because he was okay with his fate.

Be damned if she was.

She fought to get to him, ignoring the shooting pain as her arm wrenched from its socket.

Her eyes were stinging from the fire's smoke.

Ethan, run! For me, run!

Oh, God, why doesn't he run?

The heat was so intense it burned her skin even from this distance. She struggled to free herself. As she wrestled with her bindings, she recognized the metallic clanging sound.

Handcuffs! She'd been cuffed to a metal pole. A sign post. And she'd hazard a guess they were police-issue Smith & Wesson, double-lock cuffs.

Ethan's cuffs.

At her feet was the key. Carelessly tossed after the job of restraining her was done. Or perhaps not carelessly. Perhaps deliberately. As though she'd need to be freed at some later time, but not by him.

Why had he done this? *Why?*

The beast closed the final distance, the sky exploding above her as the fiery wings of Hell climbed Ethan's body and set his hair aglow. He didn't flinch; his back was straight, his shoulders square. His eyes shone through the dark gloom of swirling smoke, full of love and devotion. They radiated.

With a sense of purpose.

They didn't waver from hers, and she knew he wanted her to be the last thing he saw on this earth.

Flames licked at his shirt until it fell to burning pieces at his feet, leaving his chest exposed, the chest that had lulled her to sleep with the beat of his heart just last night.

A round metal pendant hung from a silver chain around his neck. A crystal wand dropped from his hand. The smell of burning hair, burning flesh, assailed her senses. The only indication he was in any pain was the white-knuckled clenching of his fists. Otherwise, his face was serene, his eyes soft as he stared, stared long into hers.

"Don't cry," he mouthed. "This is for you. This is all for you. *And her.*"

A gentle smile played around the corners of his lips. His expression more reminiscent of after they'd made love than of the agony he must be feeling before his imminent death. Her stomach clenched violently, tears blinded her, and she angrily blinked them back, not wanting to miss a single second of him either. *Why?*

Why was he doing this to *them*?

And who was this *her* he referred to?

Sage's voice was a croak, scratched up and unrecognizable from shouting, from begging, from the stinging smoke.

"I love you," he said. How could his words reach her ears when hers couldn't reach his? "I won't ever stop. I can't. Not now. Not ever."

She knew he meant in what was beyond this, and what was left of her heart shattered. Her black-and-white "just the facts" detective was counting on something else being there for them both.

She didn't want to see him then, dammit.

She wanted him now! In *this* life. They still had so much left to do.

"You and me." Ethan said, his face barely visible now. He made the eternity symbol over his heart. The figure eight. Then held up his crossed fingers. A symbol of them eternally entwined.

And then the beast had its way.

Sage screamed. And didn't stop.

———— ♦ ————

Something touched her face, and she slapped it away. Sitting up, Sage blinked rapidly. She was in the dead center of the circle. How had she got in there? Liquorice was pawing at her, mewling pitifully.

Hurry. We have to leave. Now.

His warning pressed urgently into her mind, triggering a rush of adrenaline. Rising to her feet, Sage picked Liquorice up, holding him firmly in one arm. The grimoire was lying open to the picture of the stones. When had she got it out? She grabbed the book and tucked it back into her bag.

What she'd just seen, that nightmare—no, premonition—clung to the edges of her consciousness and refused to clear. She'd never had visions before, especially nothing like that. It had felt so *real*.

Sage was drenched in sweat and chilled to the bone. Her hand shook as she pushed dampened cobweb-like strands of hair off her face.

Hurry, Liquorice said.

She stepped between the waist-high rocks that now felt and looked like the inanimate objects they should be. They were no longer vibrating, and they certainly weren't breathing.

Releasing a long breath, she willed her racing pulse to calm. Darkness had long descended on the area, and the bush around her cast the trees in shadows that made eerie shapes. She'd lost around two hours. Maybe more.

By the light of the moon, Sage navigated through the bush, following the trail to make sure she didn't lose her way. She didn't relish the idea of spending the night out here. And Ethan must be frantic with worry.

Reaching into her bag, she pulled out her phone. It was on again. There was no reception, but one of its features was a little flashlight. She turned it on. It put out a surprising amount of light.

That familiar tingle started between her shoulder blades. *He* was watching her again. Perhaps he'd never stopped? It was unnerving, sensing someone watching your every move. Waiting for you to slip up.

Liquorice sensed him too and bolted from her arms. He landed with a soft thump on the ground. Hackles up, he hissed, then growled, low and menacing, into the trees.

Her heart clenched. "I know, little guy. I feel the same about protecting you. But we have to pick up the pace. Stay close."

Sage hurried along the track. Suddenly she heard a different type of movement behind her. Something refreshingly not supernatural. But she moved even faster.

Lucky had abducted her once; did he mean to do it again?

The *whop whop whop* of a helicopter's blades sounded in the distance. Was that the police? Had Ethan sent them to look for her? They wouldn't be able to see her in this thick brush.

Dry leaves crunched again. Closer behind her now. Her heart almost pounded out of her chest. She was being followed, while unseen eyes watched her from the shadows. Enjoying her fear, feeding off her terror.

Switching off the flashlight, Sage broke into a run. Whatever it was, it was gaining on her.

She soon reached the clearing. Sage had never been so pleased to see a graveyard in all her life. She rushed through the maze of graves, silently apologizing if she accidentally stepped on one. To her left, a pair of yellow eyes peered at her through the darkness of the trees.

She hurried away to the right when a large form stepped into view. The yellow-eyed thing on her left was not of this world, the shape to her right was human. Which way did she turn?

The figure to her right moved in a determined path in her direction.

Lucky?

But the person was easily a head and shoulders taller than Lucky and moved with confidence, a relaxed stealth that came only with absolute belief in one's personal power and ability.

Ethan!

Her knees almost buckled with relief.

Before she could blink, he was at her side, arms protectively around her shoulders. He positioned her slightly behind him, sheltering her body with his. Possessive. He made a hand signal, and four large men, heavily decked out in combat gear appeared as if from nowhere on the edge of the clearing. Ethan's Special Ops unit. Taipan.

"Clear."

"Clear."

"Clear."

"Clear."

One of the men she recognized as Nate.

The chopper's noise intensified as it hovered overhead, the rotor wash stirring up dust and dry leaves and flinging them into the air. Its searchlight bathed the area where she and Ethan stood, and she squinted against the harsh light. Ethan made some type of signal with his hand, and helicopter banked hard and flew off.

Taipan approached, separate individuals who somehow moved as one. Their weapons drawn, their movements smooth and stealthy.

The air was still thick, heavy and oppressive. *He* was still watching. Sage sensed his excitement.

As a clear breeze blew in, her tension began to ease.

He was retreating.

For now.

The atmosphere in the area returned to normal. Animal and insect sounds started up all around them. It was a regular spring's evening once more.

But before *he* left, intentional or not, she'd caught an impression. A glimpse, maybe, of his true intention. It was the reason he'd remained in the background, doing nothing but watching. Yes, he'd enjoyed the fear he'd elicited from her while doing it. But he was only toying with her tonight. Playing.

It was Ethan he'd been waiting for all along.

———◆———

Ethan's priority right now was taking Sage home to where she was safe and under the protection of his men. If he lived to be a hundred and twenty, he never wanted to experience that debilitating feeling of discovering her missing.

Again.

The wound was still too raw. Too fresh. The first time she'd been out of his sight since that night, she'd disappeared. The terror of wondering if Lucky had got to her again, of what he would do to her this time…

He crushed that train of thought. Had to. It was too painful to contemplate. As it was, he was unable to still his shaking hands as he helped her into the passenger side of the Land Rover.

"I'll head back with Sean," Nate said, understanding without words Ethan's need to be alone with Sage.

Ethan hesitated before closing the passenger door. He ran his hands down Sage's hair, over her cheeks, across her trembling shoulders.

She met his eyes, and her smile faded. She'd read something in his expression. He couldn't be sure what it was. He didn't understand himself what his dominant emotion was.

All he knew was that now she was safe, unharmed.

Thank God.

Now that the fear had receded, something else flooded to the surface, taking the place of relief. He wasn't entirely sure where this tsunami of emotion should be directed yet, but he knew one thing.

He was angry as hell.

Chapter Seven

Ethan's jaw was set, his expression a frozen mask of chiseled steel. And Sage was the cause.

His energy made the Land Rover feel cramped. She opened her window, and a rush of cool evening air washed over her face. Breathing deeply, she filled her lungs, deliberately attempting to relax. Looking down at the ball of fur in her lap, she stroked a hand over Liquorice's silky coat.

"How are you feeling?" Ethan flicked a concerned glance in her direction. As upset as he was, he still worried about her. That was a good sign. Wasn't it?

"Much better. Thank you for asking." Her tone was cool. She hadn't intended it to be, but she didn't deserve his current temper. Of course she understood he'd been worried when he didn't know where she was, but his reaction was over the top.

"Is your migraine still troubling you?"

"No," Sage said, realizing that was true. Despite the angry man beside her, she'd never felt better. Physically.

"I'm sorry you worried about me," she said after another charged silence. "I forgot all about Craig being out front. When I remembered, I was already halfway to the gravesite. I tried to call, but there was no reception. I tried again when I got to closer to Nan's, but the call wouldn't go through. And then I got distracted when I found the circle..." Her voice trailed off. Her explanation wasn't softening his expression. He clenched and released the steering wheel, and a muscle twitched along his jaw.

He said absolutely nothing.

Sage refused to be around him in this mood. "Take me back to Nan's." She'd apologized. He could either get over it, or come back for her when he *was* over it.

"No."

"Excuse me?" Sage spun to face him, barely reining in her desire to tell him where to go and how to get there. "You don't get to tell me what I can and can't do, Ethan. I don't know where you got the idea that you can. I—"

"Goddamn it, Sage." His words exploded like a grenade in the confined space. "Give me a moment, will you?" He thumped the steering wheel, before again taking it in a vise-like grip.

Liquorice hissed and Ethan cast him a dark look. "Not you too."

Sage hugged Liquorice to her chest. "It's okay." She didn't know whether she was reassuring the cat, or herself.

Ethan let out a breath. "I've just spent the better part of two hours thinking you were in the hands of a serial killer. Trying not to think of what was happening to you. What he was doing to you. Whether you were already dead." His voice broke, and he swallowed hard. "Excuse *me* for needing a bit of time to get over that."

Sage slumped back in the seat. How could she continue to be angry with him after that?

Silence descended again, the only sound the low rumble of the motor, the change in revs as Ethan moved through the gears, handling the large 4WD with ease and confidence. On his left wrist was an expensive sports watch, and on his right was a plaited, black leather band. She'd wondered about the band for a while. He didn't strike her as someone who wore things for the sake of fashion.

"I like your wrist band."

He said nothing for a long moment. "I bought it the day of my dad's funeral."

"It reminds you of him?"

"I wear it in memory of both my parents. It reminds me why I do this job. Why it's worth the risk."

"Did they ever catch him?" Sage asked. "The man responsible?"

"I did." His tone said "subject closed" in capital letters.

Sage's throat constricted. She had so many questions about his family, but now was not the time.

"Where we are going?" she asked instead, when they passed the hotel. He took a turn to the left, along Railway Road. Gum trees lined the less-used rough bitumen road. She glanced in the side mirror, the convoy of black 4WD Land Rovers behind them. It was an impressive sight. "Are all your team here?"

"Yes."

"I only saw four tonight. Five, including you."

"Jake was in the chopper," Ethan said.

They were searching for me. She'd assumed they were looking for Lucky.

How formidable Ethan's team had looked when they'd stepped out from behind the trees. So fierce, with their wide stances and their weapons drawn. Sage would never wish to be on the wrong side of those men.

Ethan included. Not that her stony-tempered detective would ever hurt her. Not intentionally.

"Where are we going?" Sage repeated, realizing he still hadn't answered her question.

"We're here." He stopped at a large iron gate and left the Land Rover idling while he stepped out to open it. As the gate crossed the cattle grid, the screech of metal on metal seemed abnormally loud in the still evening air.

Sage recognized the property. For some reason, Ethan had brought her to the Muellers' place. He yanked up the rusty *For Sale* sign and tossed it face down to the side. Someone had finally bought it?

Ethan slid back behind the wheel. "It's mine now."

"Why would you buy a farm?" Sage blinked at him. He couldn't have surprised her more.

"I bought a house that happened to come with a bit of land. The team needed a proper base. I can't run the operation the way I need to in that old hotel."

"How did you buy a property in one day?"

"It was a few days." He shrugged. "Was surprisingly easy, actually."

He must have been arranging this over the days she'd been unwell. Every time she'd woken up, he'd been tapping away at his laptop intently.

"But surely you didn't need—"

"I *needed* somewhere safe for you. A place for you to stay while I handle this." Her heart pierced at the slight tremor in his normally steady voice.

"While *we* handle this."

He slanted her a look. "We."

"You don't get to take this over, Ethan. Don't you go heading off doing things without discussing them with me first."

"Likewise."

Sage opened her mouth and closed it again. "I said I'm sorry."

He reached out and squeezed her hand. "You scared me, babe. I can't help but react this way when it comes to you."

They pulled up in the homestead's large horseshoe driveway. Ethan opened the door for her and held her hand to assist her out of the car. She placed one foot onto the ground. Dried leaves crunched under the sole of her shoe, and a twig snapped loudly in the cool evening air.

She stilled. Senses on high alert, she looked around.

The darkened clouds began to swirl in the sky, moving much faster than normal. A sudden breeze picked up, dumping a wave of humidity over them. Ethan shook his dark locks from his eyes and looked at her in question.

She appreciated his efforts in arranging a place for her to stay. Close enough to town, yet far enough away to be private. It should have been perfect.

But for reasons she couldn't explain, her feet wouldn't move. She had an overwhelming impulse to retreat into the warmth of Ethan's car and surround herself with his comforting scent.

She fantasized them driving away from here. Fast. Taking the road back into town, through town, out of town. Getting on the highway and never stopping.

She couldn't be here.

She met Ethan's gaze. He waited on her; he'd take her away if that was what she truly wanted.

He'd already done too much on her behalf in this whole situation. He'd only come to town to solve a murder, and now he was neck deep in prophecies and demons. She thrust back her shoulders and gave him a tentative smile.

"You guys coming in, or are going to stare at each other all night?" Nate called out from the veranda.

Hugging Liquorice tightly in her arms, Sage stepped away from the car.

———— ♦ ————

At the front door of the homestead, Liquorice jumped out of Sage's embrace and landed with a hiss, hackles up. A deep warning growl came out of him, and Sage immediately bent down to comfort him.

I know, Sage told him without words. *I have the same feeling, but it's not polite for you to be so ungrateful to Ethan.*

Liquorice lowered his stance, but backed away, growling fiercely.

"He did the same thing at Nan's if you remember," Sage said. "I'm sure he'll settle down once I get him comfortable."

Ethan walked around the side of the house and came back with a bench seat similar to the one Liquorice had slept on in front of Nan's shop. He positioned it on the same side of the door, mirroring what Liquorice was used to.

Sage's heart warmed as her large, serious man, gun holster and weapons clearly visible, wordlessly arranged the furniture for her cat, keeping his team waiting.

Ethan went inside and came out with a blanket, which Sage arranged on the seat. She placed Liquorice on the comfy pad, and he stopped growling.

"Thanks, Eth," Sage said. "Is it okay if I stay out here with him a little bit? I'll be in shortly."

Ethan hesitated, scanned the area in front of the house, then nodded. "Don't wander off."

Sage bit down on her tongue, hard, to avoid a reply she might regret later. Ethan was still pissy with her, but he needn't think she'd let him get away with speaking to her like that next time. When he stepped inside and closed the door, she let out a breath.

She needed a moment, not only for Liquorice, but for herself. Everything that had happened—the strangeness of the circle, the terror she'd felt during the premonition, the sheer force of Ethan's mood, even though she understood where it came from—had thrown her off balance. She trailed her hands over Liquorice's fur.

She didn't like this house, and wished Ethan hadn't bought it. If it had been just somewhere to stay, she'd feel much better about asking to stay somewhere else. But he'd bought it for *her*. To keep her safe. So what did she say to Ethan? To the members of the special-operations team that waited inside?

"You don't like it either," Sage murmured to Liquorice. "Why?"

Liquorice was silent for so long, Sage thought he wasn't going to answer. Maybe he couldn't put it into words either.

Then something flashed into her mind. Something dark, disturbing, like disjointed stills of a movie played out of sequence. Lucky's playroom, the cottage where Lucky had taken her, only it wasn't. The same tools were there—the Bunsen burner, the metal brand, the knives, the circles of black cloth—but the walls weren't timber, they were concrete. A black and white dog barking. Blood. Blood sprayed everywhere, on the walls, the floor. Bloodied handprints on white doors.

Liquorice mewled and shuddered, and Sage withdrew her hand. The images receded. "What did I just see?" Sage asked as a chill skittered across her skin. "Where did you see this?"

He was here.

"The demon?" Sage asked, her voice barely a whisper. "The demon was here too?"

Oh mother of all things holy, now she *really* didn't want to go inside.

But how could she not?

Liquorice clawed the bedding and yawned. He looked exhausted.

She leaned in and kissed him on the head. "We'll be okay. We only have to get through until Sunday. At least we're not at the shop. You're safe out here."

We're not.

Sage's stomach fisted.

"What will you have me do?"

Leave.

"Oh, Liquorice, if only it were that simple."

Sage was going inside. She had to. How would she face the demon himself on Sunday, if she was scared of a house he'd been in long ago?

She covered Liquorice with the blanket and scratched him behind the ears. "Stay warm. I'll see you in the morning."

Standing, Sage dusted off her clothes and smoothed her hair back.

Forced her feet to move to the front door.

Took a deep breath and stepped inside.

Chapter Eight

The scent of sizzling steak and sausages filled the room, as did the five large, muscular men standing around a bench-top hot plate, beer in hand. The room was warm, and the cooking smells comforting. The unease Sage had felt moments ago outside largely disappeared.

She let her gaze travel the room. Ethan's men, Taipan, were big, but something about their presence made them seem even larger. Despite their casual attire, only a fool would be unaware that these men could be lethal. With or without weapons.

The conversation died off and heads turned in her direction as she closed the door behind her.

Sage scanned the room for Ethan, annoyed that she wanted him by her side. She'd never had any problem being on her own, but she wouldn't be human not to be a bit intimidated by these men, who were largely strangers to her.

Not seeing Ethan, she sought out Nate. At just over six foot, Ethan's partner and best friend had striking blue-gray eyes, light brown hair, and an easygoing temperament. And he was seriously good-looking. He flipped the steak on the hot plate, then passed the tongs to a man the size of a Sherman tank with a scar that ran through his lips and over his chin.

"Don't burn them this time," he said, then crossed the room to her.

"Hey, Sage." Nate planted a chaste kiss on her cheek and draped an arm casually around her shoulders. "Just in time for dinner."

"Smells good." Her stomach rumbled in echo of that statement. She hadn't eaten since breakfast. Nate caught her staring at the hot plate they'd opted to use in place of the stove.

"Just like Scouts, we come fully prepared." Nate grinned and her tension eased.

Remembering the supplies Ethan kept in the back of his 4WD, the blankets and packaged food, she smiled. Like his team, he was prepared for all contingencies.

As though conjured up by her thoughts, Ethan finally appeared. He crossed the room to wrap an arm proprietarily around her shoulders and pulled her in to his hard body. Nate's arm fell away, but his grin grew.

Ethan's possessive gesture was not lost on one single man in the room.

Although no one spoke, brief glimmers of surprise crossed their faces. Sage had no doubt Ethan had told his team about her, but apparently he hadn't made their relationship clear.

Until now.

"Gentlemen, this is Sage Matthews," Ethan said, without releasing her. "Sage, these men are Special Operations, Taipan. More than colleagues, they're my mates." The men nodded in mutual acknowledgment.

"To your left, is Sam Wells, or Spiderman," Ethan began. "When you see him in action, the nickname will have meaning." Slim and athletic, Sam appeared to be the youngest of the team, his blond hair short at the back and long at the front.

"The two men on the barbeque are Jake Brown and Sean Wynter." Jake was the huge one who had taken over the barbequing from Nate. A solid six foot, with some serious tattoos to go with that scar on his face.

Sean shared the same "don't fuck with me" look. Also heavily muscled and tattooed, he had a shaved head and goatee, along with amazing baby-blue eyes.

"At the table is Daniel Smith, and the German Shepherd next to him is Max." Daniel was also tall, with closely cropped brown hair and a neatly trimmed beard. Like Nate, he was handsome, but not quite as strikingly so.

Sage greeted the men, then smiled at the dog. "I've left my cat Liquorice out front. Will he go after him?"

"Not at all," Daniel glanced down affectionately at the dog. "Max doesn't move a muscle without a cue from me."

"May I?" Sage asked. After receiving permission, she ran her hand down Max's thick, sleek caramel and black coat. The tag on his collar had the police force logo on one side and his name and rank on the back. "He's beautiful."

"He's the seventh member of Taipan," Daniel said, pride evident in his tone. "Even though every one of us would lay our lives down for each other, I'd go as far as to say that Max is the most fearless. The most loyal and dedicated of us all."

Sage ran her fingers over Max's jet-black pointy ears. Sensing his slight unease, she reached out, but his thoughts were closed. He looked at her warily, so she backed off.

"Meat's ready," Jake announced. "Sage, you'll join us? I threw on an extra few snags, or you can have Blade's steak."

"Sausages will be fine," Sage said, standing.

"Sage will have my steak." Ethan pulled out a seat for her at the table.

"We'll go halves," she countered.

Ethan came back a short time later, with her plate loaded with barbequed meat. "Help yourself to the salad," he said, indicating the large bowl of lettuce, tomato, cucumber, and onion. A loaf of bread sat in the center of the table next to a squeeze bottle of tomato sauce.

Sage sliced part of her steak into tiny pieces and took it out to Liquorice.

"What would you like to drink?" Ethan asked when she came back in.

"There's beer in the fridge," Jake said, wrapping a sausage and onion in a piece of bread. "That's about it at the moment."

"Beer's great, thanks." Sage smiled.

"Mrs. Coote will be stocking the cupboards tomorrow," Ethan said by way of an apology.

"Glass?" Jake raised his brow, cold beer in hand.

"Bottle's fine." Jake handed her the beer, the bottle frosted damp with chill.

She sat back, chugged her beer, and began to relax as small talk and friendly banter went on around her. For such serious-looking guys, they were highly entertaining. Jokes and one-liners had her laughing and enjoying herself.

Everyone joined in, except Ethan.

He'd barely said a word throughout the meal, and more than one curious glance had been directed his way. He'd been polite, courteous, but he clearly wasn't joining in. Tension radiated from him in almost tangible waves.

"So, Sage. Tell us a bit about yourself," Sam said, taking his plate to the sink.

"Not much to tell. I'm not that interesting."

"Doubt that," Sam replied, seating himself back down at the table. "Something about you has caught Blade's eye."

A look passed between Ethan and Sam, and Sage shifted in her chair uncomfortably. *Could he still be upset with me?*

To hell with that. She'd apologized already for making him worry, but she wouldn't apologize for doing what she needed to do. While being abducted by Lucky wasn't something she was keen to repeat, she couldn't have her wings clipped so much she couldn't fly. She needed a certain amount of freedom to figure out and explore the prophecy. There was so much she needed to discover, to learn, before Sunday.

Sage spared Ethan a brief glare. If he didn't snap out of it soon, she was going to have to give him a piece of her mind.

———— ◆ ————

Ethan listened as Sage told his team a little about herself. How her parents had died when she was young, how she'd been brought up in Cryton by her grandmother. Her love for her nan, as she called her, shone through loudly. Sage explained how she'd come back to town for her grandmother's funeral, the strange things that had occurred in her grandmother's house, and the subsequent paranormal investigation by Collins and his team. She told them what she'd discovered from her grandmother's diary about the demonic entities and what had happened to Pia during the investigation. Her story concluded with how she'd been captured by Lucky and held in his cabin.

Ethan studied the faces of his team. To an untrained eye, their expressions seemed neutral, impassive. But Ethan knew these men, and though he'd already briefed them on the paranormal aspects of the case, he could see they were struggling to swallow the prophecy concept. He resisted stepping in, instead letting Sage keep the lead.

"And just how does the prophecy suggest you send this demon back to Hell?" Sam asked, but his question didn't contain sarcasm. Purely curiosity.

"I'm to perform a specific ritual as outlined in the grimoire at midnight on the blood moon. That is when the doorway, the veil between our worlds, is the thinnest. The ritual is complex, time sensitive, and involves Lucky, or rather the demon that has possessed him. That's why you can't kill him. Ethan did tell you that you can't kill him, right?"

"Yeah," Sam drawled in amusement. "He might have said something along those lines. But what I don't quite understand yet is exactly why."

"Sage needs him in the circle on Sunday night," Nate explained.

"Yes." Sage threw Nate a grateful glance for his support. "I don't need Lucky in the circle, so much as I need the demon who is possessing him in the circle," Sage said. "If you kill Lucky, then the demon becomes—" She waved her hands, searching for the right words. "A black mist? A dark shadow? An energy that I have no idea how to capture."

"So you need the demon in the circle on the blood moon," Jake said. He was leaning forward, elbows on the table, giving Sage his full attention.

"Yes. The ritual I need to perform is a process. Much like an exorcism. It takes place in the circle, because that is the portal, the doorway to another dimension. A world of darkness."

"Like Hell?"

Sage shrugged. "Perhaps." She went on to describe what had happened last Wednesday night at the cabin, where she'd had the first confrontation with the demon. The flaming wings of fire that had towered high in the sky. What had happened to her, the energy she'd summoned, and how the demon had effortlessly held Ethan suspended off the ground before flinging him against the cabin's exterior.

Ethan leaned back, observing how well Sage dealt with his team. Their sheer size and presence alone cowed the most hardened criminals. But Sage spoke to them as she would to the woman who owned the bakery, not afraid to give a bit of attitude back to Sam when he provoked her in that way of his.

The team slowly warmed to her, their body language softening as she spoke. Something inside him shifted too, relaxed. He knew now that his team would do anything to protect her, not because it was their job, their mission outline, but because they'd accepted her. Sage had more effectively assured their protection than any order he could issue.

"That is an incredible story," Daniel said. Max was now asleep at his feet. "I'm not saying I don't believe you, but I'd like to take a look at this with fresh eyes. Analyze everything that happens now with a technology and perspective that clearly they didn't have a hundred years ago. Those times were still steeped in superstition, based on fear and paranoia. Any report or document we have from that time must be viewed with that perspective, something you need to keep in mind when reading those old diaries."

"Good point," Sage said. "And I'm glad you're taking that angle. You can keep Ethan company." She tossed him a speaking glance.

Ouch. He supposed he deserved that after what he'd put her through, all that time he'd spent arguing on the side of logic, but he was behind her a hundred percent now.

"Speaking for myself," Sage continued, her chin slightly raised, "I'll be following what's written in the grimoire and Nan's recommendations, and do what I *know* worked last time. Killing a whole town of innocent people in a church certainly didn't shut the portal or stop the demon."

The men inclined their heads, acknowledging her criticism of the department they took their orders from. Although Ethan had already given them the background, he was glad it was Sage who told them about the prophecy, the grimoire, and what she needed to do come Sunday.

"So, tell us," Sam said, grinning. The shift in his body position and the teasing tone in his words broke the tension. Ethan sucked in air, grateful to be able to breathe again. "How'd Blade handle the fact his girlfriend aided and abetted the escape of a serial killer?"

Ethan groaned. He'd wondered when they were going to ask details about that night. How they'd let a serial killer go.

"I... uh—" Sage looked up at him then, met his gaze. He merely raised an eyebrow in response. She sighed. "I think he took it reasonably well, considering."

Laughter erupted around the table.

Sage stiffened her spine. "Don't be like that. It's not like I had a choice."

"Uh-huh," Jake added, clearly amused. "So you obstructed justice. Interfered with a lawful arrest. Not to mention the crimes you committed the day before that weren't in the official file." Jake was talking about how Sage had broken into Ada's house to retrieve the grimoire, a fact that Ethan had noted in the file he'd prepared for the team. As far as the local police went, the perpetrator was unknown.

Jake flicked his gaze briefly at Ethan, then continued in the same jocular tone. "You were on quite the tear. B&E on a property sealed for crime-scene investigation, unlawful entry, property damage, interfering with a crime scene, larceny—"

Sage held a hand up. "Don't. It doesn't sound good when you put it like that."

"How should I put it to make it sound better?" Jake raised one dark brow.

"Technically, it wasn't larceny, because I'd been given permission to have the book."

"By the deceased," Nate said, joining in. "After her death. Not sure how well that will hold up in a court of law."

Everyone burst out laughing.

"Technicality." Sage waved her hand dismissively to another round of laughter. "Come on, Nate, back me up here. You know as well as Ethan that I didn't have a choice when it came to Lucky. I had to step in front of Ethan's gun. If I hadn't, he would've killed him."

Silence greeted Sage's pronouncement. Ethan didn't think he'd ever seen his whole team speechless at once.

"*That's* how you helped Keyton get away?" Sam asked, jaw dropping. "You stepped in front of Blade's gun?"

Ethan inwardly groaned. He hadn't put *that* in the report either.

"Well, fuck." Jake eyed her with a different sort of expression. Something more like respect.

"I didn't have time to think about what I was doing," Sage said, raising her chin.

"You've got some serious balls," Jake said. "Are you aware that Blade is a highly skilled marksman? One of the best the department has?"

"Known to be a little trigger-happy too, on occasion," Daniel added.

"I... uh—" Sage broke off and glanced at Ethan. "Thank you for not shooting me."

The table erupted in laughter.

"Well, Blade, you've certainly found your match," Sam said when the volume died down.

"He sure has," Nate added, grinning at Sage.

The knot in Ethan's gut uncoiled a bit more. His team now knew everything: the history, the current situation, and the truth about Sage and what she needed to do on Sunday.

And by some miracle, they were all on board. She'd managed to take an unbelievable situation and make them believe. More than that, she'd managed to wrap each one of them around those beautiful fingers of hers.

Sometime during the conversation, Max had left Daniel's side and crept across to Sage's feet. It was only the distance of a meter or so, but Ethan had never seen that before. Sage tossed her head back and laughed at something Sam said and stroked her fingertips across Max's head.

There was a certain something about Sage. An innate quality that captivated people. Especially him. It wasn't merely her beauty. Ethan had been with many beautiful women over the years; for example, Jenny, his ex, was a stunning dancer in a men's club. Everything about Jenny screamed sex, and men turned to puddles around her. Their relationship had been satisfying and mutually beneficial, until Jenny wanted something *more*. It was the something more that Ethan didn't have to give.

Until Sage.

Ethan's throat closed as he remembered this afternoon. The paralyzing fear that had flooded his body when he'd received notification that Sage was gone.

Subject missing.

Lord help him, he didn't know how he'd survive if Keyton took her again. Next time, Ethan knew for sure, she wouldn't escape. File pictures of the serial killer's mutilated victims transposed themselves over Sage's body. The blade of the knife that had permanently lodged in his gut since he'd arrived in Cryton plunged even deeper and twisted.

How will I take my next breath, if something happens to her?

Ethan fingered the woven leather band on his wrist. He'd told Sage the truth about it when she'd asked, but there was more. The band wasn't just a reminder of the deaths of his parents, of why he did this job. It was also a reminder of what happened if you allowed someone in. Losing his parents had closed that door. He'd meant it to stay that way, forever. And yet, Sage had managed to sneak herself in through the back entrance.

Mine.

He hoped she knew what she'd done, because there'd be no other for him. Not now.

He'd seen the hell and destruction his father had spiraled into after Ethan's mum was killed. The anger, the frustration, the powerlessness of not being able to change what had happened, the bitterness, because it should never have happened... the blame, *the responsibility*. The bottom of a bottle didn't numb knowing someone had lost their very life because of you. *Over who and what you were.*

Mum had dealt with a lot being a cop's wife: the late-night calls, the dark moods over a case his dad had been working on, the grief over something he may have witnessed during a shift, his absence on important occasions.

And then to lose her very life because some scumbag wanted revenge on the cop who'd put him away?

Ethan had been the one to find his mum the day she'd been murdered. He'd also been the one to find his father the day he'd killed himself.

He'd never forget either day. What he'd seen. How it *felt*.

After his father's suicide, Ethan had channeled everything he had into protecting decent people from the evil that walked amongst them. And he was good at it. It had become his identity, his sense of purpose. It was who he was.

He wore the black band to remember.

And then fate stepped in, and with an ironic wink, gave him a case he couldn't solve and made him fall in love with a woman he couldn't protect.

The evil in Cryton was in a different form. It wasn't human.

And he couldn't stop it.

The whirlpool of emotion he'd been holding back all night bubbled to the surface in a rush. Ethan rose from the table. "Angel? We need to talk."

Sage cast a glance in his direction, then a regretful glance at his team.

"Don't expect us back out tonight." Ethan took her arm and led her toward the bedroom.

It was time to make her understand that she couldn't bloody well take herself off wherever and whenever she pleased.

Chapter Nine

In the bedroom, Sage sat on an antique leather chaise as Ethan kicked the door shut behind him. A stunning crystal candelabra sat atop the mantel of the corner fireplace. The original, Sage guessed. The hearth gave the room an air of romance, and she imagined it with the warm glow of a winter fire, the scent of freshly cut logs in the cane basket in the corner.

Sage sighed and tugged the tie from her hair, freeing it from her ponytail. Romance appeared to be the last thing on Ethan's mind. With his back against the solid timber of the door, he took a deep breath and eyed her. Resisting the urge to squirm like a bug under a microscope, she tried to read his mood.

"I know you're upset with me," Sage blurted. "I know you were worried when you couldn't get through to me. I get that. But sporadic mobile reception is hardly something under my control. I tried on several occasions to call you."

Sure, in hindsight, she could have turned back when she first realized she hadn't informed Craig of her plans. But if she had, she'd never have had that experience with the circle. Whatever had happened there tonight was deeply personal. And somehow necessary. An experience perhaps, she'd never have had if someone else had been with her. She didn't understand it, but the energy in the circle had done something to her. Altered her in some way.

It had been *preparing* her.

Ethan merely stared at her, saying nothing.

"Look, I've already apologized for making you worry, but I have other things to put my mind to at the moment." Despite the unwanted attention by the demon, she'd made it out safe. After all, she'd been on her way back when he'd found her.

"I'm not used to having a babysitter; it's not surprising I forgot Craig was waiting for me." She never intended on getting used to being followed around. The current situation was clearly an exception. Freedom was important to her, and something non-negotiable.

Was Ethan ever going to speak again?

Sage jumped when he pushed off the door abruptly and shrugged out of his jacket. He tossed it carelessly onto the chaise beside her, the ripple of air wafting across her skin. He tugged his T-shirt free of his jeans and unclasped his watch, placing it on the bedside table. Her traitorous pulse kicked up and her mouth dried as it always did at the sight of him. She turned away and rose, kicking off her shoes and heading to the window.

As she passed the grand four-poster carved bed, she ran her hands over the soft black fabric of the quilted cover.

Outside the window, the waxing moon cast an even glow across the property. Ethan's property. It was hard to believe Ethan now had ties to the town she was so eager to escape.

It was a clear, starry night, a gentle breeze stirring the leaves of the towering gum trees.

She heard him padding up behind her, felt the heat of his body an instant before his arms wrapped around her. He tugged her flush against him, her back to his chest, and rested his chin on the top of her head. For a long moment, neither one spoke.

"The view is beautiful from this window," Sage whispered.

Ethan made a sound in the back of his throat. "Believing Keyton had stolen you from me today ripped my heart right out of my chest." His voice was deep and raw.

She turned in his arms and peered up at him. Their eyes connected, and she took the hit like a punch to her stomach. Electricity sparked, crackling between them.

"I arranged Craig for a reason," Ethan said, his voice breaking. "Damn you for not knowing what it would do to me to be told you were gone."

"Eth—"

He closed his eyes, shoved his hands through his hair. When he opened them again, they were glistening. "I can't ever experience pain like that again, Angel. It killed something inside me. I believed I'd failed you. Again. And that thought sickened me. More than hating Keyton, I hated *myself* in that moment. For my incompetence. My inability to keep you safe... *for one fucking day*." The words were bullets to her very soul.

"And then—" He swallowed, lowering his voice to just above a whisper. "And then I discover you'd just waltzed out the back of the house, went on your merry way without so much as a thought about how I would feel. How I would react. What it would *do* to me."

Oh dear God. She'd really hurt him. "I'm sorry." The words were a mere whisper as they squeezed past the constriction in her throat. A tear rolled down her cheek. Hurting Ethan was the last thing she'd intended. This situation was taking a terrible toll on both of them.

"I'm sorry," she repeated. She reached for him, but he stiffened, and she let her hands fall back to her sides. They were at an impasse.

His body was coiled with tension, like a python ready to strike. As if he needed a physical outlet for the turmoil inside. The way he looked at her both excited and frightened her.

"Where do we go from here?" Sage had no desire to fight with him over something she couldn't change. And her body seemed to have checked out of the conversation. Being so close to him like this, every cell of hers seemed to be tingling with awareness.

Sage licked dry lips, and he watched the movement with eyes that contained a volatile cocktail of emotion. His fists clenched at his sides as though his control not to grab her and ravish her senseless teetered on a knife's edge.

She knew on which side of the edge she wanted him to fall.

He fisted the collar of his shirt, pulling it over his head and tossing it in the corner.

He stepped closer, and with one hand braced on the windowsill on either side of her, he caged her. Having him so close, so powerfully male, stole her breath.

"Where do we go from here?" Ethan repeated her words with an edge she hadn't used.

She trembled, but not from fear. The part of him that was pure primal male rolled off him and scorched her skin.

"There are many things I need to say to you about what happened today, but I don't know the words to convey everything to you so you'll understand. I only know how it feels inside." He tapped his chest, over his heart, with a closed fist.

"And words can be misinterpreted." There was no denying the raw sexuality in his tone. He took his hands off the sill, dropping them to the collar of her V-neck T-shirt. "I'm going to show you instead."

With one quick movement, he ripped the fabric down the middle, exposing her lacy black bra, and she gasped. He held her arms back, trapped in the torn material, his eyes darkening as he watched her chest rise and fall.

Brushing his palms down her arms, he shoved what was left of her shirt to the floor. He trailed his fingers across her collarbone, barely touching the parts of her breasts that swelled over the top of her bra.

"Fuck, Sage, you make me want to be anything but gentle."

"I don't remember asking you to be."

The room became unbearably hot. Sage grabbed the waistband of his jeans and tugged him closer. The rich, spicy scent of him blanketed her, filled the space between them.

Their chemistry was overwhelming, animalistic and primal. Her nipples tightened painfully. With a flick of his wrist, he had her bra undone and on the floor.

"You want me just as much as I want you." It was not a question, and she hissed in a breath as he pinched a hardened nipple between his thumb and forefinger. White hot pleasure speared between her thighs.

She wound her arms around his neck, tangled her hands in his hair a little too hard.

He gazed at her body with a predatory gaze. *"Mine."*

Sage moved forward, pushing him back a step toward the bed. *"Mine,"* she repeated back to him. His lips twitched with amusement and his eyes took on a wicked gleam.

With seemingly no effort, he lifted her up and threw her onto the bed. She laughed as she bounced and pulled herself up onto the pillows. Ethan slowly walked around the bed, took a lighter out of the pocket of his jeans, and lit the candles on the mantelpiece. With unhurried movements, he divested himself of the remainder of his clothes. Goose bumps skittered across her skin, her muscles tense, her body alive and tingling with anticipation.

He knelt on the bed, knuckles brushing the soft skin of her stomach as he unbuttoned her jeans. Pulling them down her legs, he discarded them on the growing pile of clothes on the floor.

He licked a trail up her inner thigh, lingering at the lace of her panties. He lifted off her long enough to tear the tiny scrap of fabric, leaving it to fall away, before continuing a trail up her waist, to her neck, her jaw, then her lips. His mouth was warm, and her pebbled nipples brushed against the hard muscles of his chest. As his tongue licked deep into her mouth, she ran her hands across his shoulders, down his back, to his perfectly sculpted ass. She raised her hips, pressing herself against his erection.

He sucked in a harsh breath, captured her hands, and roughly pulled them above her head, holding her wrists in a gentle, but steely grip.

"My chest has constantly ached since I met you." His breath was warm puffs on the sensitive skin of her neck. She shivered, as the fingers of his free hand brushed her hair back to fan over the pillow.

"At no time since my mother died have I ever felt I belonged. Never even wanted to. But when I'm with you—" His throat moved as he swallowed. "When I'm with you, I somehow know I'm exactly where I'm meant to be." The rawness in his eyes shredded her.

"That's how I feel about you, too," Sage whispered. "And I have ever since you first walked in the door of Beyond the Grave to investigate Nan's murder. There's always been something there between us. Even then. A... connection."

Ethan nodded, as if knowing exactly what she was trying to describe. "I can't predict the future. Hell, I can't tell you what's going to happen tomorrow. But I don't want anything to distract me from right now." He pressed his lips to her forehead. "This moment." He licked a trail down her neck. "This second, this time that I have with you." He mouthed her nipple, gripped it between his teeth, and for an intense second, her body burst into flames.

He looked deep into her hungry eyes. "I won't waste a single kiss, not a single touch... or bite." He nipped her other nipple, then crushed his mouth to hers. Sage swallowed the sob his words wrung from her. When he released her hands, she cupped the back of his neck. His kiss was urgent, ravenous.

He raised himself up on one elbow, while his other hand cupped her breast, exquisitely rolling her nipple between his fingers. Her body was no longer hers. It was his.

It always had been.

She was helpless to the urgent cravings of her body, her need for Ethan. She gave in, surrendered to the pleasure he wielded with each caress of his fingers.

His strong, capable hands splayed across her stomach, causing the muscles to jump and contract. His finger circled a spot in the middle of her belly, setting fire to her very core.

His touch became rougher, more urgent, reminding her of his earlier words, the ones that had stung her eyes with tears. They'd not been romantic utterings, clever poetic words. They'd come from a place deep inside him. A place beyond the conscious mind, a place where there was nothing but raw, brutal honesty.

He made a low sound in the back of his throat, pressing his hardness painfully against her stomach as if he were losing control.

His weight lifted off her for a moment, while he reached for something on the bedside table. Something metallic clicked a split second before it was secured around her wrist. Her eyes widened. He'd cuffed her. It should have scared her, but God help her, it turned her on. She trusted him, but relinquishing all control turned her into a breathless, writhing, mass of wanting.

He caught and restrained her other wrist, securing the handcuffs to the wooden headboard. Before Ethan, she would have said she didn't get turned on by being dominated, but ever since he'd mentioned cuffing her the first night they'd slept together, the idea had lingered at the back of her mind. His too, apparently, and thank God for that. The strong independent woman inside her was on her traitorous back with her legs spread wide begging, *Please!*

"What I wouldn't give to keep you here like this," Ethan said, eyeing the effectiveness of his restraints. "To know where you are. That you're safe. To know that when I come back, I'll find you here on my bed. Naked and waiting."

"That is the most chauvinistic thing I've ever heard," Sage said, but her words were hollow posturing. What she wouldn't give to be his sex slave for a week. Hell, if he kept looking at her like that, he could keep her here forever.

He sat back, one solid thigh on either side of her body. She tested the restraints, the cool metal digging into her wrists, and the heat in his eyes burned even hotter.

"My God, Ethan, whatever you're going to do to me, will you do it already? You're killing me." It was harder than she would have imagined to see his naked splendor and not be able to run her fingers across his heated skin.

He touched her cheek. "Keep your eyes on me. Don't look away. I want you to see what you do to me. How you affect me. I need you to know the power you have over me. Maybe then you'll understand."

"You have the power. I'm the one restrained, remember."

"No." His eyes darkened. "Even like this, you have the power. One word from you, and this ends."

Dear God no. If he stopped now, she'd die for sure. She squirmed, the only thing she could do. Her brain had stopped thinking coherent thoughts the moment the cuffs went around her wrists.

"You want me to fuck you?"

"Please."

"Then be a good girl and lie still, while I have my way with you."

Ethan lowered his lips to her body, kissed and licked every inch of her bare skin. Sage whimpered as his tongue stroked and teased, the sensations intense. His fingers and mouth were everywhere, sometimes light feathering touches, sometimes rough squeezes and nips. She was drowning, her senses unable to cope with the sexual onslaught. Her need for him was agonizing. Pure, exhilarating torture. She couldn't move, was powerless against the pleasure he evoked within her.

When his tongue found the heated place between her legs, she cried out, then bit down on her tongue. Oh God, his team could probably hear every noise she made! Ethan inhaled deeply, then kissed and suckled on her swollen clit. Boneless, she could do nothing but ride the waves of ecstasy he called forth. Her orgasm struck hard and fast, catching her unexpectedly. Ethan held her hips, continuing to suck and caress as the last wave subsided.

"Uncuff me. I want to touch you," Sage managed to whisper, her voice barely recognizable as her own.

"No."

He repositioned their bodies, and rested above her, one arm on either side of her chest. He stilled, his cock paused at her entrance, and found her eyes. Held them. If hands could caress a body, his eyes could caress her soul.

With a single, controlled roll of his hips, he entered her. She cried out. In both pleasure and pain. He filled her so completely, it took her breath away. He waited for her body to adjust to accommodate his size.

"Angel," he said, his voice deep, rough. Her muscles contracted around his length, as he remained still inside her. "Do you know what it feels like to think I've lost you?" Raw emotion, jagged and sharp, lurked beneath his desire.

Oh God! "Ethan, you'll never lose me." His cock twitched inside her, and she writhed beneath him.

Ethan withdrew slowly, the full length of him, then thrust powerfully back inside. He nipped her hard on the shoulder, then soothed the bite with a lick of his tongue.

"Do you know what it does to me, not knowing where you are?" Eyes on her, he pulled out, then thrust deep inside her again. Hard. She cried out with the deliciousness of it. His words were slicing up her very soul, while her body focused on the pleasure he was wielding.

"Do you know what it's like not knowing if the woman you love more than life itself is in danger?" His words were raw, ragged. Breathless. Another powerful thrust. "Wondering whether I could get to you in time. What I would find if I did. What it would be like for me if I didn't."

He thrust again, and this time didn't stop. She sobbed. In both relief and from his words. The bittersweet combination of pleasure and raw emotion sent her reeling.

"Can you imagine what it's like wondering if you were calling for me?" He squeezed his eyes shut and thrust again. Hard. "Believing I had failed you."

His words stung, even through the pleasure pulsing through her body. She arched her back as words of apology lodged in her throat. Tears stung her lids and rolled down her cheeks as his eyes turned a stormy gray.

"The relief when I found you whole and well hurt almost as much as when you were gone." He traced a finger down her cheek, even as he thrust harder. It was almost too much. His words. This pleasure. This pain.

"And then came the anger. The frustration, the torment of knowing that I had my heart ripped out needlessly. That you left my protection and deliberately put yourself in danger."

His eyes glittered, his skin glistening with a sheen of sweat. He was close too; in the tremble of his muscles she could feel the tenuous rein he had on his control. He ruthlessly held back his release. And hers. As though wanting her to know what it was like to need something that was being withheld from you.

Even as the pleasure built, swirling violently around them, she knew his frustration stemmed as much from last Wednesday night as it did today. They'd both been terribly scarred by what had happened. By almost losing each other.

And by knowing it could happen again.

She sobbed, even as her orgasm built to a powerful height deep inside her. She was high on that precipice of release.

"I love you, Sage."

Tears streamed down her face as she struggled against the restraints. She resented the cuffs now; they stopped her from touching him. Comforting him.

"I love you so much," she rasped. The metal cut into her wrists.

He reached up and held her arms still. "Stop, Sage. You'll hurt yourself."

"*You're* hurting me," she cried. But she understood. He needed her to fully grasp just how deep his feelings for her ran. That losing her was not an option.

"I don't mean to, babe. Just... don't do it again." His voice broke.

And then he gave them what they both wanted. He surged inside her, and the most powerful release she'd ever had shook her body, wave after wave of ecstasy shredding her emotional control.

When the last wave of pleasure left them and her damp skin began to cool, Ethan tenderly uncuffed her and kissed the reddened skin of her wrists. He rolled to one side and pulled her flush against him.

She pressed her head against his chest, heard his heart hammering as he held her tight.

"I don't just love you," Ethan said, his voice thick with emotion. "I need you more than I need my next breath. And you could be taken away from me at any single moment, because I have no fucking idea how to keep you safe."

A single hot tear landed on her shoulder and ran down her back. Nothing could have affected her more.

Destroyed her more thoroughly.

"We'll survive this," Sage said with more confidence than she felt.

Somehow, some way, they had to make it through this alive without tearing each other apart.

Chapter Ten

Tuesday Three a.m.
Dead Time

Across town, Luke Keyton contemplated his new work environment. Dougie Roberts's basement bedroom was large, but came sloppy seconds to his secluded cabin in the bush. What choice did he have though? The detective had his goons all over his place. Lucky let out a low growl. He didn't have much in this world, but what he did have, he needed. Lucky had an important job to do.

And time was running out.

Lucky fingered the silky strands of the Angel of Light's hair in his pocket. Sensed Sage's presence across town. Hair retained the energy of the being it belonged to. With his new powers, which were increasing with each sacrifice to the Dark Master, Lucky could tap into that energy to find Sage anywhere. Any time. A great tool to monitor his nemesis.

On Sunday night, Lucky would be given the honor of performing the grand invocation ritual. By then he'd have performed seven sacrificial offerings, and Sage would be dead. The grand ritual would not be performed here in the basement, but behind Lucky's cabin. He'd rather practice there, but he couldn't risk being caught. On the actual night, he'd take care of any interference, but the kid's basement would work for what he needed now.

At midnight on the blood moon, the gateway would open, and the Dark Master would be free to enter the earthly realm. Finally, the Dark Master and the other poor condemned souls banished for eternity would be free to roam the earth once again. To take what was rightfully theirs.

Lucky tamped down his excitement, drew in a deep, savoring breath, and faced the new recruits. They wore black coats and black fabric masks with eye holes cut in them. Although their faces were hidden, Lucky knew who they were. All thirteen. Lucky had kept the black circle cut-outs from their masks to use in sacrifices. The eyes, after all, are the windows to the soul, and it was souls the Dark Master demanded.

There was a tally on the chalkboard on the wall, for the Dark Master kept score.

The new recruits, in their excitement, hung on his every word, worshipped every breath he took. Such was the gift of power the Dark Master had bestowed on him.

The group had already been tested by the Dark Master before they reached him. The master had tapped into their minds, given them tasks to determine their suitability. Not all had passed. The ones who remained were excited. Honored to have come this far.

Just for fun, he raised his arms, causing thirteen black candles to flame.

They gasped, mouths hanging open in awe.

Fools, every single one. But *He* needed them, and Lucky would oblige.

"Congratulations. Many have failed, but you are the faithful. The chosen." Thirteen pairs of eyes tracked his every moment, and Lucky reveled in his power over them.

"In total darkness, the scent of blood is the strongest," Lucky said. "Removing sight intensifies the other senses: smell, taste, touch, hearing. Tonight, once again, the fragrance of blood is fresh. Rich. *Human.* Animal sacrifices are for the lower circles. Not ones who hold the highest honor of being closest to the Dark Master."

"The Dark Master," they repeated in unison.

In the center of the basement, in a circle drawn with salt, a woman lay bound and gagged. The sounds she made, her fear-driven groans, excited Lucky physically. Terror was a powerful aphrodisiac. But it was necessary to ignore his baser instincts and stick to the ritual. He was training the new recruits, after all.

"Tonight, we have a woman," Lucky said. "The offering brought to us by Blood Fox." Blood Fox was the reborn identity of Dougie Roberts, his protégé. "Blood Fox, I'll let you begin. Speak the verse, and cover her eyes with your circles."

After Dougie had finished, Lucky continued. "Fill the chalice with the blood of the sacrifice," Lucky instructed Blood Fox. "Stir it six times. Change direction, then stir it six more times, then repeat."

Blood Fox completed the remaining steps of the ritual flawlessly, without prompting. He'd learned well.

For many in the room tonight, this was the first time they'd seen a human sacrifice. Animal sacrifices didn't generate anywhere near the same power. Each participant would leave tonight filled with a dark elation and an unquenchable thirst for fear. And death. They would feed on it, and seek to elicit it every way they could. They were free to act upon those impulses. However, only the sacrifices were to be performed in a ritualistic manner.

He felt the Dark Master smile as Lucky's protégé sipped the blood of the sacrifice.

"You have done well, Blood Fox. He is pleased." Dougie smiled, and the blood stuck gruesomely to the plaque on his teeth.

"I saw the Angel," Blood Fox said. "Can I bring her?"

"No!" Lucky's fury bounced off the basement walls. "The Dark Master has promised her to me. No one but me touches the Angel."

Lucky made sure he received acknowledgment from everyone present. Lucky would love to have ordered her brought to him, but he couldn't trust any of them to do it right. To not kill her or attract the detective's attention.

The Angel of Light was too important. There could be no more mistakes.

"You may enjoy tonight's sacrifice, and the ones that follow this week," Lucky said. "But the Angel will be mine."

———— ◆ ————

Sage hadn't been asleep for more than five minutes—or so it seemed—when she was woken up by Max's barking. Not just barking, but growling viciously as though about to attack.

"Max. No!" Daniel's sharp command to Max carried through the walls. The furious barking silenced, but the dog continued to let out agitated growls.

Ethan sat up, his hand immediately reaching for his weapon on the bedside table.

Sage rubbed her eyes and glanced at the digital clock. Three a.m.

Dead Time.

The same time she'd experienced the most attacks from the demon when she'd been staying at Nan's. Pia had explained to her during the paranormal investigation of the shop that three a.m. was Dead Time. The hour between three a.m. and four a.m. was when people experienced the most paranormal activity, because it was the time of night when it was the quietest, when the veil between the worlds was the thinnest.

The time *he* was able to assert the most influence in the earthly realm.

"Wait here," Ethan said, slipping out of bed and into his jeans, sans underwear. He met Daniel outside their bedroom, and through the slightly ajar door, Sage heard their muffled voices.

"What's going on?" Ethan asked.

"Not sure. We were both asleep, then all of a sudden Max took off down the hallway."

Sage turned on the light and peered around the room. Nothing was out of place. Although she'd not felt uncomfortable at all during the dinner with Taipan, her initial reaction to the place, and Liquorice's warning about the house, returned full force.

Sage took a deep breath to slow the fluttering, erratic beat of her heart, reminding herself that she had nothing to worry about in a house filled with the elite of the police force. She doubted the prime minister had as much protection.

The internal rationalization didn't work. The hairs on her arms were standing on end, and she rubbed them with her palms. She was freezing. She looked out the window at the balmy spring night.

He was becoming stronger.

Or was she just able to sense him better now?

"Go away," Sage said to the empty room.

Ethan and Daniel were at the doorway in an instant.

"Angel? Did you call me?"

"Uh, no... yes. Can you feel that?" Sage asked.

"Feel what?" Daniel frowned.

Couldn't they at least sense something was "off"? Sage knew Ethan could; she saw him shiver.

He was watching her, like a predator stalking his prey through the night. Of course, she'd never be able to direct them to a flesh and blood intruder. But she knew just the same that he was there.

Forget her eyes, forget recording technology. The way her body reacted to the unseen energy was the best indicator she had that he was near.

Max lowered himself to the ground, bared his teeth, and growled viciously at the chaise in the corner of the room.

You can see him, can't you, Max?

Max flicked his gaze at Sage and acknowledged that he'd heard her.

"You okay, Angel?" Ethan crossed the room and sat beside her on the bed.

"I just feel uncomfortable," Sage said. "Like I did at Nan's. Like the entity is here too."

But even as she spoke the words, the sensation of the demon's presence left her. Her goose-fleshed skin returned to normal, and her pulse settled. She inhaled a lungful of air, relieved she could *breathe* again.

It was like walking from one environment to another, going from a cold stormy night into a room heated by a blazing fire. The contrast was immediate.

"It's normal to feel a little spooked in the middle of the night," Daniel said.

He's gone, Max said.

I sensed that too, Sage replied.

But he'll be back.

Sage's stomach clenched at his warning, even though it wasn't a surprise.

Ethan rubbed a palm up and down her arm. "You're worrying me," he said, and Sage was conscious of Daniel watching them from the doorway.

Sage tried for her best reassuring smile. "I'm fine." She had a feeling that *he* had left for the night. As though his visit was a reminder. That he knew where she was. That he would find her, no matter where she went.

Sage was being hunted.

"You're safe, Sage. The house is secure," Daniel said. "No sign of entry."

Sage glanced at him. "I've got the whole of Taipan here. What have I possibly got to worry about, right?"

"Right." Daniel grinned. "But I'm still concerned over Max though. He's never acted like this before."

"Maybe it was Sage's cat," Ethan said. "He was hissing and snarling at something outside."

"Max doesn't bark at cats." Daniel was clearly offended.

"Animals can sense things humans can't see or hear," Sage said.

Daniel raised his brows, confused by her comment. "That's why he's the seventh member of Taipan. He always hears things before we do, and he can track a perp from nothing more than the scent on a piece of clothing."

Sage sighed. "I wasn't talking about humans."

Daniel frowned.

"It's okay, mate," Ethan said to Daniel. "You go back to sleep. I've got Sage."

"Nah, can't sleep now." He issued a command to Max, and the dog sat at attention at his side. "I'm taking Max out for a walk, see if I can work some of this tension out of him. See you both in the morning."

Ethan came back to bed, but didn't lie down. He left his jeans on and sat up, pulling Sage's head into his lap.

"You saw him here, didn't you?" Ethan asked.

"I felt him."

She sensed his mind working as he ran his fingers through her hair. "Close your eyes," he said softly. "I'll watch over you while you sleep. There's nothing to worry about. You might have sensed him, but he can't hurt you here. You're safe. I won't let anything happen to you."

Ethan turned off the lamp, and her eyes took a moment to adjust. The moon cast its glow through the open curtains, turning the objects in the room into gray shapes.

Sage closed her eyes. Despite his words of reassurance, she doubted she would sleep. Ethan's hand stroking her hair was soothing, but his muscles were a wall of tension. His eyes continually scanned the darkness.

In the distance, carried through the quiet stillness of night, the dogs of the town began to howl.

Chapter Eleven

Morning light was filtering through the open window when Sage woke with her head on Ethan's lap, his fingers sifting through her hair.

"Morning, Angel."

Sage murmured a greeting, rolled off him, and stretched her neck. "You didn't sleep?"

"I do my best thinking at night." His lids were heavy, but his eyes were alert. Though his overlong dark hair was mussed, he looked all the more sexy for it. The golden light streaming in highlighted the well-defined muscles of his bare chest.

Sage took a sip of water from the glass on the bedside table. "Did you think up anything I should know about?"

Ethan released a long breath and ran his fingers through his hair. She took another sip of water. "Perhaps."

"Oh?"

She was about to press him for details but a tingling at the base of her spine demanded her attention. An instinct that refused to be ignored.

Sage peered around the room. Something wasn't right. She hugged her arms and shivered.

Fragments of the dream she'd been having when she awoke surfaced in her mind. Sage frowned as she struggled to remember; something told her it was important, so she tried to catch the pieces before they blew away.

She'd dreamed of a tall man with a long dark cloak standing over her while she'd slept. Here. In this bedroom. He'd stared at her with round eyes that were blacker than black, the orbs beckoning. Calling. His eyes were windows; in them, she glimpsed a time and place filled with terrible evil and suffering. Sage had forced herself not to stare, fearful they would suck her straight through to the darkness on the other side. Knowing it was what he wanted.

Her spine turned to ice—she'd seen that shadow figure before. It was the same image that had been captured in Mark's pictures taken during the investigation at Nan's house. The dark shadow in nearly every picture he'd taken of Sage that night.

At the time, Sage had assumed the figure had something to do with the house, that investigation. She'd not wanted to allow herself to believe it could *follow* her.

He had been here. Max had seen him. And now she'd seen him in a dream too.

And then she saw something in the here and now that stopped her heart dead in her chest.

"Ethan," she croaked out.

"What is it?" Ethan sat up straight, instantly alert.

She pointed with a shaking hand, drawing his attention to the chaise in the corner. Ethan's black leather jacket had been thrown over it, his utility belt on top, his black boots on the floor to one side.

On his jacket sat a child's toy. Something not from this time, but an antique from a life lived a hundred years ago. The teddy bear was in poor condition, as though held often by filthy, grotty fingers.

It had no eyes, only two black holes.

Its eyeless face had been positioned in a way that it seemed to be "looking" at them.

"What the hell is that?" Ethan asked, swinging his legs off the bed. "A dead animal?"

"That…"—Sage swallowed the lump constricting her throat—"*thing* wasn't in that chair last night."

Although Max had been barking at the chaise a few hours ago, she hadn't noticed the bear there then.

Ethan crossed the room, picked up the toy, and turned it over in his hands. "It's a teddy bear, made from real animal hair. Like an amateur taxidermy project."

Sage slid out the opposite side of the bed and pulled on her jeans. "I'm not touching it." The very look of it unnerved her. She found her favorite T-shirt of Ethan's and slipped it over her head.

"It must be very old," he murmured. "Early 1900s, maybe. Late 1800s even. The arms and legs are jointed. I wonder if Mrs. Coote found this somewhere in the house?"

"Mrs. Coote didn't put that there."

"What makes you so sure? We likely didn't notice it last night," Ethan said. "We were kind of busy…"

"Because it was sitting *on top* of your leather jacket." Ethan's face creased into hard lines, as he reconsidered the bear.

"Max was barking at that chaise last night," Sage said, absently rubbing her neck.

"Yes, he was." Ethan frowned.

Sage took a step closer to the teddy. It looked more like a dead animal than a child's toy. "It stinks." Sage held her hand to her nose to block the odor emanating from the gruesome object, a mixture of sulfur and dead animal.

"That it does."

"Eth, someone... *something* was in here with us last night. While we slept." The dark shadow figure in her dream. He'd disappeared, but he'd left her a *physical* message. A reminder. He might be of another world, but his ability to affect her reality was growing stronger.

"Impossible."

"Then what made those marks on the wall?"

Behind the chair were three deep gouges in the plaster, beginning halfway down the wall and extending in the direction of the bear.

Three fresh scratch marks.

"Impossible," Ethan repeated. "I've been awake since the incident with Max. No one was in the room, Sage. I'll stake my life on it."

"Don't," Sage demanded, then took a breath and softened her voice. "Don't say things like that."

"Angel." That one word, the tone he used, was a caress to her soul.

When Ethan moved closer to examine the wall, Sage swallowed her revulsion and took the bear from him. The fur beneath her fingers was rough, and held none of the softness of today's manufactured teddy bears. The stitching was crudely done, the thread stained with something that looked like dried blood. As if the stitches had closed wounds to living flesh. Her stomach roiled, and bile rose in her throat.

Her response to the bear might appear an overreaction to anyone witnessing it from the outside. It was, after all, just a child's toy. But it was so much more. The energy flowing off this bear triggered her fight-or-flight response. As though the thing had been imbued with evil. *Or cursed.*

Whatever it was, this bear was *wrong.*

"I wonder who it belonged to?" Ethan asked, turning back from his examination of the scratches on the wall.

The angel around her neck was reacting, a vibration radiating outward from it. As though protecting her from whatever this thing really was.

Ethan must have been having the same thoughts because he immediately crossed to her and took the bear from her hands. "I don't want you touching this."

"I don't want you touching it either." After all, she was the one with the amulet. Ethan was unprotected.

"I'll burn it," she said, "just like I did the Ouija board." She'd show *him* just what she thought of his gifts. Sage tried to grab the bear from Ethan, but he held it high out of her reach.

"Leave it, Angel," he snapped. "You can't burn it; it's evidence. And it might be important. Hold vital clues."

Taking a step away from her, he straightened the right arm of the bear and froze. Sage knew what he'd found before he showed it to her.

On the palm of its right paw was the symbol, a circle with three curved lines radiating outward in thirds.

Six. Six. Six.

The serial killer's brand.

Ethan swore. "Guess we know whose bear this is. The question is: How did it get in here?"

---◆---

The scent of freshly made toast filled the kitchen, and Ethan stepped past Sage and hit the switch on the kettle to make coffee. Sage could faintly hear voices outside, and guessed the team had decided to take breakfast alfresco since it was such a lovely morning.

Searching the cupboards, Sage located a Tupperware container with a tight-fitting lid. "Shove that thing in here."

"I have evidence bags—"

"In here," Sage repeated, relieved when he did as she instructed. On impulse, she searched the pantry to see what seasonings it contained. She found thyme and some cloves of fresh garlic and crammed as much as she could in with the offensive object and sealed the container.

"Sage, what are you doing? You've just contaminated evidence."

Sage shrugged. "We've already handled it. And you know as well as I do that there's something not right about this bear." *Not right* seemed the understatement of the century. The thing was utterly vile. "It needs something."

"Isn't garlic for vampires?" Ethan frowned as he poured steaming water into their coffee cups, and added a dash of milk. Once that comment would have been a joke, but Sage could see him actually wondering if it would work.

"Got a better idea?" Sage asked seriously.

Ethan considered the bear. "No. But I'm less concerned about the bear itself and more about how the hell it got into our bedroom."

Sage took the container and set it next to Ethan's laptop and bag on the table in the front room. "Well, the bear concerns *me*. It's creepy. There's an energy coming off it. Something bad. You won't let me burn it, so that's the best I can think of."

"It might still be useful, despite your additions." He placed her coffee on the kitchen table. "Someone was in here last night, and I will find out who or—" Ethan paused, then spoke through clenched teeth. "Or *what* it was."

A muscle around his eye twitched, and Sage knew what it cost him to concede that whatever had been in their room last night was likely not of human form. Despite all the precautions Ethan had put in place, the hideous teddy bear had managed to make its way into not only the house, but his bedroom undetected. If that wasn't a slap in the face.

In addition, Ethan had remained awake until morning. Unless the bear's arrival had happened before Max started barking? Perhaps that was *why* Max was barking.

"The fur won't be helpful as far as lifting prints goes," Ethan said, "but you never know what Zach will turn up. He's found more from less."

Ethan appeared relieved to be falling back into usual police routine. She couldn't take that from him; what else was there for him to do? A man like Ethan took charge. He was the protector, the executor of justice. He wouldn't stand being made to feel powerless, much less a victim.

"Well then, send the damn thing to Zach."

She took a seat and emptied the contents of her bag on the table to find her phone. She'd arranged to meet Pia in a couple of hours and wanted to make sure she hadn't cancelled.

Sage was going to ask for Pia's help and desperately hoped she'd give it. Aside from Pia possibly being able to offer some valuable advice about the paranormal aspect of what she was up against, Sage wanted her to help with the protection ritual for the circle on Sunday. She needed seven, and she had three definite: Joyce, Pat, and Mona. She couldn't get just anyone. It was more than just chanting the words; the person needed to believe *absolutely* in what they were doing. Belief and *knowing* were needed to project their energy outward, to add to the power of the circle itself. The energy of the seven in this realm would protect the gateway, the portal, while Sage performed the banishment rite outlined in the grimoire. Without protection, Sage would be vulnerable to attack by the master demon and his minions.

A glance at the phone's screen told her the battery was dead. She moved to the table in the front room and plugged it into the charger, keeping it as far away from the Tupperware container as possible.

When she walked back into the kitchen, she found Ethan with the Milo tin in his hand. He must have picked it up from the table where she'd placed the contents of her bag. She reached for it, but he held it up out of her reach and grinned at her.

"Milo, Angel? You forgot to bring your toothbrush, but you brought your own *Milo*?" Ethan was clearly amused, and her heart fluttered at the smile that played at the corners of his lips. "I'd have thought you'd bring coffee, if anything."

Sage placed her hands on her hips. "My toothbrush fell off the vanity and into the toilet, which was the fault of that poky hotel room, not me." She raised her chin slightly. "Getting back to the point, it's not Milo. It's grave dirt."

The amusement in his expression drained away.

"Of course there wouldn't be chocolate drink in this Milo tin," Ethan said, lowering his arm. "Whatever was I thinking? *My* girlfriend is going to carry around grave dirt."

"Don't drop it," Sage said, snatching the tin from his hands and placing it on the table next to the grimoire.

Ethan lowered himself into a kitchen chair and stared at the coffee cup in front of him.

The silence between them stretched.

"Ah hell." Ethan thrust both his hands through his hair. "I'm a cop, and interfering with a grave is a federal offense. I wasn't going to ask, but I can't not. Whose grave did you get the dirt from?"

"His name is... *was* Lance—"

"You steal anything other than dirt from Lance's grave?" Ethan asked, eyes narrowed. "You didn't dig up the poor guy's coffin by any chance?"

Sage looked sharply at him. He'd used his cop tone of voice, and it raked across her nerves. No doubt he was thinking of when she'd ripped up the floor of Ada's kitchen looking for the grimoire. What Sage considered a necessary part of her journey, Ethan saw as breaking and entering and property damage.

"There was no grave to dig up. He was cremated," she said, feeling her irritation rise. Actually, he'd been burned to cinders by the ritual; what was buried in the grave were the ashes and debris that Mary had scraped from the circle after that night. She had known it would be needed in another hundred years, and she'd followed the grimoire's instructions to preserve it.

Sage would have liked to have discussed all that with Ethan, but given the stern look on his face, she remained silent. She also wanted to let him know what she'd discovered about that grave—that he was Lance Virgil *Keyton*. Related somehow to Lucky. She'd wait for another time, when Ethan was in a better mood and not pissed off with her about the apparent legality of interfering with a grave. Besides, she didn't like talking to him when he was in his bad-ass detective mode. Seemed most of her plans broke one law or another.

She frowned at him over the rim of her cup and took a long, deep sip of her coffee. It had cooled and sloshed over the sides as she pushed it roughly away.

When she glanced up, he was still looking at her with that cold, unreadable cop expression. "What?"

"Anything else you need to tell me before I hear it from the boys down at the station?"

"Not yet." Sage stood, the chair scraping across the wooden floor loudly. "But the day's still young."

Ethan made a sound of distress in the back of his throat.

Sage glanced at his defeated expression and took pity on him. It mustn't be easy having her as a girlfriend. While other women were focusing on their careers, families, and social lives, Sage was digging around graveyards and fighting demons. "I'm sorry, Ethan," Sage said gently. "I know I keep asking you to overlook what I'm doing, my *offenses,* and that I'm asking you to go against everything you believe in. And I appreciate you doing it. I really do. In my defense, I have rarely broken the law before this. I don't even have a parking fine." Sage took a deep breath. "But I needed dirt from the grave of the serial killer from a hundred years ago. Grave dirt contains the energy of the occupant. It's needed for the banishment ritual."

Ethan's expression eased, and he nodded his head. "Of course. I remember reading that in the grimoire. How did you know who the killer was?"

"Nan found out. It was written in Mary's diary. Mary needed to do with Lance what I need to do with Lucky. She needed to bring the demon to the circle as part of the banishment rite. Afterward, she scraped his remains from the circle and put it in a grave marked with the symbol from the grimoire. There were also stones and crystals placed around the grave, no doubt to protect it from harm until now. When it was needed again."

"Jesus." Ethan leaned back in his chair.

"Mary wrote me a letter before she died."

Sage fossicked in her bag and came up with the letter she'd found in the back of the grimoire. She handed it to Ethan. He read it aloud.

To the future seer's daughter,

At the beginning of the first eclipse of the tetrad, the lead-up to the blood red moon, the veil between the dimensions will rapidly begin to thin. The master demon will have found a soul to possess. A disturbed soul, fashioned to the darkness, like a wood carving, through living a tortured life.

I don't believe babies are born evil. I can't. I'm a pastor's wife. I have to believe that life is a series of events and choices. That sometimes circumstances of life can be so cruel, way too much for a gentle soul, and that soul becomes hardened. Bitter and resentful. The hurts and injustices suffered so great that they manifest as powerful anger and violence. From there, it is only a gentle slide into pure evil.

The soul, once pure and white, is now bitter and black. It becomes vulnerable to the negative energies of another world. A world of dark entities spending eternity tortured by watching us play in the sunshine.

Hell is watching happiness that can never be yours.

They sit behind the veil, restless. Watching and waiting for that chance, that brief opportunity that arises every hundred years when the veil is thin enough to slip through.

At first the entities come through and begin attempting possession of humans. They enter through the portal in Cryton, growing in number in the lead-up to the blood moon. Although they may seem to be through, they are still not fully in our dimension. They are still only spirits at this time. Their evil is persuasive and can affect the mind and actions of the host, but they are not fully manifest.

They won't be until after the door to the portal closes on the fourth blood moon of the tetrad.

This is where you play an integral role, future seer's daughter. The master demon must be identified, captured, and brought into the circle, and the rite of exorcism followed precisely before the portal closes. If done correctly, the demonic entities will be sent back to their world. The timing is critical. You will encounter many obstacles. For evil can manifest in a multitude of ways.

This occurrence is not as rare as one would think. Similar happenings have been documented throughout history, but are usually written off as natural disasters, or the atrocities of a depraved human. No one makes the connection to the portal, or if they do, they don't make it publicly.

But there are those who know. Those who are aware and work quietly and independently to do what they can to keep these entities in their own world. Their work must remain secret so as not to cause mass panic of the general population.

The master demon enters exactly twenty years before the portal opens and chooses a host to possess. 1815 is the earliest record I can find of the demon in Australia, but more may be part of Aboriginal legends.

Know that there have been portals in other parts of the world; many have been closed permanently, but not all. Pray forgive my selfishness, but the sacrifice required to close the portal permanently is too great. You will suffer for my weakness, for the choice I have made has sealed your destiny.

I have documented as much of my journey as I can with the hope it may help you in yours.

Though my journey is ending, I pray for you and yours.

"Where did you get this?" Ethan asked, looking up from the letter.

"It was in the grimoire."

"And you're only showing it to me now?" Ethan asked. "Never mind," he said, interrupting her before she could speak. "I know I haven't exactly been the easiest person to speak to about all of this, but I hope you know that isn't the case now." He pierced her with his gaze. "You do know that, right?"

"Mostly," Sage said. "You do have a tendency to slip into cop mode at a moment's notice."

Ethan worked his jaw. "That's who I am."

"The seer's daughter is who *I* am."

Their gazes met. Locked. A long, charged moment passed, then Ethan released a sigh.

"Just so we're on the same page. The letter mentions the master demon; I take it that refers to the entity that has possessed Lucky."

"Yes."

"Who was the person possessed a hundred years ago, whose grave you collected the dirt from?"

"Lance Virgil Keyton."

Ethan froze, his eyes narrowed in focus. "Virgil?"

"That's right. Are you okay?" Ethan's eyes were wide, and Sage could almost see his mind working.

"Things are beginning to fall into place. Keyton kept referring to a 'Virgil' when I interviewed him. Claimed that Virgil was telling him what to do, who to kill." Ethan placed his palms heavily on the table. "He used Virgil as his goddamned alibi."

Ethan fired up his laptop. "I'm feeding the name through to Zach. Let's see what else he can turn up."

Nate, Sam, and Jake walked in just then, carrying empty plates from their breakfast.

"You look like hell," Ethan said, eyeing Nate's unusually disheveled appearance.

"Couldn't bloody sleep." Nate pulled out the jar of coffee and put a couple heaping teaspoons of instant espresso into a large mug. "I thought country air was supposed to be good for the soul."

"Maybe, but not in this town," Jake said.

"I know we need to keep vigilant, but can whoever was walking around the house take your damn boots off first?" Nate asked.

"Wasn't me," Sam said casually.

"Nor me," Jake said. "And Daniel left with Max after he started barking for no apparent reason. Sean went with him."

"Wasn't me," Sage said.

"It wasn't a woman's walk," Nate said, brow wrinkling in confusion. "They were a man's footsteps. Heavy. Confident. So if it wasn't one of us, then who was it?"

"The same person... uh *thing* who put the scratches on the wall and the teddy bear on the chair in our bedroom," Sage said.

Sage felt the weight of their collective gazes as they turned their full attention on her. "Someone put a teddy bear in your room?" Jake asked, raising his brows.

"It isn't just any old teddy bear," Sage said, suppressing a shudder. "It's fucking creepy."

"It's in the container next to my bag," Ethan said. "Take a look for yourselves."

"No one was in your room last night," Nate said, looking briefly at Jake and Sam for confirmation. "No one but us was in the house. We checked the camera footage thoroughly at the time Max was barking, then double-checked again this morning, in case we missed something. It's unlike Max to bark for no reason."

"There was a reason," Ethan said. "Just not one we're used to. I'm going to arrange with Zach for some night-vision security cameras to be sent down. We have the outside covered, but it now seems inside should be our focus."

"But—" Jake began.

"I'm not talking human intruders, Browny."

The comment certainly gave Jake pause, but he didn't say anything.

"PRI might have some spare equipment," Sage said, referring to Paranormal Research and Investigations, Mark's team. "I can ask Pia when I see her a little later."

Ethan's jaw worked, a muscle on his bicep bunched. "No need."

He then spoke directly to Nate. "Zach will have it here tonight. You and Daniel will need to establish the best areas to install them for maximum coverage."

"On it."

Sage wasn't surprised Ethan had refused PRI's assistance. Nothing irritated Ethan more than the mention of Mark Collins after what had happened. Although, Ethan hadn't liked Mark even before then. Did he have some instinct not to trust Mark? Or was it a simple personality conflict?

Either way, after what had happened Wednesday night, Ethan would be beyond furious if Mark turned up here again.

The men joined them at the table. Jake took out a small black computer and typed in some commands. "Taking the bird out," Jake said, referring to the black helicopter, the Eagle, in the rear paddock. "See if I can't catch a slippery serial killer for Sage." He flicked a friendly gaze in her direction and despite the morning she'd had, her chest warmed. It meant a lot to her, to have the support of Ethan's team. What she was asking them to do could get them fired.

"Is there a train stop in town, or does it pass straight through?" Sam asked, taking a bite from an apple.

"There's not a stop in town," Nate said. "Blade and I have secured every way in and out of this place. I don't remember mention of an active train at all."

Clearing a space in front of him on the table, Nate pulled out a well-worn map of Cryton.

"There isn't one," Sage said, feeling a heaviness in her stomach. "The train stopped running through here years ago."

"Well, it sure as hell was running last night," Sam said. "Heard it clear as day. Maybe you missed something. Assuming Keyton made it out of town, perhaps that was how he managed it."

"Sam," Sage said. "When I said the trains stopped running through here, I meant it literally. I was here when the station was decommissioned years ago. It was quite an event. In fact a whole section of the track was removed to make way for the phone tower that was installed last year."

"Christ," he muttered. "I heard the fucking trains running, clear as I'm hearing you right now."

Or maybe you were hearing an echo from a hundred years ago? Was it a symptom of the veil thinning?

Sage put the grimoire and the diaries back in her bag and stood. Time was ticking away, and now she *really* needed to speak to Pia.

At the front table, she unplugged her phone from the charger. She held up the Milo tin and called back to the men in the kitchen. "I'm leaving this here. Don't touch it. And whatever you do, don't try to drink it. It's not Milo."

"Don't ask," Ethan said to the others.

A phone rang. "Blade," Ethan answered. "Be right there."

When Sage made it back to the kitchen, the men were on their feet, strapping on weapons, grabbing bags, and checking equipment.

"What is it?" Sage asked.

"Veronica Coote's body was just discovered in the bush not far from here," Ethan said. "Same MO as the others. Seems Keyton is still in town."

Sam glanced at a chunky watch on his wrist that looked like the time was its least important function and jotted something in a notebook.

"Nate?" Ethan said. A wordless exchange transpired between the two men. Ethan had wanted to accompany her this morning, but it seemed his plans had just changed.

Jake drained his cup and took it to the sink.

"Be careful," Sage said, moving to Ethan. She grabbed his arms and pulled him down and into a kiss.

When he stepped back, he was looking at her intently. "It's me who will worry about you, Angel. Not the other way around."

"You can't tell me not to worry about you, Eth." She placed her hand on his chest, felt the beat of his heart through her palm.

He softened, stone melting into lava. He hugged her tightly, then looked her directly in the eyes. "Dammit, Sage, don't take any unnecessary risks today. Don't go wondering off on your own—"

Nate put a hand on Ethan's shoulder. "Relax, mate. I won't let her get so much as a scratch."

"Thank you," she said to Nate.

"Don't let that ghost-busting freak get anywhere near her, Ryder," Ethan said. "If he turns up, call me."

"Eth, you've given me Nate. I can handle Mark."

Ethan looked ready to object, but Nate slapped him on the back and winked at Sage. "Blade, chill. You know she's safe with me."

Appearing tortured, and without another word, Ethan turned and walked out the door, followed closely by Sam and Jake.

"Right, then." Nate turned to Sage. "Lead the way."

As if she had the faintest idea what she was doing.

Sage hitched her bag up on her shoulder and patted the comforting solidity of the grimoire stowed inside. She had to trust in what Mary said, in what the grimoire said, and pray that they were right.

And pray that somehow she could convince the only genuine psychic she knew to risk her life helping Sage save the world.

Chapter Twelve

The temperature was overly warm in Nate's car, and Sage turned on the air-conditioning, enjoying the cooling blast. They drove the short distance into town with Liquorice curled up on her lap. Like Ethan, he also didn't want to let her out of his sight.

"I can't believe Mrs. Coote is dead," Sage said with a heavy feeling of sorrow. Mrs. Coote had frequently sought her nan out for spiritual readings, and she'd always been nice to Sage.

"Did you know her well?" Nate asked.

"We weren't close in the way I am with Nan's friends. I grew up with them. But I knew Mrs. Coote quite well. She came around the shop a lot. How sure are you that it was Lucky?"

"As sure as we can be, I suppose," Nate said, a slight frown wrinkling his brow. "According to his last text, Blade has all but ruled out a copycat, because of details that weren't made public. Either it was Keyton, or someone closely involved with him. Blade is pissed. He doesn't take kindly to a murder taking place under his nose."

"I forgot to say something to Ethan, but you might want to look into Dougie. Douglas Roberts, that is. Don't get me wrong," Sage said quickly. "I'm not implying he's responsible for the murder, I just wanted to mention it while I remember. I had an interesting encounter with him at Joyce's house. I believe he could be involved somehow with the satanic cult you're following up."

Nate glanced her way, raised an eyebrow. "Interesting in what way?"

"I don't have anything substantial to tell you. It's just... instinct, I suppose. There was something off about him."

"Oh?"

"His voice had that strange base note to it like Mark's did at the cabin, and when he threatened me—"

"He threatened you?" Nate's head whipped around, his eyes flashing.

"Well, it wasn't exactly a threat," Sage said quickly. Although she'd most certainly taken it that way. "He just said 'See ya around, Angel of Death,' but it was the way he said it, not out loud, but directly into my mind. It was creepy as hell."

"I'll look into it," Nate said, his voice tight. "He won't get anywhere near you from now on."

They reached Cryton's main street. To an outsider driving through, it was a pretty town, looking much the same as it had when she'd grown up there, albeit a whole lot quieter. The town used to be a hive of activity, the residents stopping on the main street to chat over the purchase of their morning milk and newspaper. But lately... even the tourists seemed to have disappeared. The service station was empty, something she had rarely, if ever, seen.

Cryton had turned into a ghost town. Literally.

Sage shivered. There was something sinister about her hometown now. Something that caused the hairs on the back of her neck to stand on end and her heart to beat erratically in her chest. Could the people driving through sense it too? Did it trigger a subconscious urge to keep driving, to stop somewhere else? The residents were being affected by the energy, just like Mary had noted in her diary. What happened with Mark, with the moving guy, with Dougie... Sage suppressed a shudder, not wanting to imagine what would happen if the satanic activity escalated into the horrors Mary had described. The bonfires and the human sacrifices in the main street.

As they pulled into the driveway of Nan's shop, Beyond the Grave—Sage's shop now—Sage looked at the hundred-plus-year-old façade in desperate need of some TLC. When this was over—supposing she survived it—she'd need to give some consideration to the shop and what she wanted to do with the rest of her life. At the moment, it was impossible to look further than Sunday.

The gravel crunched beneath their shoes as they headed to the shop. Sage inhaled the fragrance of the potted geraniums as they climbed the splintered wooden steps that led to the entrance.

Liquorice jumped from her arms and ran onto the porch, immediately finding and curling up in his favorite place on his wooden chair. He wasn't coming inside. Animals were smarter than people in that way.

Pia Williams pulled up in the driveway and stepped outside her small black Audi. PRI's psychic medium made a striking first impression. Shorter than Sage by a full head, with long, straight red hair and blue eyes you could drown in, exaggerated by her pale skin, blood red lips, and eyeliner artfully flicked up at the corners of her eyes, Pia, along with Mark, was the star of their paranormal research and investigation show, *Debunking Reality*.

"Pia, you remember Nate, don't you?" Sage asked, unlocking the front door to the shop. She stepped inside and stilled. The air was so thick and heavy, she struggled to take a single breath. She was abruptly claustrophobic. The shop appeared the same visually, but it had a totally different "feel" to it than when she'd been there looking for the journal yesterday.

Pia didn't enter, just stood by the door, fidgeting with the strap of her handbag. Did she feel it too?

Sage hurried through the shop, opening up all the blinds and windows. *I still can't breathe.* She became light-headed, dizzy. Beyond the window, the afternoon was still, not a breath of air to so much as ruffle the white lace curtains. Sage turned on the oscillating fan and tiny dust particles sprang to life, dancing in the rays of light streaming through the windows.

"Come in," Sage called over her shoulder to Pia and Nate.

Hesitantly, Pia entered the room, scanning the corners.

"You didn't tell me *he* was going to be here," Pia said.

Nate appeared surprised at the comment, but he offered her a hand in greeting. The air between them crackled, as Pia ignored Nate's outstretched hand. She turned her back on him, moving to sit down at the kitchen table.

"Nice to see you too," Nate mumbled, dropping his hand.

Sage frowned. She hadn't expected Pia to be rude to Nate. Was it because he'd restrained her the night at the cabin when Mark had been possessed? Pia had tried to get to Mark, but at Ethan's request, Nate had held her back for her own safety.

"Thank you for meeting me," Sage said, hoping to cut through the tension.

Pia shrugged. "You want my help, but I'm not sure how, or even if, I can. Or should."

Pia had a certain… *way* about her. Quietly confident, she had a self-assurance that Sage envied. Pia always seemed to know the story before everyone else.

Today, she appeared uneasy, her right leg bouncing restlessly. Like she would up and bolt at any second. Was it Nate? Sage? The house? Or a combination of all the above?

"I'm not sure what I can do for you," Pia repeated.

"I just want to talk." Sage didn't want Pia to feel pressured, but she really hoped she could get Pia's help.

"About what?"

Sage went to the kitchen and offered drinks, hoping to make this feel more social and less like an unwanted interview. She found some Anzac biscuits in a tin and took a bite to test their freshness. They weren't as crunchy as they could be, but they'd do. She carried them to the table with the coffees and Pia's green tea.

"Please, Nate," Sage said. "Come and have a seat." Nate was standing back from the table, arms folded across his chest, looking uncharacteristically formal.

"What's he doing here?" Pia asked again, glaring as Nate reluctantly sat down. The tension between them wasn't helping Sage's cause.

"Got a question to ask, I'm right here." Nate leaned back on his chair and stared at Pia in challenge. She didn't look away.

"I could have asked you," Pia agreed coldly. "I *chose* to ask Sage."

"Do you need a minute to sort this out?" Sage asked, looking between them.

"Not necessary," Pia said.

"I'm good, if she is," Nate said.

"I'm staying with Ethan and Nate," Sage said. "Ethan had some things to take care of this morning, and Nate was nice enough to accompany me here." Sage smiled at Nate. "While Lucky is still out there, Ethan is a little... overprotective."

Given Ethan's dislike for Mark, it was probably best that he hadn't come. However, she hadn't expected this tension between Pia and Nate. Nate had such an easygoing nature, she couldn't imagine him having a problem with anyone. Yet the air between the two of them was saturated with a mix of emotions Sage couldn't quite decipher.

"Can't he wait outside?" Pia asked.

Nate's brows rose. "He can. But he won't."

"Then he's an ass."

Sage interrupted before Nate could respond. "Which one of you would like to explain what's going on? What have I missed?"

"I don't understand why you brought him here if you want my help." Pia rose to leave.

"My presence here is not negotiable," Nate said. "Blade couldn't be here himself, and I am here in his stead. Sage stays with me until such time as I deliver her back to him safe and unharmed." Nate took a breath and continued. "My presence here has absolutely nothing to do with you. This is about Sage. If I wasn't here, Blade would be. Would that have made you more comfortable?"

"I've had enough of you already," Pia said. "Your arrogant ass of a partner as well. I'm not comfortable around either of you. Especially after the way you treated Mark."

"The same Mark who held a knife to Sage's throat?"

"Mark is my good friend, and what happened wasn't his fault. And if you think I was involved in Sage's abduction, why would I have told you where to find Sage? Do you know what would have happened to her if I hadn't? Lucky had escaped custody and was on his way back to the cabin. I saw the images in his mind. Saw what he had planned for her."

Nate stood and stared down at Pia.

"Guys?" Sage said, desperation bleeding into her tone. She couldn't afford to have Nate scare Pia away. Sage doubted she'd be ready to face the demon on Sunday without her help.

"Nate," Sage said. "Please sit back down."

Several emotions crossed Nate's face as he looked at Pia, then he glanced at Sage and let out a long breath.

"Our conflict is not helping Sage. I apologize if Blade and I were abrupt with you that night, but there were extenuating circumstances. I don't doubt your ability. But your *good friend* Collins turned out to be the bad guy, so don't go playing the victim here."

Pia narrowed her eyes, but Nate continued. "That night, Blade was beside himself with fear for Sage, understandably so. We didn't know where to go, who to turn to. He was uncharacteristically sharp with you, and for that I do apologize," Nate said genuinely.

"You don't apologize for your own sorry ass?"

Nate clenched his jaw. Released it. "I apologize if I offended you, as well. We were all on edge. I may not have believed in your abilities before that night, but I certainly believe in them now." Sage watched the pair intently. Nate was known for his people skills, his ability to defuse and negotiate. Although his apology to Pia sounded genuine, it was still strained. There was something deeper going on here. But what?

Pia stared at him a full minute before declaring, "I'm going to pretend he's not here."

"That's very generous of you." Sarcasm laced Nate's words. He lowered himself into the chair, leaned back, and crossed his arms over his chest.

Although Sage would have preferred they got along, she had neither the time nor the inclination to play peacekeeper.

"Thank you for leading Ethan and Nate to me that night," Sage said, placing her hand on Pia's. "You no doubt saved my life." Sage had already thanked Pia that night at the police station, but she felt it needed to be repeated.

"You're welcome," Pia said, casting a pointed glance at Nate.

Something caught Sage's attention out of the corner of her eye, but when she turned to look, there was nothing there. It might be gone, but the icy sensation that flooded her veins remained.

"Did you see that?" Sage asked Pia.

"Yes," Pia said. "But it's interesting that you did."

"Did you see it?" Sage asked Nate.

"See what?"

"What was it?" Sage said, turning her focus back to Pia.

"Who," Pia said. "There are a few entities in this house. Not all of them evil."

"Can you tell who is here?" Sage asked. Was it the demon? The black-cloaked figure?

"There's nothing here now, but a very dark entity has been here recently. Its stench clings to the walls."

The coffee in Sage's stomach sat uncomfortably, although she was relieved to know the demon wasn't still here.

"You asked to meet me today," Pia asked. "What is it you want from me?"

Sage took a deep breath and told her the complete story, leaving nothing out. She told Pia about Mary's diary, the prophecy, and the grimoire. She finished by telling her what had happened afterward at the cabin, when she confronted the demon within Lucky and what the demon had done to Ethan.

Throughout Sage's story, Nate had been listening intently, even though he'd already heard it when she'd told Taipan. His forearms resting on the table in front of him, his eyes sharp. As though analyzing her story for holes, discrepancies. Appearing satisfied, he now sat back in his chair.

Sage took out the grimoire and placed it on the table. "The prophecy is outlined in here."

At midnight on the night of the blood moon, the veil between this world and a far darker one will be at its thinnest, unsealing a doorway that should never be opened, allowing the unspeakable to come through and unleash hell on earth.

"The rituals I need to perform on the blood moon are all in the grimoire. The banishment ritual is at the end. That's the one I need to prepare for on Sunday. What I need Lucky for."

Pia, her eyes wide, appeared slightly stunned while Sage recounted the events that had led her to this point in time. Silently, Pia pulled the book toward her. She traced delicate fingers across the embossed symbol on the front, then almost reverently opened the old leather cover and began sifting through the pages.

"Fuck, Sage," Pia said in awe. "This is the real deal." A dozen different expressions flickered across Pia's face, then she squeezed her eyes shut.

"This was the book you were worried about when you were in the cabin, when Lucky had you?" Pia asked, opening her eyes.

"Yes. I thought I'd lost it." Ethan had found the bag she'd dropped when Lucky had dragged her out of Ethan's car.

"And that," Sage said, "brings me back to your original question about what you can do for me."

Pia sat up straight. Sage had her full attention.

"Will you be with me on the night? I need seven to protect the circle, and I have three. You're familiar with things like casting a circle and rituals of protection, aren't you?"

"Of course."

"I'm not," Sage said, swallowing a rush of anxiety. "This is mostly all new to me. Although there is a lot of detail in Nan's and Mary's journals and the rituals are in the grimoire... Well, I imagine there's a lot of basic knowledge that needs to be understood before performing that stuff. Mary was like Nan; they'd both lived their lives familiar with this type of thing. I spent my life running away from it."

Pia acknowledged that with an incline of her head. "Performing any type of magic ritual generally takes years of practice."

"I don't have years. I have days. I hope I'm not asking too much, but will you please give me some of your time? Help me understand the magic side of things? The power I'm supposed to summon is a lot of responsibility for a novice like me."

"I'm not sure—"

"And I'm even less sure." Frustration bled into her tone. "I know I'm asking a lot, especially as you don't really know me. If you don't want to be there on the night, will you at least help me with the practice? I know on a psychic level, you can answer some of the questions I have. Like how an old teddy bear suddenly appeared in our bedroom last night, when no person could have gained access to the house. Why Max barked for no apparent reason and a scratch appeared on our wall."

Pia sat forward, and Sage pressed on, knowing she'd piqued her curiosity.

"In addition to what I have to do on Sunday, something happened to me on a physical level which I don't understand either. I came face to face with whatever demonic entity was inside Lucky Wednesday night, and out of fear or sheer desperation, I activated something inside me, some gift I've been told has been there all along but I'd denied. The energy was overwhelming and quite frankly scared me, although I was too flooded with it at the time to notice. It was later, after the energy was gone, that I knew it was out of hand. Untamed."

Sage swallowed, as memories of that encounter flashed through her mind. "I know that I can do this on Sunday. Well, at least I'm willing to give it my best shot. I'll follow what's in the grimoire to the best of my ability because I know it's whatever is inside me that is needed to stop him. It's just that—"

This was the part that worried her the most. Sage swallowed hard and sucked in a deep breath.

"What I'm worried about is: What if I can't do it again? I know I *can* do it, because I did it before. But what if I don't know *how* to do it again? What happened was an accident. A fluke. I don't know how to make it happen again when it counts. I need to practice, to understand."

Sage briefly closed her eyes, took a breath. "I know I'm asking a lot. Probably far too much. I don't know why you'd even want to help me. It will be dangerous. We're dealing with a very evil entity from a dark dimension I don't understand. But you likely do."

Sage looked away, angrily blinking back hot tears. She didn't want to beg, but she didn't know what else to do. "The plain truth is, I don't know who else to turn to."

Pia was silent. For a long, horrible moment. Finally she spoke. "Of course I'll help you. I'm sure I won't have all the answers to your questions, but I'll share whatever I do know."

"Will you help me on Sunday?" Sage hoped she wasn't pushing her luck. "Will you be one of the seven to cast a circle of protection around me? Your energy is particularly powerful, and if that part doesn't succeed, everything else I try will be in vain."

Pia took a deep breath and looked into Sage's eyes, as if searching for something. Finally she nodded. "I will."

The rush of relief made Sage feel light-headed. "Thank you," she said, grabbing Pia's hand.

Pia appeared startled, and began to withdraw her hand, then she closed her eyes. A warm tingling of energy spread through Sage's hand and up her arm.

Eventually, Pia opened her eyes. And smiled.

"Well then, that was interesting. Buckle up, Sage. You're in for one hell of a ride."

Chapter Thirteen

From his vantage point, parked high on a hill, Ethan looked down on the town of Cryton. At what he could see of it anyway. The whole town was covered in a blanket of low-lying fog. When he'd first driven through it, he'd thought it was smoke because of its opaque gray color, but it didn't smell like smoke. It didn't have the moist, cool feel of fog either. It didn't swirl, or roll through the town. It was still. Cloyingly, deathly still.

A murky shroud of gloom.

He now knew the foggy haze was part of what caused the disturbance in the electromagnetic field over Cryton. Something related to whatever power was being generated from the circle.

That was why he had been forced to drive all the way up the hill to get phone reception.

He filled his lungs with fresh air, but the three hundred and sixty degree view didn't make him feel any less closed in. Leaning against the hood of his 4WD, he withdrew his phone from the inside pocket of his leather jacket. Three bars of reception. Enough.

He scrolled down his contacts list and tapped on the one he wanted.

"Blade," his boss, Chief Superintendent Ian Hallow, said in greeting.

"Thanks for sending Taipan," Ethan said, straight to the point.

"I didn't," Ian replied.

"Even though you said you would. 'Tell me what you need, and you've got it,' I think your words were. I asked for my team, and you said I'd have them. And then lo and behold they arrive, but not because you kept your word."

"Jesus, Blade. Don't take that tone with me. That conversation happened before things changed."

"What things changed?" Ethan asked coldly. "Seems everything is still the fucking same. Nate and I are out in the middle of fucking nowhere, assisting you in a government cover-up, and you can't find it within you to stick to your word and send me the backup I need." Ethan couldn't keep the hurt of the betrayal out of his tone.

"It's out of my hands. Blade, I can't tell you what's going on, but I'll tell you this because your father and I went way back. I've always looked at you like a son."

"Family don't screw each other like that."

"I told you, the decision wasn't mine. It's been taken out of my hands."

"Whose hands is it in then?" Ethan demanded. "Who do I need to talk to, to get the resources I need?"

Ian was silent a beat, then two. "You need to move out, Blade. If what you say is true, and you have Taipan there, they need to leave as well. Immediately. This is bigger than me, and a whole lot bigger than you."

"I'll ask one more time," Ethan said, his voice lethally quiet. "If you can't help me, who do I need to talk to? The commissioner? The fucking prime minister? Oh, I know, *the media.*"

"Blade, you don't want to play games like that."

"There's nothing like a press release to make things real messy," Ethan continued. "How does this sound? September 1915, the police were called in to investigate a string of serial killings in Cryton. Unable to work out what was going on in town, and unable to successfully solve the case, they decided to make the problem disappear. Men, women, and children were herded into the town church and murdered like—"

"Blade!" Ian's voice whipped down the line.

"Is there a problem with that?" Ethan asked coolly. "The journalists will dig and discover that it's the truth."

"But it's not the truth. Not the whole truth anyway. And you know it."

"The fallout will be beyond comprehension," Ethan continued. "There will be worldwide headlines within the first hour. There'll be public outrage, a royal commission will commence, and Internal Affairs will dig out every file Taipan ever buried. What else will they find? How many will lose their jobs over this? Tell me, Ian, what will the powers almighty say about that?"

"You don't know what you're messing with."

"And yet, here I am, doing what I've been assigned to do. Solve the case. And just when I begin to get a handle on exactly what this is, you rip the rug out from underneath me. Tell me, Ian, just how do the almighty plan on solving the problem this time?"

"I'm not at liberty to say." Ethan could hear Ian's teeth grinding.

"You can't tell me. Well, let me tell you how this is going to go down." Ethan took a breath. "You are going to give me until Monday."

"Can't do that."

"And yet you will. You'll also leave Taipan with me."

"You're asking the impossible," Ian growled.

"Never stopped you asking it of me."

Ian cursed heavily. "Just to clarify. You want me to take your threat to them. Do as you say, or you'll go to the media and expose them? Do you have a death wish, Blade?"

"Better me than three hundred innocent people in this town."

"You have until 0600 Monday."

———◆———

"That feels so much better," Pia said, extinguishing her smudge stick. She'd spent the better part of the last hour wafting smoke into every nook, cranny, and corner of Beyond the Grave. Pia repeated the circuit she'd taken with her smudge stick, this time using the musical vibrations from a sound bowl. She then placed crystals in a special grid formation, the points all pointing to a larger, master crystal she'd placed on a table in the center of the room. The entire time, she recited words softly in a musical tune.

Sage filled her lungs. The place *did* feel better. Every window and door was open and Sage was positive the house felt… lighter somehow. Whether it was a placebo or not, Sage embraced it. There was great comfort in believing she had a place to go where she was safe from the entity.

"I'll bring something different tomorrow," Pia said. Pia's whole demeanor had changed. To Sage's relief, Pia seemed to have fully embraced her promise to help. She was a formidable ally. Though Taipan also had Sage's back, bulk and muscle didn't help when it came to fighting something you couldn't see.

"What I've got back at the hotel is also white sage, but I've customized it by mixing in other herbs I've found effective in removing evil spirits when we've encountered them on Mark's investigations. I made it after our last investigation here, the night I was overpowered. I'll bring something for you too. To use in that house you're staying in. I don't like the sound of that teddy bear turning up in your room." Pia looked thoughtful. "I'm going to do a reading later, see if I can shed any light on it."

"Thank you," Sage said, understanding that Pia meant a psychic reading. "I'd appreciate it. That bear creeped me out. I put it in a Tupperware container with garlic and thyme."

Pia smiled. "At least that will stop a vampire from stealing it."

Sage grinned, despite herself. "I didn't know what else to do."

"I'll let you know tomorrow. Hey, can I take the grimoire, read it tonight?" she asked abruptly.

Sage shook her head. She picked up the grimoire, her fingers tightening on the worn, comfortable leather. "No. But I'll bring it again tomorrow. We'll go through it some more together then."

"Mark would love to see it," Pia said, and Sage involuntarily stiffened.

"I'm not sure I'm ready—" Sage began.

"Absolutely not," Nate said, interrupting and startling her. Sage had almost forgotten he was still in the room. He'd taken himself off to a corner and had watched quietly as Pia cleansed the house, but he'd stepped forward abruptly at hearing Mark's name.

"Blade was very clear in his instructions that Collins is not allowed anywhere near Sage," Nate said, his tone brooking no argument.

"Is that so?" Pia and Sage said at the same time. Their gazes met briefly in acknowledgment.

"'Fraid so," Nate said, but he squirmed slightly under the intense scrutiny of two unamused females.

Sage wasn't overly eager to see Mark either; the memories of his demon-possessed expression as he'd held the knife at her throat were still vivid. But if and when she was ready to see Mark again was her decision, not Ethan's.

"Don't worry," Pia said, placing a hand on Sage's arm and glaring at Nate. "This is a useless argument anyway. Mark isn't even here. He took off soon after they released him, and he hasn't returned even one of my calls." Pia's brilliant blue eyes shone bright with unshed tears. She turned to Sage. "You know he'd never hurt you, right? I need you to know that."

Sage looked away briefly, then sighed. "I know Mark wouldn't have hurt me, but there were times that night when he wasn't in control."

"If Mark was really a bad person, he wouldn't be feeling so terrible about what happened," Pia reasoned. "You saw his face when he learned what happened. What he did. I've never seen someone so... wrecked. He's off somewhere hating himself right now, and I don't know how to reach him. He's hurting, Sage. You know that. This will be killing him."

"I know." Sage sighed. A wave of sadness washed over her. Sage liked Mark, she really did. And she knew Mark liked her. Maybe a little too much, to judge by his attempts at flirting with her. It was just that once someone had held a knife to your throat, it was a little hard to look at that person quite the same way again.

"Perhaps he just needs a little time to himself," Sage said, feeling sorry for Pia. "I'm sure he'll be back soon."

"I hope so," Pia said. "I'm really worried about him. The longer he closes himself off, the more concerned I become."

"Can't you see where he is?" Sage asked.

Pia shook her head. "We've been friends for a long time; he learned how to throw up a mental block that shuts me out. Our friendship wouldn't have lasted this long otherwise." Pia smiled wryly. "It's no picnic having a psychic for a best friend. He's an empath and has learned to be quite intuitive himself. I just wish he'd come back." Pia released a long, sad breath.

"But not here. Not this house, or around Sage," Nate said firmly.

Pia turned to Nate, who was standing with his arms crossed. It was a cop stance, a posture that denoted he was drawing a line you'd better not step over.

"Don't be such an ass." Pia glared at Nate. "Look at you, on your high horse. It could just as easily be one of your team that gets possessed the next time. It would serve you to remember that."

"Don't bet on it." Nate glared back in challenge.

Sage inwardly sighed. She took the empty plates and cups to the kitchen sink, and let them have at it. When she came back, they were still arguing. Pia threw her hands in the air and turned to Sage.

"As you found out firsthand," Pia said. "This demonic entity is more powerful than anything that has come before. *None* of us is safe. Not your detective, his team, or that tosser." Pia flicked a hand to indicate Nate behind her.

Sage rubbed her temples, her head beginning to pound.

"Are you okay?"

"Yes." Sage suppressed a wince. "I've suffered migraines, to varying degrees, my whole life. But since Wednesday night, they've been excruciating. The tablets barely take the edge off anymore."

"That's it!" Pia said, pleased. "You just said you've had migraines all your life, right?"

"As far back as I can remember."

"And you have also fought the acceptance of your gift all your life. Your denial has been a blockage of energy."

"I'm not sure I'm fully following."

"On Wednesday night, you opened a very powerful channel. You've always had access to a higher energy, as did your mother, but on that night you summoned it in a major way."

"It surprised me at the time," Sage admitted. "But when it came, it felt so... *right.*"

"The need to save Ethan overrode any conscious notion on your part. You reached outward with sheer will, and the power answered." Pia looked thoughtful a minute. "I understand to a certain degree what happened to you, how you accessed a higher energy. It's how I access psychic information. Although on a much, much smaller scale."

"Except, I'm not psychic," Sage said. She absolutely knew that to be fact. Nan, like Pia, could look into the future and "see" things. Like Pia had "seen" where Sage had been locked in the cabin. Sage had never experienced things like that. She didn't know what exactly the energy that came through her was.

"No," Pia said. "You're a healer."

The words slammed into her. And yet, they felt true.

I'm a healer. She tested the words, felt them resonate with the core of her very soul.

So many injured and sick animals had somehow recovered after she'd held them in her hands. She'd been able to revive withered plants that had seemed past the point of saving. But most of all, she remembered cradling Ethan's head against her chest that night the demon had hurtled him against the wall. He'd been limp as a doll in her arms, nearly lifeless. And she'd been determined that he wasn't going to die. Had she somehow helped heal him? Or had he come to on his own?

She'd suspected something then, but hadn't quite wanted to believe it.

Was this the gift she'd spent her whole life avoiding?

A *healer.* Of course. The sense of knowing came in a rush.

She was a healer. Not a freak.

"Please consider not taking any more of those tablets," Pia said gently.

"When the headaches come, try letting the energy flow through you and out of you. Breathe it in, then let it flow out. I know if I don't want to see something a spirit is trying to show me, I feel the pressure. You gift is far more powerful, and you are resisting it, causing physical pain. Possibly even damage."

Pia touched her arm. "I can show you some techniques that work for me. Think of energy like an electrical current. We are all connected to a universal power source, say forty volts. The receiver in *your* body, Sage, can receive a higher amount of electricity than say the normal person's, but your fear is like a regulator, restricting the flow of electricity. On Wednesday night, your desperation to save your detective summoned the full flow of electricity. Your body was flooded with a full two hundred and forty volts."

"That makes sense." That was exactly how she'd felt. How the energy had flowed through her, continuing throughout her lovemaking with Ethan the following day.

"Your body wasn't used to the higher voltage, to keep using that analogy. And afterward, when you were tired and your body was healing, your lack of understanding over what happened scared you. You've put the resistor on again, are stopping the energy, and it's backing up, causing the migraines."

Sage sank back in the chair. "And the tablets are helping me block that energy."

"Yes. That's why when they wear off, your body feels even worse. The only way you're going to ease the physical symptoms is to stop resisting and allow the energy to flow."

"I've felt so strange since that night. Like I can hear sharper, smell more, taste more." Her libido and sexual response had been off the charts as well, especially during the first twenty-four hours after that night.

"All your senses are heightened at the moment," Pia said. "They'll likely settle down as you become accustomed to the higher flow, but they'll always be more sensitive from now on."

It was good to understand what was happening. "Thank you, Pia." Sage gave her a grateful smile.

"I didn't do anything," Pia said, returning her smile.

"What you said helped lots of things slide into place. I appreciate that more than you know."

Pia waved a hand dismissively. "Glad to help. This is going to be fun."

Okay, maybe fun *was pushing the envelope...*

Pia glanced over at Nate. "Are you going to bring *him* back tomorrow?"

Sage followed Pia's gaze. It wasn't the first time Pia's eyes had strayed his way during this afternoon, and Sage was beginning to suspect Pia's preoccupation with Nate had nothing to do with simply his presence here.

Nate was strikingly handsome, especially his blue-gray eyes, which, like Pia's, seemed to miss nothing. When he drew himself up to his full height, he made an imposing figure. And he positively towered over Pia. Not that she seemed a bit intimidated.

"Depends what Ethan's got on," Sage said. "They're dealing with... a spike in crime at the moment."

"Relating to devil worship and occult practices."

"Yes," Nate answered. "How'd you know that?"

Pia simply raised her brows as if to ask, *Really?*

"There's always been a higher occurrence of it here," Pia said. "But now that the veil is thinning, access to that dark dimension is much easier. Those who summon the darkness will find it."

"Make a deal with the Devil, know he will be back to collect," Nate said.

Pia looked at him in surprise. "Yes."

Nate raised a single brow in return. Was it her imagination, or did Pia's lips twitch at the corners?

"The energy *he* is spreading through town is getting stronger every day," Pia said, turning back to Sage. "It's what drew Mark's attention in the first place. Then when he received the call from Ada about your grandmother's house, he jumped at the chance and took that angle for his show."

All the pieces of the puzzle were falling into place. Sage had always thought the small country town she couldn't wait to leave was boring and uneventful. To hear that there was an ongoing dark side to Cryton intrigued her, but somehow didn't surprise her. Demons aside, she'd experienced her fair share of evil here.

"Your grandmother was very aware of this; that's why she kept the shop here. Lots of people sought her counsel. And protection."

Nan had always had people coming to her for advice. How had Sage not known the extent of what had been happening?

"You didn't want to know," Pia said, answering her unspoken question.

Pia's words were a fist to Sage's stomach. That she had been so willfully naïve sickened her. *Never again.*

She'd make it a point to learn everything she could. The veil had been ripped from her eyes. Good or evil, she was willing to see it all. Knowledge was power.

"Let's meet back here tomorrow," Sage said, leaning in to hug her new friend.

"Take care," Pia whispered. The words felt more like a warning than a well-wish.

———— ◆ ————

Liquorice snuggled into Sage's lap as Nate drove them back to Ethan's house. Lost in thought, she scratched Liquorice's ears. "What do you think of all that?" Sage asked.

"She may be beautiful, but she's got one hell of an attitude." Nate slid her a glance. "And... that's not what you were asking."

Sage felt her lips curve up at the corners.

"She frustrates me," Nate admitted. "Makes me madder than anyone I know." His hands tightened on the steering wheel. "But at the same time, I believe her. I believe every word that falls from those blood red lips."

"I believe her too," Sage said. "She knows her stuff. I'm glad I have the chance to work with her over the next few days, to help me get ready."

Nate reached over and squeezed her hand. "You've got Blade, but you've also got me, Sam, Jake, Sean, Daniel, and Max too."

Sage's eyes stung. "Thank you, Nate. That means a lot. More than I can put into words." How ironic that she had more true friends being different than she ever had while trying to be normal.

"No need to thank me. You've already done enough. You make Blade happy. Something we all thought we'd never see. He's always operated on the principle that you can't get hurt if you won't let anyone in." Nate looked her way, holding her eyes for a moment. "And then you came along. I've never seen him the way he is with you. He's almost human." Nate grinned, then turned serious. "It would kill him if something happened to you. And I'm not speaking metaphorically. We just won't let anything bad happen to you then, will we?"

"It's certainly not my intention."

"Just be careful. I know today helped you. A great deal. There's a confidence in your eyes that wasn't there this morning. Just don't forget what happened with Collins, when you decide just how much trust you give her."

"You believe her, but you still don't trust her."

Nate exhaled loudly. "I don't know what to make of her exactly. She gets under my skin though."

Sage suppressed a small knowing smile.

Now she recognized the expression on his face when he'd been watching Pia cleanse the room.

It was the same one she saw on Ethan's face when he looked at her.

———◆———

Nate parked his black 4WD in the driveway of Ethan's place, next to Ethan's and two others. He got out and headed toward the house, but Sage lingered in the vehicle.

She looked up at the homestead, again experiencing a heavy sense of foreboding. What was it about this house that caused such a strong internal reaction? She'd almost give anything to not have to get out of the car and go inside. The pricking of Liquorice's claws through her jeans told her he felt exactly the same way.

The images he'd shown her last night flashed again in her mind, the disjointed stills of a movie played out of sequence. The sharp tools, the circles of black cloth, the black and white dog. And the blood, the blood sprayed everywhere...

For a moment, she thought she was remembering what Liquorice had shown her, but as she met his direct gaze, she realized he was... *reminding* her.

"What do you want me to do?" Sage asked Liquorice. "Ethan has made this place a fortress. Look at the additional security cameras he's had installed. There's even one above your bed. That's to keep you safe too," she told him.

"I don't know any other neighborhood cat with his own personal security."

Liquorice turned his head away, unimpressed by Sage's attempt at humor.

"Sage? Coming?"

Nate had come around to her side and opened her door, clearly wondering what the delay was.

"Yes." She looked back at the house. And stilled.

Someone was in the attic. The attic that had been boarded up years ago.

The blood turned to ice in her veins. For a heart-stopping moment, there was a figure in the attic window. She blinked and it was gone.

It must have been one of the guys. They must have opened the sealed doorway in the hallway. That was all.

So why didn't that slow her racing pulse?

Sage stepped out of the car. Her hand shook as she slung her bag over her shoulder.

"I see you guys managed to get into the attic."

Nate stopped, looked up at the window, and frowned.

"I didn't know that. But it doesn't surprise me that Blade would search the house top to bottom."

"Where is he?"

"His message said you'd find him out back. You all right to go, or do you want me to take you?"

"No," Sage said. "I'll be fine. Thanks for today, Nate."

Nate smiled genuinely. "Pleasure, Sage. I'm enjoying getting to know you. I can see what Blade sees in you."

She touched his arm, then headed around the house to look for Ethan. But she had to force one foot in front of the other, like she was slogging through concrete.

Sage fought every natural instinct she had, deliberately ignoring the chilling sensation that the house was... *watching* her.

———— ◆ ————

Sage found Ethan out back, where Nate said he'd be. Sweat beaded on his forehead as he used one of the lower limbs of a large tree to do sets of pull-ups. His muscles bulged and clenched and Sage's mind blanked. Demon who?

She placed her bag on the small outside table and sat down.

Ethan was shirtless, his shoulders wide and broad, his muscles rippling powerfully as he moved with precision and control. Sun glistened on the sheen of sweat that coated his tanned skin, and her mouth dried.

She must have forgotten to breathe because she found herself sucking in a huge lungful as she tried to regulate her heartbeat. Goddamn. Ethan Blade was nothing short of magnificent. Watching him work out was a dessert of the finest caliber. She relished the moment to study him unnoticed, enjoying the beauty of a male in peak condition in the prime of his life.

Ethan twisted, dropping from the branch and landing so that he was facing her directly. She should have known he'd sensed her presence. It wasn't possible they weren't aware of each other.

He swiped a black towel from the top of a nearby sports bag and drew it over his face, then tossed it and swigged deeply from a bottle of water. His hair fell over his forehead and hung in damp waves around his face.

She couldn't move, couldn't breathe as he turned toward her. "Angel." He licked a drop of water from his lips, the glimpse of his tongue sending a wave of heat throughout her body.

He approached, all masculine strength and pure male power. She felt every effortless step closer as a physical caress. As he neared, the scent of his workout sparked another wave of desire. Ethan overwhelmed her. How could he not? He began to pull a shirt on over his head, but she took it out of his hands and tossed it onto the nearby chair.

"Don't."

She stepped forward, placed one hand on his heated chest and traced his face with her other. She trailed her fingertips along the chiseled contours of his cheekbones, then down to his jawline and over to his full sensual lips. She pressed a finger in his mouth and he nipped it, surprising her out of the trance he had her in.

Grinning wickedly, he caught her hand, pulling it to his mouth. He separated her fingers, then staring directly into her eyes, sucked long and deep on each one. His tongue circled and licked before releasing each finger, and pleasure pooled hot and demanding between her thighs. His heart was hammering beneath her hand on his chest, its racing beat matching her own.

Her knees weakened, and his arm circled her waist and pulled her flush against him. She felt his hardness, the proof of his desire, against her stomach. His skin was hot, his breathing fast. Sweat from his chest dampened her T-shirt, making it cling to her body.

"I want you," she breathed.

She took his mouth in a hungry, urgent kiss. She was gone, her mind incapable of registering anything but the urgent need to give her body the satisfaction it craved. The pleasure only he could provide.

She distantly registered the sound of Daniel coming back from his jog with Max. Thought she heard Jake call out to Ethan, then change his mind. Had he seen the darkly intense expression on Ethan's face as he looked at no one but her?

It was with single-minded focus that Ethan scooped her off her feet and carried her with freshly pumped muscles back into the bedroom.

He kicked the door shut, threw her bag on the chair, and tossed her onto the bed. He had her jeans off before she'd even made herself comfortable on the pillows.

She looked up, and the weight of his stare stole her breath.

A lump lodged in her throat. "Can you feel what this is between us?" Sage asked, her voice reduced to a strangled whisper.

His eyes darkened, his lids heavy. "Yes."

"Does it... Have you felt that spark with anyone else?"

"No." The reply was instant. He didn't even need time to consider. "I've never felt any of the things I feel with you."

She tried to find the words to describe how he made her feel. Needed to know he felt the same. Not just passion. Not just sex, or even love. There were a lot of different types of love in the world. With Ethan, it was... something else.

"Eth?" She pulled back again, as his lips sought hers.

He sighed patiently. "Yes, Angel?"

"Do you think there's something deeper between us than our love? A... *connection* to something bigger than us?"

His eyes shifted from her lips to her eyes. Held. "Can we not talk about anything paranormal tonight? I'm not sure I can take much more today."

Sage frowned. What did that mean? Did he feel what she did?

"What I want right now," Ethan said, his voice low and husky. "What I need to feel, is us. Nothing but us. I want what I can see. What I can touch." He trailed a finger from her chin, along the column of her throat, across the swell of her breast, to the top of her nipple, and down her stomach. "What I can taste." His tongue languidly traced the path his fingers had just taken.

The energy that arced between them was an electrical current through water, crackling with a positive charge. Every cell in her body called to each of his. She felt whole, complete, in his arms. Her heart a hollow void that only he could fill. She craved him powerfully, her body physically ached for him.

Would it always be this way between them?

She opened her legs, inviting him in.

They didn't resurface again until the morning.

Chapter Fourteen

Wednesday
Four Days to the Blood Moon

A towel wrapped around her freshly showered body, Sage padded from the bathroom to the bedroom. They'd slept almost peacefully last night, and it was with relief that Sage woke to discover no unexplained objects or scratches on their wall.

Strangely, for the first time since last Wednesday night, Sage hadn't dreamed a thing, at least nothing she could remember.

It was a warm spring day with the merest hint of a refreshing cool breeze. Sage smiled and headed off to meet Ethan in the kitchen. Halfway down the hallway, she saw something that stopped her dead in her tracks.

The door that led to the attic was still crudely boarded up. Large raw pieces of timber had been bolted and criss-crossed over the opening. She eyed it intently, desperately trying to find signs that it had been opened and resealed.

"Eth," Sage called. He appeared at the end of the hallway, fully dressed in cargo pants and a T-shirt that fit tightly across his chest. His weapon and cuffs were visible on his belt, but they'd be covered by his leather jacket when he left the house.

"Angel?" he asked as he approached.

"Have you been in the attic?"

"No. Why?"

Sage swallowed hard. "I know when you first brought me here, the attic blinds were down. But when I returned with Nate yesterday afternoon, the blinds in the attic were up, and it appeared the windows were open. I... I saw someone standing up there, Eth."

Ethan's brow creased as he considered her words. "You sure?"

"Positive. Nate saw it too."

"I had planned to go up there, but I was tied up with Veronica Coote's murder and didn't get a chance. You don't think the noises, Max barking, the teddy bear in the room... You think the son of a bitch is in here? Hiding in the attic, under our very noses?"

"The door is boarded up," Sage pointed out. "Haven't you wondered why someone would go to all this trouble to board up the attic like this in the first place?"

"It was common to seal off unused rooms years ago."

"This is hardly a mansion. We're not talking about closing off a whole wing. And why not just keep the door closed and simply not go up there? Why board it up like that?"

"If someone was up there," Ethan said slowly, "that would explain why we experienced everything the night before last but nothing last night. Bet he watched us install the cameras." Ethan placed his hands on his hips and cursed. "There must be another entrance. A secret doorway." He tugged on her arm. "I need you out of here."

"Ethan," Sage said, pulling away. "I'm going to meet Pia at the shop. Can I at least get dressed first?"

He must have been preoccupied, because he looked at her wearing nothing but a towel as though he'd just noticed.

His eyes darkened. "I'll help you. Then we'll go find Nate together. I want you away from here, stat. If he's up there, we've got him trapped in a cage of his own making. There's no way he'll get out undetected."

Sage allowed Ethan to "keep her safe" while she got dressed; she even held her tongue and tolerated him personally escorting her into Nate's car and settling Liquorice onto her lap.

As they drove away, her tension only increased.

There wasn't a serial killer in the attic. Sage stroked Liquorice's fur and thought of the images he'd shown her.

There was a reason someone had gone to all that trouble to seal off that doorway.

———— ◆ ————

Later that morning at Beyond the Grave, Pia looked up from the grimoire, her eyes wide. "Wow. This book is amazing."

"It is pretty special." Sage had to force a bit of enthusiasm into her voice. Watching Pia flick through the grimoire's pages filled her with anxiety. Why? She'd needed Pia's help.

Maybe it was because of the amulet. As soon as Pia had picked up the grimoire, the amulet around her neck heated up and began to vibrate. Not unlike what it did when the demon was around. Was it not happy with anyone else touching it?

Except Ethan, she mused. It didn't protest at all when he held it.

"The ritual is rather intricate," Pia said. "The most detailed I've ever seen. Do you have everything you need?"

"I still need a few things. Some white candles, a few herbs I haven't heard of before, some essential oils. I've found all the crystals I need in Nan's boxes."

"I should be able to help you get the rest," Pia said. "Work out a list, and let me know what you still need."

"Thank you."

Pia flicked back a few pages to the banishment ritual. "You noticed that in addition to needing Lucky, you also need the demon's name. You need to summon him to banish him."

Sage nodded, beginning to feel the pressure. "Yes. I haven't seen it referenced in the diaries, and Nan's friends didn't know either when I asked yesterday. They said they'd done a séance the night before Nan died to try to find that information." Sage continued, her voice tight. "They believe it was the séance that brought the demon down on Nan."

Pia briefly touched Sage's arm. "I'm sorry."

"I need seven to form a circle of protection," Sage said, pushing past her grief. "I have four."

"I'll help," Nate said.

"You will?" Sage hadn't even considered asking Nate. Perhaps it was because, before these meetings with Pia, he wouldn't have suited. But he seemed to really believe now, an essential requirement. "I'm sure Blade will want to support you as well."

"Thank you, Nate." Sage's smile reflected the warmth she felt for him. Of course, she'd fully expected him to be there on the night. There was still the very real concern over any action the government officials might take. But it was another thing entirely to be willing to participate in a ritual that necessitated the summoning and banishment of a demonic entity.

"Who are the others?" Pia asked, as though she didn't want to have to consider including the detectives.

"I now have potentially six of the seven. You, Nate, Ethan, Joyce, Pat, and Mona."

Pia raised a perfectly plucked brow. "The Wiccan witches?"

"What?" Sage's brows knitted together. "No, Nan's friends."

"Yes." Pia nodded, smiling. "They're the ones."

"They'd told me my mother and my nan were witches, that I was one too. But I didn't realize they were witches as well. They told me they didn't have gifts like the women in my family."

"That doesn't matter. Wiccan magic centers around helping others, and healing. That was certainly true for Celeste's coven. Witches are spiritually open to the 'more' that there is to life. They are open-minded, tolerant, and have very strong ethics."

Sage felt a surge of excitement. That would surely mean they would add a powerful energy to the circle on Sunday night. *Don't underestimate us*, Joyce had said.

Sage suppressed a grin and concentrated back on the grimoire. "Okay, for the banishment rite, the final section. It refers to a chalice."

"I have one if you'd like to borrow it."

Sage nodded in thanks. "And a few pages over, after a section in Latin I can't read, there's a picture of a wand. A specific wand, judging by the detailed description."

"That's underneath the section for the alchemist's son."

Is that what that Latin title says?

"Wow," Sage mused, tapping the page with her finger. "So I'm not alone in this. If I'm the seer's daughter, who is the alchemist's son?"

Pia shrugged. "Not sure."

"Does this mean I'm not going to be able to defeat him after all?" A rush of disappointment rolled through her. "I didn't see any mention of an alchemist's son in Mary's diary."

"That section is after the banishment rite," Pia pointed out. "From what I can work out, that is the section on how to finish this forever, not just for the next hundred years."

"I didn't even know that was an option. Read it for me?" Sage slid the book back to Pia.

"When the moon first turns to blood, the doorway opens. A portal allows travel in both directions. For sixty minutes, no more, no less. The spells in the grimoire, if performed effectively, control the action and direction of flow. Using his name, be sure the demon is on the right side of the door. Before the sixtieth minute, the demon must be banished, to protect the next century. Or choose the way that's forever…"

"The next section I can't read."

Sage's amulet began to vibrate, and she curled her fingers around it.

"I can read Latin, but this…" Pia considered the page. "I'd say this is a cipher."

"What's a cipher?"

"It's something written in code," Nate said. He was so quiet, just sitting back observing them, or mainly Pia, and Sage was so focused on unraveling the prophecy, that she kept forgetting he was even there.

Pia flicked over to the next page. "From what I can work out, the seer's daughter can stop the demon for the next hundred years, like Mary did, but if she joins with the alchemist's son, they can stop it forever."

Sage sank back in her chair. The possibility of ending this forever was enticing. But who was the alchemist's son?

"Someone who comes from a family of magicians, alchemists," Pia said, staring off into space, as though Sage had voiced her question out loud. "Know anyone like that?"

"No," Sage said. "What is alchemy?"

"Alchemy is white magic, like Wicca, but powerful. I'll think on it. Maybe do a reading, see if I can get a vision."

A rush of hope filled Sage. "Yes. Please do. If we can stop this forever, even if it's just a slim possibility, we should give it a try."

"Agreed," Pia said.

"Speaking of visions and knowing things, are you able to shed some light on what's going on in town?" Nate asked. "At Blade's house, we're hearing heavy booted footsteps during the night, and a train running through the town, even though we know the train stopped running years ago. Blade keeps seeing this goddamned dog that isn't there, and his reaction makes me reach for my weapon every bloody time, which is starting to piss me off. And then of course, there's that... creepy old bear that was left in Ethan and Sage's room. Obviously this is all related, but what exactly is it that we are seeing?"

"Do you want me to see if I can get you some answers?"

"Answers would be good," Nate said.

Nate's face was impassive, but his blue-gray eyes were intensely focused on Pia. Energy crackled in the air, like it always did, a constant charged arc between them.

Pia pulled a black velvet pouch from her handbag and withdrew a stack of cards. She began to shuffle, eyes closed, and took a series of deep breaths.

"Tarot?" Nate said a little too loudly.

"Yes, tarot," Pia said, opening her eyes. "But not just tarot. The cards help me create a connection to my guides. The connection helps the answers flow." She paused in her shuffling and narrowed her eyes at Nate. "There's no scientific proof I'm correct. Do you want me to stop?"

"No!" Sage said.

"Jesus Christ," Nate growled. "I believe in your ability, damn it. Excuse me if I don't understand what it is you do and how. Why do you always want to pick a fight with me?"

Pia looked surprised. "I... I don't know." She stared at Nate for a heartbeat. Two. Then slowly shuffled the cards. "You irritate me."

"Yeah well, the feeling's mutual. Get on with your... tarot thingy. Please," he added.

"Then keep your trap shut for a minute and let me concentrate."

Pia closed her eyes and took another series of deep breaths. Then she began to slowly lay out the cards facedown in a specific way. When she was satisfied, she lifted up the corners of several cards and looked at them before turning them fully over.

"That dog. It's a black and white cattle dog."

"It is," Nate confirmed. "That's how Blade described it too."

Pia continued. "The dog used to live on that property where you're staying. Belonged to a previous owner. I can't quite see who."

"A cattle dog is haunting the place?" Nate asked.

"No. It's not intelligent. It's an imprint. I think, anyway." She held up her hand to stop him asking more questions, then continued. "As far as the other things you mentioned, the train you're hearing, that's definitely an imprint from a hundred years ago. You have no reason to fear that. It's an echo from the past. It feels to me like the times are overlapping, the separation of time is blurring. Merging. The portal is bringing the past to the present, the present to the past."

Pia flipped over another card. She turned to Sage with slightly unfocused eyes. "The outcome has yet to be determined. Sunday night can still go either way. There is no guarantee, even with preparation, even with the grimoire and everything you need. He is strong. Much stronger than he was a hundred years ago or the hundred before that. And don't forget, he has an advantage over you. He's been through this before, many times, and he's had a long time to ruminate on his defeat. He's furious, and determined to win. And your abilities are new. Untried..."

Sage swallowed hard, but remained silent. The situation weighed heavily on her shoulders, but she refused to dwell on *his* perspective in all of this. She pushed the image aside and brought her attention to her part. New and untried or not, failure was, quite simply, not an option.

"Should you not succeed," Pia continued, "and should the demonic entities manage to enter, and they are legion, by the time the full moon has turned new, they will be firmly established in our reality. Their power will continue to increase, as will their numbers. Hatred breeds evil, and that evil will spread through the town, then radiate outward like a deadly virus. I suppose in that respect the government a hundred years ago wasn't that far from the truth."

"Christ," Nate muttered.

Even though little of what Pia said was new, it was still chilling to hear it spoken aloud like that, in that way.

Pia reached across the table and grabbed Sage's hand, startling her. "That house. Oh my God, Sage. That house. Get out!"

"You mean Ethan's?" Sage asked, even though Pia's words echoed Sage's own instincts. Her deep primal urge to flee, her conviction that there was something very wrong with that house.

"Yes."

"Why?" If Sage were to leave, she wanted to provide a solid reason. "Ethan bought it to keep me safe from Lucky. His team are stationed there. I couldn't be safer if I was the President of the United States."

"There's far greater danger for you there than Lucky."

Pia whipped her head to the side, as though something caught her eye.

Sage had seen it too. The raised hairs on her arms were a physical reaction, an internal confirmation that she'd sensed dark energy.

"Pia?" Sage asked, darting a nervous glance around the room. "Did you see something? We cleansed, right? There shouldn't be anything here anymore."

"It's no longer enough. Not now that the gateway is thinning. And you're a beacon. Plus, he has something of yours. Something he's using to link his energy to yours. To track you. He's never far from you. The others too." Pia looked to a space just to the right of Sage's shoulder. "He's watching. And waiting."

Sage's mouth had completely dried up.

"Perhaps you're bringing them here with that tarot stuff," Nate said. "You should stop. Look what it's doing to Sage."

"I'm okay," Sage said, pulling herself together. "Nate, I need this." Then she addressed Pia. "Please continue. If not Ethan's house, is there anywhere I can be safe?"

"Sage, you're safe there with Ethan. He—" Nate began and Sage raised her hand to silence him.

"Outside Cryton, maybe," Pia answered. "Maybe not. You're too much an integral piece of the prophecy. He's becoming more brazen every day as the veil is thinning."

"The bear?" Sage asked.

Pia turned another card. "The bear is a warning. No." Pia turned another card, then silently turned another. Anxiety was burning a hole in Sage's stomach. Eventually Pia spoke. "The bear is a threat. A direct threat to Sage. Please, don't ask me any more about it now."

The look in Pia's eyes would have been enough to silence her without her request. What was the threat?

"There's a place where satanic practices and demon worshipping are occurring," Pia continued.

"We have Lucky's cabin secured. He hasn't been back since last Wednesday," Nate said.

"He has moved somewhere else. He is gathering a circle of seven helpers, much like you are, Sage," Pia said, her eyes taking on a faraway look. "He needs to perform seven ritualistic sacrifices to be strong enough to enter through the circle on the blood moon. He's already done four... no five. He's done five. There'll be two more sacrifices before Sunday. One of those will be a child."

Pia's face contorted as though the images she was seeing disturbed her greatly. "And a betrayal," she added, widening her eyes at Nate. "Who, is unclear, but make no mistake. A betrayal is coming." Pia turned over more cards.

"There is someone else too," Pia said, tapping a card on the table, her eyes again closed. "Someone close to Lucky. He's still here. But he's laying low. The other is the one spreading evil, recruiting more townspeople. During Dead Time, his magic is the strongest. He's cunning, ever watchful, awaiting the slightest opportunity." She leaned forward. "Dead Time. In the house. If you don't get out—"

A loud crash upstairs saw Nate on his feet in an instant.

"Stay here," he said and, gun drawn, ascended the stairs three at a time.

"What did you see?" Sage asked.

But Pia's eyes had cleared. "Something bad is going to happen in that house. *He* caused the distraction deliberately. He doesn't like what I'm doing."

"What do you mean, something bad is going to happen? Can you see what?" Pia blinked for a moment, her expression clearing. She was now fully present and out of her trance. The session was over.

Pia's hands shook while she put the cards back into a pile and tied them with a black satin ribbon. "What's he think he's doing up there?"

"Looking for what made that noise, I assume," Sage said.

"Uh-huh."

Nate appeared at the bottom of the stairs, sliding his gun back into its holster. "Appears to be all clear."

Pia spared him the briefest glance as she rose from the table. "He hasn't learned much yet, has he?"

"What do you mean by that?" Nate glared, but shifted his feet uncomfortably.

"What do you think you're going to do with that gun? Shoot a shadow?" Pia asked. "Entities don't have bodily mass. Have you not listened to any of what I've been saying?"

"I had to bloody well check it out, didn't I?" he growled. "It's all fun and games until there's a serial killer upstairs, and I didn't so much as get off my ass and take a look. Keyton *is* flesh and blood, and by your own admission, still after Sage."

"He makes a damn good point there," Sage said.

"Whatever." Pia dismissed Nate with a wave of her hand, and color rose in his cheeks.

"Sage, you must leave that house. Things happened in the attic. The basement. The things he wants to do. To you..."

There's a basement? Sage's stomach bottomed out as she remembered seeing the figure in the attic. The attic Ethan was searching today, in the hope of finding Lucky. "What happened in the attic?"

"It's where he put them. Until it was time to take them to the basement."

"Who?" Nate asked.

"*Him.* And he's still there."

"Give me a name."

Nate's phone signaled an incoming call. "It's Blade," Nate said, glancing at the screen. "I have to take this." He walked across the room, listening intently. After a moment, he disconnected the call and turned to Sage.

"I have to go. Blade needs me. Sam will replace me."

"Is everything all right?"

"There's been another murder." Nate looked at Pia. "The sixth sacrifice, right?"

"No," Pia said.

"Toby James," Nate said, reciting impatiently by ticking off his fingers, "was the first, the fifteen-year-old boy. Roy Peterson was number two. Celeste Matthews was number three, and her friend Ada Slatterley, number four. Veronica Coote was number five. So this murder will make it the sixth."

Pia straightened in her chair, rubbing her eyes as though the reading drained her in some way.

"The murder your partner just called you about is not a sacrifice. It was the murder of somebody in the demon's way. Lucky needs to make seven sacrifices, and they must be performed according to a specific ritual, before the blood moon. I can't see who they are, but he knows already. There'll be two more."

Sage shuddered, Pia's words echoing in her mind. *One will be a child.*

Chapter Fifteen

Another murder. Different MO, but most certainly connected. This one, a middle-aged man, David Roberts. Sam had been following up the tip Nate got from Sage about the son, Douglas, when he spotted the body through a window.

Ethan and Nate walked through a flock of clucking chickens roaming free in the front yard of an old farming homestead on the outskirts of town. Sam was waiting for them on the porch.

According to Zach's report, the stone house had been in the family for generations, and Mrs. Ross had bequeathed it to her grandson David twelve years ago. Content with country life, David Roberts had married a local girl and found employment at the hardware store in town. He was one of the best sheep shearers in the area, and had extra income come shearing time. Roberts lost his wife to cancer twelve months ago, and had one son, a sullen teenager named Douglas.

Weapon drawn, Ethan swung the front door open. The smell of burnt flesh, heavy and pungent, saturated the air. In keeping with the style typical of houses in the area, the front door led straight into a corridor with rooms branching off to either side. They followed the stench across faded linoleum to the sitting room at the rear of the house.

Ethan stood at the entry to the room, and with a gloved hand, flicked the light switch. A threadbare, three-seater fabric couch was positioned against the window and faced a television that dominated the room. No flat screen here. A large black unit on a free-standing trolley. A filthy rug lay claim to the center of the floor, covered in stains that overlaid older stains. A chipped laminated coffee table squatted on top. The most modern items were nudie pictures taped in various locations around the room. The magazines they'd been ripped from still littered the floor.

But it was what was in the corner of the room that had Ethan's attention.

A large circle, defined by white powder, surrounded what Ethan could only presume at this stage to be the house's owner, David Roberts.

Or what was left of him.

At first glance, it appeared that Roberts had burned himself to death; perhaps an unattended cigarette had caught the chair alight. Only, Roberts hadn't merely suffered third-degree burns. There was nothing left of him but greasy black gunk and one intact and preserved right hand and forearm to the elbow.

Nate began taking photos, and the flashes from the camera freeze-framed the scene, like graphic stills from a horror movie. When he'd finished the initial round, Nate opened the window so they'd be able to breathe again. Ethan was used to the smell of decaying flesh—as used to it as one *can* get—but this odor was foul on another level. The melted fat particles hung in the room, leaving a rank taste in his mouth.

"Jesus, Blade." Nate stood as close to the window as possible. "The temperature of a fire needed to incinerate a human body is near a thousand degrees Celsius, and yet nothing else caught fire."

Beneath the decades-old threadbare carpet was a timber floor. Candles burned around the room like eerie tributes. "Blow out those candles, will you," Ethan said to Sam, "before anything else goes up."

The smoke from the extinguished candles mingled with the scent of burnt flesh.

"A house fire can be caused by a single candle flame or a short in a faulty electrical device," Nate said. "So why didn't the whole house burn?"

"Spontaneous human combustion," Ethan murmured. He'd been skeptical of the phenomenon, but this had all the hallmarks. And nothing would surprise him in this town.

He picked up a large jar filled with something blackish red. "Or someone dabbling in something they shouldn't," Ethan murmured. Everything about this crime scene screamed "not right." He held the jar out to Sam. "Get this to Zach, ASAP. I need to know if this is blood, and if so, human or animal."

"Blade, take a look at this." Ethan followed the sound of Nate's voice to the hallway, where he was standing with a door open at the top of a set of stairs. "Wanna bet we'll find our answer down here?"

Their heavy boots creaked on the aging timber stairs as they made their way down to the basement. The light switch didn't work, and they flicked on their Maglite torches.

The room was large, the temperature easily ten degrees cooler than upstairs. It was dark, a fact enhanced by the concrete walls, which had been slathered with black paint. An unmade single bed was pushed against the left-hand wall, and three large shelves lined the other walls. Cluttering the shelves were statues of mythical creatures with demonic tails, a large inverted cross, and numerous pillar candles in various sizes. All black. Black feathers decorated the walls, as did inverted pentagrams and pictures that could only be described as scenes from Hell.

In the middle of the room was a table surrounded by six chairs. On the table was a Ouija board and next to it, six black candles. Dark wax had pooled around their bases and dripped onto the floor.

Off to one side was a tall bench set up like an altar. On it were more black candles, a large bowl filled with feathers, entrails, and a beak from a black bird—a crow?—alongside several knives, and bottles of dark red liquid.

"Roberts's teenage son lives here, right?" Nate asked. "Wanna bet this is his room?"

"Can't imagine he brings many girls home," Ethan murmured.

"And yet, look at that." Nate pointed to a pair of women's panties on the pillow of the bed. Ethan moved closer. They were lacy pink, and icy fingers raked down his spine. Didn't Sage have a pair very similar to this?

He lifted them with his pen, and dropped them into the open clear evidence bag Nate was holding. "These are not to be run through the system. Send them to Zach with the jars. I can't wait for a report; I need this information back today. Tomorrow at the latest."

And if the panties hadn't disturbed him enough, in the center of the Ouija board he spotted a few strands of blonde hair. He'd need forensics to positively identify it, but he knew whose hair it was. He'd recognize that color and texture anywhere.

"Goddamned son of a bitch." Ethan's hands clenched into fists. He wanted to pound something and fought a powerful urge to rip into the room.

"Keyton must be hiding out here," Nate said.

"Perhaps," Ethan conceded. "But my money is on the teenage son, Douglas. The missing section of Sage's hair is considerably larger than these few strands. I'd say Keyton is connected in some way to whoever's been using this room, and whatever he needed the hair for, he's kept some for himself."

There was a good chance Douglas Roberts—and possibly Keyton himself—would come back to this room, as long as they felt it was still safe.

"Get Jake and Daniel here. Jake can give us a hand inside, and Daniel can sit surveillance out back. In case they return and one of them makes a run for it, Max can follow their trail."

"What about the mess upstairs? We call it in?"

"No." They couldn't risk even Ian finding out about this. Ethan would bet that the unusual circumstances of David Roberts's death had something to do with the Ouija board and the apparent satanic practices that were taking place down here.

He didn't need the obvious visual confirmation for that. There was a dark energy in this place; he'd breathed it in the moment he walked through the front door. There was a heavy feeling in the air, anger and hatred so strong he could taste it. It hung in the room and clung to the walls, and triggered something matching deep inside him.

"We keep this with Taipan only," Ethan said. "If we have this place crawling with cops, whoever is using this space will stay away. You can bet that person is our link to Keyton. And judging by the hair and underwear, there could be an imminent threat to Sage. We'll do our own surveillance. Whoever is using this space will be back soon, I can guarantee it. All we have to do is sit tight and lay in wait."

Ethan and Nate slipped out of the house and blended into the shadows of the trees.

———— ✦ ————

After Nate left to meet Ethan at the scene of the latest murder, Pia and Sage spent an hour re-cleansing Beyond the Grave. They'd opened all the doors and windows, and Pia had walked around several times, using different tools: a bell, a singing bowl, and more white sage. She said it was overkill, but they both felt the difference to the energy of the room when she was finished.

Pia went out front to get something from her car, but when the door opened, it wasn't Pia standing in the doorway.

Sage looked up, her heart stopping dead in her chest. There, his finely honed body encased in denim jeans, leather belt, and tight black T-shirt with the Debunking Reality logo, stood Mark Collins.

A strangled cry choked her throat, and her fingers sought the angel around her neck. For a moment she was back at the cabin, Mark's arm locked around her, the blade of his knife at her throat.

Breathe. It's just Mark. Not the demon.

Sage told herself her reaction was typical of a victim seeing her attacker for the first time since the incident. Except Mark wasn't a rapist, nor was he a criminal. He'd been a victim himself that night.

She looked into his face now, seeing only a handsome man with movie-star charisma. But all too clearly, she could recall when he'd been possessed—his eyes glassy, vacant, and unfocused, his smile chilling. It was the personality change that had been the most disturbing. Like meeting someone's identical twin. The same, but not. And Mark's twin had been a psychopath. She stared for a long moment, looking for signs of the other Mark, but found nothing other than an expression of true regret.

Mark slipped inside the shop, but kept his hand on the door handle and didn't advance any further into the room. He was gauging Sage's reaction, assessing her response.

She should tell him to get the hell out. Stay the fuck away from her. Ethan would expect her to do just that.

But she couldn't.

This Mark was the man she'd grown very fond of these last few weeks. The sweet and genuine Mark who'd stood by her side and kept her safe during the nights of the paranormal investigation.

This Mark standing at the door was her friend.

But if he'd been possessed once, what was there to stop it happening again?

Sage stood on shaky legs and wiped the palms of her hands on her jeans. She had to trust that Mark would remain himself. That he'd taken precautions.

She refused to let the demon win.

Holding her gaze, Mark let go of the door and took a step toward her.

"Hi Mark." Sage's heart kicked in an irregular beat, but her voice was reassuringly strong. Steady.

He crossed the room and crushed her against his chest.

Startled, she pushed down a rush of panic, then let herself relax against him, the strong rhythmic beat of his heart soothingly regular. Comforting. *Normal.*

There was nothing suggestive in the way he was holding her, but she pulled back anyway. Mark gripped her shoulders, capturing her gaze.

"I'm sorry," he said roughly. "I'm so goddamned sorry." His eyes glistened and his face contorted in pain, his agony all too clear in the lines of his face.

Mark had not been in control that night. He'd been used, nothing more than a pawn in an evil game. The demon was responsible for what had happened to Mark, just as he was responsible for the deaths of her mother, grandmother, and others.

"I don't expect you to forgive me," Mark said. "I don't know if I'll ever forgive myself. But know that even in the grip of that demon I never would have hurt you. I'd have let him kill me first."

Sage heard the truth in his words. And she believed him. He'd whispered something similar in her ear while fighting the demon's hold. And yet, the small scar on her throat was a reminder she carried. Did he too have burns from the cigarette lighter she'd used to escape? But greater than the external scars were the internal ones. The ones they both needed to set aside so they could move forward.

"You look even remotely possessed again, and I'll kill you myself." Sage managed a small smile to soften her words. She'd kept her tone light, but the raw honesty in her words was clear. She was taking no further risks when it came to this demon.

There was too much at stake.

"Mark," Pia said, walking in through the front door. When she came forward to give Mark a hug, Sage realized Pia hadn't been surprised to see Mark today.

"You knew he was coming?" Sage asked when Pia stepped back. The betrayal stung.

"You wouldn't have stayed if I'd told you."

"It was my decision to make," Sage said through clenched teeth. "Not yours."

"Was it?" Pia gestured for Sage and Mark to follow her to the table. "Look how well it turned out." She sat at the table and poured Mark a drink like it was her house.

Sage crossed her arms. "How did he get past Sean?"

"I had to ask Sean a question. I guess he was preoccupied and didn't notice." Pia shrugged nonchalantly and straightened the neckline of her shirt.

"Pia," Sage said sharply. "I don't appreciate being steamrolled. It's cost me a lot to trust you. And Mark too, for that matter. If we're going to work together, I require honesty. Do something like this again, and I'll shut you out."

"Sorry," Pia said, not looking sorry at all. "Sometimes you need a little intervention to smooth over a rough patch."

"What happened last week was more than a 'rough patch,' Pia. Mark was under the influence of something that could have proved fatal to me." Sage's cheeks burned. "You won't make choices for me in the future. Are we clear?"

Appearing surprised by the vehemence in her tone, Pia nodded. "I'm sorry. I just know Mark will never hurt you. I'd never have invited him back otherwise."

She looked so confident. So certain. Sure, she was a psychic, but that hadn't helped Sage last Wednesday. Well, not until it was almost too late.

But she'd let it go for now. Nothing would be gained by arguing. And she desperately needed Pia's help.

They spent the best part of the next hour catching up. Sage discovered that Mark hadn't been willing to come back until Pia had left him a message yesterday saying that Sage didn't blame him. When Nate had left to help Ethan, Pia saw that as an opportunity for Mark to see Sage, so she'd called him and arranged their little ruse to sneak him in.

Sage still wanted to be angry about it, but she had to admit it felt good to see Mark again. Now that she'd got over her initial fear, she remembered how reassuring his presence had been during the paranormal investigation.

Mark hadn't been idle while he'd been away. He'd thoroughly researched Cryton's history, and he hinted that he'd learned a number of interesting facts that were pertinent to what was happening now. Sage should have known he wouldn't give up his quest, his driving need to document proof of the paranormal for the unbelievers.

Mark cracked his knuckles, adjusted his watch, and cleared his throat. Then he looked at Sage. "You're not going to like this, but I want to set up the cameras again. I believe we can get some real good stuff here. This is a once-in-a-lifetime opportunity. Plus, I want to catch what happens on the blood moon."

Sage sank back into her chair, boneless. He could take his cameras and shove them. His reality TV show was the least of her concerns. And yet...

It might just be advantageous to have documentation of what transpired over the next few days. Especially if the government moved in like they'd threatened to. There would be no cover-up this time.

"You know what, Mark? Stick your cameras wherever you want, but I have two stipulations. One, the ritual can't be interfered with in any way." Sage leaned forward on both hands. "Two, none of this will be aired until it's over. Until after the blood moon. The slightest leak would be disastrous. I can't afford anything to get in the way of what I need to do Sunday. I need your promise." Media attention before the blood moon would force the hand of the authorities.

"Done."

Sage narrowed her eyes. That was a little too easy.

126

"What? Don't you think if I'd intended to do that, I couldn't have done it already?" Mark lowered his voice. "I know you need to learn to trust me again. Look at it this way. I want the scoop. This is my exclusive. Why would I tip off anyone else?"

Sage slowly nodded. That did make sense. "Okay. Set up your cameras."

"Can I put some cameras where you're staying now?"

Sage's stomach bottomed out. Again. She knew how Ethan would react to Mark being in town. "Why would you ask that?"

"In my digging around, I found out something pretty interesting. Creepy interesting, that is."

"What?" Sage asked.

"That house you're in, the Muellers' house, was once owned by..." Mark leaned in, lowered his voice for emphasis. "Lance Virgil Keyton, known as Virgil. Lucky's great-grandfather, who just so happened to be the serial killer almost exactly a hundred years ago. How bizarre is that?" Mark asked. "What are the chances that DS bought that very house? Are you sure you can trust *him*?" Mark referred to Ethan by his nickname for him: Detective Skeptic, or DS for short.

Sage's muscles tensed. "Of course I trust Ethan. He couldn't possibly have known the history of the house. It's a coincidence."

"Pretty big coincidence, don't you think?"

Sage frowned. "What exactly are you implying?"

"DS bought that *particular* house. Not any of the others on the market. That particular one. And he *bought* it. Didn't rent," Mark said, leaning forward for emphasis. "I'm just saying you want to be careful about who you trust. I'm speaking of course, firsthand. I've had experience with demons and ghosts over the years, and yet I still fell victim. How easy would it be for the demon to influence someone unsuspecting? *Unbelieving* of the possibility?"

Sage refused to even consider it. Ethan was too strong of mind to ever allow something like that to happen. Wasn't he?

"That fits in with the vision I had earlier while reading the tarot cards, Sage," Pia said urgently. "Virgil still haunts the house, has attached himself to you. He influenced Ethan to buy the house. He wanted you there, Sage. He kept his victims tied in the attic, torturing them, until it was time to take them to the basement." Pia closed her eyes against the images she appeared to see all too clearly. "His playroom."

Sage swallowed, hard.

"You can't go back there tonight," Pia said.

"I have to." Sage swallowed a wave of anxiety. "Look, I don't feel comfortable there either, but Ethan bought it to keep me safe. He's put crazy security on that house, mostly for me. But his team also needs a base to work from. It's somewhere safe for all of us."

"I still think it's too risky." Pia touched her arm. "Virgil is fixated on you."

"I'll cleanse the house then. That'll work, right?"

Pia seemed to consider. "It might. But Virgil's attachment to the house is strong."

Mark rose to his feet. "I need to get back to the hotel. There's something else interesting that I'm working on."

"What?"

"I'll fill you in tomorrow. When I bring the proof to back up my claims, you'll be blown away. I know I am. You coming?" he asked Pia, and she nodded.

"We good?" Mark asked.

Sage smiled. "We're good."

He pulled her in for a friendly hug.

"Wait," Sage said. "You can't go out the front. Sean will see you." Sage wanted to be the one to tell Ethan Mark was back.

"Follow the path that goes behind the shed in the backyard. It will take you to the graveyard. Turn right, and it will lead you back to the main road. Pia, you can leave out the front, and pick Mark up down the road."

Sage ignored a stab of guilt and tried not to think about what Ethan would do if he found out Mark was back in town.

When he found out...

———◆———

Later that night, Sage jerked awake, her heart pounding. Ethan made a sound in his sleep and tightened his embrace, but she wriggled free so she wouldn't disturb him. She sat up, her skin coated with sweat brought on by the terror of a nightmare.

She'd been in the cabin again. No... it was somewhere else. Another playroom. The same, but different. Mark's image blurred with Lucky's, then blended into the demonic entity with black fiery wings. *He* was close now.

I can feel his presence, so strong, when it's as quiet as this.

Not a single sound broke the silence. Even the nocturnal creatures outside had turned quiet as death.

Wiping her clammy hands on the sheet, Sage consciously relaxed her shoulders. Moonlight entered in wafer-thin slices from around the blinds, allowing her to see the gentle rise and fall of Ethan's chest.

I should have told him Mark was in town.

She'd wanted to. Intended to. But when he'd returned, it was late and she hadn't had the energy to fight. He'd looked exhausted, his eyes dark and shadowed.

He'd phoned her as he'd left the crime scene he was working on. She'd had just long enough to perform the same cleanse of the house that Pia had done at the shop. It was Sage's first cleanse, but she felt confident she'd done a good job. It had worked at the shop, so it stood to reason it would work here too. Wouldn't it?

They'd had a quick meal and made love instead of talking. It was what they'd needed more.

She'd tell him over breakfast.

The digital display on the bedside clock clicked over to three a.m. A series of footsteps sounded overhead, and she lifted her head to listen.

There was something on the roof. No, the attic. Not something. *Someone.*

The footsteps were too heavy to be those of an animal. Her chest tightened and she listened, barely breathing.

She then remembered that Ethan had intended to open up the attic today. With everything that had happened during the day, Sage had forgotten to ask.

Clearly, he hadn't found Lucky or another individual. She would have heard about that for sure. Most likely, he'd discovered an empty room. Visually empty anyway.

The past is bleeding into the present, the present into the past.

Pia had said the times were overlapping. Lance Keyton had kept his victims alive in the attic, before taking them to the basement.

Just what horrors was Sage listening to? What was he doing to them?

For a while there was nothing but a long drawn-out silence.

Then, the creak of a large heavy door being opened sent her pulse racing. It was so loud, she at first glanced at her bedroom door, but it had come from overhead. More sounds: something being dragged, a bump, something being dropped, then a sound that chilled her blood.

A muffled, disembodied scream.

If Sage had believed even for a second that it was someone who needed help, she would have woken Ethan in an instant. But the noises were coming from the attic, the unused attic. They were not from this time, but echoes from the past.

Her chest ached. She'd felt what Virgil's victims had felt, trapped and waiting for the serial killer to return. Imagining what would happen when he did.

Sage struggled to breathe.

They are not from our time. Sage repeated the words to herself, over and over, but kept her eyes squeezed shut.

A dog howled somewhere in the distance, and the noises overhead grew louder.

She pulled the quilt up to cover her ears, buried her head in the pillow, and tried hard not to think about what was happening in the attic. What the dragging noises and the screams meant. Desperately tried to blank out the images Liquorice had projected into her mind.

Pia had warned her she couldn't stay here. But if it was simply time overlapping, an imprint, as she called it, it couldn't hurt her. Could it?

And then, something changed.

A different sensation came over her. Something that triggered panic deep inside her, and had her gasping for breath. Someone wasn't just in the attic.

Someone was *in the room.*

Even beneath the quilt, she felt its menacing presence.

Go away, she silently screamed. *Go away. Go away! Go away!*

But still, the sensation of being watched remained.

Blood thrashed past her ears. She couldn't breathe, and she was trembling uncontrollably.

She didn't want to look. Couldn't bring herself to do it.

But she had to.

Slowly, she inched the blanket down. And froze.

There, at the foot of the bed, stood a tall dark figure in a black coat. She squeezed her eyes shut, but when she opened them, he was still there. She shivered and let out a whimper.

Her limbs refused to move. She couldn't alert Ethan. She was paralyzed, unable to do anything but stare. And will it not to move. Not to come closer.

Who are you? she demanded silently. *What do you want?*

You. Slowly, he raised an arm. Reached for her.

She hissed with pain as though he'd touched her. He couldn't have reached her from that distance, but still her chest burned.

And then he was gone.

Outside the window, the night wind brought with it howling, agonizing cries and screams of pain. They were pleading. But not with him.

With her.

Help us! they demanded. The wail of many tortured souls, calling, begging for release. Pulling at her with fingers rigid with death.

She closed her eyes. But still they came.

Their hands, their fingernails, were sharp claws of desperation that pierced her flesh. Their cries all the time becoming stronger. Louder. Until they were a deafening roar in her ears.

She could not help them. And she could not stop them.

She pressed her hands to the sides of her head and inwardly screamed.

Leave. Me. Alone!

Ethan stirred restlessly.

And then abruptly there was silence.

Outside the window, the souls receded, disappearing back into the earth. The attic turned silent. The night was again black as pitch and silent as death.

And she knew.

She didn't have until the blood moon.

The dance with the Devil had already begun.

Chapter Sixteen

Thursday
Three Days Before the Blood Moon

Blade, you awake?" Daniel's voice carried through their bedroom door.
Sage looked at the digital clock on the bedside table. Five fifteen a.m.

Ethan was already sliding into his jeans as he called out, "Coming."

Something had upset Max. Furious barks were interspersed with vicious growls.

"What's going on?" Sage asked, immediately sitting up in bed.

"I'm about to find out." Ethan glanced her way, then whipped his head back in a double-take.

"What is it?" Instantly uncomfortable for no apparent reason, Sage pulled up the sheet to cover her naked chest. "What's wrong?"

"What the hell happened to you?" Ethan moved to her side, the bed dipping as he sat next to her. Gently, he unclenched her fingers from the sheet and lowered it so he could see.

Sage became aware of what had concerned him. Could feel a stinging burn across her chest. Her hand went immediately to the spot.

"Angel, let me see." Ethan took her fingers in his and moved her hand out of the way. His eyes were narrowed, his jaw clenched. She lowered her chin and looked down.

Three angry scratches ran from her collarbone toward the center of her chest. A mark of aggression, pointing to where the angel pendant rested.

She traced the scratches and flinched. "It burns."

"Christ, what did that?"

Sage reached for the angel around her neck. "Last night. I dreamed about him. Again. He was here. Standing at the foot of our bed."

"Again?" Ethan's jaw clenched.

Sage struggled to speak past the constriction in her throat. "I'm not just imagining him, am I?"

"Blade!" Daniel called out again. More urgent this time.

"I have to see what he wants." Ethan stood, his hands fisted at his sides. Clearly, he didn't want to leave her. "I need to know you're all right."

"I'm fine," Sage managed. "Go. Daniel needs you."

Ethan crossed the room and grabbed his weapon.

"Stay right here. I'll be back."

Sage slipped out of bed and grabbed her jeans off the floor.

"I want you to stay here until I advise otherwise," Ethan ordered, looking back at her from the door.

Yeah right!

She ignored him, but her hand shook as she fumbled with the button on her jeans.

Abruptly, her stomach roiled.

"I have to go to the bathroom." Sage said, dashing in that direction. She barely managed to shut the door behind her before she was violently ill.

The scratches burned intensely. Had the entity somehow sickened her, infected her with his dark energy?

—————◆—————

Ethan hesitated, torn between wanting to help Sage, and needing to respond to Daniel's call. There might be an intruder, they might even have Lucky. Leaving the bedroom door open, he hurried to the kitchen to find Daniel unsuccessfully trying to calm Max, who was straining against Daniel's hold to get to something on the table.

"What the hell's going on?" Ethan quickly scanned the room, saw no visible signs of a break-in, no disturbance of any kind.

And then he saw it, and knew at once what had upset Max.

"Jesus Christ," Ethan said, snatching the offending object off the table. "Don't let Sage see this." He remembered her reaction when she'd first discovered it while packing up her grandmother's shop.

"Don't let me see what?" Sage demanded, stepping into the room. Judging by her expression, she was far from impressed that he'd been trying to hide something from her.

"Ethan Blade, what have you got in your hand?"

No way was he telling her. She had enough to worry about. He turned on his heel and headed toward the door.

She rushed in front of him, placing herself between him and the outside, her green eyes flashing.

The object in his palm began to burn, and he smothered a hiss of pain.

"Sage, move out of my way." He was going to smash this thing to pieces once and for all.

"After you show me what's in your hand."

His palm was on fire, burning as though he held a fistful of hot coals. He'd be lucky if he wasn't incurring third-degree burns. He resisted the urge to drop it. He needed to get it out of the house.

"Move," Ethan demanded.

"No."

"Goddamn it, Sage." With his free arm, he pushed her aside. She stumbled and fell.

"Jesus, Blade!" Daniel growled, doing his best to hold back an agitated Max.

Seeing Sage land on the floor was enough to make him forget everything else. He tossed the burning object to the ground and rushed to her side. He hadn't meant to hurt her. He'd hardly used any force at all. Or so he'd thought.

Tenderly, he pulled her to her feet and checked her over. When he'd convinced himself she wasn't hurt, he pulled her into him. "Sage. Goddamn, I'm so sorry. Are you all right?"

Her shock fading, Sage pushed him hard on the chest. "Get your hands off me." He instantly released her.

Her eyes came to rest on the gargoyle figurine on the floor. Her jaw dropped, her face turning ashen.

Ethan cursed and put his arm around her rigid shoulders, but she shrugged him off.

Nate was at the door, gun in hand, and Jake moved in behind him. They stood at the entrance to the room, trying to get a read on the situation through the chaos.

"Dan! Take Max outside," Ethan shouted over the dog.

Daniel picked up his barking dog, restraining Max in his arms. As soon as the door closed behind them, Max silenced.

"What the hell is going on in here?" Nate demanded. "Blade, tell me I didn't see you push Sage."

Sage backed away from the object on the floor. "How did that get in here?"

"What is it?" Nate asked, moving closer. "Damn, Sage, you're as white as a ghost. Did Blade hurt you?"

"Fuck you, Ryder," Ethan growled. But he raked his eyes over her again anyway. He'd die before he'd hurt her.

"How did that get in here?" Sage repeated, her voice shaking.

Nate picked the gargoyle up off the floor and abruptly dropped it, bringing his palm to his lips. "What the fuck?"

Sage was frozen to the spot, unable to take her eyes from the wicked-looking beast with pointy ears and a forked tail.

Cursing heavily, Ethan snatched up the metal kitchen tongs, picked the ugly statue off the floor, and took it out to the woodshed. He placed the grinning creature on a wood block and could have sworn its eyes were glowing red with intelligence as it looked at him.

His hand stinging, he picked up the axe, swung it high over his head, and smashed it precisely onto the gargoyle. He could still see the fear on Sage's face, the shock when he'd pushed her. He had hurt her. The creature's evil had seeped into him, just for an instant, but an instant was enough.

He continued to wield the axe until the thing was an unrecognizable powder.

And he'd be damned if it didn't laugh at him while he did.

———— ◆ ————

A short time later, Ethan entered the house. The smell of breakfast was in the air: coffee, bacon, and eggs, which Sam was just serving onto plates. Sage was sitting at the table smiling at some story Nate was telling her. Her eyes briefly met Ethan's, and he received the reassurance in them that she was okay. He rolled his shoulders and stretched his neck.

Judging by the small talk, the tension in the house was easing. It was one of those rare moments when the whole team was together. Daniel was sitting at the end with Max lying quietly at his side. Sam and Nate were at the barbeque, turning over the bacon and cooking eggs. Toast popped up and Sam grabbed the slices from the toaster and put them on a plate. Jake was sitting across from Sage reading the local paper, and Sean was typing something into his laptop.

Wordlessly, Ethan moved to the kitchen and set about making Sage a cup of coffee. Through the kitchen window, Ethan stared at the shed where he'd taken to the gargoyle with an axe. He gripped the bench top and tried to understand exactly what had just transpired. He'd pushed Sage. He'd hurt her, the woman he loved. The woman he wanted to protect.

He couldn't be sure, but when she'd tried to stop him, he could swear that something had whispered to him, set a match to his temper. But had it been the gargoyle itself, or just the intense pain in his hand?

All he knew was that the damn thing brought out such rage in him. What scared him the most was that he'd *enjoyed* crushing that gargoyle. Bringing about its death. But objects weren't alive. Objects didn't have glowing eyes and wicked laughs either. As impossible as it was, Ethan knew what he'd seen and heard. He also knew what it had made him *feel*.

The spoon hit the side of the cup as Ethan stirred the coffee. At the table, he handed Sage the steaming mug and was surprised when she gasped.

"Ethan, look at your hand!" Sage grabbed his hand in both of hers and turned over his palm.

Ethan glanced down to where Sage was tracing her fingers across the burns that had begun to blister. She blinked up at him with wide eyes.

"It was hot." He shrugged. Another reason that something about that object was not right. The heat had been searing, like the gargoyle had been pulled out of a raging fire. Nate had felt it too. It wasn't all in his mind.

Jake looked up from the paper. "Wasn't last night."

"You?" Sage's coffee cup landed hard on the table, and liquid sloshed over the rim. "*You* brought it here, Jake?" The hurt in her voice stabbed Ethan's heart. "Why would you do that?"

Her hand was shaking and she placed it in her lap, covering it with her other hand. If Ethan was disturbed by the gargoyle, Sage was even more so. The gargoyle had haunted her on more than one occasion these last two weeks.

If Jake was surprised at her curt tone, he didn't show it. Ethan swallowed his surprise. Jake was a tough man, but he wasn't callous. It wasn't like him to be oblivious or uncaring to someone's obvious distress. And it wasn't as though he wouldn't have noticed. Reading people was what made them good at their jobs.

"I found it at that house we were in yesterday," Jake said casually. "The boy's bedroom, Blood Fox. It was on the table with the candle and the skull with the hole in it."

"Blood Fox?" Sage's forehead creased into a frown.

"Douglas Roberts, I mean."

Ethan sat forward, placing his forearms on the table. "You took an item from that house yesterday? Brought it back here?"

Sam took the pan off the heat, and Nate stopped slathering butter on toast.

Jake frowned, as though the question confused him. "I. Uh... Yes, I guess I did."

"Why?"

Jake met Ethan's gaze. His eyes clouded before clearing. "I don't know."

"Did you take anything else from the site?"

"No," Jake said, clearly offended now.

"You appear surprised I asked, and yet the gargoyle is here," Ethan said. "In the center of the table, where it would be seen by Sage when she awoke. Brought into this house by you." Ethan lowered his voice to a dangerous level. "I ask you again. Why? Why would you do that? And why did you choose that object over any other?"

"And why did you think his name was Blood Fox?" Sage asked.

"Sage has a good point, Browny."

Slowly, Jake raised his head, gave Sage a glare that chilled Ethan to the core. Ethan's hands clenched into fists, and he felt his control slipping. Forcibly he reined in his temper and gripped the edge of the table.

"Sage asked you a question," Ethan said, to take Jake's attention away from Sage and bring it back to him. The way he was looking at her was just not right.

Jake didn't look away from Sage. "What's got your pretty little knickers all bunched up?" Jake sneered. "It's just an ornament." He sat back in his chair and crossed his arms over his chest, his tattoos rippling as his muscles flexed.

Ethan's chair slid back noisily as he stood.

Blood roaring past his ears, Ethan placed his palms on the table, leaned over so that his face was level with Jake's. Thrusting back his shoulders, Jake pushed out his chest, refusing to be intimidated.

No one said a word. The room seemed to pulse with a volatile electrical charge. As though at any second a grenade would go off, killing everyone in the room.

"Fuck you, Blade." Jake's breath stank like he'd just eaten a long-dead animal.

Ethan fisted the material of Jake's shirt at the collar. "You don't want to do this," he said, his voice low and barely controlled. "Stand down." Fury swirled inside him, and he resisted a powerful urge to beat Jake senseless.

Ethan's head pounded, and the room tilted, and for one shaky moment, he didn't even know what he was angry about. Only that a beast inside him, a beast he could usually keep buried, had been unleashed. That beast wanted to kill Jake. To tear him limb from limb.

Jesus Christ. Ethan abruptly let Jake's shirt go and pushed him roughly into his chair. What the fuck was happening to him? Ethan thrust his hands through his hair and took a deep breath. It didn't help. The urge to cause Jake physical harm was a wildfire in his veins. He wanted to punch him. Kick him. Pulverize him. Just like that bloody gargoyle.

"Next time you bring something that belongs to those sick fucks into my house, I'll kill you with my bare hands." Ethan turned and paced across the room. He needed to get out of there, but he couldn't back down. He couldn't.

Ethan moved back to the table, opened his mouth to speak, and froze. Jake's image blurred, his face turning into something inhuman. It happened so quickly, Ethan couldn't be sure he didn't imagine it.

Raising his palm, he slapped Jake in the face. Hard. Jake barely flinched, but he blinked, bringing his hand to his reddening cheek.

He stared up at Ethan, his eyes gradually clearing. "Did you just bitch-slap me?" Jake appeared to be in shock. He looked at the floor, as though not understanding what had happened.

Ethan knew the feeling. Sure, he was pissed that the gargoyle had been brought into the house, but to want to kill over it? A member of his own team? His mate? Someone he loved like a brother?

When Jake rose to his feet, his eyes were bloodshot. Shattered.

"Fuck, Blade. I'm sorry."

It was the gargoyle. It had to be. It had made him push Sage. It had made him want to kill it. And the rage it had stirred inside him had made him want to kill Jake.

Ethan inhaled deeply, then exhaled long and slow. "It wasn't you." Ethan knew the truth in those words. But it wasn't just the gargoyle. Something evil was in the house, and it was bringing out the evil inside them all. "I'm as much at fault as you." Ethan stepped forward and embraced Jake with a manly slap on his back. "I'm sorry too, mate."

"I don't know what came over me," Jake said, seating himself heavily in the chair. He looked at Sage. "I'm so sorry."

Sage nodded. "Ethan's right. It wasn't you. Either of you. That... *thing*, it's evil. And it brings evil with it."

"Let's move on," Nate said, and slowly the room filled with sounds of normality. Plates being placed in the dishwasher, the metallic clink of a spoon landing in the sink.

"Right, then," Sage said, standing. "I'll leave you guys to it. I can hear a shower calling. Thanks for breakfast, Sam."

Jake's eyes were still downcast, and Ethan's chest tightened. His team was the most important thing in his life. After Sage.

They would put it all behind them and move on.

"I know we have a full day ahead, and we're all eager to set off. But if you would pull up a chair, boys, and give me a moment, there's something I need to discuss with you."

Something he should have discussed with them already. Something he could put off no longer.

Ethan faced his team. His mates. He was well aware they didn't have to be here with him. *Shouldn't* be here with him. They'd given up their leave to do so.

Although Ethan had verbally secured permission for them to be here from Ian, there was a chance that permission could flip on a dime. If it hadn't already done so, behind closed doors. Ethan had threatened the powers almighty, and that was no small thing. The threat could cost him his job, possibly his life.

But this had long since ceased to be a case for Ethan. It was personal. Hell, it had taken over his life. He couldn't eat, he couldn't breathe, he couldn't sleep without the case invading his thoughts. He could do nothing else until this was over. Until Sage was safe.

But Taipan being here gave him a little perspective. To them, this was still a case. Granted, a strange case. But they worked for the government, not Ethan, and they had orders.

Ethan looked around at his team. "I want to thank you. All of you for answering my call for help. Even though you should be on time off."

The guys frowned and grumbled unintelligible words.

Ethan rested his eyes on Nate. "My last conversation with Ian didn't go well. Although he's verbally agreed I can have you until 0600 Monday, permission was given... under duress." Ethan cleared his throat. "That conversation no doubt cost me my job. I have no right to put you in that position. This case is being watched closely by people in very high places. And to say I pissed them off would be an understatement. I'll take the fallout from my actions. I don't expect you to."

"What are you saying, Blade?" Nate asked in disgust. "That I'd go and leave you in this hell so I can kiss some ass? Fuck that."

"I've upset some pretty serious people."

"Understood." Nate folded his arms across his chest. "Still not leaving."

"Nor us," Daniel said. "Right?" His eyes traveled around the room, and he received a chorus of agreement.

For a moment, Ethan didn't respond. "I threatened to go public," he said, wanting them to fully understand the gravity of the situation. The consequences. "To expose the cover-up. That part is on my head, but staying might reflect badly on you. I have… coerced permission for you to be here, but I want you to be fully aware of the fallout and consider any potential ramifications for yourselves."

"Still staying," Daniel said.

Ethan's chest tightened as he looked around the table. At his unit. His mates.

"You sure?"

"For you?" Nate said. "Abso-bloody-lutely."

"Same goes here," Daniel agreed.

"Too bloody right," Sam said. "Ian shouldn't have even considered leaving you here unsupported in the first place, given the gravity of the situation. I'm surprised."

"I'm staying until the end. You don't give cases time limits." Daniel ran a hand down Max's back. "They take what they take. Have you told Ian what Sage believes she can do to save the town?"

Ethan looked down at his clenched fists and consciously relaxed them. "Yes. In an earlier conversation, when he first agreed I could have you. And I think he actually believed me." He spoke through a clenched jaw. "But someone higher up is calling the shots now. Ian was very clear about not giving anything away, mentioning no names. That fact alone speaks volumes. Ian's in a very tight, very uncomfortable, spot."

Sean shook his head. "What a mess."

"Just so I'm clear," Ethan said. "You're all staying? Even if it means your careers?"

"We don't leave our own." Daniel all but growled the words. "You know that's not how we operate. You wouldn't leave us."

Ethan inclined his head. "No. I wouldn't." But that decision would have been easier for Ethan to make. Even though being part of Taipan was important to him, he'd always been more or less a lone wolf. Rules were just things that annoyed him until he found a way around them. How many times had Ian overlooked Ethan's blatant disregard for procedure because he got the job done?

"So you're all potentially unemployed at this current moment."

Silence greeted that statement, then each man nodded. "I guess we are." Nate shrugged.

"Damn," Daniel said, then looked up. "Shit happens."

"Nate knows I've been planning to set up my own security and investigations company for a while now," Ethan said. "Gentlemen, welcome to the official opening of Blade Security and Investigations. If this all goes to shit, and you lose your jobs, it just so happens I'll have five positions open. Sorry, Max." He grinned at the German Shepherd. "Six positions. They're yours if you want them."

He waited for his words to sink in.

"You're leaving Taipan anyway," Daniel said.

Ethan nodded. "Think that decision is a given." Depending on what happened over the next seventy-two hours, Ethan was going to need to watch his back pretty closely.

"I've been thinking about going out on my own for some time," Ethan continued. "This situation is just the catalyst. You guys are free to choose. Wait until this plays out to make your decision. You all know there's nobody I'd rather work with. If we do this, we'd still do the work we've been trained for, but we'd work privately. We'd operate as efficiently as we always have. But we'd do it our way."

"Hell, yes," was the resounding response.

"But," Ethan said, holding up a hand to silence their enthusiasm. "We're not there yet. Depending on what transpires, we may be going up against the force. They may even call in the military. They may decide we've gone rogue and handle our keeping them out as a hostage situation. And knowing who we are, they'll bring in heavy reinforcements. They will have more people, more resources, more weapons."

"Jesus," Jake swore.

"I do have considerable resources available to me. More than sufficient funds for this. What you need, you'll have. That being said, it will still be a David versus Goliath situation."

"They're David, right?" Sam asked, and laughter greeted his comment and eased some of the tension.

"Remember, it's not too late. You can still change your minds. You haven't resigned; no one knows. I'll not hold it against you if you walk away. Hell, it's the sensible thing to do. I'd go so far as to recommend it." Ethan sucked in a deep breath and continued. "Think about it before 0600 Monday, and let me know who's in."

"I'm in," Nate said immediately.

"I said *think* about it," Ethan said, his chest tight.

Nate glanced at the ceiling and back. "Thought about it. I'm in."

Ethan leaned in and gave him a manly slap on the back.

"I'm in," Daniel said. "I'll speak for Max too."

"I'm in," Sam said.

"I'm in," Sean said.

"I'm in." Jake pumped a fist.

"Looks like you've just got yourself your five employees, Blade," Sean said, grinning.

"Six," Daniel said. "Don't forget about Max."

Chapter Seventeen

"You've really got to get out of that house," Pia said for the umpteenth time, looking at the three scratches across Sage's chest. They'd burned fiercely when she'd first noticed them, and again as the water had hit them in the shower. The shadow figure had the power to not only visually manifest around her, but to *mark* her as well. *He* was growing stronger by the day. What would he be capable of next? Where did she go that was safe? If he was following her, was she really safe anywhere? Even worse, the amulet hadn't appeared to protect her from the attack last night.

"It is less painful than it was." Sage rubbed at the area.

"It's like an angry swipe," Pia said, frowning. "As though it wanted to rip that pendant from your chest."

"That's what it looked like to me too."

"It's a demonic entity," Mark said. "He wants you to remember that the veil is thinning, and his power to hurt you is growing."

"He's trying to scare you, Sage," Pia said.

Well, hell, it was working. The scratches were more than physical; the pain she felt blackened her very soul. Would it ever fully heal?

"He's without a doubt following you," Mark said.

"Which is why it doesn't matter where I am. Ethan's house is as safe—or unsafe—as anywhere." Even if it was pretty unsettling to know whose house it used to be. And what had happened there.

"I want to use the crystals of protection outlined in the grimoire," Sage said. "Nan used them to protect herself from him here, and they'd apparently worked until the séance went wrong that night."

Pia considered. "It may work."

"We're following the grimoire for the banishment rite; it only follows we

140

can have confidence in the protection it outlines."

Pia nodded. "So, moving on. We have seventy-two hours to get the demon's name and/or work out who the alchemist's son is."

"Perhaps Lucky knows the demon's name?" Mark suggested. "It's a good bet."

"He might," Sage said. "It's only a matter of time now before Taipan catch Lucky, but what if we can't get the name from him? I don't want to have to rely on that. Ethan has plans to sedate him so there's no repeat of what happened when he escaped from the hospital."

Ethan had shown her the surveillance footage. The guard had made eye contact with Lucky, then stood, walked directly across the room and uncuffed him. As smooth as that. Lucky also appeared to have set the fire alarms off with his mind, activating the sprinklers, then casually strolled out the front door of the hospital.

"Ethan understandably won't take any chances," Sage continued. "What if Lucky puts up a fight and ends up in no condition to talk? How are we going to get him to offer up the demon's name? What if he doesn't know it?"

"Good questions," Mark said.

She didn't want to mention it, but they were running out of options. "Pia, you said once you might be able to do a séance or spirit board session."

"I'd love to film that." Mark smiled.

"We can do one. But not here." Pia tapped her nails on the table. "We've cleansed the house too well, and we need a safe space. The entity is strong. I don't want to call what I can't send away again. Plus, remember what happened to Celeste."

"Is there another way to get the name?" Sage said. "A spirit board session sounds riskier than I thought."

"Everything about this is risky," Pia said. "We can give it a try though. If not here, where is the best place to do it?"

"Blade's house," Mark suggested. "We can attempt communication with the shadow figure."

"That's not a good idea," Sage jumped in. "The house is too heavily guarded by Ethan's men. And I'd rather not have to explain this to them."

"You mean me," Mark said. "When are you going to tell him?"

"When I get to it."

"Which will be?"

"Soon." As soon as she grew a backbone. Ethan was going to be furious.

"Did you end up asking Ethan why he bought *that* particular house?"

"Stop bringing it up as an accusation. I've already answered that question. He didn't know. And you can't possibly believe he did. I certainly don't."

"Perhaps not consciously," Mark conceded.

"What the hell is that supposed to mean?"

"I wouldn't trust him." Mark leaned back in his chair and folded his arms in front of him.

A rush of anger spiked her blood. "Like I trusted you?"

Pia leaned forward, placed her hands together on the table. "I had another vision. A premonition. The demon will use someone other than Lucky. I couldn't make it out who it was, but the person was male."

Sage glanced at Mark. He sat up straight in his chair. "Fucking hell, I'm never going to live that down, am I? It could just as easily be DS."

"It's not Mark," Pia said. "I would have known."

"You didn't know last time."

"I couldn't see anything last time. This time I can... *ish*. But I know whoever it is, it isn't Mark. It's someone else. Besides, I've taught Mark how to protect himself against possession by an entity. Not only for this case, but for future cases he works on. It's not Mark."

Mark laid a hand on Pia's arm and they exchanged an affectionate glance.

"You can't see who it was, but can you tell me what happened?" Sage asked.

Pia released a breath. "It's all jumbled."

"Okay, I'll watch out for signs."

"I'd be keeping an eye on DS if I were you," Mark murmured.

"Mark," Sage and Pia said simultaneously.

He raised his hands in front of him. "Just saying,"

"Well, stop just saying," Sage said. "Although," she said, considering. "Something did happen that was strange. Jake Brown, one of the Taipan team, was acting out of character and brought back to the house something from a crime scene."

"What?" Pia asked, sitting forward.

"That gargoyle. You remember the one." She turned to Mark. "The one I asked you to destroy when it turned up in the attic, but then you brought it out when you were possessed in the cabin."

"What crime scene was it at?"

"I don't know all the details, but I do know it was at Dougie Roberts's house. I had an experience with him as well, outside Joyce's place when he was helping with the maintenance repairs. I'd put money on the fact he's heavily involved in this; his eyes, his voice, were strange. And he spoke directly into my mind."

"Seems as though there are several people who it could be. Be wary of everyone." Pia leaned forward, her brow wrinkling. "I wish I could be more specific."

Sage's stomach tightened. She'd need to be extra careful who she asked for help, especially help with the circle. Ask the wrong person...

Mark. He certainly believed. But could she trust him? *Really* trust him?

Though who else was there to ask? It's not like she had weeks to find someone.

"Mark, I need seven to protect the circle. Right now I have six, including Ethan and Nate. Would you be the seventh on Sunday night?"

"Of course," Mark said, his eyes shining. He knew what Sage asking meant.

She reached over and touched his hand. She'd done it. She'd have to trust that it was the right decision, and not a big mistake.

Decision made, she focused on the final issue still to be resolved.

"Getting back to the demon's name. It's not mentioned in the grimoire, Mary's diary, or Nan's journal. I think that leaves us no choice other than to attempt this spirit board session. I've been meaning to ask. Is a spirit board the same as a Ouija board?"

"In a way," Pia replied. "My spirit board is used to contact high spirits, angels, guides, loved ones who've crossed over. I go through those angels and guides to protect me and keep me safe as I attempt to contact negative or unknown entities."

Sage thought about the Ouija board that had been on Nan's table. The one whose cursor had moved by itself during the storm on her first night back in Cryton. The one she'd destroyed and set on fire.

Had Nan used it in an attempt to get the demon's name? Sage would ask Joyce; most likely Nan would have used it with "her girls," her coven.

"When we meet tomorrow, can I bring Joyce, Pat, and Mona? I'd like us to get together to go through what needs to be done on the night."

"Good idea," Pia said.

"They had been actively involved in the journey until I took over. They were the ones who kept the grave dirt of Virgil Keyton, Lucky's great-grandfather. Nan had discovered his grave behind the shop, marked with the grimoire symbol. They'd been preparing to take on the ritual themselves Sunday night."

"Yes, I remember you telling me you had the grave dirt," Pia said. "Where is it now?"

"At Ethan's..." Sage trailed off at look on Pia's face.

Mark leaned forward. "So you took Virgil home."

My God! Sage's stomach felt hollow. "I didn't realize I was doing that."

"Of course not," Mark said. "But do you see how many supposed coincidences there are? Everything is falling into place. Like the teeth on a key turning in a lock."

"Where should I keep the tin?" Sage asked.

"Spirit energy retains an attachment to physical materials in our world," Mark said. "It's what helps me get the evidence I need for my investigations. Wood, clothing, jewelry, houses, are all materials that still contain the energy of the original owners."

"So, grave dirt—"

"Yes," Mark said. "Virgil's energy is without doubt attached to the dirt. That's why it's an important component in the ritual Sunday night."

Of course. "What should I do with it?" Sage asked. "Bring it here? I need to keep it safe."

"I'm not sure," Pia said. "Leave it for now, and let me think on it."

You took Virgil home... Mark's words echoed in her mind. Being unwittingly used made her angry.

"What about doing the spirit board session in a known devil-worshipping place?" Sage asked. "If what I think is true, Dougie is involved directly with these entities. I overheard Ethan saying he found evidence of a room in Dougie's house that had been used for black rituals. If we discount coincidences, we have to assume it's all related."

"Perfect," Pia said. "The demon's energy will already be attached to the location. We go in, tune in, get the info we need, then get the hell out again. Where is this place?"

"Within walking distance, if you don't mind a bit of a hike."

Sage considered calling Ethan, then cringed at how she imagined the conversation would go. *Hi, babe. I'm off to do a spirit board session to trick the demon into giving me his name. Oh, and Mark will be helping me.*

Yep, she could just imagine how Ethan would take that call.

Some things it was best he didn't know.

If all went well, she'd simply tell him tonight that she now had the demon's name, and he'd tell her they'd captured Lucky.

Sage tapped her phone, checked the time. Three p.m. Ethan had messaged her earlier to let her know he was going to be out of contact for a while. There had been another murder. Ken Baker, from the hardware store.

Sage squeezed her eyes shut as her gut clenched painfully. She hadn't had to ask Ethan for the details. She'd seen Ken's death when she'd touched him at Joyce's house while he'd been doing the repairs.

She'd had a vision of something dark. Sinister. A knife with a black, ornately carved handle. The scent of burning flesh. And the blood. The continuous poor of thick red liquid. The splash it made when it landed in the jar, how it clung to the sides before pooling at the bottom.

The vision had been brief; she'd touched Ken for just a second, but the images had terrified her. Of course she'd not understood what she'd seen back then. Had she, would she have been able to prevent his death?

Sage didn't know how Pia lived with that gift. That responsibility.

There'll be two more sacrifices before the blood moon, Pia had predicted when they'd heard about David Roberts's murder. *One, a child.* Assuming Pia was right, after Ken Baker, there would be another sacrifice before the blood moon. *A child...*

Sage placed her hand on her stomach as it twisted painfully.

"Can you see who the next sacrifice will be?" Sage asked. There must be something they could do to prevent it. *Please God, not a child...*

Pia lowered her eyes and shook her head. How cruel to be given the gift of knowledge but with not enough detail to alter the event.

Sage dragged her mind back to the issue at hand. Ethan would take care of Ken's death. The only thing Sage could do was focus on winning on Sunday so the demon couldn't harm anyone else.

Ethan would be back at six. That meant she had three hours.

Jake was in his vehicle out in front of the shop.

Sage squashed the memory of how desperate Ethan had been when he'd discovered her missing on Monday, the day she'd taken the rear track from Joyce's house to the circle. She'd hurt him, and she'd promised not to do it again. But what other choice did she have? He'd never let her do the spirit board session.

144

"How long will this take?" Sage asked, rubbing at the warning ache in her stomach.

"In a normal spirit board session, up to twenty minutes. But if we're going into a place used recently for demonic summoning, I imagine we'll connect with... *something* almost immediately."

What was the alternative? Without the demon's name, she would fail.

She'd be back here as soon as she could. She'd walk out the front door, check in with Jake, and Ethan would never have to know.

"We've got two hours tops. I want to be back here by five at the latest." That was safe. Sage couldn't imagine Ethan finishing up before then. Plenty of time to recap after.

"We can't drive, or Jake will be tipped off. It's a fifteen-minute walk if we hurry. That means we've got an hour and a half." Sage couldn't imagine wanting to spend any longer than that using the board. The whole idea gave her chills.

Pia stood, grabbed her bag.

"I'll bring basic equipment, just camera and voice recorder," Mark said. "With any luck, we'll get some good EVPs, or even better, some footage. Give me a sec; I'll swap batteries to make sure everything's fully charged."

Neither woman paid him any attention. Sage abruptly reached out and placed a hand on Pia's arm. "Are you sure this is the right thing to do?" she whispered. "What will we do if Mark becomes possessed again?"

Pia released a breath. "He knows how to protect himself. It will be fine. And if it's not, better to know that before Sunday."

Oh God! This was not a good idea. There was no way to know what they were walking into and what would happen when they did. "But what if we start something that wasn't meant to begin yet? What if—?"

"We need the demon's name," Pia cut her off, her face pinched with concern. Or fear. "We're out of time, and I can't think of any other way to get it, can you?"

"No." The knot in Sage's stomach tightened fiercely.

"Then we've got no choice."

Well then. If there was no other option, there was no use worrying about it, was there?

Someone ought to tell that to her racing heart.

Sage snuck out the back of the shop with Pia and Mark. *Ethan, please forgive what I'm about to do.*

What if he couldn't?

He had to, right?

But what about this morning, the way he'd pushed her, the way he'd gone after Jake? Ethan had finally got himself under control, but just barely.

What if she put him over the edge for good?

She just wouldn't tell him.

As they passed by the graveyard behind the shop, Sage looked through the headstones to the faint track on the other side. The path that led to the circle.

Something peered at her through the darkness, watched her with a keen interest. An icy chill hit her skin and seeped deep into her bones.

Yellow eyes glowed with otherworldly intelligence from smoky darkened shadows, shadows that seemed blacker than black.

"Hurry, Sage!" Pia called out, having no doubt sensed the same thing.

The shadows eagerly watched.

Then followed.

———◆———

The track behind Nan's house led to the rear of the Roberts place. Sage climbed the three painted concrete steps up to the wide veranda.

Pia pulled the small metal catch on the screen door, and swore when she tried to enter. "The house is locked."

Sage inwardly groaned. Of course it was. Who didn't lock their houses these days? She'd been so worried about the wisdom of their decision, she hadn't even considered a basic thing like access.

"But this window is not," Mark said, hefting a large window up in its frame. "Hurry."

Sage climbed through after Pia and tried not to imagine what Ethan would say. Was it breaking and entering if the window wasn't locked? No doubt he'd call it something like unlawful trespass.

The first thing that hit her when she crawled through the window was the awful stench of burnt flesh. She slapped a hand over her nose and gagged.

This was a bad idea. Not because it was illegal, but because something about this house was *wrong*. Terribly wrong.

"Pia?" Sage's voice came out weak and shaky.

"I feel it too," Pia said. "Imagine yourself surrounded in white light. The protection, like I showed you to do for Sunday night. We don't have time for second thoughts. We're here for a reason." Pia disappeared into another room.

Sage rounded the corner and stopped dead in her tracks. The thick, cloying stench of burnt flesh filled the air and left a foul taste on Sage's tongue.

Pointing to globs of charred remains, Pia said, "Dougie's father," through the hand across her mouth. She paused a moment, then continued. "He walked in on Dougie during a ritual and grounded him."

"Dougie killed his own father because he got grounded?" Sage managed to say, trying not to inhale.

"Remember, it's the demon inside the person that's calling the shots," Pia said. "Be careful of everyone until this is over."

Sage followed Pia out of the room and down the hallway. Pia stilled at the top of a set of stairs that led to what was obviously a basement.

Pia pointed into the murky darkness. "Can you feel that? The energy is so thick you can taste it." Sage swallowed. The air rising up the stairs vibrated, as though the darkness itself was alive.

The light switch didn't work, so Pia pulled out a lighter to provide them some illumination. Sage forced her fear aside, and followed Pia and Mark down the stairs. The temperature dropped as she descended, and instinctively,

Sage began reciting the protection passages from the grimoire. The space smelled of mildew and the earthy tang of mold.

In the flickering light, their shadows rose up the walls, reminding Sage of the tall, cloaked figure from her dreams, and her heart started to race. When they reached the bottom of the stairs, Pia lit a few candles that had been placed at the base of the wall.

It wasn't hard for Pia to find more candles to light. The whole room was lined with them. All black. And in different shapes and sizes, with varying degrees of melted wax.

Inverted crosses and pentagrams decorated the walls along with gruesome depictions of the suffering in Hell. A bookshelf contained several books on satanic worship and the occult. Alongside the books was a chalice, just like the one she'd seen in the grimoire, and several jars containing what Sage assumed to be blood.

The gargoyle had been here too…

A whiteboard was off to one side, with some kind of tally. The heading read, *Blood Fox.*

Jake had known Dougie's name was Blood Fox…

"Holy fuck," Mark breathed, turning in circles as he took in the room.

In the center of the room was a circle of chairs, around a table that contained a Ouija board.

Sage kept her distance, but Pia and Mark moved forward to have a closer look.

"We'll use this," Pia said.

"Uh, I don't mean to rain on your parade," Sage said, "but weren't we going to use your spirit board? Angels and guides to keep you safe and all that?"

"This will give us direct access to what was just summoned through this board."

"Feels like whatever it is, it's in here with us already," Mark said.

"The dark energy in here is very strong." Pia sat down in one of the chairs and Mark sat across from her. "It's a whisper from being too much. Come, Sage, join us. We don't have much time, and I don't know how much I can take. I'm more sensitive, more susceptible, to the effect of this type of energy than most. Remember what happened the night of the investigation?"

Sage would never forget. They'd made contact with the entity, and Mark had decided to use an electromagnetic, or EM, pump, to generate energy that entities could draw on. That had been a mistake. The demon had used the extra energy to attack Pia. She'd been unconscious for over an hour.

Sage took a step closer, but remained outside the circle of white powder on the floor. A warning alarm was a screaming in her ears.

"I've never seen one quite like this," Pia said.

Pia picked up the pointer, the planchette, Sage now knew it was called, and almost reverently picked up the old wooden board and peered beneath it. "Just as I thought."

Mark pulled his video camera out and hit *record.* "We're in the basement of a house that has clearly been used for satanic rituals. Pia, show us what you're holding."

Pia shifted, lifting the board for the camera, falling easily into a familiar role.

"Can you explain what's significant about this type of Ouija board?"

"It's a double-sided board." Pia turned the other side toward the camera. "And when we came down here, the board was on the table, dark side up."

"Can you explain what that means?" Mark walked around the table, the light from his camera glowing eerily red.

"When the board is turned dark side up, it's being used for one reason, and one reason only." Pia placed the board back on the table and looked directly into the camera's lens. "Contacting demonic entities."

Sage shivered. Pia continued talking.

"The reverse side of the board is traditional. Most people who play around aren't deliberately intending to contact a dark entity. The majority of attachments that occur are a pure accident. A Ouija board is a portal to another dimension. For an untrained user, playing on the board is dangerous, because they may inadvertently allow dark entities in. Souls who have not gone into the light. Entities that remain, even thrive, on the opposite of the light."

Mark spoke. "And this board has a side specifically designed to contact dark entities, spirits that are demonic in nature."

"Yes. Sage, come sit with me."

Sage sat, and Pia pointed to the board again. "If this board has been used recently, it shouldn't be hard to tune in to the entities that were contacted. And I damn well bet it's the same demonic entities we need."

"You always use the plural," Sage said. "How sure are you that there is more than one?"

"There are usually several on any typical occasion. In this town, there's an infestation. A multitude. But we need only one name."

"So, you'll use this board and contact them directly rather than try to go in cold through yours," Sage said. "Are you sure that's wise? You said your board could offer you protection."

"Sage does have a good point," Mark said.

Pia considered. "There is that concern, yes. But one of my reservations over using my board was that I would pick up an attachment, or the energy would somehow imprint itself onto my board, and I'd have to cleanse or destroy it after we finished. This way, I use their board, and we simply cleanse ourselves after."

"Okay, if you're sure." Mark looked at Sage. "What do you say, Sage?"

"It sounds far from a good idea, but I trust that Pia knows what she's doing. We connect, get the master demon's name, and we log back out."

Pia laughed. "It's not a computer, but I catch your drift, and I'm with you on that. I have no intention of holding the connection any longer than is necessary."

Mark set the camera on the table, hit *record*, and took a seat. He placed his hands palm up on the table, and Pia took one of them. Sage hesitated, feeling the weight of their stares. *Don't be silly*. After all, they were here for her.

The banishment ritual on Sunday would not work without the demon's name.

She grabbed their hands and completed the circle.

———— ◆ ————

Ethan slid behind the wheel of his 4WD, started the vehicle, and pulled out onto River Terrace, which would lead directly to the highway that ran through Cryton. Ethan and Nate had just revisited the place where Ken Baker's body had been found. Ethan had discovered that the body had originally been dumped on the side of the road behind some bushes, but at some point after that, the local animal residents had dragged it out onto the road and treated it as a meal.

The killing had the same MO as the others: the body drained of blood, eyes removed, puncture wounds in the shape of a cross on the chest, the symbolic six, six, six branded into the palm of the right hand. Was dumping the body where it would be easily found a warning? Was the killer becoming overly arrogant? Or had the body just simply ceased to be important once it had served its purpose?

Ken Baker was the latest sacrifice, with the satanic ritual having taken place last night. The tape across the mouth indicated that Baker was likely alive at the time of the ceremony. Ethan believed the killer removed the duct tape when he disposed of the body to hide his fingerprints. Perhaps he couldn't stick the tape on the victim while wearing gloves? Perhaps he wasn't wearing gloves at some stage while he was handling the tape? Either way, there was a total lack of evidence left on the bodies.

The only thing they knew was that Douglas Roberts had been working for Baker yesterday, doing maintenance jobs around town. He was the last person known to have seen Baker alive. Considering that Douglas Roberts's father was also deceased, Sage's suspicions about the teenager seemed dead on. Now all they had to do was find him. Ethan was looking forward to having a chat with the boy, sure he was connected somehow to Lucky. The kid would break, and they'd have the demon for Sage. He'd promised her he would.

He didn't intend on breaking that promise.

Which is why he still hadn't gone back to Adelaide to look through his father's things for the pendant. The two latest killings and his work with Taipan to catch Keyton had taken precedence.

He couldn't put crimes directly relevant to this case on hold while he went back to his house to search for a pendant. And what if he was wrong? It would waste valuable time needlessly. It had, after all, been several years since he'd seen it. And even if it matched the symbol on the grimoire, what would that mean anyway?

Still, there was a low niggling in his gut he couldn't ignore. Something was pulling at him to go home, and he would. He just needed to speak with Douglas Roberts first.

The hands-free beeped with an incoming call. "Blade, Ryder," Ethan answered, and Sam's voice came through the car's speakers.

"You'll never guess who just entered the Roberts house through the back window."

"Don't let them come out," Ethan said, pressing his foot hard on the accelerator. "Hold surveillance, get close enough to try to see what they're doing, but don't be seen. I don't want them to bolt." A rush of adrenaline shot through his veins. This was his chance to speak to the kid. Nate stuck the blue flashing light on the roof of the car.

"Blade," Sam said. "I think you misunderstood. It's not the teenage son."

"You think I'm in the fucking mood for riddles?" Ethan snapped.

Sam audibly cleared his throat. "The three people who entered the house are Sage Matthews, Pia Williams, and Mark Collins."

What the *fuck* was Sage doing with Collins?

Ethan swerved, correcting hard to get the vehicle back on the road.

"Same orders." Ethan's voice was as black as his mood. "Don't enter. Keep surveillance. The only exception is if Roberts or his cult turn up. Otherwise, sit tight. I'll be there in—" Ethan glanced at the digital readout on the console. "Fifteen minutes." He pressed the pedal as far to the floor as it could go.

By the time Ethan disconnected, Nate had already sent instructions for the rest of Taipan to meet them on site. He then dialed a number via the car's Bluetooth, so that Ethan could handle the call hands-free.

"Blade," Jake answered.

"Where's Sage?" Ethan's voice was quiet.

"Inside. What's up?"

"Then how is it Sam just saw her enter the Roberts house?"

Jake let out a string of curses, and they waited, hearing nothing but muffled booted footsteps and slamming doors and more cursing.

"She's not here." Jake sounded short of breath.

"No shit. Stay there. Don't move a fucking muscle until I advise otherwise."

Nate disconnected the call.

"Any idea what she's up to?" Nate asked.

Ethan released a long breath. "Not a fucking clue. But Collins is about to regret the day he was born."

---- ◆ ----

Pia began speaking the prayer, or ritual, of protection from the grimoire, and Sage instinctively joined in. Pia surrounded them in white light, asking her angels and guides to keep them safe. They repeated the verses three times, and although the words spoke of love and light, Sage's insides clenched around the sinking rock in her stomach. But she wouldn't leave. Not when they were so close to getting what they'd come for.

Pia opened her eyes and released their hands. "Now."

They all reached forward and placed their fingers lightly on the planchette.

The air in the room stirred, pressing down on them with a palpable weight. The floor softened beneath Sage's feet, listing and rocking gently like a ship at sea.

Pia's eyes were focused on the board, but her breathing changed, and Sage knew she felt the same things too.

"Who is here with us?" Pia asked.

The planchette began to move on the board, making circular motions. It was a strange feeling, and Sage immediately tried to work out which one of them was pushing it. But it soon became apparent that no one was. Just as her fingertips were barely touching the wood, Mark's and Pia's were as well. Neither of them were applying enough pressure to move it, especially as they'd need to alter the position of their fingertips to change the direction of the planchette. Laws of physics.

Sage was forced to concede that the planchette was indeed moving by itself. Or more accurately, being moved by something other than them.

"Tell us your name," Pia demanded.

The planchette continued to move in a rainbow motion.

"It's getting used to the energy of the board," Pia explained. "It obviously has something to say."

"Who are you?" Pia asked, speaking to the room.

V.I.R.G.I.L.

"Virgil," Pia repeated. "We know who you are. Lance Keyton. Lucky's great-grandfather."

"What are you?" she asked.

D.E.M.O.N.

The temperature plunged, as if they were surrounded in pure ice. Malice, thick as oil, filled the air. Sage's muscles had gone rigid, her insides quivering.

"Demon, as in singular?" Pia called out.

P.L.U.R.A.L.

"Legion, as I suspected."

The heavy air, foul and sour, swirled around the room. Sage's stomach roiled, and she closed her mouth to stop her teeth from chattering. All she wanted was to toss the board over and run screaming from the room, and she thought the demon smiled at the image that flashed in her mind. Squeezing Pia's hand briefly, she mirrored Pia's position and sat up straight, refusing to be cowed.

"What do you want?" Pia asked.

T.H.E.G.R.I.M.O.I.R.E.

Sage gasped, her eyes darting to the bag at her feet.

"You can't have it," Pia said.

The planchette pushed upward suddenly, hovering an inch above the board, vibrating with power. Sage's fingers slipped off.

"Ooh, you don't like to be told no, do you?" Pia said tauntingly. She applied pressure to the planchette, and it lowered back to the table. After a moment's hesitation, Sage swallowed and placed her fingers back on the wood.

The second she did, the cursor circled the board. Once, then twice, before positioning itself back in the center.

"Do you not like us in your space?"

A chill skittered across Sage's skin, and a low, deep laugh seeped through the walls.

Heavy footsteps sounded on the stairs, and Sage's heart stopped dead in her chest.

"Someone's here," Sage whispered.

Was it Dougie? Sage normally wouldn't be scared of a teenage boy, but the kohl-rimmed eyes that had peered at her were not those of a seventeen year old.

A figure arrived at the base of the stairs, and at first Sage was relieved it was a human form. Until she saw who it was.

There stood a man, with dirty blond hair and a grimy polo shirt.

Lucky.

Chapter Eighteen

Lucky stood at the bottom of the basement stairs. Accompanying him was a stench of rotten eggs, sulfur mixed with a bucket of prawns rotting in the hot sun. The air turned stone cold with the icy claw of death. Sage gagged, her stomach heaving.

Hundreds of black candles around the room suddenly flamed.

Sage gripped the table with one hand and the angel around her neck with the other.

Instinct told her to summon the power. Evoke whatever she had called upon Wednesday night.

But it was too early. They still didn't know the entity's name. She had to trust Pia. Sage gripped her angel, her amulet.

Lucky bared his teeth in a smile that was anything but pleasant.

"That's him," Sage said, surprised her voice sounded so calm when she felt so shaky inside. "That's Lucky."

She planted her feet on the ground, digging in her toes. She'd see this through to the end. Not that she could leave anyway. Lucky was blocking the only exit.

"Yes," Pia said. "I know."

Of course she does.

Pia and Mark's fingers were still on the planchette circling the board. "Ignore him," Pia whispered urgently. "I can feel another entity coming closer. He is what we came here for. This is our chance to get the name."

Sage turned back toward the board, but kept watch on Lucky out of the corner of her eye. She eyed the large cast-iron candelabra on a nearby table. If Lucky approached, Sage was lunging for the makeshift weapon.

"Tell me your name," Pia demanded with a bravado Sage envied. "Don't you want to take credit for your crimes against humanity?" Pia called out, taunting the entity they couldn't see, but could *feel* with them. "Come through and tell us who you are, unless you don't even have the power to do that."

The board vibrated, the planchette scraping heavily in a frenzied blur. The air was charged, brittle with crackling electricity. Hatred and anger moved in a malevolent circle around them. Through them.

Lucky pushed off the wall, taking a single step closer to the board, and Sage eyed the candelabra.

Sage might not be able to escape, but she sure as hell was going to fight.

Take one more step, you crazy possessed psychopath...

Sage was watching Lucky so intently she hadn't noticed that Mark had taken his hand off the planchette, his energy no longer needed. Instead, he was pointing the camera between Lucky and the board, trying to document it all.

Pia continued to taunt the unseen entity.

The energy, vile and furious, circled the room; it was heavy, alive, its path through the room slow and deliberate. The candle on the table flickered, then its flame grew, turning into two horns. The overwhelming stench in the confined space turned Sage's stomach, threatened to overpower her.

"I know you're here," Pia raised her voice over a dull roar that surrounded them. The sound grew louder until the concrete walls were screaming with the sounds of a thousand wailing, tortured souls.

"Who are you?" Sage demanded. "Tell us your name."

Lucky hadn't moved, but his eyes were glazed and he had a strange slack smile on his face. Mark had his camera focused in that direction, documenting everything.

"There's something else in the room with us. Can you feel that?" Pia asked. "There are two entities attached to Lucky. Seems the master demon is manipulating Lucky's great-grandfather Virgil even after death."

Sage could feel the second entity Pia was referring to. It was the same one she'd felt in the cabin with her that Wednesday night.

"The second one, the master demon, is the one we want to communicate with," Pia said.

"Leave us, Virgil," Pia continued loudly. "You are nothing but a devil's plaything. Go away and let the real evil come forward."

B.I.T.C.H. the board spelled out.

"Oooh," Pia mocked, calling out to the room. "Think I've never been sworn at before? That all you got?"

Lucky began speaking, talking in a strange language Sage didn't recognize. It sounded like a chant, an ancient summoning.

Whatever he was doing, it wasn't good.

"Pia!" Sage whispered urgently, tugging her arm. "Something really bad is about to happen." The tension in the air was like being inside a pressure cooker about to explode.

Sage's blood pounded past her ears, and a sheen of sweat covered her skin even though she could see her breath in the freezing air.

"Shh!" Pia snapped at Sage then continued tormenting the unseen entity in room. The entity might not be visible, but the anger and menace that were whipping at her body terrified her.

Even Mark was looking uneasy, his camera darting around the room.

I hope to God Pia knows what she's doing.

And more importantly knows what to do if this gets out of hand.

"Stop hiding behind Lucky and Virgil, you weak pussy. Who are you?"

G.E.T.O.U.T.

"Make us," Pia challenged.

Sick laughter filled the room, echoed off the walls.

"Oh you laugh," Pia taunted it. "But you don't even have the power to push your name through to the board. I'm not scared of you. My name is Pia Williams."

"My name is Mark Collins," Mark said.

"My name is Sage Matthews."

"So, demon. You know who we are. *Who are you?*"

Lucky began gagging, and his hand rose to his throat. The candles flamed high, then low. The stench of rotten flesh, of sulfur, was so thick Sage couldn't breathe, and feared suffocating.

Pia glanced her way in concern. There was a pressure on Sage's chest, something was crushing her, forcing her down into the chair. Unseen hands were around her neck, choking her.

"What are you doing to Sage?" Pia demanded. "Does that make you feel tough? Come on! Take credit for what you can do. Tell us who you are!"

The angel around Sage's neck burned her skin as she struggled to breathe.

Mark was filming, but took the camera away long enough to look at her with more than a little concern. "Is she all right?" Mark asked Pia.

"We're so close," Pia whispered back.

Lucky's head fell back on his neck and when it righted itself, his eyes were a fiery red. He hissed, bile bubbling from the corners of his mouth, and he bared his rotted, yellow teeth. "The Dark Master has come!"

The cursor flew across the board, too fast for Pia to keep up. Her hand fell away, the planchette no longer needing the energy from her touch.

S.Y.T.R.O.L.I.U.S it spelled. Then continued to spell the same letters over and over.

The pressure around Sage's neck tightened even further, and she began to feel light-headed. They might have the name, but she was surely going to die.

"Welcome, Dark Master," Lucky said, his voice sounding far off in the distance. "Is it time to take the Angel?"

Oh dear God, this really is the end. She wouldn't even be able to put up a fight, the lack of oxygen was making her so weak.

Lucky lunged for her, and something exploded.

For a moment Sage thought it was the house. Instinctively, she crouched and covered her head with her hands to protect herself from falling bricks and objects.

Shouted commands barked out around her; men, more than one, their steps heavy, flew down the stairs. Lucky moved, but she couldn't see where to.

Until someone cranked her neck backward and a dirty hand covered her mouth. She didn't have time to think; she simply reacted by sinking her teeth as hard as she could into Lucky's filthy flesh.

It startled him, and he released her. She took the split second of his surprise to wheel around and knee him hard in the balls. The connection must have been good because he doubled over instantly. Using both hands, she shoved him backward into the wall. His head hit the concrete, the force sending objects on the shelves crashing to the floor.

An inverted cross flew past Sage's head, catching the tip of her ear. Other items careened around the room and into the walls. Pia screamed, and Mark was held pressed against the far wall.

Ethan, Nate, Sam, and Sean stormed the room, four towering forms of pissed-off male being hit from all directions with flying debris. The large cast-iron candelabra hit Sean in the head, sending him to the ground.

Pia began chanting, her voice loud and confident, her eyes wide and frightened. Sage caught phrases about closing the circle and casting the entity out. Sage joined in, following her lead, adding as much of her energy to Pia's as she could.

Eventually, the objects stopped flying and fell to the ground instead. Was that because of what Sage and Pia were doing, or had the demon reached the limit of his influence at this time?

"Keyton!" Ethan's voice whipped through the room. "Get your fucking hands up where I can see them."

Lucky didn't move. Couldn't. He was out cold from when Sage had thrown him against the wall.

Nate crossed the room and used more force than was necessary to wrench Lucky's hands behind his back and cuff his wrists. He pulled a syringe out from somewhere and plunged it into Lucky's arm.

Stillness. So sudden it was shocking.

Sage's head jerked forward with the release of force, as though someone had turned the machine off in a wind tunnel.

Ethan was the first to react.

"Collins." The word bounced off the walls. "What the fuck are you doing here?"

Ethan's eyes narrowed as he took in the scene. The Ouija board in the center of the room, the scent of recently extinguished candles. His eyes moved from Mark, to Pia, then finally, finally to Sage. The connection stole her breath.

Though Ethan's face was a solid mask of granite, his gaze scorched through to her very soul. Sage had betrayed Ethan's trust, inflicted an untold amount of damage. On him.

On us.

She never wanted to hurt Ethan. Lord knows it was the last thing she'd ever want to do.

And yet, it was exactly what she'd done.

Will he ever forgive me?

Could she expect him to? What did you really have if you didn't have trust?

Betrayal.

The word tasted bitter on her tongue. Sage could *feel* the demon's pleasure that she'd wounded Ethan, his laughter echoing in her mind.

Had this been the demon's intent all along? Had Dougie been just another pawn in the demon's twisted game? Had all the events that had played out so far been leading to this point, so *he* could watch with depraved pleasure as a wedge was driven between Ethan and Sage? Weakening their bond. Strengthening the demon's position for Sunday.

Ethan's hands were fists at his sides. Her pulse raced in a staccato rhythm past her ears, her heart fluttering erratically in her chest. She wanted to run to Ethan, grab his face in both her hands, and make him talk to her. Make him tell her that he understood why she'd done what she did, and that he was hurt, but they'd get past this.

I need to know we'll get past this.

But as she held his gaze, his focus wavered. His lids closed, and he turned his head, shutting her out on a level deeper than physical.

The pain of a thousand razor blades sliced through her insides, leaving her raw and bleeding, a broken and bloodied shell.

It didn't matter that they had the demon's name. That they'd captured Lucky.

She'd potentially ruined the one thing that meant more to her than anything else in the world.

And if that were true, how would she ever manage to forgive *herself?*

Chapter Nineteen

Ethan and Sage pulled to a stop at the lookout atop the tallest hill just outside town. The tourist spot provided a perfect view overlooking Cryton, the little town that was concentrated around a point on the highway, its farmhouses and crops of wheat, its paddocks of sheep and cows, sprawled as far as the eye could see.

The little town that appeared normal on the outside but was far from it underneath.

Sage was reminded of the last time Ethan had brought her here, the night after they'd finished giving matching—incomplete—statements to the police regarding Lucky and his escape. That night, Ethan had held her so tight it had hurt, as though it would kill him to let her go.

This was where he'd first told her he loved her.

Ethan killed the motor and stared out the windscreen. The silence that filled the confined space was louder than any rock concert she'd ever been to. Less than an arm's length away, Ethan was as inaccessible and removed as if he were in another state.

How do I reach him?

His hands pushed off the steering wheel, startling her, and without so much as a glance in her direction, he slid out of the vehicle. Leaving the door open, Ethan moved to the back of the 4WD, returning with a small foldable picnic table. With practiced ease, he set up his laptop, phone, and files. He shrugged out of his leather jacket, and without looking, tossed it carelessly on the grass beside him. Holding his phone up, he checked for cellular reception, then bent his head as his fingers flew across the keyboard of his laptop. A lock of dark hair fell forward into his eyes, and he pushed it back.

Sage ached to go to him, but the distance between them was not going to be resolved by being physically close. She'd been preparing for angry, would have welcomed the explosion rather than the silence.

Though she'd considered how Ethan would feel before she'd made the decision to seek out the demon's name, imagining it and living it were two very different things.

When she'd unintentionally slipped away from his security detail, he'd released his excess emotion physically, shown her how much it had hurt through a powerfully intense sexual connection.

Her blood heated, and her chest ached as she remembered that night. It had been a turning point in their relationship. Ethan had opened himself up and laid himself bare. She'd breathed in the hurt he'd expressed, and he'd allowed her to glimpse that protected vulnerable space deep inside him. His trust had moved her. He'd begged her not to put him through that pain again, showed her what it would do to him. And yet she'd done just that.

She wished she could prize open her chest so he could see just how much her heart was breaking too.

She glanced at him, hunched over his laptop in stony silence, a muscle twitching along his jaw. Tension followed the hard lines on his face. He was a powerful man on an average day. Authoritative and commanding, he had an innate presence that compelled attention. A man people were immediately aware of the moment he entered a room. But when he was feeling an extreme emotion, like now, his presence was overpowering.

Ethan had yet to say a single word since they'd left the Roberts house. After Sean and Sam had taken Lucky away, Ethan had separated her from Pia and Mark, then questioned them all like the detective sergeant he was, his face impassive, giving nothing away. There was no special treatment for her, nothing to indicate they were anything other than detective and perpetrator. She'd almost believed he'd lock them all up.

He'd issued no formal charges, he'd not even wasted his breath issuing a warning.

His cool indifference had *hurt*.

She'd answered his direct questions with honesty. They all had, even Mark.

Ethan had said nothing when Pia issued a desperate warning that Sage not stay at the homestead tonight. He hadn't responded to any of Pia's pleas for him to take Sage somewhere else. Anywhere else.

He'd asked question after question with dispassionate reserve, recorded every answer in his notebook, then clicked his pen closed and slid it in his pocket.

A brief nod in Sage's direction was the only indication she'd had he was finished and expected her to accompany him to his car. And now, here they were.

But where do we go from here?

Sage stepped out of the car and took a deep breath of fresh air; it was cooling, no longer having the warmth of the setting sun. She picked up his jacket, flicked off the dirt, tiny sticks, and dry grass that had clung to the fabric inside. On impulse, she held it to her face. The worn leather was still warm with his body heat and soft beneath her fingers. She inhaled, and his masculine scent filled her lungs, but couldn't fill the gaping hole inside her. Instead of putting the jacket in the car as she'd intended, she changed her mind and put it on.

She should march over to him, get in his face, and force him to talk to her, shout at her. Something. Anything. His silence stung.

But she couldn't summon the strength. She was emotionally wrung out. In the peace and stillness of the early evening, she felt no desire for confrontation, only a deep heartache. And if she was honest, she didn't believe he was acting this way deliberately. Ethan wasn't emotionally manipulative; he wasn't that type of man. He wasn't punishing her with his withdrawal. He was struggling to cope with something inside himself.

Sage left him to his computer and moved to the passenger side of the car, leaned against the door, and looked out across the view. There was no doubt Cryton was beautiful, and tonight, the sunset held an artist's palette of every shade between orange and red. It was postcard perfect.

Yet somewhere beneath that beauty, a demonic entity was at work, manipulating a satanic cult whose members thought they were powerful, inflicting their evil on others and committing heinous atrocities. In truth, they were nothing more than pawns, caught in a battle between light and darkness older than time.

The evil lurking in Cryton jarred with the peaceful landscape, and for a moment Sage could not believe it was real.

She didn't turn, but was aware the moment Ethan started to make his way to her. He stopped a few inches away, mirroring her position, and leaned against the car and looked out at the view. She risked a glance his way. His expression had softened, its hard lines settling into resignation.

"It's so still," Ethan said.

Sage nodded. There was not even the slightest hint of a breeze. She pulled the leather jacket tightly around herself. *Deathly still.* She hadn't even noticed the background droning of cicadas until it was absent.

She felt his gaze sweep over her and shifted so that she was facing him.

"You look so good in my jacket."

"I think I'm going to keep it," she said without thinking. She'd intended the comment to be light, but the underlying implication that he'd be leaving her hung in the air between them.

Sage cleared her throat, swallowed the pain that had made its way up her chest. "Are you still mad at me?"

He closed his eyes and released a breath. When he opened them again, they were a dark tempest of emotion.

"Oh, I'm wildly mad at you. Make no mistake about that. But I'm also wildly in love with you, and I don't know how to reconcile the two. Or if it's even possible." His eyes took on a sheen and he shifted, moving behind her and pulling her back against his chest. He touched his lips to the top of her hair, and a tremor ran through his body. She wanted to study his face, read behind his words, but he'd chosen this position so she couldn't.

"Damn you for not knowing what it's like for me to not be able to protect you." His voice was a broken whisper in her ear and a knife in her heart. "For deliberately making it harder than it already is."

"I needed to get the entity's name," Sage said softly. "I didn't know how else to do it." Ethan exhaled against her back. "On the positive side, you caught Lucky."

Ethan released her abruptly, moved so that he was facing her. "He attacked you."

"It worked out."

"But what if it hadn't?" His voice cracked, and his tortured eyes captured hers.

She had no answer.

"Damn you, Angel. This feeling—" He shoved both hands through his dark hair. "The way I feel scares me to death. Now that I have you, I won't breathe the air of a world without you in it."

She closed the distance between them and placed her hands on his chest. "I don't know what to do but keep moving forward. The ritual takes place on Sunday. I don't get a redo. I have to succeed. There's no other choice. For any of us."

His hands moved inside the jacket and around her waist. He tugged her against him and held her tight.

"I need you in my life, Angel. My need to protect you is all-consuming, and yet... I've never felt so powerless."

She pressed her lips against his chest and looked up at him. "You are not powerless."

"I'm not?" His voice grew sharp. "How can I keep you safe when you make it impossible? My best men watch over you, and you slip away, with Collins of all people, to go into the basement bedroom of a boy who killed his very own father, a boy who's practicing the occult, and summon this energy to you, in a concrete cell with only one exit. An exit that was being blocked by Keyton himself when I arrived."

"Who we now have—"

Ethan held up a hand, cutting her off. "Oh, I can catch a serial killer. But that's not even the problem. He's not the real threat to you, is he?" Ethan exhaled harshly. "It's the demon part that I'm struggling with, Angel. How do I protect you from that?"

"Maybe you just have to let someone protect you for once."

He stared at her for the longest time.

"Loving you has turned my whole world upside down," he said.

"Do you regret it?"

"You can't truly love someone if you're too scared to fall." He turned her around again so that her back was against his chest, his arms wrapped tightly around her. "And before you ask, yes, I fell." The vulnerability she heard in his tone made her knees weak. "I've jumped off the tallest building, hurtling at high speed toward earth, and I don't know when or how I'll land on the ground. Or what condition I'll be in when I do. But it's too late to stop. The momentum is already carrying me."

Tears welled up in her eyes. "I'm sorry. I'm so terribly sorry. I never meant to hurt you."

He inhaled deeply, his expanding chest pushing against her back. "I know, Angel," he said on his release of breath.

They were silent for a while, both lost in their own thoughts. They'd both been scarred already, and the real battle was yet to be fought.

Sage didn't want to ruin the tentative reconciliation between them, but she needed to address the heart of the issue still lying between them.

Out of everything she'd done today—sneaking away from Ethan's security detail, breaking into a crime scene, participating in a séance to summon the demon—it was doing all of that with Mark Collins that had affected him the most.

"I'm sorry I didn't tell you about Mark."

Ethan tensed, his fingers digging into her flesh. "That cut," he said, his voice low and rough. "And so does everything that stems from that."

"What do you mean?"

"I can't help but wonder why you didn't tell me? What else are you hiding?"

Sage stiffened. "Don't." She barely managed to force the word out of her constricted throat. "Don't do that, Eth. I'm not hiding things from you. You've got to believe me…" Her voice trailed off.

How can I ask him to believe me, after I broke my promise to him? After he'd bared his soul?

Sage had known how important it was to him, and yet she'd done it regardless.

"I don't blame you for not trusting me," she said sadly. "Trust has to be earned, and I broke yours. All I can do is explain what I did, why I did it, and hope you understand that it arose from fear of time running out, of not being ready for Sunday. I never meant to hurt you, or deceive you, and for that, I apologize."

"*Angel.*"

Sage hurried on. "I wanted to tell you about Mark. He came into the shop yesterday when I was with Pia, and I can't say I was excited to see him. But after we talked, I realized that he was a victim as much as I was. I'd intended to tell you last night, but you came in so late and looked so worn out, I decided there was no harm in letting you eat your dinner and come to bed and tell you in the morning. But then after the scratch from the demon, the gargoyle, the fight with Jake… it just never happened."

"You trust Collins?" Ethan asked tightly.

"I do. I need him to be the seventh in the ritual on Sunday. He agreed."

Ethan made a low sound in the back of his throat, and for a heartbreaking moment Sage thought he'd push her away. She braced herself for the loss, the emptiness, but for the longest time he remained so still she barely detected a single intake of breath.

"Pia warned me not to let you come back to the house," he said, and Sage understood that while he was not happy about the Mark situation, he was setting aside his feelings and trusting her judgment. That he would do that, after everything, meant so incredibly much.

Sage blinked back the sting of hot tears. "Pia gave me the same warning."

"What do you want me to do?"

She touched her chest, where the scratches still burned. The shadow figure had touched her, physically hurt her, after all the noise she'd heard coming from the attic. Was the entity drawing power from something up there? "What did you find in the attic?"

Ethan's palms moved up and down her arms. "Nothing. At first. It was filled with unused furniture, and we searched every inch. I knocked on the walls, looking for a loose brick, a doorway, something along those lines, when I discovered a false wall." He hesitated for a second, then said, "Behind that wall, we found six bodies."

"Oh God," Sage said, thinking of the closure their families never got. Her stomach twisted. "What did you do?"

"We've recorded, documented, and photographed the scene. I've removed the bodies from the attic. People I can trust have taken over that side of the investigation, but it's all off-record until after Sunday."

"Thank you," Sage said softly. "I know you keep breaking rules for me."

"Angel," Ethan said, his voice low. "You have no idea."

"What do you mean?"

"What do you want to do about Pia's warning?" he asked in lieu of answering her question.

Sage considered. "I have to admit, I've never liked that house. I like it even less now that I know what happened there."

"Agreed."

"Where are Taipan?" Sage asked. "Are they staying?"

"We discussed this earlier, and they've all voted to stay. The crimes after all were committed a hundred years ago, and different families have lived there since without incident."

But that was before the portal began to open...

"Perhaps Pia's premonition was about the bodies in the attic," Sage wondered out loud. "She couldn't give me details. Couldn't tell me what to watch out for."

"And we have Lucky now. Perhaps Pia had seen something to do with him? He's sedated in the concrete cool room behind the house. With the security we have in the house, and my team there, no one can get to you." Sage knew the room he was talking about. Built beneath the ground, it had been used to store meat from the farm.

The scratches worried her. It was clear the entity was gaining power, enough to be a physical threat in itself. But even Pia had said *he* was following her. He'd followed her from Nan's to Ethan's. Was there anywhere he couldn't go?

Instead of trying to hide, it was a much better option to learn how to protect herself. After all, she'd be facing the demon on Sunday night. She had to not only protect herself from a direct attack then, but banish him as well. Plus, she still had a lot to do before Sunday; she couldn't spend her time ducking and weaving.

"There's a section in the grimoire for protection against the demon," Sage said. "It details a cleanse I can perform. Pia did it at the shop and it worked successfully. I tried to do it at the house last night, but it must not have been strong enough on its own. There's also a layout with crystals I can use in conjunction with the cleanse. I have the crystals I need, since Nan had used the same layout in the shop, and it had been working until I packed up the crystals; I hadn't understood what they were for at the time. I'm following everything else in the grimoire; it stands to reason this should work too."

"So you're staying."

She nodded. "Let's all stick together. You, me, Nate, Jake, Sean, Sam, Daniel, and Max. Lucky is no longer on the loose, so we don't have him to worry about. I'll lay out the crystals of protection and do the cleanse. Hell, I'll do it twice. We can't outrun the demon, but maybe we can shut him out."

Chapter Twenty

Friday Morning
Two Days Before the Blood Moon

The sky was beginning to lighten when Ethan reached for Sage. He knew at once she wasn't there, even before his hand landed on an empty sheet. Instantly awake, he willed his racing heart to slow. The rush of adrenaline interfered with his ability to think clearly.

Where was she?

The bathroom was silent. She might have gone to make coffee. He strapped his watch on his wrist and glanced at the time. Five fifteen. He hadn't even realized he'd drifted off. A light sleeper ordinarily, he should have stirred when Sage got up.

He slid into his denims and strode sans shirt and shoes into the kitchen. The lights weren't on, and a palm on the kettle revealed it to be cold. He checked the reinforced locks on the front door and did a sweep of the house, looking for signs that Sage had perhaps been sitting and reading because she couldn't sleep. Back in the bedroom, Ethan double-checked the bathroom and toilet cubicle. Both empty. He picked up Sage's handbag and with a mental whisper of apology, looked inside. Keys to her grandmother's shop, her phone, her money, the grimoire, and the diaries.

His pulse quickened. Sage wouldn't go anywhere without the grimoire. She must be in the house somewhere. He walked back to the front room.

"Sage!" he called out.

Sam and Nate came out of their rooms.

"Seen Sage?"

"No," they answered in unison.

Ethan unlocked the door and stepped out onto the front porch. The morning was still, and already humid. It was going to be a warm spring day.

Sage's car was out front. No visible additional tire marks or footprints. No obvious signs of disturbance or activity anywhere.

"Sam," Ethan said. "Check the video footage from last night."

"Already on it."

Ethan left Sam sitting hunched over his laptop while he proceeded to search the house. Nate accompanied him up to the attic, although it would be highly unusual for Sage to have wandered up there by herself, especially after he'd told her what he'd discovered.

The attic, somehow ice cold despite the outside heat, was empty. Nothing appeared touched or moved. Ethan's anxiety rose and he gripped a bench and breathed deeply.

"Blade," Sam called out below.

"Got something?" Ethan took the stairs in two steps, landing heavily at the bottom.

"You'd better take a look yourself."

He crossed the room in swift strides and looked over Sam's shoulder. It wasn't outside footage as he might have expected; it was footage from the night-vision camera set up in the hallway outside Ethan's room.

There was silence, and he held his breath while the camera showed nothing but an empty hallway. The digital readout on the bottom left-hand corner clicked over to three a.m.

The bedroom door opened. Sage emerged, wearing only his T-shirt, the soft gray material hanging to mid-thigh. She glided out the door, down the hallway, then her image disappeared off screen.

"Where the hell is she going?" Ethan asked, impatience riding him hard. "Did you check the cameras at the rear of the house?" He found it hard to believe she would take off out the back of the house in the middle of the night wearing nothing but his T-shirt. And for what purpose?

"Of course I've checked the outside cameras." Sam sounded clearly offended. "No one left or entered the house the whole night."

"Then where did she go?" Fear clenched his gut with an iron fist, squeezing and wringing. "I've searched the whole damn house, even the attic."

"Blade. Take a closer look." Sam, who'd been playing the image over and over, pressed a series of buttons and the camera zoomed in on the lower half of her body.

Ethan leaned forward, his palms resting heavily on the desk. As Sam played the scene again in slow motion, what Ethan saw brought his whole world to a shuddering halt.

Throughout the short journey down the hallway from Ethan's bedroom to where her image disappeared off screen, Sage's feet were six inches off the ground.

———— ◆ ————

166

Sage woke to find herself in a darkened room, a low glow coming from an old oil lantern in the corner. As her eyes adjusted, she had a strong sense of déjà vu. For a horrifying moment, she thought she was back in the cabin, Lucky's playroom. She scrambled up and found the door. Of course it was locked. After all, why would someone bring her here, if not to hold her for some reason?

Her back against the door, she scanned the room. It was similar to Lucky's playroom, but different. There were no windows in the room's concrete walls. This wasn't a timber cabin, and the work bench was metal, not wood.

The items on the bench were the same, however; saw, hammer, surgical knives, except... Except they were old.

Not old, *old-fashioned*.

Lucky's handsaw in the cabin had been a modern variety; she remembered its jagged blade clearly. The saw on the metal bench before her was handmade. She traced a finger along it. Old, but not rusty. These tools had been lovingly cared for.

Though at first she'd thought she must be seeing things as they were a hundred years ago, these were not images, imprints, as Pia had called them. Not echoes of a time gone by. They were tangible, physical objects.

Sage ran her fingers across a scalpel. The metal was cold, hard.

Real.

Had she been transported back a hundred years ago? Through the blending of time? Was that even possible? If so, where was Ethan? How did she get back?

Her mind raced, and her heart skipped erratically in her chest. She took a series of deep breaths. *Don't panic.* Someone had managed to bring her here, and they'd locked her in this room with a selection of weapons. Sage chose a scalpel and palmed it.

The memories of her abduction Wednesday night were still fresh and too quick to rise to the surface and mingle with this new reality. Forcibly, she pushed the flashbacks away. She needed to think clearly.

The last thing she remembered was going to sleep in Ethan's arms. That was it.

She ran her fingers along the soles of her feet. There was no dirt; it didn't feel like she had walked outside. Was she still in Ethan's house? How had someone managed to get past Taipan to get into the house? How did they get past Ethan next to her in bed? Her stomach clenched. Dear God, she hoped he was okay. The only way he'd allow someone to take her was if he were physically unable to stop them.

She mentally scanned her body. Despite wearing no underwear, it didn't feel as though she'd been physically assaulted. She would know, surely. Whether she'd been unconscious at the time or not.

She heard footsteps overhead, and instinctively held her breath.

Overhead.

Were they coming from an attic? No, the footsteps sounded heavy, creaked on timber.

She was in a basement.

The basement.

Pia had told her Virgil had kept his victims in the attic until he was ready to take them to the basement.

She listened, the only sound the rapid pounding of her heart. Virgil. The dark shadow figure who'd stood at the end of her bed.

But how could a spirit from a century ago lock her in here? It couldn't have been Lucky. He was sedated and under lock and key and constant guard from Taipan.

Sage shook her head. She couldn't waste time wondering how she got in here; the more pressing concern was how to get out. She tried the handle of the door again, pulled and wrenched at it until she twisted something in her shoulder and was forced to let go.

The door was solid. And locked. Despite the early 1900s surgical instruments, strangely the door and its lock were modern. She was not getting through it without a weapon of some sort. If only she had Lady Smith, she'd be able to blow the lock to pieces. Then put a bullet in whoever walked down the stairs. There was nothing as beneficial as a gun. Except a bigger gun.

There was no advantage to remaining silent; whoever had brought her here knew where she was. If she was still in Ethan's house, there was a chance that the footsteps overhead were from someone other than her abductor. Ethan, or Taipan, if she was lucky. She had to take the chance. If she alerted them to her presence, she might have a chance to be saved.

If it was her captor, he'd know she was awake and that might bring him down there. But that would give her a chance to escape.

Standing with her back against the wall by the door, she clutched the scalpel in her palm, opened her mouth, and screamed.

——— ◆ ———

At the sound of Sage's scream, Ethan felt simultaneous elation and gut-wrenching fear. Max began to bark, the sound coming from outside. Then Max raced in through the open front door, almost knocking Ethan over in his haste to push past.

Where was Max going? He rushed to catch up.

The scream came again.

"Ryder!" Ethan called for his partner, as he hurried after Max. He heard Daniel calling out for Max, but he didn't turn around.

Max was barking at a place on the floor, in the hallway at the rear of the house.

"Blade?" Nate drew to a stop next to him.

"Max!" Daniel ordered, placing a hand on his dog. Max began to paw at the floor in a windowless pantry alcove with solid concrete walls. A cool room from the days before refrigerators. Beneath a heavy wooden crate filled with empty jam jars, they found the edge of a basement trapdoor.

"Jesus Christ, she's been here the whole time." Relief almost buckled his knees. *She's alive. She's close.*

Another scream rose up from the floorboards. His gut twisted. That son of a bitch was torturing Sage right beneath his nose.

Ethan heaved a large wooden box to one side and found what he was looking for. He grabbed the metal ring and lifted. The timber door opened to expose a ladder. Ethan didn't take the steps, opting instead to jump the distance.

"She's down here," Nate called out to the team from the top of the stairs. "We're going in."

"Grab the kit," Ethan called back, referring to the medical kit. There was no way to know what condition they'd find Sage in.

"Goddamn it, Blade. Hold up," Nate shouted behind him. Ethan couldn't wait. The difference between life and death was often a single second.

There was a large wooden door in front of him. It was locked. And her screams were coming from the room behind the door.

"Stand back," Ethan shouted before discharging his weapon at the lock. The door sprang open, sending chunks of wood flying.

The stench hit him first, a pungent mix of sulfur and rotting flesh. Evil was in the room with him. Unseen, but no less present because of it. He'd become familiar with the entity.

The moment Ethan stepped fully into the room, the door slammed shut behind him, locking out Nate and the rest of Taipan. Nate shouted and banged on the door while Ethan scanned the dimly lit room for Sage. At last he spotted her. "Sage!"

Before he could reach her, something threw her back against the wall and dragged her up to the ceiling.

Ethan lunged forward, but smacked into an invisible wall. No matter how hard he punched and kicked, he was unable to breach the barrier.

Sage was held suspended, her torso pressed to the ceiling, gravity causing her limbs and hair to hang down. She looked like a rag doll.

An *unconscious* rag doll.

Ethan knew the display of power was to provoke him. Fury overwhelmed him, causing his vision to distort. He fought for control. Failed. Again, he attempted to rush toward her, used everything he had, only to abruptly hit a solid mass of energy. An unseen wall that tossed him to the other side of the room.

Ethan roared, wild in his anger, the sound that rose out of him a deep, primal declaration of war.

It laughed.

"Come on," Ethan shouted, jumping to his feet. "Fight me, you son of a bitch. Or is the minion of Satan too much of a pussy? Does taking on a woman make you—"

Ethan broke off as his body was picked up and thrown back against the door.

"Blade, open the door!" Nate shouted through the thick wood.

Ethan tried to push forward, but the entity held him, as if with a giant hand, and pressed him back against the only exit.

The temperature of the room plummeted. The bitterly cold air seethed with a mass of swirling, menacing energy. If the entity was pissed before, it was murderous now.

"Bring it on." Ethan's voice was a mere rasp. The entity was compressing his torso to the point where he could barely breathe. "Let her go and fight me. Man to... beast."

His vision blurred, the air in the room becoming opaque. The metal table in the corner was now covered in surgical tools. The style was old-fashioned, yet they weren't rusty or tarnished. They were brand new. Light that didn't come from the room reflected off the blades.

Impossible. Ethan blinked to clear his vision. When he opened his eyes again, the room was covered in blood—sprays of red spurted up the wall, bloodied hand prints smeared downward.

Sage! The bastard had murdered Sage!

Rage formed red spots in his vision, and he hurled abuse at the unseen entity. Without realizing, the tirade became a Latin passage he remembered from the grimoire. He felt something shift in the air. The change was subtle, but noticeable. Ethan repeated the passage. Something unseen reacted violently. Various objects flew across the room. He jerked his head to one side, narrowly avoiding a scalpel, and something sharp pierced his thigh.

A dark shadow now floated above him. He continued to recite the words. Gobs of spittle flew into his face, and he closed his eyes, the saliva splatting on the floor with the pooling blood.

And then he heard a sound that made him open his eyes.

Sage's voice had joined his.

She wasn't unconscious! She was pressed face first to the ceiling, her head at an odd angle, but she made eye contact with him, and he gave her whatever strength he had inside him. The pendant around her neck was glowing, and the glow spread to became a cocoon of white light.

Their words became a repetitive chant. Initially, the passage had made the beast angry; now it seemed to be weakening him. The mass of energy in the room slowed, and something screamed with a thousand voices. A figure appeared in Ethan's mind, a human body with the head of a goat. Two horns protruded upward, and its mouth opened wide, its sharp teeth covered in blood-laced spittle.

And then it was gone.

Abruptly, he was released. As he slid from the door, he realized he'd been inches off the ground. He doubled over in pain and sucked in huge lungfuls of air. With a sickening thud, Sage dropped from the ceiling to the floor, where she lay in a crumpled heap. Holding his stomach, Ethan fought his way through a thick fog to Sage.

Afraid of what he'd see. Terrified of what he'd find.

Sage had landed in a pool of blood that disappeared before her eyes. As did the arterial sprays and the bloodied handprints, some as small as a child's, that marked the walls.

The door gave way, and Taipan burst through, guns drawn.

The bright lights mounted on their guns temporarily blinded her, before she was crushed against a solid, heaving chest. Ethan's heart was pounding too hard, his breath gusting across her face.

"I've got her." He pulled back to look at her. "Angel. Are you all right? Talk to me. Are you hurt?" He somehow managed to scan and check her over without releasing his grip.

"I... I think I'm okay."

"Clear," Nate called out. He'd been searching the room.

"Why did you lock us out?" Nate snapped.

"I didn't."

"The door you busted through was shut tight, even though the lock's smashed apart. Something was pushed up against it."

"Me," Ethan said dryly. "But it wasn't intentional."

"Put her down, Blade," Nate said softly. "Let me look her over."

Sage's bare feet touched the cold concrete floor. Her knees buckled briefly, then her legs firmed. She wiped her hands on her T-shirt and tugged at the hem, suddenly conscious she was wearing nothing beneath it.

Ethan flicked on the beam of his Maglite torch as Nate felt along her limbs, his eyes serious, his touch as impersonal as a doctor's. He appeared satisfied. "Nothing seems broken. I'll check you over properly upstairs."

"What happened to your leg?" Sage gasped. Blood was seeping out of a wound on Ethan's thigh, little rivers of blood tracking down the denim.

"I'm going to have to stitch it," Nate said, eyeing the injury the best he could through the hole in Ethan's jeans.

"Bullshit. Nothing but a scratch," Ethan said. "Help me get Sage out of here."

Ethan wrapped his arms tightly around her, half supporting, half carrying her as they made their way to the door.

Following the beam from his torch, Sage could see the room was composed of four roughly plastered concrete walls. No doors other than the one they'd entered through, not even cupboards. The only items in the room were bare timber shelves and the empty table in the center.

"Wait!" Sage pushed away from Ethan and stood in the center of the room. Ethan immediately moved to her side, as though unable to be parted from her even that much.

"What is it?" Ethan whispered urgently.

"This bench was covered in tools." She could describe in minute detail what the saw had looked like, its wooden handle and sharp teeth. She'd touched the saw, taken a scalpel. But her hand was empty, and only a bare metal slab stood before her. The shelves that had been crowded, a jumble of jars and clutter, were barren.

"I saw them too," he said softly.

There was no stench, no thickness of the air to raise the hair on her arms. It was as though nothing had ever happened.

Her heart was slowing to normal, as if she'd jumped from a great height but was now safely on the ground.

"Pia said the times were blending, that the past was the present, the present the past. I thought she meant we'd see visions, an imprint of times gone by. The cattle dog, the trains running through the night. I had no idea that evil could reach out its hand from a hundred years ago and touch us in the now. None of us are safe."

Ethan held her so tight he was bruising her, but she needed the connection as much as he did. The pain reminded her that he was here. That he was real.

"I know I'm stating the obvious, but I guess the cleansing and crystals didn't work," Sage said. Or perhaps she'd made a mistake with the cleansing ritual? The placement of the crystals? The house was so big. Maybe they needed twice as many as Nan had needed? Or maybe the evil in the house was just too freaking powerful, too saturated with the trapped energy of the pain, suffering, and death inflicted here for the ritual to work. Or perhaps it was because she'd brought Virgil home?

"Would have been a better idea to just heed Pia's warning," she said.

Tension radiated off Ethan in waves. He made a sound in the back of his throat that reminded Sage an injured animal. Her heart broke for him. Everything about this case seemed designed to wound him. And then to wound him a little bit more.

———— ✦ ————

The scent of freshly brewing coffee filled the front room.

The whole team, except Sean who was watching Lucky, had returned, and they'd gathered in the front room of Ethan's house. The house that he'd bought to ensure Sage's safety but that had turned out to be the very thing that had nearly killed her.

Not only had the house been owned by the serial killer a century ago, it had also been his torture chamber and execution room.

How was Ethan supposed to deal with the fact that he'd had such a strong impulse to buy this particular house in the first place? He'd bought the potential murder weapon, fully loaded. If they hadn't found her, how long would Sage have stayed sucked in its gruesome belly before it killed her? And what would it have done to her before it gave her that relief? An image slipped into his vision. Of Sage pressed against the ceiling, her long blonde hair dangling away from her face, which was contorted into an expression of pure terror.

He tried to push it aside, but it joined the Polaroid stills of the other images: the ones of Sage in Lucky's cabin surrounded by a serial killer's tools of torture; the one of Collins's knife blade at her throat. The hideous gargoyle, the surveillance video of Sage floating down the hall, feet six inches off the ground. His gut heaved, and despite shaking his head to clear it, the images kept coming. Shouting at him louder and louder, drowning out the voices of his team in the room.

Disjointed sentences, incredulous murmurs, and shocked exclamations floated in and out of his hearing as Sage filled the team in regarding what had happened behind that closed basement door. What he heard didn't make sense, the words overlaying the stills in his head like a movie production edit gone seriously wrong.

"Ethan, the crystals of protection are still in place," Sage called out. "I guess they just weren't strong enough? I'm sure I placed them correctly, I triple checked. Perhaps the entity is just far stronger now?"

Sage was across the room, but her voice was coming from a long way away.

Or perhaps Ethan had unwittingly helped the demon by bringing Sage to *his* house.

I've been a damn fool to think I could protect her here.

Was the demon laughing in his face right now?

Sage could have died.

Ethan's heart was racing, his fists clenching; he was flooded with a ferocious energy. The violence inside him didn't have an outlet, and it was sending him mad.

He didn't recognize this new self, didn't know what to do with this agitated, highly strung version. The old Ethan was cool and calculating. One step removed from the situation was the best perspective for clear thinking. How many times had he said: "You can't help a victim while you're sympathizing with their grief. You have to give yourself a little distance. You have to look at the evidence and think like a killer. That was how you caught them. A case is a case. It's not personal."

Except this one is.

And his blood was not running cool. It was fiery hot. Goddamn, he couldn't even touch, let alone kill, what had done this.

Sage sank down onto the couch. Her lovely green eyes, which could sparkle like diamonds and stop the very heart in Ethan's chest, were cloudy and downcast. She picked at the threads on a cushion she was hugging to her chest, and flicked the odd concerned glance in his direction.

He should go to her, comfort her. She shouldn't be hugging a pillow. She should be hugging *him.*

But he was as useless to her now as he'd been at protecting her while she'd been lying in his very bed.

From his position across the room, he watched as Nate handed her a coffee and she took it with two hands, giving him a small smile and thanking him. Ethan was grateful to his partner, but Nate's helpfulness compounded his frustration.

He should be the one over there, reassuring her, making her smile. But he couldn't. He was a fraud. There was nothing he could say to reassure her, reassure even himself.

She was supposed to be safe here.

What the fuck did he do now? The goddamn son of a bitch had stolen her from his very arms.

His very bed.

Was there anything more emasculating than that?

It was Friday, 0600. Sixty-six hours until the blood moon at 2400 hours Sunday. Until Sage faced off against the demon. And what was he supposed to do? Stand back in a pansy circle, chanting in Latin, and watching while the woman he loved went into battle alone.

How the fuck was he expected to stand back and not take action? Beat him, starve him, cut him to pieces, that was what he'd trained for. That's what he *did*. He fixed things.

If he could, he'd dive right into the fiery pits of Hell and rip that fucking demon to pieces. End this once and for all.

Ethan stilled. And that, that was the other thing he'd tried not to think about. In the back of the grimoire was a cipher. There *was* a way to end this forever. Not just for the next hundred years. The cipher spoke about the alchemist's son. He was the one who could ensure this ended, this time, once and for all. No more future government cover-ups, no more serial killer, no more ritualistic deaths.

Ethan wanted that. He wanted that so bad he could taste it.

He'd considered the section more than once. Nothing about this case had been a coincidence. From Sage's arrival in town, to everything that had happened up to and including Ethan buying the serial killer's house.

And now, Mark Collins had returned.

Was that son of a bitch the alchemist's son?

What did Ethan know about Collins? His background hadn't indicated anything related to magic; his father was a businessman who wanted his son to be an accountant. But Collins did have a passion and a calling toward the supernatural, toward this very area.

Did that mean Collins had a special bond with Sage? He'd certainly done everything he could to win her affection since he'd arrived. Would this be what it took for him to succeed?

Would Collins be the one to help Sage where Ethan couldn't?

The front door handle was in Ethan's hand, then it slammed against the wall as he flung the door open. The force he'd unintentionally used created a hole in the wall, flinging plaster across the timber floor.

He was conscious of his action silencing the room, but he couldn't stop. He'd used the last ounce of his self-control to make it outside.

Across the porch, down the steps, around to the backyard, and over to the tree where Sean had suspended a bulletproof vest to form a makeshift punching bag. Almost blind now, Ethan drew back and took the first swing. The hessian bag of sand hurtled backward, the tree bending against the force, and a flock of squawking birds exploded from the branches above. Waiting for the bag to swing back, Ethan clenched and unclenched his fists, then he swung again. The force he expended took the wind from his lungs. But he lunged again. And again. And again.

He pummeled the bag with both fists and everything he had, giving the animal inside him free rein. He became wild, an untamed, savage beast.

At some point, Ethan became aware of Nate watching him. It was a sixth sense they'd developed through years of having each other's back. Nate would be concerned, but he wouldn't intervene. Not unless Ethan gave him cause. Nate wouldn't let him go too far.

Ethan heard laughter in his mind, as though the Devil himself were watching, pleased with the anger and hurt he'd caused. The laughter intensified Ethan's focus, his punches becoming more direct as he imagined his fists sinking into the goat's face. It was at this point, at the height of his fury, that he finally understood.

This conflict was not only about Sage.

The beast was equally after him. Hurting him through her.

The Kevlar jacket was stained red from his bloodied knuckles before the tidal wave of emotion eased. Ethan's fists dropped to his sides, and he bent over, dragging in huge lungfuls of air. When there was nothing left inside him but a bitter hollowness, his head began to clear.

This demon was not going to beat him.

Just because he didn't know how to defeat it—yet—he wasn't going to let it have the advantage. The demon might have won the round last night, but Ethan wouldn't let him take another.

Like any predator, Ethan needed to learn about the demon. Knowledge was power, and the more studied his opponent, this entity, the more likely he was to discover a flaw.

There was sure to be one. Nothing in life was without its weakness. Everything had a vulnerability.

Ethan's, the demon had already discovered, was Sage.

What was the Beast's?

Dry leaves crunched beneath his feet as he walked back to the house. He slowed when he reached Nate. Wordlessly, Nate rested his hand briefly on his back, before falling into step beside him.

Nate didn't bother with words. What was there to say? He simply reminded Ethan of his unwavering support. His strength.

They'd get through this. And they'd succeed. Ideas began coalescing in Ethan's mind.

He'd be damned if he'd let that son of a bitch win.

A plan started to form.

———— ♦ ————

Sage was relieved when Ethan returned, accompanied by the bushy scent of outdoors and the masculine smell of fresh sweat. The room fell silent as the men walked in and Nate casually took his place at the table. Ethan's eyes immediately sought hers, connected. She took the hit, steadied herself from the intensity. Being the recipient of his focus was a physical blow.

He ate up the space between them, knelt in front of her, and kissed her on the lips. Hard. Possessive. He tasted salty, his skin damp with sweat.

It was an apology.

But also a reassurance. She pulled back, cupping his cheeks in her hands. His hair framed his face in loose, dark curls. His eyes held hers with a tenderness that stole her breath, but that tenderness was tinged with hard steel.

"I'm sorry I lost control," he whispered, resting his forehead against hers.

"Everyone loses control from time to time, Eth."

He stood, and she grabbed his wrists. Silently, she looked at the bloodied mess of his knuckles, then softly touched her lips to them. She glanced up, met his heated gaze, and a slight tremor moved through his body.

Rolling back his shoulders, he moved to stand at one end of the table.

"Slight change of plan today," Ethan said. "Nate will replace me at the Roberts place, but will be on call should I need him. I'll be with Sage today, so there'll be no need for any additional protection."

His gaze flicked to hers.

She gave him a smile in return.

After last night, she didn't want to be apart from him either.

Chapter Twenty-One

Mark's large black Paranormal Research & Investigations van was parked in front of Beyond the Grave, and Sage saw Ethan stiffen, even though he'd known Mark would be there. Sage had told Pia where to find the spare key earlier, so she and Mark had already been there a good hour or so, cleansing and preparing a safe working space for Sage. After Sage had filled her in on what had happened last night, Pia said she wasn't taking any risks.

Sage squeezed Ethan's hand as they walked to the front door. Seeing Mark would test his already stretched control.

"Morning, beautiful." Mark breezed in from the small kitchen at the back of the shop and embraced her briefly, placing a kiss on her cheek. It was a standard Mark greeting, just his way. Ethan made a low sound in the back of his throat.

"It's afternoon," Ethan said. "And you've been told to keep your hands off her."

Mark met Ethan's narrowed look head on. "We warned you about that house. Pia doesn't say this shit for fun. I learned long ago, if Pia gives you a warning, you ignore it at your own peril. Your stubbornness could have seen Sage killed last night."

"Yes, it could have. And your actions could have managed to get her killed yesterday."

"And yet, here I am," Sage said, spreading her arms out in front of her. "Neither of you is at fault, because—hello?—I make my own decisions. The reasons I went into Dougie's house were mine, and they were sound. Likewise, I chose to go back to Ethan's house last night. The responsibility lies with me, so you can both stop trying to blame each other."

As if she hadn't said a word, Ethan and Mark were still staring each other down. Ethan was taller and had a more solid build, but Mark, as always, stood his ground, refusing to back down. Mark was a law unto himself, as though his oft-disparaged profession had made him immune to the criticism of others.

Still, Sage detected a slight tremor in his hand as he placed it on his hip. He wouldn't have been human if he'd been unaffected by Ethan in his current frame of mind.

Sage softened her voice, wanting to defuse the situation before it became one. "Please. I need both of you to set aside your differences so we can all work toward a common goal. Can you do that?"

Sage raised her brow at Mark. "Yes," he conceded. "Anything for you."

A muscle along Ethan's jaw twitched.

"Eth?" Sage asked more gently.

"Of course, Angel."

Sage inwardly sighed. The power play between the two men would probably never cease, but at least she had their agreement to work together.

For now.

It was as good as it was going to get.

"Who wants coffee?"

———— ◆ ————

Sage ran her finger down the moisture that beaded the outside of her water glass, then pushed it aside and took a large mouthful of coffee instead.

At the small kitchen table, Pia, Mark, and Ethan discussed at length what had happened last night.

"The protection ritual and crystals didn't work," Sage said.

"He's too strong now," Pia said. "It's too close to the blood moon, and I don't want to say I told you so. But that house... I told you so."

"I thought you didn't want to say it?" Ethan raised a brow.

"I lied." Pia shrugged nonchalantly.

Ethan closed his laptop after having just played Mark and Pia the footage they'd captured last night of Sage gliding out of her bedroom. Icy tremors had raced down Sage's spine as she'd watched. There was something sacred about sleep, an implied trust that when you closed your eyes, you'd be in the same place when you awoke.

The knowledge that she could be taken to a separate location, into danger— unaware—was a unique type of torture. She couldn't imagine sleeping at all until this was over.

Mark leaned back in his seat. "Very good, DS. The footage is almost perfectly clear; you must have used good quality night-vision cameras."

"The best available, I believe."

"If you ever get tired of crime-fighting, you could come work for me."

Ethan narrowed his eyes, but remained silent.

"Initially, I thought I was alone in the basement," Sage said. "I heard footsteps overhead and wondered who had locked me in. My mind was confusing Virgil's playroom with Lucky's at the cabin. The items on the table were so similar, and the air in the room…" Sage tried to put the experience into words. "Reality was kind of wavering. No, 'rippling' is a better description. It was hard to focus, and my memories of the night at the cabin became confused with the present. I was waiting for someone to come back, when I realized no one was coming back. He was already in there with me."

Ethan took her hand, entwined his fingers with hers.

"At first he seemed to just enjoy feeding off my fear. And then when it became clear Ethan was coming down, I sensed the entity's excitement." Sage glanced at Ethan. "I know that doesn't make sense, but somehow I got the impression that it was Ethan he was waiting for all along, and not me."

Pia leaned forward. "What makes you say that?"

Sage fidgeted with her empty coffee cup and tried to make sense of her thoughts. "The moment Ethan entered the room, the door slammed shut behind him. Locking out Nate and the rest of Taipan. At that exact moment, I was thrown back against the wall and dragged up to the ceiling." The memory caused her heart to beat wildly in her chest, but she forced herself to continue. "It was horrific, that feeling of being suspended."

"Powerless," Ethan said softly.

"Yes." And Ethan would know. He'd had the same experience Wednesday night at the cabin. Rendering a man like Ethan powerless would be the worst type of torture.

"Seeing you like that—" Ethan broke off, his voice low and laced with emotion. "I couldn't get to you. You were in the room, but out of reach. Nothing was between us, but something was. I was pinned to the wall. My fury was all-consuming. Debilitating."

For a moment, Ethan looked tortured. "The hatred for this… beast. Over what he was doing to you. You have no idea what I would have been capable of in that moment. Things I never would have imagined myself able to do. They scared me. Because if I ever acted on those thoughts, with my training, I would carry them out in an extremely proficient and effective manner. But that's not who I am," he finished softly. "And yet… perhaps there's not as much separating good from evil as we think."

"Eth—" Sage's heart ached for him. "Don't let him make you question who you are and what you stand for."

"It's what *he* wants," Pia said, tapping her nails on the table. "What you're saying is starting to make sense of some strange visions I've been having. Ethan, you are more a part of this than you realize. In the back of the grimoire, there's a section about the alchemist's son."

Ethan nodded. "Yes. The alchemist's son is the one who can end this forever, not just for a hundred years. Do you know who it is?" Ethan asked. An expression Sage couldn't read crossed his face, and he flicked a glance at Mark.

"Ethan, I hate to say this," Pia said slowly. "But I think it's you."

———— • ————

179

Ethan leaned forward in his seat, attention fully on Pia. "Are you on drugs?"

Pia was wrong. Dead wrong. Why didn't she suspect the alchemist's son was Collins? Given Collins's background, he seemed the logical choice.

Instead of being offended by his comment, Pia's eyes gleamed. "You're not the first person to wonder that. Just makes it harder for them when they realize I'm right. Which I invariably am."

Ethan's jaw worked. "Okay, then. What makes you think that it's me?"

"Think about this logically. The demon's been after you, as much as Sage, perhaps more so all along."

Ethan considered. A large gum tree branch had almost taken him out the very moment he'd arrived in town. Then there was the rabbit with the strange glowing eyes that had darted in front of his car, causing him to swerve violently and barely escape running his vehicle at high speed into a tree. The vicious hit on the back of his head when Sage had been abducted by Lucky. Being suspended in the air and thrown against a building with a flick of the demon's hand. He was sure Sage's healing gift was responsible for his recovery; would he have survived otherwise? And those were just the first things that sprang to mind. There would no doubt be others if he gave it more thought. Could Pia be right?

"If that's true," Ethan said slowly, "Why?"

"Why you, you mean?" Pia asked.

"Yes."

"Because you are the alchemist's son, the one who can close the portal forever."

"My God, Pia!" Sage said, her eyes wide. "Are you sure?"

"I told you before," Pia said to Ethan, "the night when Sage was abducted, the night I proved my abilities to you, that it was no accident that you were here. At that time, I knew you were destined to be here, but I didn't know why. Now I do."

"Are you messing with me?" Ethan asked, feeling his spine stiffen. "Ha ha, very funny, joke's on me. This issue is serious, though. Sage could have been killed last night. This situation is hard enough; can we just stick to facts?"

"I think you might need to consider that as fact," Pia said seriously. She closed her eyes and stretched her neck from side to side. Raising her hands up to her temples, she took a couple of deep breaths. Then she went still. After a while, she nodded her head slowly. "Yes. Yes, it's true. You have always had a heightened sixth sense. Everyone who knows you, knows that about you. You call it your gut, but even you must concede your intuition has always been stronger than what's considered average. You have an unprecedented success rate in solving cases. In your work, you never rely on a report, always saying you can't get a gut feeling unless the person is in front of you. That's because when you are with someone, you're tuning in to your higher senses. You also 'know' things others don't. You call it a hunch. Where do you think the ideas come from that solve these cases? You may have always called it something different, but it is still the same thing. Part of being psychic is developing heightened senses."

"You think I'm psychic?"

"Not psychic. Although, I believe you could have been had you had a different upbringing. With your raw and undeveloped naturally heightened senses, I believe your abilities, had they been nurtured, would be quite impressive by now."

Did she really believe this?

Ethan sat up straighter and rested his forearms on the table. Glared at a smug-looking Collins, then turned to Sage who, to his irritation, seemed to be quite entertained. Was it the idea, or his horrified reaction that was causing their amusement?

He opened his mouth, then closed it again. Sage's smile faded away, and she looked at him with a twinkling in her eyes. His heart skipped a beat.

"What do you think?" Sage's voice was slightly breathless, and he had the strong urge to make her breathless from something else entirely. With his life spiraling out of control, he wanted Sage naked in his room, where he would call the shots.

As though she could read his mind, her eyes took on a darker shade of green.

Ethan swallowed past the lump that had formed in his throat.

He loved the way she was looking at him, and the thought that he could actually help her was something he sorely wanted.

But the alchemist's son? Me?

He held up his hand. The idea was preposterous.

"Pia," he said seriously. "You know I highly respect your ability. But having a good instinct is a bloody long jump from being a... what? A witch? No, a male witch is a what—a warlock?"

"I never said you were a warlock. I said alchemist. Warlocks generally apply low magic. Alchemy is a very high magic. Not the same as Sage's, but similar in vibration."

Ethan was speechless. Pia sounded so goddamned serious. If she was taking the mickey out of him, she was a bloody good actress.

"I thought the alchemist's son was Collins," Ethan said, ignoring the stab in his stomach. It would kill him if Sage looked at Collins the way she'd just been looking at him.

He grabbed Sage's hand and held it.

You are mine.

He'd be dead before he'd let Collins anywhere near her in any capacity other than what they needed to end this.

And then, Ethan remembered what the cipher said... The sacrifice that was to be made.

Ethan looked at Collins with fresh eyes. Collins had strong feelings for Sage. But did he love her? Enough to make that type of sacrifice?

"It's not Mark," Pia said with a confidence that brooked no argument. Ethan's brief elation dissipated with her next words. "It's you."

He sat back in his chair, his eyes seeking out Sage's. Their gazes met and held, as they usually did. A deeper connection flowed between them. Something powerful. Something ancient.

Her eyes flared, the pulse beneath his fingers raced, and he knew she recognized it too.

"Yes!" Pia said, watching the interaction between them, visibly pleased. "When you both join on the night, it will raise an enormous amount of power, far greater than either of you could raise alone. And your love for each other will make that power even stronger."

"You're not shitting me?" Ethan asked. "I'll be real pissed if you are."

"Ethan," Pia said, angry now. "You read the grimoire, right?"

Ethan indicated that he had. Sure, he'd skimmed over most of the spells and rituals, but he'd read everything in between.

"Then you know more about the alchemist's son than you've told Sage. The alchemist's son," Pia said, leaning forward with emphasis, "is you. Even the grimoire is meant as much for you as it is for Sage. You need Sage as much as Sage needs you. Sage is the yin to your yang. Your destiny. Everything that has happened these last hundred years has come full circle."

Ethan's worlds collided in that very moment. Something very strange happened inside him. Something clicked. Like Pia's words were the key unlocking the heart of who he was.

Except that would mean... How could this prophecy change who Ethan was? Who his ancestors were?

It couldn't.

"Wait!" Ethan's head was spinning. How easy it would be to get swept along with a theory. The appeal of being able to help Sage and not just watch was too much temptation.

But any theory was just a theory without proof.

"Pia," Ethan said slowly. Patiently. "The flaw in your theory is that my father wasn't an alchemist. Couldn't have been." The idea that his stalwart, hard-headed father could be an alchemist was beyond amusing.

If Sage thought Ethan was black and white...

Ethan realized he was smiling, and slid his detective mask back on. Impassive. Unreadable. He leaned forward, his forearms on the table for emphasis.

"My father was a highly decorated chief superintendent. His name was Simon Blade. Perhaps you've got your wires crossed?"

"My wires don't get crossed."

"Sorry, Pia. But I think you might be wrong on this one. My father was not an alchemist. He didn't believe in anything at all unless it involved police work or fishing. Trust me. I went fishing with him, and he certainly wasn't bringing those fish in the boat by magic." Ethan released a breath. If Pia was wrong about this, perhaps she was wrong about other things too.

"Perhaps so," Pia acknowledged. "But as Sage knows, denying your innate abilities doesn't make them less so."

"Dad was adamant about the subject of anything airy-fairy," Ethan said. "It was one of the things he impressed upon me, like making sure I ate my greens and looked both ways before crossing the road."

"Ever ask why your father was so strongly set in his beliefs about the paranormal and supernatural?" Pia said.

"Life experience?" But it was just as likely the same place most children's core beliefs originated. Their parents.

Ethan's father had criticized people who believed in ghosts as kooky. Much like what Ethan had done to Sage and to Collins, he thought with a twinge of guilt. He'd acted on a core belief, a childhood program he'd never questioned.

"Your great-grandfather worked the case a hundred years ago with your boss Ian's grandfather, didn't he?"

"Yes."

"Do you think that was an accident?" Pia asked, clicking her long black nails on the table. He tried not to let it irritate him. "Do you think your being here now is an accident? Your strong attraction to Sage, a recognition that goes beyond the physical to something deeper?"

"I don't believe in accidents," Ethan said, his mind racing to put all the pieces together. His ordered life was being shattered before his very eyes. "What exactly are you saying about my great-grandfather?"

"When you forced me to prove my abilities to you, the night Sage was abducted, I told you that your grandfather was often with you on cases. He is not the only spirit that stays close to you. Your great-grandfather has chosen to speak to me now. He says he made a horrible mistake. He tells me that he was an alchemist. But what he saw here in this town a hundred years ago caused him to refute his power. The demon was too strong, too powerful. Your great-grandfather was torn between his loyalty to the force and what he 'knew' from other sources."

"Much like you are now," Sage said quietly.

"The difference with you," Pia continued, "is that you've found Sage. That's why it can be different this time. Mary didn't have the alchemist's son. Sage does."

Sage's fingers entwined with his. He glanced at her, and the look in her eyes told him she understood the emotions warring inside him.

Was it possible that Ethan, just like Sage, had been kept in the dark about who he really was?

"Your great-grandfather did not know about the prophecy, and that it would be repeated in a hundred years. He thought that renouncing his power was a way to keep his family safe."

Ethan had been aware of his family's tragic past, how the men had all died in the prime of their lives. He'd assumed the cause had been their careers in law enforcement. Law-enforcement officers took their lives into their own hands every time they stepped out the front door.

Was it possible that something outside everyday life had been targeting his family? If so, it made sense that one of his ancestors would decide that the best chance the family had of surviving was if they gave up alchemy.

What Pia said made perfect sense in a disturbing way. But surely, if this was true, wouldn't he have had some idea of who he was? Of what was in his blood?

As if he'd spoken aloud, Pia said, "You've suppressed your natural abilities. Like Sage. If you'd been encouraged to look within yourself at an early age, you could have cultivated your gift."

"Ethan, you're known in the force for your uncanny ability to read people," Sage said. "You've mentioned to me that communication is ninety percent nonverbal. You just wrote off your gift to having good gut instinct. But unlike me, you've used your gift every day."

"Christ." Ethan sat back in his chair. Hard. The upshot of this whole conversation hit him at once. "So I really am a fucking spook."

Pia visibly stiffened. "No offense taken," she said, her brilliant eyes flashing a warning. "I bet as well as your heightened intuition, you have keen eyesight and hearing, and a heightened sense of smell, taste, and touch. Your base senses. More so than most people."

Ethan shrugged. How could he assess that? "My eyesight is twenty/twenty and my hearing is sharp. Can't comment on touch, taste, and smell."

"You are extremely organized and methodical. Ethical to a fault. These are all innate characteristics for a natural alchemist. There are many variations as to what exact line you are descended from, but I can say for certain its high magic, otherwise you wouldn't be compatible with Sage. Plus, I bet if you dig into your past, you'd discover your ancestors used natural magic."

"High magic sounds better than the alternative," Ethan said wryly. "What does the natural part mean?"

"Alchemists traditionally practiced high magic, as opposed to witchcraft, or black magic. Natural magic involves working with elements of nature, such as plants, water, and earth."

"Sage of Earth." Ethan glanced over at Sage and covered her hand with his.

"Everything is tying in together," Sage said. "The phases of the moon are also an integral part of natural magic. That's why Sunday's blood moon is so powerful."

"And there's the amulet," Ethan said. "My father had a talisman with the same symbol as on Sage's amulet." Strangely, instead of complicating things, Pia's theory was bringing everything into focus. He'd recognized the symbol on Sage's pendant and the grimoire instantly.

Ethan had planned several times to make the trip back home and retrieve the pendant from his father's things, but every time he'd thought he'd get the chance, there was another murder for him to attend to.

Had that been a deliberate move on the demon's part to distract him? If so, what else was the demon frightened he would find out? He had to search his great-grandfather's and grandfather's belongings for anything else that might help. Any notes his great-grandfather might have made from his time here in Cryton. He'd get Zach to dig deep into the Blade family's history.

"An amulet, or a talisman?" Pia asked. "An amulet contains power; a talisman is for protection." Then she shook her head. "Never mind, it's both. You'll need it Sunday."

"I'll have the pendant," he said, hoping he'd be able to locate it. If this demon wanted him, he was going to make himself available. Do whatever it took, if it meant keeping the demon away from Sage. But Ethan wasn't a fool. You fight fire with fire, magic with magic. Like a gun and a Kevlar vest, if he had access to something to protect and help him, he was going to make sure he was armed with it. Being held against a wall was not going to happen again.

His mind was already turning. Making plans. It meant a trip out of town, but he had time. He didn't want to leave Sage, but he couldn't see the alternative.

"Eth—" Sage had visibly paled.

"Angel, what is it?"

"I just remembered something." She choked back a sob. Ethan was instantly alert.

"What?" Pia prompted. Sage was looking at him with eyes that were wide and an expression that tore at his heart.

He squeezed her hand. "It's okay, Angel. Tell us."

"I had a premonition. At the circle." Sage blinked up at him. "It was about the blood moon. Ethan was there, surrounded in fire. He was walking into the flames, I was screaming at him to stop. But he was... happy. Well, not happy exactly. 'Resigned' is a better word. We... we said goodbye." A tear slipped from her eye and rolled down her cheek.

Ethan's heart stopped dead in his chest, but not because of Sage's distress.

His eyes locked with Pia's. Did she know?

Pia nodded. "Tell her."

"Tell me what?" Sage asked.

Ethan released a breath. *Oh God, it was true.* "The cipher, the way to end this forever."

Sage took out the grimoire, flicked to the section at the back about the alchemist's son. She slid the book to him, pointing to a page and tapping it forcefully. "Tell me. Read this to me."

"Angel, you have enough—"

"Read it."

Ethan cleared his throat. "I'm going to interpret it into modern language, so we all understand the message." He looked down at the page and read it aloud.

The Alchemist's Son.

With the heart of a warrior, the alchemist's son will enter via the flames to the fiery pit of Hell and stab the beast through the heart with a sword of light.

To achieve this, he must have made a choice. For only love as pure and as intense as the demon's hatred can void the curse. Not for just the next hundred years, but forever. His death will test the strength of his bond to her.

"What is the sword of light?" Pia asked.

"I'm not sure," Ethan replied, but he was looking at Sage. She was deathly pale, frighteningly still. He reached for her, and she gripped his arm.

"Ethan, no," Sage said abruptly, as though coming out of shock. "You will not! Promise me you won't." She dug her nails into his skin so deeply they drew blood.

Ethan looked to Pia for help.

What was he supposed to say? Earlier, they'd all thought it was a great idea that the alchemist's son could stop the demon forever. Now he was supposed to promise Sage he wouldn't do it, without any thought? Any consideration? He didn't like the sound of it either, but maybe it wasn't as literal as the cipher made out? "Sage, I don't—"

"Damn you, Ethan Blade." Sage stood up so abruptly her chair fell over backward. Tears streamed down her cheeks and she clawed at her hair. "I saw you, Ethan. I saw what you did. I won't let you. Goddamn you, Ethan, I *won't* let you." Her eyes were wild, her hair coming free from her ponytail. Whatever she'd seen in that vision terrified her.

His instinct was to stop the pain, so that was what he did. He pulled her close, held her shaking body flush against his chest. "Shh, Angel," he murmured. "I promise. I promise." She shuddered, choking on an intake of breath.

"Say it again."

"I promise," he said, hoping he knew what he was promising. He had one role in this prophecy, and she was making him promise he wouldn't fulfill it. He'd go through his great-grandfather's box, see what he could learn, what other nonliteral interpretations the cipher might have. The cipher after all could well be a metaphor. If he discovered that, he'd revisit this conversation with Sage again.

He held her for a moment longer, and when she was calm, he let her go, watching as she sat back down. She pulled a tissue from her bag and dabbed at her nose, but her spine was straight and her chin was slightly raised.

Ethan sat down. He also affected an outward calm, but his stomach churned. What had she seen?

"Sorry about that," Sage said, shifting in her seat.

Collins rubbed her arm. Ethan barely resisted snapping Collins's hand off.

"So we have the grimoire, Lucky, and the demon's name," Sage said, seemingly determined to move on. "And now we wait, right?"

"Practice," Pia said. "You have to get a lot stronger before Sunday. You are like a child with your power; somehow we have to cram years of knowledge into two days."

"I looked the demon up," Collins said. "Sytrolius is the most powerful demon ever to enter our dimension."

The room vibrated, as if the demon had heard his name and drawn near. Ethan instinctively moved his chair closer to Sage's, took her hand in his.

"What can you see about him?" Mark asked Pia, leaning toward her.

"Sadly, not much more than that," Pia said. "I can't tune into him. We were fortunate to get his name the way we did. I'd say that cult did us a favor, seasoning the board like that."

The kitchen window rattled with a thud, and everyone turned to look. Through the part in the white lace curtains, they could see a flying bug, perhaps a cricket, crash into the window hard enough to splatter its guts everywhere. Another bug followed, then another, then another, then countless others in a furious fusillade.

Pia stood abruptly, her chair scraping back. She walked to the window and closed the blind.

"He's listening, but he can't get past the protection," Pia said with some satisfaction.

The noise continued behind the blind, growing louder as bugs pelted into the shop's front windows as well.

Sage closed the blinds on the front windows, trying not to wince in disgust.

"Ignore it," Pia said. "I'll increase the protection later to include the outside of the house."

"But the fact that it's working is a great thing," Sage said. "I only wish I could have done something so effective at Ethan's last night. Well done, Pia!"

"Come, sit back down." Pia laid her hands on the table palms up. "Let's show the strength of our unity."

Ethan locked gazes with Collins. He didn't like the ghost buster and probably never would. He'd never forget what Collins had done to Sage, possessed or no. But if they were going to beat this demon, they were going to have to set their differences aside and do their best to work together. He just had to get through the next two days. He'd do it for Sage.

"I owe you an apology," Ethan said to Collins. "I shouldn't have belittled your life quest to record evidence of the paranormal. I understand what you're doing. Where you're coming from. The show is valid, and I wish you well with it."

Collins didn't reply and for a long time simply stared, as if assessing the authenticity of Ethan's apology.

"Yeah, well," Collins said eventually. "I'd say you're going to be living your penance for that." His face broke out into a movie-star grin. "Karma's a bitch, ain't it?"

Ethan groaned.

Collins placed his hand on the table, palm up, and wiggled his fingers, winking at Ethan. Ethan released a breath and joined hands with Collins.

Completing the circle of hands.

It was then that Nate walked in.

"Well, this is cozy," Nate said. Suddenly self-conscious, Ethan withdrew his hand from Collins's grasp.

"Bug problem?" Nate asked, raising one foot and looking at the crushed bodies of various insects on the bottom of his boot. He had insect splatter on his shirt and a cricket crawling in his hair. He wiped a dark-green spot of goo off his cheek and grabbed the squirming insect, holding it between two fingers. The thrumming of bugs hitting the window had stopped, but evidence of the carnage remained.

Nate leaned down, said something only Ethan could hear.

Jesus Christ. The room spun and Ethan gripped the table. It was coming true, everything Pia had predicted. His whole life had turned to quicksand beneath his feet.

And what of Sage's premonition?

He couldn't breathe.

"I... I have to go." Ethan said, standing abruptly. His legs were unsteady, but he'd be damned if he'd fall apart in here.

"Ethan?" Sage asked. The concern in her voice pulled at him.

He didn't meet her gaze, wanting to hide the turmoil raging inside him. He closed his eyes and pressed his lips to hers.

Then he clapped Nate hard on the shoulder. "I have to go," he repeated. "Goddamn it, look after her." He wanted to say more, but he couldn't.

"It was the child, wasn't it?" Pia asked. "A little girl. The seventh sacrifice."

The expression on Nate's face said it all.

The demon was prepared. And waiting.

————— ◆ —————

Sage watched Ethan leave. He'd tried to act normal, but his energy was off. She could feel it. He shouldn't be alone.

"Nate?" Sage said. "Shouldn't you go after him?"

"Nope." He gave her an easy grin. "Blade's a big boy. He knows what he's doing. Never questioned him before. Not going to start now."

"But—" she started, then reconsidered. Telling Nate about Ethan's "energy" was going to sound daft. "You don't understand. He found out some things today that have shaken him up pretty badly."

"Wouldn't shake him up as much as if something happened to you. And looking after you is what he's asked of me." Nate effortlessly swung a chair around and straddled it, leaning his forearms on the back. "So that's what I'm here to do."

"Who was the little girl?" Sage asked.

"A three year old by the name of Susie Rafter."

Sage gasped. "No!"

Pia seemed to have gone inward for a second. "She was descended from a witch."

Sage's throat closed over.

Nate reached out to cover her hand. "Sage, you knew her?"

"Yes," Sage said, remembering the bright, bubbly little girl with blonde curls and big blue eyes. "She's Pat's great-granddaughter."

Pia spoke. "The demon wanted blood that is pure for his rituals."

Sage ran to the bathroom and was violently ill. Pia's comment had created an image in Sage's mind she'd never un-see.

Oh Pat. She would be devastated. She'd doted on Susie.

Joyce, Pat, and Mona had been right. They'd been targets. But the demon hadn't settled for a direct attack. He'd done something far worse.

He'd taken an innocent. And Pat would know that Susie's death was her fault.

Sage looked in the mirror, wiped at her tears. Tears would solve nothing.

Damn this demon!

Making a fist, she pounded on the porcelain sink, each blow sending pain up her arm.

Damn him!

The air seemed to vibrate, and her skin tingled. *He* was near. Listening, laughing, drinking in her anger, feeding on it.

She took a deep breath. She couldn't change what had happened. Death was final. But she could win on Sunday, and stop him doing this to anyone else.

And she was damn well going to do it.

"I'm going to need to see Pat," Sage said, returning to the table.

Nate shook his head. "Not now. Blade is over at Pat's house, where they found the body. The place is swarming with uniforms. There's nothing you can do. Pat is currently with Susie's mother, Amanda, in Glenbrook."

Glenbrook was about thirty minutes' drive from Cryton. Sage didn't know Amanda very well, except through stories she'd heard over cups of tea. But why had Susie been staying with Pat?

"It's strange that Pat would have let Susie stay at her house with everything going on."

"She didn't," Nate said. "From what we know at this point, Amanda turned up on Pat's doorstep last night asking her to watch over Susie while she went into the hospital for overnight monitoring and tests. She's pregnant, and had some bleeding," Nate said. "Pat agreed to help, but offered to go to Amanda's house to do it. Apparently she didn't want to take the risk of Susie being in Cryton. But Pat woke the next morning to discover Susie gone. Vanished from her bed. She went into a panic and called me, and about an hour ago, Jake found Susie's body in Pat's bed. Here, in Cryton."

Sage scrubbed a hand over her face, unable to stop the tears that were silently rolling down her face. Her vision had clouded around the edges and she clenched her fists so tight, her nails dug into her palms.

"How did Jake know to look at Pat's?" Pia asked.

Nate shrugged, seemingly unconcerned. "This is what we do. Taipan, I mean. Jake is damn good at his job."

"Uh-huh." Pia's brow wrinkled.

"I just feel like I should do something," Sage said. "I should go to Joyce, to Mona. They'll be feeling this too."

"Blade wants you to stay here for now. Let him do his job."

"But—"

Nate cut her off. "Sage, your energy is better spent practicing. You are the one with the power and... responsibility to make sure he can't do this to anyone else."

And then Sage had a thought. A selfish thought she hated herself for having. Would Pat be able to be at the circle Sunday night? Sage had been relying on the strength, the power, a coven of witches could summon.

Had this been part of the demon's plan? A way to weaken her?

If Pat couldn't do it, who would make a seventh? Sam, Sean, and Daniel wouldn't be suitable; their belief and understanding of the paranormal wasn't strong enough. Belief was the accelerator pedal on the engine of energy. How deeply you believed determined how strongly the energy flowed. Doubt and uncertainty were the brake pedal. Sage needed to go full throttle on Sunday night.

Jake? Sage pondered. Perhaps. If Pat wasn't able to make it, Sage would ask Jake.

Sage turned to Pia. "Nate's right. The only way I'm going to beat this demon is to be in top form. Let's practice."

Sage used the heavy emotions swirling inside her and channeled them into learning the rite. Not just the words, but invoking the power. Testing it, tasting it, as it tingled through her blood. Her body was responding to the words now; whereas when she'd first begun learning them, she'd felt a little light-headed and dizzy, now her blood fizzed, like an effervescent soft drink.

Over two hours had passed by the time she next looked up from the grimoire. Mark had taken himself off somewhere, mumbling about exciting research he was doing for the taping of Sunday night's "event." It rubbed her the wrong way, how he was referring to the life and death battle she was undertaking as a show, or event, but she supposed for Mark, the coming conflict was the ultimate proof he could hope for. The culmination of his life's work.

Nate had retired to a corner of the room, tapping furiously away at a keyboard. It eased some of her tension to know Nate had stayed here in Cryton with Ethan. Ethan trusted him to make sure she was safe, but Sage was equally grateful for Nate because she knew he wouldn't let anything happen to Ethan either.

"You've done a fantastic job memorizing the rites," Pia said. "Anyone would think you were a seasoned witch."

Sage smiled. From Pia, that was high praise. "I wouldn't go that far, but I think I'm at least pronouncing the Latin correctly. Ethan has been helping me."

"I can tell. How about the focus exercises I gave you?"

"I think I'm doing okay there." She hadn't spent as much time on those as Pia had asked her to, what with everything else that was going on. Quieting your mind was a whole lot harder than it sounded, she'd discovered.

"Try working on that next. You may very well have been given the greatest natural gift known to mankind, but if you don't know how to harness it and focus, you won't be able to use its full potential. The demon will be at his most powerful on the blood moon. He's had many lifetimes to build his strength. You can bet your ass *he's* prepared. You need to be too. He'll exploit any weakness, however small, Sunday night. You can't afford even the slightest of errors."

"You make me nervous when you say things like that." She didn't want to ask, but she needed to know. "Do you think I'll win?" She studied Pia's face, looking for any sign of hesitation.

"I need to believe so. But I think that if you do, you'll win through sheer determination. Much like what happened Wednesday night when you saved Ethan. With as little experience as you've had, the power inside you is a largely unknown quantity. You'll be relying on instinct rather than strategy."

"So you're saying if I win, it will be more ass than class?"

Pia laughed and relief washed over Sage. Pia had tiny dimples when she smiled, really smiled, like she was doing now.

"I haven't properly thanked you yet," Sage said. "You don't have to be here. You don't owe me anything. And yet you're going out of your way to help me." Sage's eyes welled up and her voice thickened. "I just want you to know how much I appreciate you."

Pia placed a hand over Sage's, giving it a light squeeze. "We will always be friends. This is only the beginning."

"I like that thought."

It sure beat thinking of it as near the end.

Feeling a strain across her shoulders and down her neck, Sage stretched her arms over her head.

"We should also do some exercises to strengthen your body," Pia said. "Remember how much of a hit you took last time?"

Sage nodded. She'd been physically wrecked and emotionally wrung out, bedridden for days.

Nate stood up from his keyboard. "I'm just going out back to make a call so I don't disturb you in here. I won't be far. If you need me, you only need raise your voice and I'll hear you."

As soon as he stepped out, Pia motioned Sage closer. "Sage," she whispered. "I was shown something else last night. Something important. It's going to be hard to take."

"Compared to what's happened in the last twenty-four hours and what we're still facing, it can't be that bad."

"You haven't heard it yet."

Chapter Twenty-Two

Sage had thought she was ready for anything. She had no idea how wrong she was. Pia's words had hit her like a blow. Her ears were even ringing.

"Say that again?"

"You're pregnant," Pia repeated slowly.

Sage sank into the chair, stunned. Of all the things she'd imagined Pia hitting her with, that was the last.

"How?"

"Well, if you need me to explain..." Pia grinned.

But Sage couldn't return her smile. She swallowed, suddenly aware that her mouth had dried open.

Pia's expression turned serious. "Are you okay? I mean with this? That you're pregnant?"

"I... uh." Sage swallowed. "Are you sure?" Pia could be wrong, couldn't she? Psychics weren't infallible. Sage sat up in her chair. "Pia, Ethan and I... we always used condoms." She tried to remember when she'd last had sex before Ethan. It'd been months. She'd had several periods since then.

"The condom broke," Pia confirmed.

"No, it didn't." Then a vague memory pressed into her mind. That day after she'd used her energy to defeat the demon. She and Ethan had had unrestrained, *very* physical sex. Had the condom broken then?

"Wow," Sage said. "Wow, wow, wow."

What would Ethan think?

"But it's early right? Too early to know for sure." *Too early to tell Ethan?*

"It is extremely early, yes. But it is so, just the same."

"But what if?" Sage broke off and took a deep breath. She was going to ask Pia if she could be wrong. But something in Pia's face told her it was pointless.

192

"You're not wrong, are you?"

"I'm certain. At this very point in time, you have life growing inside you. I can see it clearly in your aura. I saw a change before, but I thought it was just from you having accessed your power. But now the new life is becoming distinct."

Sage sat in stunned silence for a while, letting the reality of that life-changing statement sink in.

"I wouldn't normally tell people stuff like this, but with what you are about to face, I thought it in your best interest to know."

"Is it—" Sage broke off. She was about to ask Pia if it was a boy or girl.

But then it came to her. It was a girl. It was *the* little girl Sage had been visited by at various times throughout her life. The one who came to her while she slept, held her hand.

"Do you want to know?" Pia asked.

"Yes."

"It's a girl."

Sage's throat closed over and tears stung her eyes. She blinked them back, but they fell regardless.

I'm pregnant!

With a *girl*. One hand went to the angel around her neck, the other covered her stomach. Her own little angel. Tears spilled from her eyes and wet her cheeks. Now there was more than ever riding on her getting this right.

Pia wasn't rejoicing with her. Instead, she was looking more and more concerned.

"What aren't you telling me?"

"The power you'll need to summon will be far greater this time. Remember Wednesday when you received two hundred and forty volts? Now, think lightning strike. You'll need everything you've got. You'll need to access the maximum you're able."

Sage's heart skipped. "Do you think that will harm the baby?"

"No, but..." Pia broke eye contact and looked down.

"Pia," Sage said firmly. "Tell me."

"I'm sorry, Sage. This isn't something I wanted to tell you the same time I broke the news about your pregnancy."

"What. Is. It."

"Sage, the demon knows about the baby."

Sage sucked in a lungful of air. "How do you know?"

"That teddy bear in your room?" Sage slowly nodded. "It was a message from the demon. A threat. Not only to you, but to your daughter."

Sage felt the color drain from her face, and Pia was at her side in an instant. "Sage, are you all right?"

Sage took a series of deep, fortifying breaths, brushed off Pia's hands and stood.

"Oh no, he won't." Sage walked to the kitchen and pulled out a glass. Instead of pouring herself a glass of water, she gripped the counter, uncaring of the pain as her nails broke. "No fucking way will I allow him to hurt my baby."

And what sliced her up even more was that *he* had known about her baby before she had.

Sage pushed off the sink and turned to face Pia, one hand settling protectively over her flat stomach.

"He's not going to get anywhere near her. He'll have to kill me first." She'd never experienced such intense fury in her whole life.

The bell on the front door clanged and Mark entered. Nate appeared almost instantly to see who'd arrived, but he just nodded at Mark and went back out to continue his call. Sage exchanged a meaningful look with Pia, who understood without a single word spoken. No one was to know until she'd had a chance to speak to Ethan.

"Guess what I've just discovered?" Mark's light-blue eyes twinkled with excitement. He was so eager to share his discovery, he seemed oblivious to the heavy emotion between Pia and Sage.

"What?" Sage asked, with a sinking feeling. Sage rarely enjoyed the things Mark found exciting. She pushed away thoughts of the demon and his threat to her baby and tried to focus.

"Ever heard of ley lines?" Mark asked.

"Maybe," Sage said. "But somehow I don't think it matters because you're going to tell us about them anyway, aren't you?"

"Ten points to the beauty on my right," Mark said, every inch the showman he was. "Ley lines are invisible lines of energy that run through the earth. They run through the sky as well, but the ones I'm talking about are the earth ones."

"What have you found out?" Pia asked, sounding impatient.

"I've been doing a little digging about this town, tracing ley lines in the area. I found something interesting, but considering everything that's happening, not surprising."

"Get to it," Pia said. "We're not getting any younger here."

"You do know how to wreck a bit of fun." He gave Pia a hard look, then continued. "There are ten ley lines in this area, and guess where they intersect?"

"This house?" Pia guessed.

"Nope," Mark said, enjoying himself a little too much.

"The circle," Sage replied dully.

"Another ten points!" Mark grinned.

"Do you know what that means for us?" Sage asked. "Will that impact us in any way on Sunday?"

Mark frowned. "Well, not exactly. It's just interesting to note, that's all. I mean haven't you ever asked why? Why *this* town and not any other?"

"Mark always wants to look for scientific evidence to preface the show," Pia explained.

"And the proof is here," Mark said again, waving the pages he'd printed out. "With the footage I'm going to capture on the night, plus the history of the town..." He glanced at Sage. "Yes, I knew what the government did back then before Pia told me. How they covered up killing innocent people. It isn't hard to find when you know what to start looking for."

"Mark—" Sage said warningly.

"An epidemic doesn't kill an entire town overnight. But I guess they thought no one would pay that close attention to how sloppy the death certificates were."

"You can't—"

"Ah, don't worry your pretty self. I won't say anything, I know it would jeopardize Sunday night. And I don't want to do that. But after you whoop his demon ass on Sunday, and I capture it all on video, I'm going to have the hit of the century!"

Mark took a seat, sitting backward on the chair, long legs on either side. "The demon's entry point needs to be near a sacred site. That's the graveyard, where Virgil and the others are buried," he clarified. "The Murray River that flows alongside it also carries energy. Water accumulates, then amplifies, the power. The ancient circle has power of its own, and that power will be most acute with the energy of the blood moon. This house, the residual energy left in the soil from the confrontation a hundred years ago.... All these elements combined are what make this town right. That's why the demon can enter here, and not say, somewhere in London."

"No, that would be werewolves," Sage said dryly. "Although you will probably find it interesting to know that Mary had mentioned in her diary that there were other portals in other parts of the world. This is not the only one."

Mark's eyes lit up, and Sage could almost see him plotting a whole future season of *Debunking Reality*.

"Ah, come on," Mark said, glancing between Sage and Pia. "You have to admit that this is more than a little exciting?"

Sage met his gaze. "I'll let you know Monday."

———— ◆ ————

After Ethan had finished doing as much as he could on Susie Rafter's case for the day, he picked up Sage and Liquorice from the shop and drove to the local sports oval. Waiting for them, motor idling, in the middle of the grassy field was the Eagle.

Ethan held Sage's hand tightly as they crossed the field. The rotors kicked up bits of dry grass and blew her hair every which way. Liquorice stiffened in Sage's arms, but she reassured him that he would be safe. After Ethan assisted her into the helicopter, he said a few words to Jake, who slapped him on the shoulder and left to drive Ethan's 4WD back to the farmhouse.

Ethan strapped her in, then performed a series of checks. After flicking some switches, he placed his hand on a central stick, eased the helicopter off the ground, and swept them up into the sky.

After what had happened last night, Ethan was not willing to take a chance having her anywhere near his house, no matter how much protection or magic she could theoretically generate.

Sage was absolutely on board with that decision. Even if she had been an accomplished witch, she wouldn't have risked it. This close to the blood moon, the demon's strength was too powerful, and she was not giving him an opportunity to hurt her baby.

There was a fair amount of turbulence until they were out of town, and during that time Ethan's face was etched into harsh lines of concentration.

One hand on the safety handle, the other on Liquorice purring softly in her lap, Sage's gaze was hardly on the sweeping landscape. She didn't appreciate the squares and rectangles that defined the hay crops from the sheep grazing paddocks. She barely noticed the tractor parked in the middle of the field where a farmer had left off work for the day, or the group of kangaroos resting beneath a group of trees.

Sage's attention was more focused on the man beside her than on any of the stunning views below. Dark locks of hair fell in front of Ethan's sunglasses, the golden light of the setting sun reflecting off his watch. Despite the helicopter lurching sideways, the engine straining against the turbulence, she'd never felt so head over heels in her life.

Ethan was a pillar of strength and competence as he handled the bird with unshakable grace and control, and Sage's body heated with desire. She inwardly chastised her wayward thoughts. She ought to be worried about Ethan landing this thing alive, not thinking about what her body would like to do to his.

He glanced at her, as though reading her thoughts.

Would it always be this way between them? Their connection was no less powerful because it was unseen. It existed as surely as gravity and the orbits of the planets.

Soon, the turbulence eased, and Ethan lowered the chopper onto a grassy hill outside town. The landing was gentle, a contrast to the bumpy ride. After he turned off the engine, the silence was complete.

He came to her side and assisted her to the ground. The place he'd brought her to was nothing short of magical. Or did it just seem that way after spending day after day in the nightmare that was Cryton? She'd almost forgotten there was a world outside. People living their lives in the normal way. Going to work, tucking their children into bed.

Ethan spread out a large blanket and popped the cork on a bottle of wine. He placed Liquorice's rug directly next to theirs. Liquorice immediately hopped out of Sage's lap and went to it, turning circles several times before curling up.

Ethan sat down next to Sage, and opened the lids to containers of cold roast chicken and salad.

"How did you manage to arrange this?"

"I can't take the credit. Jake picked these up when he brought the Eagle."

Sage took a bite of potato salad, recognizing the tangy onion flavor as being from the local bakery. "It's a beautiful spot to spend the night." Using the chopper was a great idea. It meant that they could get a significant distance from the town, but not have to spend too much time on travel.

"Jake recommended it. He's spent quite a bit of time these last few days mapping out the area, and he thought it might suit us. Not too far out, but far enough," Ethan said, echoing Sage's thoughts.

He took her empty plate and poured her a glass of wine.

Jake had bought them a bottle of wine? So thoughtful. But… Sage's hand automatically went to her stomach. As much as she longed for the wine to take the edge off her nerves, she'd give it a miss. "Do you have any juice?"

Ethan set the glass aside, and peered into the cooler bag. "Orange juice?"

"Thank you," Sage said, taking the small bottle and popping the lid. "Uh, Eth—" she began, and stopped. How did she tell him? Should she lead up to it? Something like, *Remember how we were Thursday, after fighting the demon?*

"Angel?"

"I've got something to tell you."

"I worked that out already. What is it?" She had his complete attention, and it made her nervous. What if he wasn't happy? Perhaps she should tell him after Sunday night.

Sage started to speak, then faltered and blurted, "I love you."

"That's not what you were going to say, and, you'd better tell me fast. You're killing me here."

She sucked in a deep breath, filling her lungs with fresh country air. The sun had just disappeared beneath the horizon, leaving a rainbow of color in its wake.

"I think I might be pregnant." Sage closed her eyes, so she didn't see his expression. It would kill her if she saw disappointment cross his face.

He was silent for so long, she wondered if he'd even heard her. She cracked open one eye and peeked. She was hit with the full intensity of his dark gaze.

"Angel, just to be sure I heard you correctly, you'd better say that again."

Sage's hand shook as she took a sip of juice. "I'm pregnant. If Pia is correct, that is."

His eyes darkened even further, a lock of hair dancing at the edge of his face. The way he was looking at her stopped her heart and left her breathless. The fierceness in his gaze pierced through to her very soul. He didn't look excited, he didn't look not. His face was a mask, completely unreadable.

"Say something. Anything. I was just as shocked when Pia told me. And I argued with her. Told her it wasn't possible. I—" Sage swallowed. "She told me it's a girl."

He crushed his mouth to hers. She was startled, then relaxed into his arms as his soft lips moved over hers. She wrapped her arms around his neck, and he pulled her closer.

It can't be all bad if this is his reaction, can it?

And then she understood. The kiss was Ethan's way to process this. He wasn't upset; he was *emotional.*

And he conveyed everything he couldn't put into words through the kiss. He'd always professed not to be good at expressing himself with words, but she was becoming used to him expressing himself in this deeply personal way. The honesty, the unadorned emotion he displayed, was powerful.

Eventually, they broke apart. She looked up at him, feeling raw. His face was still unreadable, but she was surprised to find his eyes shining with unshed tears.

She tried a different tack. "You don't look surprised that it's possible."

Ethan inclined his head. "On the contrary, I am surprised. But not shocked. It certainly is possible."

"It was Thursday, wasn't it?"

"Yes," Ethan confirmed. "That morning after I brought you back to my hotel. You were insatiable."

"Me?" Sage asked playfully.

"Yes, you." Ethan grinned back. "You forced me to make love to you all day and then some."

"Ethan!"

"Okay," he said, holding up a hand. "I may have been a little into it myself." His grin faded slightly. "One of those times, the condom broke. You'd fallen asleep in my arms. Too exhausted to notice."

Sage sucked in a deep breath. "You didn't tell me."

"I didn't want to worry you."

"Are you worried?"

"Are you?"

Sage smiled. "Would it make any difference if I were? Let's just add it to all the other things I've got to worry about at the moment."

The smile drained from his face and he looked at their joined hands, his thumb rubbing back and forth across her knuckles. A muscle jumped along his jaw.

"Eth, look at me," Sage whispered. She waited until he met her gaze. "You can't let this change anything."

He made a strangled noise in the back of his throat and jumped to his feet. She let him go, her heart wringing painfully as she watched him take a series of deep breaths, his hands clenching and unclenching at his sides. "Angel," he said brokenly. "Don't get me wrong, I'm happy, but this changes everything."

She stood as well, but let him have a little distance.

Ethan turned to her, and she drew closer. He choked, then swallowed a couple of times before speaking. "Good God, I thought I couldn't love you any more. But heaven help me, I somehow do. And to know what you—God, it's like being in a car that's hurtling out of control. Not knowing if you'll make the corners or keep it on the road."

He cursed, then tenderly reached out and touched her stomach. The simple gesture was almost too much.

"Jesus, Angel. How will I be able to bear Sunday night now?"

"The same way you intended to before."

His jaw worked, and his eyes traveled the full length of her body, then back again to meet her gaze. She shivered, and he mistook it for her being cold. Ethan shrugged out of his leather jacket and held it while she slipped her arms inside. She inhaled, enjoying the jacket more for his comforting scent than its warmth.

"Eth, there's something else."

Ethan spun her around, her back to his chest and pulled her close. "Something else, Angel?" His arms tightened around her.

"Except... You won't be as happy to hear this."

"Tell me." Ethan bit out the words.

"The demon knows.... about the baby."

His body went rigid. When he spoke, his voice was lethally quiet. "What makes you say that?"

"That creepy teddy bear was a message." Sage swallowed. Hard. "Pia said it was a threat."

Ethan exploded with an outpour of curses. Helpless, she hugged the jacket tightly around herself and waited. He walked a short distance away, and she let him go. Eventually, he returned, drawing to a stop just in front of her. His face was a study in chiseled anger, his eyes narrow and hard.

"This changes everything." Ethan repeated his words from earlier, only this time a chill rolled down her spine.

"What do you mean?"

"This ends Sunday. I won't have the son of a bitch doing this again to our daughter's great-grandchildren."

The implication of his words ripped through her. Her knees wobbled, and she dug her feet into the ground. "Ethan, no."

He nodded slowly. "Yes. You can't tell me I'm the alchemist's son, with the power to end this, and then tell me not to do it. That's not who I am."

The earth shifted beneath her feet. Sage's whole world was crumbling. What was supposed to be a happy moment, a small glimmer of hope in a time of darkness, had destroyed everything.

He couldn't do it; she wouldn't let him. Panic clawed its way up her body and lodged in her throat.

"Ethan, how dare you say that? You are not leaving me!" Her voice was a ragged rasp. She pounded her fists against his chest and he caught her wrists in his hands. Gently, tenderly, he kissed her palms, then lowered them to her sides.

"Angel," he breathed.

"Don't you 'Angel' me." Sage blinked back stinging tears. "I'm not doing all of this only to lose you. Goddamn you, Ethan. If you are the alchemist's son, you'd bloody well better find another way."

Ethan's brow furrowed. "Perhaps there is," he said. "Tomorrow's Saturday. I'm running out of opportunities before the blood moon. Regardless of anything else the demon throws at me, I'm going to head back home to go through my grandfather's and great-grandfather's things."

"Nothing like the last minute," Sage said.

"Yes," Ethan frowned. "I'd intended to go tonight. But then the little girl..." His hands curled into fists. "Don't you think it strange that every time I've made the decision to go back to Adelaide, something comes along to detour me from that path? The demon gives me something to chew on, something to distract me. That gives me hope, Sage." He straightened his shoulders. "There must be something he doesn't want me to find. Something that's important. There may be another way to end this; the cipher may be a metaphor, remember that."

Sage clutched onto that thread of hope. Maybe the premonition, no matter how vivid, was only a possible reality—one that existed before Ethan knew he was the alchemist's son. Tentative hope welled inside her. "You think so?"

"The more I think about it, the more I feel I'm right. The demon doesn't want me to find something. Something that will help shed some light on this situation. Give us another option. Another way."

"I hope so," Sage said, her knees buckling in relief. There was no guarantee, but at least Ethan was looking for alternatives. He'd scared the fuck out of her a moment ago.

He led her back to the blanket and packed away the uneaten food. Neither of them had an appetite anymore.

Once they'd set up the tent for the night, Ethan turned on a lantern and asked for the grimoire.

Sage reached into her bag, took out the three books, and handed it to him.

Ethan silently read the old book from start to finish, then read it again, as Sage did with Mary's diary and Nan's journal, looking for anything she'd missed. Unable to sleep, they then spent the hours until dawn going over and over the ritual, reading and rereading the verses and making notes. Sage double-checked the list she'd made for Pia of things she needed for the ceremony.

The whole time, she sensed Ethan's mind churning. Like her, he was desperately trying to work out a way that they could all make it through Sunday.

If Sage lost him… No, she refused to give airtime to that thought. There had to be another way. Ethan would find it tomorrow in his ancestors' belongings.

Wouldn't he?

Chapter Twenty-Three

Lucky woke with his back pressed against a hard concrete wall. He was dizzy and his head was spinning.

He felt different. Weak. His eyes were heavy, like there were coins on his lids, and he struggled to open them the merest crack.

Where am I?

Lucky couldn't remember where he'd gone to sleep. He was cold, and he wished he had his blankie.

Where is my blankie?

Lucky concentrated, but couldn't remember where he'd put it. He started to cry. He always needed his blankie after his daddy had visited his room. And he must have been in here, because Lucky was ice cold. And sore. His body ached all over.

Lucky's fingers scrabbled in the space around him, searching for the soft crocheted blankie that the granny had made especially for him. What was her name? Celine? No, Celeste. He remembered now.

The granny knows what Daddy does in the darkness of night.

But no one believes her either.

She wants to take me away, even tried to once, but the police got her in trouble. Big trouble.

No one believes the granny because she's a witch. Dangerous too, they said. They put steel on her wrists and took her away last time she was here.

She stopped coming with blankies a long time ago.

It made him sad.

There was no one to help him, no one to stop Daddy.

Lucky was tired. So terribly tired. He let his head loll back on his shoulders.

He prayed like Mummy told him to. For strength. For courage.

For someone to stop Daddy.

But it wasn't God who answered his prayers.

———— ♦ ————

Lucky woke with a start.

He scanned the space around him. Cold, hard, concrete walls. His head throbbed, and he remembered that the detective's goons had injected him with something, then thrown him in this empty room.

His heart pounded loud and hard in his chest, then skittered to a shuddering halt.

Where were the voices?

His head was unnaturally silent. The drugs they'd given him must have blocked the voices.

Would they come back?

Lucky needed the voices. His pulse raced and his hands shook. His leg began to make rapid jerky movements.

He fumbled inside his pocket for the packet of roll-your-own cigarettes.

Gone.

Just like the voices.

Please come back! Lucky placed his hands on his head. *Please!* The room spun around him, his breath whooshing in and out, faster and faster.

Where are you? Lucky silently called to the darkness.

It had been a relief when the voices had come to him, that night when he was a frightened little boy.

The voices had believed him about Daddy.

And when he'd been strong enough, the voices had made sure his father couldn't hurt him again.

The voices were his friends, and Lucky was no longer alone. He no longer had to fret over decisions. The voices always knew what to do.

Where were they?

And then Lucky heard something move through the darkness outside. Something familiar…

It hit him in a rush. His body buzzed, his eyes rolled back in his head.

The air in his concrete prison thickened. Crackled and came alive.

The Dark Master.

Lucky regained his new, sharper focus.

He welcomed the presence as it settled inside him. He welcomed its darkness. The angry determination it brought.

He took a series of deep breaths and felt his body acclimate. Become stronger, larger. The confines of the concrete walls closed in on him.

Despite being still imprisoned, Lucky was calm. Confident.

He was no longer slow, dim-witted Lucky Keyton. *The victim.*

He was big and powerful.

No one would dare hurt him now.

The voices gave him power, a purpose.

He reached out with his mind, and "saw" the goon standing guard outside, reached out further and saw that Blood Fox had taken over his role. He'd captured and performed the seventh sacrifice. The virgin child.

If Lucky didn't get out of there fast, Blood Fox would perform the grand invocation ritual in preparation for the blood moon.

Fuck that! No one was taking his glory.

Lucky focused on the goon. He was leaning against the tree, but was staring in the direction of the cell, as though aware of a change, but had no idea what it was.

"You can tell something is wrong, can't you?" Lucky said quietly. "But you believe your eyes, which are telling you that nothing is amiss."

Fool. Human senses were useless when dealing with Virgil, Sytrolius, and the demons of the darkness. Such entities were far stronger, without the frail limitations of humanity, of common flesh and blood.

Lucky tapped into the goon's mind. He had his fingers resting on his weapon, his eyes scanning the area, seeing nothing.

His name was Jake.

And he'd be very useful.

Chapter Twenty-Four

Saturday
The Day Before the Blood Moon

Saturday morning, Ethan and Sage set aside the grimoire and the diaries and watched the sun rise, peeking through dark storm clouds. The many hours of study, together, gave him a bit more confidence that there was a chance they'd both survive the ritual. But he wouldn't really know until he returned to Adelaide and found—or didn't find—whatever it was the demon was trying to keep him from.

Heavy drops pelted them as they folded up the tent and tucked it back in the Eagle. He didn't like flying in this weather, especially with the added difficulty of flying through the strange electromagnetic field surrounding Cryton, but he had no choice.

The turbulence as they neared the town had worsened from the day before. Would he even be able to fly the Eagle back in tomorrow? Ethan was relying on the Eagle, as he planned to spend tonight, their last night before the blood moon, out of Cryton again, out of the demon's reach. He'd have to rethink that plan if the interference got much worse. Storms were risky, but he'd flown in worse. The electromagnetic field that interfered with his equipment was an unknown.

The Eagle plunged several meters, bucking against his attempts to keep the chopper level. His gut tightened, and sweat rolled down his forehead into his eyes. He blinked at it furiously, unable to take his hands off the controls. Liquorice yowled in Sage's lap, and she stroked the cat's head, her face pale when Ethan risked a glance at her.

It'll be okay, Angel. He hadn't spoken the words aloud, but she flicked her eyes his way as though she'd heard them.

At last they reached the sports oval, and Ethan set down the bird with a heavy thump.

He drove the short distance to the shop and dropped Sage off. Jake and Nate would keep watch over her. Daniel and Max were currently guarding Keyton, and then Sean and Sam would take Daniel's place later in the day.

Despite having arranged as much protection for Sage as he could, Ethan would rather not leave her. Not for a second. He wanted Sage to come with him, but she had arranged to meet Pia, Mark, Joyce, Mona, and hopefully Pat, at the shop to go through the ritual together to make sure everyone was prepared.

Ethan had no choice; he had to go to Adelaide. Now. He had to know what the demon had been trying to keep from him.

He drove the hundred and ten kilometers to Adelaide in record time. He tapped his foot and jingled his keys as the elevator took him up to the penthouse apartment he owned. He used his key card to enter the apartment, looking around the space with new eyes.

While some of his mates had reached the age where they were buying houses with backyards and tree houses for their kids to play in, Ethan had found his setup situated in the heart of the city more suited to his bachelor lifestyle. Low maintenance, close to work and the airport, it was fully serviced by a housekeeper who kept his sheets clean and the essentials in his cupboards.

The penthouse could not be further removed from the farm he'd bought in Cryton. The place he'd be selling come Monday—provided he survived the blood moon. What would Sage think of his apartment? He assessed it with cool eyes. It was sprawling, decorated in masculine neutrals—black, white, and gray—with accents of color coming from statement pieces. The place looked like something out of a magazine-spread. Hiring designers would do that.

But compared to how he'd been living with Sage in the farmhouse, this space was cold. Unemotional. How had he not noticed that before? The penthouse was a perfect reflection of the person he was. The person he'd *been*. Before Sage.

He'd changed so much in these last couple weeks. Sage had changed him. So much so, he barely recognized the reflection that stared back at him in the mirror.

He pressed the control that opened the curtains. Normally, he appreciated the view of the city, but today storm clouds darkened the sky and heavy drops fell, thudding against the windows. The gloomy weather matched his mood.

He'd better get on with it; the clock was ticking, and who knew how long it would take him to sift through his family's belongings?

Ethan entered the spare room. In contrast to the minimalist décor of the rest of the apartment, this room was crammed with boxes. These were the things he'd kept from the house after his parents had died. He'd never opened a single box. Had never wanted to. He'd always assumed he'd take them to the place that he settled down in and someday explore them at his leisure.

When he was ready.

He'd have to look through everything, no matter how painful the task was.

He'd promised Sage he would find an alternative. He'd promised he'd stay with her, and God knew he wanted that more than anything.

Ethan took a deep breath and contemplated the task ahead of him. It was going to take hours. And it was going to hurt.

Taking the knife from his belt, he flicked open the blade. The sooner he found what he came for, the sooner he could go... where?

He was about to say "home," but that wasn't true, was it? He couldn't keep a house that had belonged to a serial killer. But he knew one thing. Home wasn't here. Like a snake who'd shed its skin, this place no longer fit him.

Home was wherever Sage was.

Hours later, Ethan sat cross-legged on the floor, surrounded by opened cartons and a mountain of packing paper, but he'd finally found the box he'd been looking for.

Inside the box was a combination of items Ethan recognized as belonging to his father as well as older things, that judging by their age had belonged to his grandfather and great-grandfather. Someone had taken his great-grandfather's belongings out of the thick old cardboard fruit box with ventilation holes he'd remembered seeing in the shed during his childhood, and repackaged them into a generic moving box.

Had his father done this? And had he sat on the floor much like Ethan was, and contemplated the objects it held? Did he wonder what the items told him about his history? About who or what he was?

Or had he already known?

If Ian had known what happened in Cryton a hundred years ago, chances are good he'd discussed it with Ethan's father. Perhaps his father had started to investigate what had happened? He'd been a cop to the core of his being, much like Ethan was. Chances were high that his father had started digging as soon as the first question was raised in his mind.

Had the demon somehow been behind his father's death? To keep the truth about who Ethan really was from being discovered? His father had been a strong man, and although Ethan had understood the power of grief, he'd always found it a tough pill to swallow that his father had committed suicide. Especially leaving behind his son. What if there was more to the story than he knew?

Ethan would have to wait to dig for those answers. He continued to search through the box. It wasn't long before Ethan found the pendant he'd seen on his father's bedside table. What he'd suspected was confirmed absolutely. It was the same symbol as the one on the grimoire.

He curled one hand around the metal charm and rubbed his aching chest with the other. Ethan had often tried to imagine just how much pain his father had been in, to choose to end his life. If the demon hadn't been involved, was it acute sadness over the murder of his wife, the love of his life? Did he feel that because it was his job that got her killed, that it was his fault? Was it grief, guilt, or a combination of both? Whatever it was, it must have been bad enough for him to feel justified in taking away his son's only remaining parent. The very last surviving member of Ethan's family.

A lump lodged in his throat. Why hadn't he been enough of a reason for his father to hang around?

Ethan stilled, as something occurred to him.

If he followed the cipher, was he doing to Sage what his father had done to him?

No. If Ethan made that decision, it would be *for* her. So that the love of his life and his daughter could go on. He would assure the safety of future generations.

He would not hurt them the way his father had hurt him. They would understand.

Wouldn't they?

He sat for a long time, holding the pendant. Pia had reached his grandfather and great-grandfather. But not Ethan's father. Why? Had he so thoroughly abandoned his son?

Ethan wouldn't do that to his daughter and Sage. If he died, he would stay near them, even if it meant forsaking Heaven for a time. He would *stay*.

His eyes stung with unshed tears, the lump in his throat hard as rock. So many questions he wanted to ask his father. No hope of answers.

Swallowing hard, he let out a breath and pressed his fingertips to his eyes, wiping away the moisture that had gathered in the corners.

He focused on the pendant. His father had kept it for a reason. Had he known anything about its purpose? Had his grandfather known?

Question upon question, stacking on top of one another. Was he prepared to learn the truth? Accept the responsibility of what he might discover?

The answers he was looking for were in this box.

Ethan placed the chain around his neck, tucked it inside his T-shirt and leaned in, inhaling the scent of old things, the smell of items in a second-hand shop. He pulled out various items: an old jewelry box, and an even older one. His great-grandmother's, he guessed. An old pocket watch; an old box of Redhead matches; a palm-sized empty tin; a larger one filled with crumbling receipts. Apparently the kitchen table he remembered in his great-grandmother's house had been paid for with twelve sheep and two cows.

And then his fingers landed on something highly polished and solid. Pulling it out, Ethan discovered it was a wooden object, the size of a small shoe box. Ethan turned the object in his hands, transfixed by the symbols carved into the rich wood—he recognized them from the grimoire. Though there was no handle, no obvious lid or release mechanism, something rattled inside the box as he admired it from various angles.

"You're beautiful," he murmured.

Ethan ran his fingers along the joins in the wood, imagining how it would open. It had to be some type of puzzle.

He'd always loved a challenge, and this box was captivating. He stroked the timber lovingly, frowning at the indentations on either side. Round indentations caused by force. Perhaps by a hammer. Someone had tried to break into this box.

Who?

"But you wouldn't have it, would you?" Ethan murmured. "No, you won't open to the wrong person."

The room melted away, the floor, the walls, the ceiling. Ethan was conscious of nothing but the feel of the smoky carvings as he traced them, caressed them.

The box began to hum, a low vibration that traveled through his fingertips and up his arm.

It's purring.

"You didn't want to open for the man with the hammer, but you want to open for me, don't you?" Ethan was not bothered by the fact he was talking to a box.

"Show me," he whispered. "Come on, my lovely. Show me what you've got."

Several timber panels slid apart, and the lid sprang open.

Ethan inhaled the scent of beeswax and dried herbs. And something old. Air from a previous time, captured in the box and released into this time. Past and present melding together.

He breathed the strange fragrance into his lungs, aware of the clouding effect it was having on his thoughts.

Or was it a clarifying effect?

Were things finally making sense?

Inside the box was a large crystal wand matching the picture in the back of the grimoire. It was the wand of light. The one the alchemist's son needed to perform the cipher. Black strips of leather wound around the base, forming a worn, well-used handle.

Ethan took the wand in his hand, noticing the engravings in the crystal, above the leather binding. Symbols. Impressed into the leather at the base of the handle was the same symbol as the one on the back of Sage's angel pendant, on the pendant around his neck, and on the cover of the grimoire.

There was no denying any longer that all these things were related. The things he and Sage were going through were different, yet inextricably tied together.

Ethan was the alchemist's son; Sage, the seer's daughter. The prophecy entwined their destiny, their fate. One thing was certain: Sage *was* his.

A wave of possessive energy washed over him. The polished crystal blade of the wand glowed, or at least he imagined it did.

The air vibrated, but Ethan didn't feel the demon. He concentrated, and became aware of several shadowy figures in the room with him, intently watching. The previous generations of alchemists. A wave of approval washed over him. Ethan was conscious of how the wand felt in his hand. How his fingers curled around the handle, how cool it felt, how the coolness traveled through his hand to his elbow.

Then he was aware of hands that covered his. He could see the aging skin of older hands, and knotted knuckles. Someone from a time past. And then another set of hands on top of those, even older, darker. More wrinkled. But kind, oh so kind.

They held his, became his.

Ethan may not have been aware of his destiny until now, but he was confident of one thing.

He wouldn't be going into this fight alone.

Setting the wand safely back in its box, Ethan grabbed the items he thought he'd need, and checked the pendant around his neck.

A journal near the bottom of the packing box caught his eye, and he pulled it out, leaning back against the wall. He opened the aged, thick cardboard cover. It was in ink pen, and the name inside told Ethan it belonged to his great-grandfather.

Ethan only had time to skim the precious book for now, but hoped to find some hint of how to defeat the master demon without having to resort to the sacrifice necessary to fulfill the cipher. Any hint of anything else he could try to succeed.

And keep his promise to Sage.

———◆———

"Okay, Sage," Pia said. "Mark and I are heading back to my place now to get the things on your list for tomorrow."

Sage stepped forward and embraced Pia. "Thank you so much for today."

Pia smiled. "You did great. You all did," Pia said, smiling at Joyce, Mona, Pat, and even Nate.

"Oh, we're looking forward to it," Joyce said. "Aren't we girls?"

Pat dabbed at her eyes. "We'll send that demon back to Hell, if it's the last thing I do."

It was late afternoon, and they'd spent the day rehearsing the ritual. Their practicing had started off seriously, everyone a little uncertain as to their roles, but once their confidence grew, they'd indulged in some light-hearted fun and banter, often at the expense of Mark and Nate, who Mona, Joyce, and even Pat had flirted with shamelessly, the men giving as good as they got. The witches lifted Sage's spirits, reminding her of how Nan had always been able to make her feel better.

Sage took everyone's plates and cups to the sink, and glanced at the time. Ethan should be back soon. She smiled as her heart warmed at the merest thought of him, then mentally *tsk*ed at herself. She was disgustingly gone over him.

"We're going to head off now too," Joyce said. "You'll be great tomorrow. Celeste would be proud."

Sage smiled as her vision blurred. "Thank you, Joyce. She'd be proud of you too. You, Pat, and Mona. You are champions."

"Let's leave the celebrating until after tomorrow," Mona suggested.

"She makes a good point." Sage smiled. "How are you getting home?"

"I'll take them home, as I was the chauffeur that brought them here," Nate said, walking over. Joyce visibly preened, touching her hair, and held onto Nate's arm as though he truly were her escort.

Sage laughed as she walked them all to the door and said her goodbyes. Watching them all pile into the Land Rover, she took the opportunity to stroke Liquorice's back when he abruptly jumped up and hissed, arching his back.

"What is it, little buddy?" Sage asked.

He's here. Run!

The hairs on the back of Sage's neck stood on end, and sweat beaded on her brow.

"Back in ten," Nate called through the window as he pulled out of the driveway. Jake waved in acknowledgment.

"Nate!" she yelled, but the vehicle didn't stop. Apparently he hadn't heard her.

Liquorice hissed again, his hackles raised. *Let's go!*

It's okay. Jake is still here, she told him.

No, he's not.

What did that mean?

And then she knew.

Sage picked Liquorice up, but before she could follow her instinct and put some distance between her and the house, Jake grabbed her wrist and yanked her inside the door. The force sent Sage sprawling on the floorboards, her leg landing awkwardly beneath her.

Liquorice jumped from Sage's arms as she fell. He landed on his paws, then turned on Jake, and claws extended, pounced on Jake's leg and latched onto it. With a low-pitched growl, Liquorice bit through the denim. Jake cursed and kicked forcefully, sending Liquorice flying out the door onto the porch. Smacking into the ground, Liquorice rolled back to his feet and prepared to launch himself for another attack when Jake slammed the front door shut. Liquorice hurled himself against the door, yowling viciously, his claws raking the wood.

Jake turned, leaned back against the wooden frame, and eyed her.

Sage scrambled to her feet, crying out at the sharp stabs of pain that ran up her leg. Jake smiled. His eyes were glazed, his lids lowered as though he were struggling to focus.

He pushed off the door. "Come with me." His voice sounded warped.

Sage backed away, looking for something to use as a weapon. She lunged for the kitchen counter and palmed a knife she'd left there. It was a steak knife, not the butcher's knife she would have preferred, but it would have to do—

She'd no sooner finished the thought than Jake had her disarmed and on the floor, hands behind her back. She'd barely had time to even register what had happened, he was that fast. Damn, Taipan knew their stuff.

Jake yanked her up off the floor, almost wrenching her shoulders out of their sockets. He kneed her in the back to get her walking.

Tears stung her lids as Jake ushered her outside. Max was on the patio, where Daniel had left him to guard the back of the building while he did some work at the farm on the chopper. He was expected to return any minute. As

Jake and Sage walked out of the house, Max was instantly on his feet and bared his teeth in a low growl.

Jake snapped a warning at him, and Max hesitated, instinct warring with his training. Jake continued his rough escort of Sage, down the rear steps and onto the path that led to the backyard shed.

Liquorice came running at full speed, claws unsheathed and teeth bared. "Liquorice, no!" Sage cried out. Liquorice pounced, and Jake kicked him. Liquorice went flying, landing with a sickening thud against one of the posts on the porch. He didn't move, his body lying in a crumpled heap.

"Liquorice!" Sage's pained cry sounded as broken as she felt on the inside.

She screamed and lashed out at Jake as he pushed her roughly forward and into the woodshed. She landed hard on bark and splinters of wood. Skin ripped off her legs and palms as she scrambled to come to terms with what had just happened. Jake was the betrayal Pia had predicted. What did he have planned for her? For Ethan?

Sunlight cast the figure at the door in shadow.

"What the fuck do you think you're doing?" Sage demanded. "Ethan's going to kill you for this." *And I'm going to kill you for hurting Liquorice.* She sent up a quick prayer that he'd be all right.

The silent figure didn't move, and Sage tried to stand, to make a run for it. She slipped, struggling to find purchase on the loose logs, but she made it to the door.

Jake pushed her back. Hard.

"What's *wrong* with you?" Sage shouted, though she knew the answer. She just hoped to somehow get through to him, the man inside. The look in Jake's eyes was the same one that had been in Mark's that night at the cabin. The night he'd been possessed.

She was in serious trouble.

"Do you really think you can get away with this? Daniel will be back any second."

"Fucking bitch. Should have duct-taped that stupid trap of yours." Jake's voice, already deep, had picked up an additional note, a deep baritone, making his voice sound more like a chord. With his large muscular frame and tattoos, he looked formidable at the best of times. Add the slightly crazed eyes of a psychopath, and he was terrifying. Jake attempted to shut the door, but Sage struck out with her foot, kicking with all her might.

Cursing viciously, he lunged forward, grabbed her legs, and tossed her back as though she were a ragdoll. Her head slammed against the timber wall, and black spots momentarily filled her vision. Hoping Daniel had returned, Sage screamed as hard as she could.

"No one's going to hear you out here, whore," Jake sneered. The door closed and Sage heard the latch slide into place. In the last second before the door shut, Sage glimpsed a flash of something metallic to her left. Her eyes adjusted to the amount of sunlight that made its way through the chinks in the crudely made structure. Enough to see the blade of a long-handled axe embedded in a stump of wood.

It took both hands, since the shed's roof was too low to allow her to stand, but she managed to dislodge the axe and swing it as hard as she could at the door. The blade buried itself into the wood and she used everything she had in her to pull it out and keep swinging.

She made a small hole and it spurred her on. As she was about to take another swing, something slithered across her foot.

The scream lodged in her throat, terror stealing her voice. She heard movement behind her as well, and realized with dawning horror that Jake had locked her in the shed with a snake. Two snakes.

Snake safety came back to her. What did you do? Stay still. Absolutely still. Allow the snake to continue on its way. But that didn't apply when you were locked in a shed with them. Where would they slither away to?

Heart galloping in her chest, she tried to steady her ragged breathing. Her grip tightened on the handle of the axe, her eyes searched the darkness for the snakes.

Where had they gone?

Perhaps she could try to summon her power? Would it surround her and protect her like it had in the attic?

Sage attempted to calm her emotions and still her mind, like Pia had shown her. But she couldn't stop her heart racing; it was all she could do to fight outright panic. She was in a woodshed with more than one potentially lethal snake. Her mind wasn't silent; it was screaming. *Get out! Get out now!*

Fortunately, she had more light now from the hole she'd made in the door. But what she saw made her blood ran cold.

There, in the corner, was a definitely lethal eastern brown snake coiled atop a nest of eggs.

Adrenaline fired in her blood. She still had the axe in her hand.

Fuck fighting, she was out of there.

Terror gave her superhuman strength, and she smashed through the door in three swings. She crawled through the opening, the bottom of her jeans snagging on the jagged wood. She fell forward, landing on her face. She writhed, kicking her legs, as she spit out blood-laced dirt.

She spun herself over to use her hands to free her jeans when she saw two snakes starting to exit out the same hole her leg was caught in.

She froze, her stomach contracting, as a tail brushed her ankle on its way out. One of the snakes slithered around the corner of the shed away from her; the other paused, studying her with eyes that were strangely intelligent.

She didn't scream, didn't even breathe.

Then she realized what she should have tried earlier.

She reached out to the snake with her mind, trying to tell it she wasn't a threat, but a wall stopped her.

He was influencing the snake. Or at least blocking her from talking to it.

She was too scared to make even the slightest movement. The snake broke eye contact and undulated toward the tree, then circled back round. Keeping her movements minimal, Sage undid the button and zipper on her jeans and, not taking her eyes off the snake, pulled herself out of her jeans.

She was free. Relief hit her in a rush. She rose to her feet and was about to make a run for it when the snake began gliding toward her. She was trapped, her back against the wall of the shed. Brown snakes struck with lightning speed; if she startled it, she wouldn't stand a chance.

Liquorice pounced from behind the shed. Somehow he was still alive. *Oh thank you, God.*

"Liquorice! Go!" She didn't want him to get hurt again. Or worse.

He ignored her, hissing at the snake, but not getting within range of its bite.

Max came charging at full run, growling and barking at the snake.

"Max! No!"

Startled at Max's barking, the snake turned, reared its head, and struck, catching Max on his hind leg.

Max yelped, but he wasn't deterred.

He growled, low and deep, bared his teeth. The snake that attacked paused, but the second snake slithered around the corner toward Sage, and Max attacked.

"Max! NO!" Sage repeated fiercely. "Stay back!" Max's jaws clamped down on the snake. A subsequent strike from the other snake hit Max on the rear leg. Max took another bite on the side of his mouth as he wrestled with the snake he'd grabbed, wildly gnashing his teeth until the snake was dead.

Tears blinded her as she hurried out of striking range and tried to call Max away.

The remaining snake hissed, capturing Max's attention.

"Max!"

But Max wouldn't be deterred. In full attack mode, he wasn't letting anything threaten Sage.

"Daniel!" If Max wouldn't listen to her, he'd listen to him. *Where was he?*

A third snake slithered out of the woodpile and advanced toward Max. When it joined the second, it raised its body off the ground, winding itself into an "S" shape. Mouth gaping open, fangs bared, it was poised and ready to strike.

Liquorice hissed, trying to attract the third snake's attention, but it was too focused on Max.

Even though things felt like they were happening in slow motion, Sage knew everything was happening in an instant.

Max was about to attack, and Sage couldn't allow that. She tried to pick Max up, but he twisted, giving her a warning nip to her arm. It wasn't a bite meant to incapacitate, but it still drew blood.

She tried again, but Max turned on her, snapping his jaws.

Sage backed away, taking herself out of danger, hoping Max would follow, frantically calling his name. Willing him to come. Reaching out with her mind.

Max ignored her pleas. He lunged again at the snakes, and was struck a fourth time.

The sound of a gunshot deafened her. The bullet hit the slithering, moving target once, twice, sending pieces of snake flying into the air. Another two shots took care of the other.

Daniel lowered the gun, and Max limped toward his owner, swaying as he did so. Blood dripped from Max's mouth as he leapt into Daniel's arms.

"Hey buddy. Have a little run-in with a snake, did we?" Daniel spoke soothingly to the dog, but his face was contorted with anguish. Cradling Max to his chest, he was already moving toward the house.

"Sage! Go. Get in the house and call Blade," he called out over his shoulder.

"I'm here," Ethan said from behind her. Sage shivered as Ethan's strong arms wrapped around her and scooped her off her feet.

"Are you okay? Were you bitten?" Ethan's eyes were wide, his gravelly voice low and urgent.

Sage shook her head. "It was Jake. He can't be trusted. He's just like Mark was. Possessed."

Ethan exchanged a meaningful glance with Daniel.

"Max protected me from the snakes. He saved my life." Her chest heaved, and she choked out a sob.

At that moment, the sun set, and gloom settled over the town. A shiver slid across her skin and down her spine as she remembered the unnatural eyes of the snakes. Ethan retrieved her discarded denims from where they had snagged on the wood and held her firm while she slid back into them. She was cold, frozen to the bone, but not because of lack of clothing, but her fear for Max's life.

Liquorice jumped up into Sage's arms, butting her with his head. *I'm sorry,* he said.

"Come on. Let's get you inside." With his arm firmly around her shoulders, Ethan followed Daniel into the house.

"Eastern brown?" Ethan asked Sage.

"Yes." Sage said. "Four strikes, two different snakes."

Ethan cursed. Sage's sentiments exactly.

Max's odds of survival were slim.

———— ◆ ————

Inside, there was a buzz of action as the men cleared the kitchen table to make a makeshift surgery. Liquorice didn't come inside, instead opting for his usual spot on the front porch. She'd hastily examined him, but he'd assured her he was okay. Just badly bruised.

Nate had returned, and he quickly retrieved the medical kit from his car. Withdrawing a syringe, he injecting a liquid into Max.

"What's that?"

"Vitamin C," Nate said. "It can delay the effects of the bite. It's not the same as antivenin, but it can help until we can get some."

Tenderly, he wiped the blood from Max's puncture wounds. "Brown snake venom causes paralysis and stops the blood from clotting."

Max whimpered softly, his pupils dilated. His trembled, and saliva frothed from his mouth.

"Any luck on the vet?" Nate called out.

"Not yet," Daniel said, punching more numbers into his phone. "There's no goddamn reception."

Sage picked up the receiver of the land line. Nothing. The phone had been in her grandmother's name, and the cancellation order had already gone through.

"Sage, nearest vet?" Daniel asked.

"In Septon, thirty minutes away. He'll be closed though. It's after five on a Saturday."

"Who've we got for after-hours call out around here?" Daniel snapped.

"I don't know. There might be a number on the vet's door. You'll more than likely have reception out of town too."

Before she could blink, Daniel had Max in his arms and made his way to the car, Nate scrambling to catch up.

———— ◆ ————

"What the hell happened?" Ethan's voice boomed like the thunder that had begun to rumble in the late afternoon sky.

Sam and Sean had arrived at the shop. "What are you guys doing here?" Ethan demanded.

"Browny said he'd take over watching Keyton," Sean said. "Said that you needed us here, that you couldn't get through to us on the phones."

"Goddamn it." Ethan briefed the men in on the situation. "Go find Browny and bring him back here. I don't care what you have to do to do it. And make sure Keyton is still secure. Give him another shot of sedative if you have to. Go!"

Ethan crossed the room to sit next to her. "Tell me exactly what happened, Angel." Doing her best to remain unemotional, she relayed the story.

"Jesus," Ethan said, thrusting his hands through his hair. "I don't believe it."

"You don't believe me?" Sage asked slowly.

"God, no. Of course I believe you," Ethan said, taking her by the shoulders. "I believe you," he repeated, softer this time.

"It's just that..." Ethan jumped to his feet, walked across the room and slammed his fist into the wall, making Sage jump. "Fuck!"

Ethan rested his forehead on the wall and flexed his swollen knuckles. "Goddamn you, Browny. What the hell happened to you?"

"The demon got to him, just like it got to Mark," Sage said.

Ethan didn't reply and Sage's face heated. Of course he'd already come to that conclusion.

"What I don't understand is why someone who knows a thousand ways to kill chose to do what he did?" Sage said.

"I'm guessing he was going to make it look like an accident. Perhaps come back and unlock the door after the snakes..." Ethan cleared his throat.

Ethan didn't need to finish the sentence. Would Jake have made it look like Sage had been walking around out back and been bitten, perhaps arranged her body after the fact? Maybe he'd even planned on being the one to *discover* her body so that no one suspected him?

The front door burst opened and Sam rushed in. "Lucky's escaped."

"Jake," Sage said, stating the obvious.

Ethan grabbed his keys and checked his weapons. At the door, he stopped abruptly, turned back to Sage, and planted a possessively heated kiss on her lips. When he pulled back, her head was swimming.

"Don't go anywhere. Wait here."

"Stay here with Sage," Ethan said, turning to Sam. "Nate and Daniel should be back from the vet's soon. No one is to come in here. *No one.* And if Browny shows up, shoot the fucker."

"No question about it," Sam said grimly.

Ethan and Sean slammed out the door. Seconds later, tires spinning on gravel, they took off.

"What will they do when they find him?" Sage asked.

For a long time, Sam didn't answer. "You don't go against your own. Going after you is the same as going after Ethan himself. Max is one of us. Same goes. I wouldn't want to be in Jake's shoes when they find him."

———◆———

An hour later, when darkness had settled on the house like a ghostly blanket, Daniel and Nate returned. Carrying Max, Daniel walked in the door, his eyes rimmed with red, his face pale, his blue eyes flat and haunted.

"He didn't make it." Daniel's voice broke on the words. Sage hurried to drag forward the large chair from the back corner of the shop and Daniel sat upon it heavily.

Sage didn't hear the words, she felt them, a powerful fist to the stomach. For a long drawn-out moment, the silence in the room was complete.

Then Daniel took a breath, his voice thick. "Sage was right, the vet was closed. The after-hours number went to a voicemail explaining that the doctor was away for the weekend and sorry for any inconvenience."

Nobody moved. No one breathed while they absorbed the implications.

"Max fought hard to hold on though, didn't you, buddy?"

A pained cry echoed around the room, and Sage realized it came from her. It snapped her out of her shock and she moved to where Daniel was sitting with Max on his lap. She knelt down in front of them, her tears wetting Max's black and caramel fur as she sobbed brokenly.

"Thank you, Max. You were a brave, brave boy. The way you stood up to those snakes. Didn't back down even after you'd been bitten. You should have run, but you didn't."

Sage heard a faint voice and bolted up straight. Liquorice was standing at the open front door.

Give it a try, Liquorice said. *Like the bird that fell from its nest at school.*

Sage was momentarily stunned. Was it possible?

"May I have a moment with him?" Sage asked. "Can you put him down, so I can reach him better?"

Daniel tightened his hold, and made a low sound in the back of his throat. "Please?"

"Smithy, let go," Nate said, coming over and gently lifting Max from his arms. Daniel resisted for a moment, then released his grip.

"Where do you want him?" Nate asked.

Sage indicated the chair and Daniel left the room, the door slamming shut behind him.

"He's taking this hard," Nate said softly, as he placed Max on the chair. "What do you want with Max? Need to say your own goodbye?"

"He saved my life."

Nate nodded and gave her some space.

Sage knelt in front of Max and ran her fingers through his soft fur. *Don't you make me say goodbye to you.*

"Be back in a bit." Nate and Sam walked out but left the door open so she could call for them if needed.

The room silent, Sage closed her eyes and laid her cheek on Max's soft fur. Through his silky thick coat, she heard the faintest flutter of a heartbeat. Or at least she thought she did.

Come on buddy, you're a fighter. Fight for me.

Unsure of what exactly she was doing, she turned her mind off and worked on pure instinct. Just like with the little bird that had fallen from its nest at school. She closed her eyes and ran a hand across his fur in a slow rhythmic motion.

She soon forgot she was on her knees, becoming unaware of where she was. Her thoughts silenced, she entered that space beyond normal consciousness and reached out with her mind. The toxin flowed freely through Max's bloodstream, and she imagined it draining away, out through his wounds. In her dream-like state, she cleansed his body of the poison and restored his damaged vital organs.

She must have fallen asleep, because when she next opened her eyes, Max was licking her face.

She'd done it.

She *was* a healer, as Pia had said.

She looked up, and through stinging eyes saw Liquorice watching her with approval from the door.

Max enthusiastically bathed her face with his tongue.

Ugh, Liquorice said. *Dog slobber.*

Laughing, she threw her arms around Max. "Hey buddy. Welcome back. You certainly gave me a scare."

Max gave her another long lick before bouncing off the couch. On hands and knees, she rolled on the floor with him. He knocked her backward and sniffed at her ear, sending her into a fit of giggles.

Sage heard someone enter the room and Max bounded away. Still laughing, she spun to see where he was going and her gaze connected with Daniel's shocked one. He was frozen at the door, staring at her in open-mouthed astonishment.

Nate and Sam arrived, looking at her with similar expressions.

She smiled shakily. "Max's back."

Daniel lowered himself to his knees and hugged the friend he'd thought he'd lost. Silent tears traced down his cheeks while Max nudged and licked his hand.

"Sage?" Nate said, making her aware of his presence at her side. "Did you do that?"

Sage shrugged. "He wasn't dead." She abruptly felt dizzy. Drained, her body weak and achy. She closed her eyes. "Can you help me up?"

Nate gave her a hand up, then supported her over to the kitchen table.

Nate poured her a glass of water and it was then that she noticed.

Mary's diary sat next to a bowl of cleansing herbs. Nan's diary was beside it.

But the grimoire was gone.

She gasped, startling Max, who let out a low warning growl. Heart racing, she scanned the area around the table.

Fully alert, Nate sprang to attention. "What is it?"

Daniel, hand on his weapon, surveyed the room.

"Did anyone come in here?" Sage asked, checking beneath the table in case it had somehow been knocked off.

"Not that I'm aware of. Are you missing something?"

"Yes. The grimoire."

Sage's hand automatically went to her neck. Her fingers touched bare skin. The angel.

It was gone too.

Chapter Twenty-Five

Saturday Dusk

Lucky donned his hooded robe, which sheathed him from head to toe in black. On the altar, he placed a lock of Sage's hair beside the chalice filled with the virgin-child's blood, which Blood Fox had retained from performing the final sacrifice in his absence.

If Lucky had been free, he'd have chosen a baby, but the three-year-old girl the boy had managed to get was close enough. And her death was another strike against the witches. Blood Fox had done well.

Standing behind his pulpit, Lucky faced his cult. He'd chosen the seven he needed, the seven strongest in conviction. Seven, including Blood Fox. The other six had been discarded earlier. They were no longer of use.

He placed the grimoire of demonic magic on the lectern and thrust his arms out, palms downward, to call forth energy from below, not above, and opened the ritual.

Lucky summoned the master demon by invoking His name. Sytrolius was the demon of one of the four elements: the master demon of fire. There were others, but only one master demon could enter through this portal, at this time, through this prophecy. Sytrolius had his legion, and they would follow him through. When they won.

"Oh almighty Dark Master Sytrolius," Lucky began. "I invite you to join with us tonight." The congregation greeted the Dark Master, bowing with reverence as they did so.

"Use me, your humble servant, to serve your every wish and wicked desire."

Lucky reached into the chalice and flicked blood in the center of the dark circle cast specifically for the invocation ritual.

"I ask you now, give me a vision of what is to come."

Images pressed into Lucky's mind. In the vision, he saw the Angel of Light's detective walk backward, into the angry flames of the Dark Master's wings. Lucky felt his master's pleasure as flames licked at the detective's flesh, His excitement keen as He observed the man's demise. Through his master, Lucky saw the detective's death, his lungs filling with smoke as he drew his final breath.

Lucky smiled. "Dark Master of fire, I thank you for appointing me this role of guiding the dark congregation. I shall do your bidding and descend into the darkness. I require no further payment than this simple honor to serve you, Dark Master Sytrolius."

"Dark Master Sytrolius," the dark congregation repeated.

Lucky opened the grimoire of demonic magic, and turned to a page near the back. The invocation ritual. Now that the sacrifices were complete, this final ceremony committed their energy, their power, to the Dark Master.

Tomorrow night, on the blood moon, the physical bodies of Lucky and his seven acolytes would be no more. They would be at one with their dark leader and joined for eternity.

Lucky addressed the congregation. "To walk with the entities of darkness, you must first purge your heart of any light, love, and kindness. The Dark Master expects you, as your ultimate gift to him, to be cleansed of all light before you are offered. We will begin that cleansing now."

Lucky picked up his athame. The double-edged blade of the ceremonial knife gleamed. He brandished it overhead, then symbolically plunged it into the heart of the body of those who formed the circle. "I hereby renounce all that is good and holy in this world and the next. I pledge my eternal soul to the Dark Master, and become one with the darkness." The seven repeated the words.

He tossed hair from the virgin child, the seventh sacrifice, into the circle.

The Dark Master was pleased with the sacrifice of the girl. He gladly flaunted His power by taking something so close to the almighty. Where was their God now? Lucky spat on the floor in disgust. Where was God when he was needed, ever?

God certainly hadn't been there when Lucky had needed him. When his father had come into his room, held him down in the middle of the night. Hadn't been there to hear the screams, the cries, of a little boy whose daddy was hurting him.

Lucky shook his head to clear the memories.

His father had paid for what he'd done. The voices inside Lucky's head had provided the help and guidance of the Dark Master. Certainly none had come from a fluffy God preaching about love and forgiveness.

Vengeance was power.

The little girl's sacrifice was symbolic twofold. Great outrage was generated over the death of an innocent. The younger, the sweeter, the greater the vehemence. That outrage provoked violence, the demand for retribution. It turned them into the very thing they claimed to abhor. And all the while, the Dark Master fed on those wild, savage, primal emotions.

Secondly, the death of the sweet and innocent was proof that the Dark Master's power was growing. A message that no one was safe. No one was protected. After they won on Sunday, the Dark Master would be unstoppable.

The flames of the black candles grew unusually large, filling with goat heads and skulls with demon horns.

Lucky tossed hair kept from all seven sacrifices into the circle. He raised his athame to the east, performing an intricate set of moves, then repeated the same facing west.

He dipped the knife into the chalice filled with the child's blood and closed his eyes as he licked the coppery substance off the blade. He then sliced his wrist and passed the blade around the congregation for them to do the same, each slicing into their flesh to add more blood before passing it on.

Their flesh and blood bodies were insignificant when compared to what they were about to experience tomorrow night.

Lucky would facilitate the murder-suicide pact, and his and these seven souls would join with the Dark Master and be free to wander the earth without the interference and restrictions of the righteous.

An eternity spent with no rules.

An existence where no one would hurt him again.

A place where *Lucky* would be the one doing the hurting.

Lucky began to chant. He raised his hands and invited his cult to add their voices to his.

In the windowless room, the air swirled thick and dark around Lucky, blowing at his cape and whipping at his hair.

All that was needed now was to eliminate the Angel of Light. She wasn't a required sacrifice, but eliminating her would ensure that none could interfere in the Dark Master's ascension to the earthly realm. If Lucky had time, the details of her death would be at his discretion.

His pleasure.

He closed his eyes and imagined branding her right hand, the hand that receives, with the mark of the beast.

He pictured removing her eyes, the mirrors to the soul. No longer needed where the Dark Master was taking her.

The puncture wounds he'd make in her chest in the shape of a cross over the heart were Lucky's personal touch, a reminder of his heart's pain when his childhood prayers had gone unheard... unanswered.

He clutched the strands of the Angel's hair; they contained her specific energy.

That was how he'd find her.

Whether or not he had time to savor her death, one thing was certain.

The Angel must die.

Before tomorrow night. The blood moon. The demon's victory.

Lucky couldn't wait to taste her tears.

Chapter Twenty-Six

The Eagle was parked on a grassy bank a short thirty-minute flight from Cryton. Far enough away that Sage felt just out of reach of the demon's sharp claws.

Darkness had fallen, and the air was unnaturally still, the calm that came before a thunderstorm. But Sage was waiting for a different sort of storm altogether.

Liquorice had made himself comfortable on his rug, and Ethan had just set up the tent.

"This isn't the end," Ethan said, wrapping his arms around Sage from behind and pulling her back against his chest.

"Oh, Eth." Tears welled up in her eyes and she clutched his arm. "I've failed. I've lost the grimoire. The amulet. And Lucky is gone. I can't see how we can possibly succeed now. The demon has so much power. So much experience."

"Angel."

"Don't bother, Eth." She wiped at her eyes and took a deep breath. "Let's face it. It's over. Nan and Ada died for nothing."

"Damn it, Sage. We're not giving up."

"We're not?"

Thunder boomed in the distance.

"No, Angel." He kissed the top of her head. "Not a fucking chance."

Sage drew in a shaky breath. She wanted to share his confidence, she really did. But it was all so hopeless now.

Tomorrow, she was going into a battle she would surely lose.

And she was tired. So very tired.

Sage shivered. Ethan shrugged out of his leather jacket and slipped it over her shoulders. She ran her fingers over the soft worn leather, filled her lungs with his scent, his warmth.

"How is it you always know what I need without me having to say a single word?"

Ethan pressed his lips to her temple and wrapped an arm around her shoulders. "This isn't the end," he repeated softly.

Sage shrugged out of his embrace. How could he be so fucking forgiving? So calm? "Why aren't you angry with me? The blood moon is tomorrow night. We are out of time. How is this not the end?"

"Slow down, Angel. Take a breath."

Ethan lowered himself to the ground, and tugged on Sage's hand to draw her down beside him. She didn't want to sit quietly; she wanted to punch something. But her body had other ideas. Responding to his command, her knees gave way and Sage found herself on the soft grassy bank beside him. Immediately, he pulled her into his side. She let him embrace her, but she drew her knees up and rested her head on them.

"I'll get you Keyton," Ethan said. "If I don't catch up with him earlier in the day, you can rest assured he'll be around tomorrow night. It is, after all, what the demon has been waiting a hundred years for."

"True. But we don't know much about the demon's power. What he will be truly capable of when he has full strength tomorrow."

"We'll be fine. We'll find your grimoire too. Or we'll manage without it. You've been practicing. You know your rites."

"Of course I have the main one memorized—the banishment rite—but there's far more I need to remember. The preparation of the circle, for example. How to protect it, how to repel the demon if he enters. The ceremony of cleansing and preparation beforehand. I think I've memorized them all. But what if I make a mistake?"

Sage's fingers were scrabbling in the dirt, and glancing down, she saw she'd created a hole in the grass. A tiny creature ran onto her fingernail, and she carefully set it aside. "And don't forget, the grimoire itself holds power."

Sage couldn't imagine going into tomorrow night without it. Couldn't go up against the demon without it in her hands. With it, she actually believed she was the answer they thought she was. The grimoire was a tangible reminder of a history of success. Without it, she was a fraud. An ordinary girl taking on the impossible.

They'd had everything in place ready to go. Now they were back to square one without the time to begin again.

She glanced up at Ethan, who was silently staring off in the distance. He hadn't reacted at all to her summation of her difficulties heading into tomorrow night. "How are you managing to stay so calm?" Sage said grumpily.

He turned to her, amusement in his eyes. He ran a finger down her cheek, and across her lips. She nipped at his fingertip, and his eyes darkened.

"What will you have me do, Angel? Giving up is not an option. Never has been. I'll do whatever it takes to see this through, and that means making the calls at the time they're needed. Not before. Worrying won't help a thing."

"Don't you feel better if you're prepared?"

"Life rarely gives you that luxury. If it does, you can consider it a bonus. Most of the time, I go into a situation on little more than a wing and a prayer. That's particularly true when working undercover. Plus, I found something when I went back home."

"You did?" A spark flamed to life in her chest.

Ethan stood, and walked back to the Eagle. She felt the loss of his warmth immediately. In a few moments, he was back, holding a wooden box about the size of a child's shoe box.

He lowered himself down next to her.

"What's that?"

Ethan handed her the box. She didn't know what it was, but she *felt* its importance. "Ethan," she said, her voice hushed. In her hands, the box vibrated just like the grimoire did. "It's beautiful. Exquisite." The symbols carved in the wood matched those on the grimoire and her amulet. "Where did you get this?"

She turned it over in her hands, and unable to find how to open it, looked up at Ethan. He was staring at her in a way that stole her breath. Dried her mouth.

"You, Angel, are what's exquisite."

Sage's pulse quickened.

"I love it when you smile," he murmured, his voice turning husky. "When this is over, my life's purpose will be to see how often I can make you smile."

"Eth—" Leaning in, she pressed her lips to his, then managed to tear her gaze away from his heavy-lidded one and focused on the box again.

"What's inside? How do you open it?"

Ethan touched the box, closed his eyes a moment, and a series of wooden panels moved and the box unlocked, the top half opening.

As if by magic.

Sage gasped.

Inside, she saw the most magnificent combination of crystals she'd ever seen, fashioned into the shape of a wand. Their clarity and perfection rivaled anything she'd ever seen in Nan's shop. Sage withdrew the wand, the same familiar symbol embossed on the bottom of its bound leather handle.

Ethan reached inside his shirt and pulled out a pendant on a chain.

"Eth, you found it!" She turned the metal pendant over in her hands. It emitted a vibration, much like her own.

Sage searched his face, anxious to know what he felt. He'd not only found the pendant, he was wearing it. He'd also come back with a mysterious box that didn't have a lock, but could somehow open, and an incredible crystal wand.

"Pia was right. I'm the alchemist's son. And this"—he touched the wand—"is the sword of light."

"Who are you, and what have you done with my black-and-white, just-the-facts detective?"

"He's still here, Angel." He gave her a smile that made her heart skip. "But I'm just... *more* now. I'll always question. It's not in my nature to accept anything I'm told without my own investigation and verification." His lips twitched. "I just have more things to investigate now, I guess."

"Nan always told me to keep an open mind, but not so open your brains fall out."

"Good advice."

Sage held the wand in her outstretched hand, the almost-full moon casting the wand in a radiant glow. Or maybe... "That glow isn't just from the moon, is it?"

"No." Ethan took the wand from her. In his hand, the wand brightened, became iridescent.

"You have everything you need for your part. Tell me you've discovered another way to end this forever."

Instead of replying, Ethan moved her so that she was sitting between his legs. He pulled her back against his chest and wrapped his arms tightly around her.

"Your hair is tickling my face," he said, grabbing it in one handful, twirling it around and setting it to the opposite side.

"You're stalling. What have you learned?"

"Your Mary grew up on the outskirts of Cryton. Rivertown, as it was called back then. Mary had two younger sisters, and her father died shortly after the youngest was born. Her family were poor, dirt poor. The holes in her shoes didn't keep her feet clean or dry on the long walk into town and school. Rain, hail, and blistering heat, the girls traipsed over the hills to school every day."

"Wait. How do you know all this?" There were few online records Ethan couldn't access, but the story Ethan was telling sounded less like official records, and more like a personal account.

"In the back of my great-grandfather's journal, I found correspondence between him and Mary."

"Wait. What? Your *great-grandfather?*"

"If you'll stop telling me to wait, Angel, I'm bound to answer some of those questions."

"Of course. Sorry. Just tell me."

"On one of these long walks back from school, Mary met Bill, my great-grandfather. She fell in love."

"If he was anything like you, I can't blame her," Sage said, snuggling back into Ethan's arms.

"He fell in love with her too. He kept her correspondence and a small brooch he'd given her."

"Shouldn't she have had the brooch?"

Ethan let out a long breath. "My great-grandfather's family weren't the type of people a religious family like Mary's wanted to associate with. Anyway, his family were just passing through. They were constantly moving from place to place, practicing alchemy and healing people in the surrounding towns."

"Alchemy," Sage breathed.

"Seems it's in my blood."

"Then how come you didn't know?"

"I'm getting to that. Back then, alchemy was often thought of as a form of witchcraft. Associated with the Devil's work."

"Pia said that alchemy was high magic."

"It is. Bill's father was a healer. A medicine man. But his power still scared people, and small towns didn't tolerate differences well. Eventually, he'd become unwelcome and have to travel on to the next place."

"Must have been a hard life for a young boy."

"I imagine it was. Especially after he fell in love with a beautiful brown-haired girl named Mary."

"They couldn't be together?"

"Mary's mother forbid her to see Bill. And for the first time in Mary's life, she disobeyed her mother."

"What happened to them?"

"Mary's mother created a huge outcry, started the rumors of witchcraft that drove Bill's family out of town. Mary was brokenhearted. Especially as she was pregnant."

Sage placed a protective hand on her own belly. "Oh no, poor Mary."

"In desperation, Mary's mother went to the town's pastor. His son was a few years older than Mary, and the parents decided it was the perfect solution, so Mary was soon married to the pastor's son, Raymond."

"Poor Mary," Sage repeated. "To not be allowed to be with your true love. But it couldn't have been all bad. In her diary, she mentioned loving Raymond very much."

"Apparently, he was a solid man, with a good heart, and he took his responsibilities as a pastor seriously. Mary had two more children with him, and Ray brought all three up as his own."

"Poor Bill. How did he take it?"

"My great-grandfather returned to Cryton as soon as he could escape the ever-watchful eyes of his father to find Mary had wed someone else. It broke his heart. She gave him back the brooch because her new husband refused to have it in the house. Bill knew she was pregnant and that it was his, and that he could never be in his child's life."

Sage rubbed at an ache in her chest. "I can't imagine."

"He turned away from alchemy," Ethan continued. "Blamed it and his father for everything wrong with his life. He too, married much later in life, and had one son, my grandfather. I thought the fact that he kept Mary's letters all these years revealing."

"That is so sad."

"When my great-grandfather renounced alchemy, he created a strong set of views that were handed down to future generations. He wanted to protect those who came after him from the hardships he'd endured. And he'd seen the demon's power, the devastation it had caused in Cryton. He didn't want his family involved in that world anymore."

"So, you are the alchemist's son, and you're here. Everything in the grimoire is coming true."

"Strangely, yes."

"Do you remember exactly what to do?" Sage asked. Ethan had the wand and the demon's name, but she had to hope he remembered his part of the ritual without the need of the grimoire.

"I believe so, yes."

"Ethan! You are the most exasperating man I've ever met. Do you have to answer just the question? Can't you provide detail without being asked for it?"

"Possibly."

Fortunately for him, she caught his lips twitching in amusement.

Sage turned and looked up at him. Enunciated her question slowly and carefully. "Do you or do you not remember what was written in the grimoire well enough not to need it for reference?"

"I do."

"Good." She pressed her lips together, then looked away. "Eth, have you worked out what the cipher means? It's not literal, is it? Tell me it isn't."

Ethan placed the wand carefully back in its box and set it aside. "If I knew of a way to stop this forever, would you want me to take it?"

His serious tone gave her a chill. "Not if the price was your life."

"Angel, you're not even showing yet, but I've already bonded with my daughter. *Our daughter.* I don't want this to happen again in another hundred years. There are only eighty years before the demon next enters our realm. I want our children to live a life where they don't have to worry about demons. I want them to live in peace. Happiness. I want them to look back on us, and say, *they won*."

A lump formed in Sage's throat. "I want that too," she said, her heart slicing in two. "But none of that matters if I don't have you. Nothing matters at all, if we don't both make it out of this alive."

She looked over her shoulder to discover Ethan's eyes had misted, their sheen picking up the moonlight.

"I vow to you, Angel. I will do everything within my power to make sure our daughter and hers are safe."

Sage's blood turned to ice. "Ethan, no." She stood, brushing off his hands.

"Don't get angry," Ethan said, standing also.

"You *promised* me. Damn you, Ethan Blade, don't you dare break it!" She grabbed him by the shirt, and he caught her hands.

"Steady on there, tiger. I won't break my promise," he said, and she knew it was the first lie he'd ever told her.

"But I want you to consider this. What price is too much to ensure our daughter doesn't have to worry about her grandchildren having to fight the demon? I can't bear to think of her going through what we're facing now. Can you?"

Tears flooded her vision. "Damn you," she sobbed, and he cradled her in his arms. When she finally got herself under control, she peered up at him.

Moonlight highlighted strands of his hair as he leaned in and pressed his lips gently to hers. The tenderness in the gesture stole her breath. He'd promised. Ethan would work out another way. She had to believe that.

He traced her lips, his eyes following the trail of his fingers. He then traced a path down her neck across her collarbone and over the lace at the top of her bra. She sucked in her breath. Started to speak.

"Shh. Can we not talk about this anymore tonight? Tomorrow will come soon enough. Let me enjoy this moment with you. Let me—let *us*—have tonight."

Tomorrow was already approaching fast, and nothing they did or said tonight would change that.

She wanted to forget, even if only for a brief moment. Tonight, there was just the two of them. No demon, no prophecy. She wasn't going to waste a single second.

Ethan moved his hand inside her shirt and cupped her breast.

The sensation as he brushed a thumb over her nipple sent waves of pleasure washing over her.

His expression changed from serious to playful, and using one hand at his neckline, he took off his T-shirt. His bare chest stole what was left of her mind, scattered her thoughts across the grass like marbles.

She was gone. It didn't matter what he asked, her response would be *yes*.

He spread his shirt out behind her and laid her back.

Sage sighed. "This is why I love you so much."

"Oh? Why is that, Angel?"

"You have a steaming hot body."

"That so?" He rested one elbow on either side of her, his breath warm on her mouth. "Not because of my potential demon-fighting capabilities?"

"Uh-uh," she said, shaking her head.

"What about for my mad flying skills?"

"Nope. Just your body."

"Well, then," he said, in a low, lazy voice that screamed pure sex, "good thing I also know how to use it. Want me to show you?"

Sage tried for a nonchalant shrug. "Whatever."

His chuckle reached her ears just before his lips covered her breast. Her nipple hardened in his warm mouth and her mind went blank to everything but the pleasure only he could give her.

———— ◆ ————

Ethan made love to Sage softly. Tenderly. Slowly. He looked deep into her eyes as she lay beneath him, her legs locked around his waist. There were no passionate screams, no bucking hips, no shouts of ecstasy.

Their lovemaking was about connection. Being close was not enough; they had to become one. He stayed joined with her, inside her, pausing only when silent tears rolled down her cheeks and she turned away. Gently taking her chin in his hand, he turned her face so that her green eyes were looking into his.

He kissed away her tears, pressed his lips to her lids, closed his mouth gently over hers. Then he continued his rhythmic slide into her body.

They didn't speak. What could they say? Words were superfluous. Her tears were clearly an overwhelming rise of emotion too powerful to remain trapped inside.

He recognized that, because her feelings mirrored his own.

Later that night, Sage dozed lightly in Ethan's arms. He drew in a breath and silently watched her sleep.

He could scarcely fathom how much Sage meant to him, how quickly she'd become his everything. His life had always been about righting wrongs. Catching the bad guys. Keeping the world safe for the decent folk. Taking a drug dealer off the streets might keep little Tommy from taking his first hit of crack, but busting a drug syndicate might save a hundred Tommys. He'd rather save the hundred Tommys. Spare a hundred mothers the devastation of watching the ruination of their children.

He'd spent his whole life content with the satisfaction he received from the happiness he gave others. Never had he wanted or needed more. Never had he even considered his own happiness.

Until Sage.

Since meeting her, everything he thought about life had been turned upside down. These last few weeks had challenged him. For once, he couldn't protect someone. Not in the traditional way anyway. Not in the way he'd been trained.

But he had discovered there was another way to protect her. It meant letting go of everything he'd ever believed, everything he'd ever known, and embracing a fact about himself that sounded crazy.

She was worth it.

Sage was about to go head to head with the greatest evil he'd ever encountered. And nestled inside her soft, warm belly was a child.

His child.

Something tangible created out of their love. Sage had already become his life. His everything. Now that he'd tasted love, he couldn't go on without it.

When your life is empty, you don't know any different. Ignorance is bliss, as the expression goes. But now he'd seen the other side; the veil had been lifted. He'd felt how life could be. Should be.

He'd thought he loved Sage an impossible amount. But now that she was carrying their child, that love had expanded.

Hell, it had felled him to his knees.

He'd always balanced extreme risk with an innate sense of self preservation. Now his own life paled in significance to those of Sage and his unborn child.

Sage made a soft sound and tossed fitfully in his arms. He held her tighter. As exhausted as he was, he didn't close his eyes. He wouldn't let sleep rob him of one second of her.

"I love you," he whispered, kissing her golden locks. What an understatement. He more than loved her.

He worshipped her.

His eyes stung, and he blinked back tears that were hot and bitter. Tears he'd never show to her. He didn't want her to think he regretted what he had to do.

He'd wondered if he could do it, but his conversation with Sage tonight had confirmed it.

He'd give his life for her, for his unborn child.

Was this then, their last night together?

He closed his eyes and inhaled each breath she exhaled. If he was leaving, he was taking a part of her with him.

Chapter Twenty-Seven

Sunday
The Morning of the Blood Moon

The sun was creeping above the horizon. Sage's wavy blonde hair was messily tied back and full of tangles, and she was nibbling on what was left of her nails. They'd been perfectly manicured when Ethan had first met her.

She was deep in thought, and he resisted a powerful urge to go to her, to feel her body flush against his, to feel her soft skin beneath his fingertips. She was gathering her strength. Perhaps even having a conversation with a higher power.

Today, one way or another, this ends.

She turned and looked at him then, and for a moment time stood still. Their gazes met and locked, the electrical current that sparked and crackled between them as tangible as a summer storm. She smiled softly, her bottom lip trembling slightly before she clenched it between her teeth.

The gesture stole his breath, and his chest ached. A choked sound rose from somewhere deep inside him, and she ran to him, throwing herself into his arms. He caught her easily and held on for dear life. It was all he could do.

It was everything he could do.

———◆———

Sage helped secure Liquorice into a pet carrier in the back of the Eagle.

"It's better for you this way," she reassured him. "It's going to be a very bumpy ride into town." Sage loved her kitty but didn't relish his claws digging into her for purchase. Plus, what if the turbulence knocked him out of her arms? The last thing any of them needed was for him to go flying around the cabin and getting hurt.

Liquorice meowed unhappily and licked her fingers through the wire, but he eventually settled down on his blanket. When he was safe, she moved a distance away and stared briefly across the landscape while Ethan did his preflight checks.

The rolling hills were quiet, the only movement a flock of birds that flew from a tree and circled in the sky, before coming to land in a different tree. Spring flowers turned their faces to the rising sun. The day felt promising. It certainly didn't feel like the end of anything.

Ethan came up behind her, crushed her tight against his chest. Like hers, his heart was beating way too fast.

She clung to him. Absorbing his warmth. His strength. Then pulled back. "You look after yourself tonight," she said, fingering the symbol on the cool round pendant. "It suits you." She released the pendant, and it came to rest against his tanned chest.

"You suit me more."

A lump formed in her throat. She could barely look at him.

"When this is over," Ethan said, his voice growing thick, "I'll take you on a holiday."

"Yeah?" She tried to smile. "Where to?"

"Oh, I think an island off the coast of Mauritius."

"Sounds nice," Sage murmured, pressing her lips against his neck. "You know, I've never been outside Australia."

"It's a big world out there. I'm going to be honored to be the one who gets to show it to you." Her eyes met his. A lock of his hair danced in the breeze, and she reached out, tucking it behind his ear. "Ready?" he asked.

She wasn't, but it was her turn to lie to him.

"Ready."

———— ◆ ————

"Eth! Are you sure the Eagle can handle this?" Sage asked as the bird dropped several heart-stopping meters in a single second. Ethan fought with the controls, his lips pressed tightly together, and the bird climbed back to a safe altitude. Liquorice yowled in his cage, and Sage sent him reassuring messages, pressing them firmly into his mind.

Ethan was flying blind. The gauges were useless, their needles spinning randomly. The inter-cabin headsets had also been rendered impotent. The town was just up ahead, the Eagle struggling through the electromagnetic field that had surrounded Cryton.

The dark, eerie mass casting its shroud over the town was clearly visible from their vantage point. Sage's blood raced hard and furious past her ears.

The closer they got to the strange darkness, the more the helicopter's engine screamed in protest. Sage held on, put everything she had into casting a cocoon of protection around them.

Ethan tightened his grip on the controls. "We'll make it," he shouted. "The risk is necessary to get you in."

You? The plan was for *both* of them to get into town. "What about you?" Sage yelled over the straining engine.

"Change of plan. It's too dangerous for me to land. The bird could tip. I'm going to drop you down and head in by foot."

He was right. The Eagle was being tossed around like an inflatable raft in high seas.

Still, she worried about them separating. In only a few short hours, they needed to do this. Needed to both be fully present and prepared, ready to confront the demon himself. The bird lurched forward and Sage's head snapped back on the seat, sending streaks of pain down her neck.

She took a deep breath, held her focus on the layer of protection she'd cast, and calmly asked, "How will you get back in?" Through heavy rolls of mist thick as smoke, Sage could see the roads into town blocked by cars and men in uniforms.

"Ian promised me they wouldn't move in until 0600 Monday morning, and only if this isn't over by then." Ethan shouted over the engine's roar.

"They seem to be pretty organized already."

"Ian knows about the prophecy, and the blood moon. His grandfather worked the case last time. He knows what we're up against. He'll be fully prepared, ready to move in at a minute's notice. I just have to hope he doesn't jump the gun." Sage was sure Ethan was more concerned than he was making out, but she didn't challenge him. She had to trust that he was prepared to deal with both the government task force and the demon at the same time.

Aside from the action she could see at the outside road block, the barricade closest to town consisted of heavily armored vehicles, and armed men were visible and in position.

They looked ready to charge in any second.

"Are you sure they'll wait? Have you seen down there? They look pretty active for men who've been informed to sit tight."

"Don't have to see them," came his terse reply. "I know how they work. Ian said I had until 0600 tomorrow morning. They are here as contingency only." Sage saw his jaw clench and heard the unspoken words, *I hope.*

The turbulence was ferocious now, the metal frame of the Eagle making disturbing noises, like the haunting moans the Titanic made as it went down.

The oval was now in sight. She didn't want to separate from him at this late hour, but there was no choice.

"Ready?" Ethan asked, fighting to keep the bird steady. They were some distance from the ground, but he was unwilling to risk getting any lower.

"I'm going to lower you and Liquorice down now. Do exactly as we planned. If the time comes, start without me. Nate will already be there; fill him in on the changes to the plan." She strapped on the harness and secured Liquorice's cage to it. "Stay with Nate until I get back to you. Don't leave his side for a single second. Promise me."

Sage nodded. Her pulse was thudding hard and fast in her throat, making it difficult to speak.

"I'll be with you soon. Nothing can keep me from you." Ethan's words were like bullets; they penetrated her chest and embedded directly in her heart. His expression was fierce. Without him having to say more, she understood the lengths he would go to reach her.

She knew, because she'd do the same for him.

The words, "Be careful," rose and died on her tongue. The warning was inadequate. She had to believe he'd make it back to her. Safe. She needed him with every fiber of her being. Not just for this, but for herself.

"Angel?" The fire in his eyes burned into her. "Don't look so worried. You'll be fine. We'll be fine. You'll do great tonight."

Sage nodded, blinked a few times to clear her stinging eyes.

The oval was directly beneath them now. Time to go.

Sage stood and stumbled, struggling to find purchase in the lurching bird.

Ethan thrust his arm out, and she grabbed on, using his iron hold for stability while she awaited his signal to jump. With the helicopter jerking so violently, her landing was going to be rough.

"You can do this, Angel." As she looked up, she was hit physically by Ethan's dark stormy gaze, so powerful she froze. His features were hard lines in granite, the muscles along his jaw twitching as he clenched his teeth. The air outside the chopper reacted. She imagined she heard the demon's growl of disapproval.

And Sage knew. This bond between them was their greatest weapon against him.

Ethan's grip on her wrist was powerfully tight, but she relished the pain, the physical proof of their connection. Using his forearm and elbows on the control, he freed his hands just long enough to slide the tangle of his black leather band from his wrist. As the Eagle dropped threateningly, he slipped it onto hers.

"This is not goodbye, Ethan Blade," she said fiercely, slipping then regaining her balance.

His expression hardened. "It will never be goodbye for us. Never. We will never be over."

Her eyes burned, and she blinked hard, refusing to blur her vision of him.

A shout from the ground broke the moment.

Nate was in position as Ethan had pre-arranged the night before. He was supposed to pick them both up, but now it would be only Sage.

Sage lowered her eyes to his lips as he spoke. She wanted to kiss him goodbye so desperately. But it was impossible in the lurching bird. It didn't stop her from craving the taste of his lips one last time.

No, not one last time.

Ethan could get back in past the barriers. He'd find the weak link in the chain and come back to her. She kissed her fingertips then pressed them against his soft full mouth instead.

"I love you." Even though she whispered the words, she knew he heard them. She heard his reply even though his lips didn't move.

Sage gripped Liquorice's cage tight in her arms as Ethan lowered them to the ground. Liquorice growled, and she felt the demon's presence close by. *He'd* been watching. Waiting.

A vile stench polluted the air. She sensed his anticipation, his excitement, and steeled herself for the night ahead.

———◆———

It had all but killed Ethan to leave her. Had there been another option, he would have taken it. But Sage's safety had to come first. With a great deal of struggle, Ethan only just managed to land the Eagle in a paddock on the outskirts of town. Even though he'd been outside the visible dark energy zone, he'd struggled to set the chopper down without crashing. The demon's power must be extending farther outside Cryton.

But Ethan refused to die before the confrontation had even begun.

He refused to break his promise to Sage.

He pushed his sunglasses up on his head. The day had turned dark, the sun disappearing behind manufactured clouds. With grim determination, Ethan strapped himself into full kit. Firearm on his hip, another in an ankle holster, knives, cuffs, Maglite. Beneath his shirt, he wore his Kevlar. The government had brought in a full task force. They weren't playing.

Every entry and exit point to town was covered.

Ethan would rather get back into town without coming into contact with any of them. He didn't want to draw attention to himself. Didn't want to give Ian a chance to change his mind. Or whoever was calling the shots above him. Better they thought he was still in Cryton. Knowing Taipan were in town was perhaps the only thing forcing them to keep their word.

A chain, he thought. The boundary was just a chain. All he had to do was find the weakest link.

———◆———

Sage watched the Eagle shudder out of sight. She'd done her best to maintain the protection she'd placed around the struggling machine, but she had no way to know if it had been effective at a distance. She had to trust Ethan would be safe and could somehow make it back to her in time.

Nate tugged at her elbow, urging her off the open and exposed oval into the safety of his vehicle.

"He'll be fine," Nate said, answering her unspoken question. But as she looked at him, his expression was as serious as she'd ever seen it. Her stomach twisted

She let Liquorice out of the cage and he hopped up onto her lap. Nate started the engine and headed in the direction of the shop.

"You think he can get back in?"

"If anyone can, it's Blade."

It wasn't much of an answer, but Nate wouldn't lie to her. It was as much reassurance as either of them could hold onto.

———— ◆ ————

Ethan took a direct line through the thick bush toward town. He had one dirt road to cross before he was back under the cover of the trees. In his desperation to get across the border, to find Lucky and get to Sage in time, Ethan didn't spend the time he needed to scope the area.

He used his visual clues only. The area appearing all clear, he took the chance and bolted across the road.

As he reached the other side, six cops in riot-squad gear appeared from within the bushes, tackled him, and took him down. A palm was on the back of his head, pushing it into the ground. He spat out a mixture of blood and dirt.

One of them spoke. "It's over, Blade. Stop fighting."

Like fuck. It took three of them to bring him to his feet: one on either side and one holding his arms behind his back.

"Let. Me. Go."

"It's over," the one on his right repeated. "This is no longer your case. You have no authority here."

"Like hell it isn't. This is my case until 0600 Monday, and I need to get into town." Ethan bit back hard on his frustration. "You can verify this. Get Chief Superintendent Ian Hallow on the phone."

"Our orders come from higher than him," said the one on his left.

"I have until 0600 tomorrow," Ethan bit out. "Let me go."

"No use crying about it," the one on his right said. "Our orders are if we see you, we're to bring you in. You've gone rogue, Blade."

"Fuck you." Ethan seethed in frustration. There was no one he could call if the orders were from over Ian's head. He was on his own.

Wrenching himself free, he held his hands out in front of him. "Come on. You know who I am. I'm a cop, for fuck's sake. You're not cuffing my hands behind my back."

The leader hesitated, then did as Blade requested.

Two of them man-handled him over to the waiting squad car. As one opened the door, Ethan looked back at the town, at the barricade of police vehicles, marked and unmarked, the flashing blue and red lights, a siren sounding in the distance.

The riot squad were getting into position, batons drawn behind a wall of shields. Now that they had Ethan, all bets would be off. He struggled against his restraints, spat some more blood.

"Get in the car," one of the cops growled. A rough hand on the back of his head pushed him down and into the back seat. He relaxed, gave the impression of being cooperative, and the three cops began walking back to the barricade, one moving to the driver's side.

The last cop shut the door, and Ethan stuck his leg out, wincing as the metal hit his shin. The door bounced back, and he took the split second of confusion to exit the car. He brought his cuffed hands down on the cop's head, and as the officer slid to the ground, Ethan bolted into the bush.

He stopped running after a couple of kilometers, zigzagging and doubling back and circling around to confuse his scent in case they used the dogs. The only way they'd find him now was by accident. He lowered himself to the ground, and digging into his pocket found his handcuff key and released himself. He tossed the cuffs and pulled out his radio.

Nothing but static. He swore.

How the fuck was he going to get back to Sage? He needed to get in. Find Keyton and bring him to the circle. If he didn't get back in, Sage would fail.

That was not an option.

He was planning another attempt to get through when he heard the blade chop of a helicopter overhead and saw the familiar black bird circling in the sky. He felt the first surge of hope all day. One of his unit must have found the Eagle and come searching for him. Perhaps Nate had heard his arrest over the airwaves and triggered the alarm.

At just the right time, Ethan stepped into sight. He knew he'd been seen because the Eagle turned abruptly, veering off to the side. Knowing the pilot was finding an appropriate spot to land, Ethan took off in that direction.

The blades kicked dust in his eyes and he kept his head low. He placed his boot on the step, about to haul himself in, when he looked up at the pilot and heat surged through his veins.

Jake!

"What the fuck are you doing here?"

"Get in."

Ethan hesitated, scanned Jake's face, unable to sense anything but his former mate. And for a moment it felt as though nothing had ever changed. That the last few days had never happened.

"Goddamn it, Blade. I'm fucking sorry. Get in."

Can I trust him?

Over his shoulder, Ethan heard shouts and hurried footsteps coming his way. He'd been seen. He was out of time.

Ethan leapt inside the helicopter, and the Eagle took off in a hail of gunfire. Strapping himself in, Ethan prayed that they wouldn't be shot down.

Jake had mad flying skills, and they banked hard and out of the line of fire.

"What the hell happened to you?" Ethan asked as they circled back toward Cryton. The closer they drew to town, the worse the turbulence got.

"You won't be able to land in town," Ethan shouted over the engine noise. "You'll have to drop me at the oval."

"Roger that."

"Well? What the fuck happened to you?"

Jake's jaw clenched. "I don't know."

Ethan faced him full on, eyes narrowing. Jake's expression was hard, but pained. "As I said, I don't know. I remember being damned angry. Filled with rage and hate. I hated everyone and everything. Especially Sage." The Eagle bucked and Jake cursed. The turbulence was even wilder than when Ethan had let Sage down this morning.

Jake flicked his eyes Ethan's way and winced. "I know it doesn't make fucking sense. I thought I'd lost my goddamned mind. I'd zoned out, like I'd taken drugs, had a bad trip or something. Then I found the Eagle, and as soon as I got inside, felt the controls in my hands, it was like a veil lifted. I remembered who I was, who you all were. I felt like myself again. The last two days are a fog, but I remember enough of it."

"Do you?" Ethan snapped.

"I'm pissed as hell at what I did," Jake continued, his voice rough. "But I was... overcome. The voices in my head—"

The bird dipped wildly, and Jake clenched the controls before he straightened it again. "You have no idea what was going on in my mind. It was fucking scary. I'd turned into the most evil criminal I'd ever encountered."

"You almost killed Max."

"I did?" Jake said, genuinely horrified. "How?"

"He took the snake bites meant for Sage."

"Goddamn." Jake let out a string of curses. "I remember the snakes."

Ethan had had a taste of the demon's power. He knew what it could do. How strong it was.

"The strange thing was though," Jake continued, "I was still in there somewhere. Me, I mean. The person *I* am. I just couldn't stop the horror. I can tell you something though. I never would have let it continue. If I didn't return when I did, I'd have taken my life."

Ethan looked at him sharply. Suicide was something he'd never thought he'd hear contemplated by any member of his team. They'd been trained to withstand torture, without breaking. A comment like that was disturbing.

"After I came to, I sat for the longest time with the Eagle's controls in my hand, my mouth over the end of my gun. The slightest hint it was back, I'd have blown my head off. I still don't know if it will come back though. Don't trust me."

Ethan couldn't hold on to his anger. Every word Jake spoke carried the ring of truth, tinged with grief and regret for what had happened. That he was responsible for it. His pride would never heal. Realizing what he'd done would have cut him up more than anything Taipan could have done to him. Loyalty was everything. For all of them. But no one would have taken it harder than Jake.

Had the demon somehow known that? Was that why Jake was his first choice of victim? Ethan couldn't think of anything that could destroy a strong man more.

"Forget it," Ethan said. "We've got bigger issues to worry about right now." The Eagle pitched and lurched. "When this is over, we'll ask Pia how to cleanse you properly. Make sure the demon can't come back. She did it with Collins."

"I can't trust myself," Jake said sadly. "You can't trust me either. None of the team can."

"We'll see you right," Ethan said. "Move on."

"Don't *trust* me," Jake repeated with vehemence. The bird plunged a stomach-tightening distance. "Trust is like a drinking glass. Once it's broken, it will never be the same again. You can put it back together, but you'll always be wondering if it will leak. I'd rather die than be the weak link in Taipan."

"Fuck, Browny," Ethan growled over the roar of the motor. "This case is distinctly unparalleled, and incomparable to anything that has come before or will come after. It could have happened to any one of us."

"But it didn't. It happened to *me*."

And that was the sticking point. For Jake, who had saved Ethan's life and had his back on too many occasions to count, his very identity hinged on the fundamentals of strength, honor, and loyalty to his unit. If he failed in that, he failed the core of his self.

The oval came into sight.

"You'll find Sage's bag behind your seat," Jake said.

Ethan reached around, grabbed the bag, and opened it. Money, phone, keys, and there at the bottom... the grimoire with Sage's angel amulet wrapped around the cover.

Hope surged through him.

Now all he needed to do was find Lucky, and he already had a plan on how to do that.

Could he trust Jake to help him? Ethan glanced at his long-time friend fighting the controls. Yes, the old Jake was back. The real Jake. Otherwise, why would he have given him the grimoire? Why would he be taking Ethan back into town? Surely if he were still possessed by the demon, he would be making sure Ethan and the grimoire were as far away from the circle as possible, assuring their failure.

There'd be a time in the future for more conversation. A conversation that would include the other members of Taipan. Ethan wasn't the only one Jake would be answering to. Besides, Ethan didn't have time to kick his ass. There'd be time enough for that later.

"I don't blame you," Ethan said. Any of them could have fallen victim to the demon. Looking back, Ethan could see the demon had been chipping away at them while they were in the house. *His house.* Ethan himself was as much to blame as anyone. Jake wouldn't have even come in contact with the demon had it not been for Ethan's buying a house where ancient evil still resided.

Jake didn't reply.

Despite the extensive training required to become part of the most elite special-operations unit there was, avoiding demonic possession was not covered. Still, Ethan knew no punishment would be enough in Jake's eyes. Somehow he'd have to get Jake to forgive himself.

Approaching the town, the turbulence hit hard, tossing the chopper around like a cork on a stormy sea. Just like Ethan had this morning, with the instruments not working, Jake was flying by visual cues alone. As the town came into view, so did a hazy mist-like fog. It wrapped around the chopper, obscuring their vision.

"Fuck," Ethan swore.

"That's far enough. Drop me here," Ethan said. "I'm inside the boundary. I'll go the rest of the way in by foot."

In between the thickening gray clouds, Ethan caught glimpses of the ground below him. They'd flown over the police barricade surrounding the town. They cops were in position, geared up. Awaiting an order.

"You don't have time," Jake said. It was uncharacteristic of Jake to argue when given a direct order, and Ethan assessed him carefully.

Jake glanced at him, and a look of pain washed over his features. "You've got to get to Sage." His voice was empty. Hollow.

"We can't see a thing. It's too dangerous," Ethan said, holding on to the steel bar above the door.

What appeared as smoky fog was actually gray clouds of something Ethan guessed was similar to static electricity. Every time they hit one of the clouds, the chopper lurched violently. The frequencies inside the clouds wreaked havoc on the Eagle, so much so that Ethan expected the engine to cut out like the equipment. The situation couldn't be more critical.

Preparing for his descent, Ethan strapped himself into the harness.

"This is far enough," he shouted over the noise.

Jake wrestled with the controls, his face fixed in steely determination as he held course. Arguing now would be a waste of time. Jake had made up his mind. They were all the same, his team. Jake was committed to his mission and nothing would deter him.

The motor whined sickeningly, and the bird tipped dangerously to one side.

The ground came closer as Jake shouted, "Now!"

Ethan glanced at Jake before he jumped, just long enough to see Jake give him the unit sign and touch his fist to his chest.

Ethan returned the sign, slid down the rope, and jumped the last few meters to the ground. The landing was hard, the impact jarring his already injured leg. He cursed and unclipped the harness, then signaled to the sky.

The bird, waiting for the sign, banked a hard left and took off. Out of nowhere, a large gray cloud surrounded the bird. Ethan caught glimpses of black, rotating blades, then there was a god-awful noise as the bird took a hard left, then dropped right out of the sky.

A second passed.

Two.

An explosion rocked the air, flames bursting up from the ground. A column of thick black smoke spiraled into the sky.

Ethan was momentarily paralyzed. Of course, Jake had been fully aware of the risks when he'd flown so close to town. He'd been trying to right a wrong. His life was his team. Taipan. And he'd failed them.

To a proud man like Jake, giving his life for them would be the only way possible to prove his loyalty beyond doubt.

It was his atonement.

What he didn't realize, was that by doing what he had done, he'd given the demon another victory.

Fixed on the flames from the explosion, Ethan's eyes misted. "You were a damn good man, Browny. Always."

Then Ethan roared into the sky, releasing his anger, his aggression into the soupy clouds.

"You'll pay for this, Sytrolius, you son of a bitch. I'll take great pleasure in sending you back to Hell."

With Sage's bag safely stowed across his shoulder, Ethan set off to do just that.

Chapter Twenty-Eight

The Blood Moon

T
he strange gloom that had descended across Cryton could almost be confused with being overcast, simple low-lying clouds, except for the way it affected the human body. The electromagnetic field Sage had traveled through on the helicopter ride in was alive and tingling with an unseen vibration that rolled through her cells and set her pulse racing.

Somewhere behind the unsettling murkiness was the moon. Full... and blood red.

Where is Ethan?

Anxiety rode Sage hard. She hadn't wanted to even consider that Ethan wouldn't be here with her at this time.

"He'll be here," Nate said, as though reading her thoughts, or because he'd been reassuring her repeatedly this last hour.

They had just left Beyond the Grave where Sage had everything fully prepared for tonight. Pia and Mark were there with Joyce, Pat, and Mona. Even without the grimoire, Sage believed she had a good chance. They'd been going through the rites all afternoon, and everyone was in good spirits.

Sage had insisted Nate take her for a drive to search for Ethan in town. He'd argued, she'd given him points for just how much, but in the end he'd thrown his hands in the air and agreed. She'd counted on the fact that Nate was worried for his partner, and it went against the grain for him to not actively do something to help his mate. Her nerves were making her jumpy, and she needed to get out of the confines of the shop.

"The guys are already out searching," Nate grumbled, driving the dirt roads around the back of town. Of course they were. But what if the demon had Ethan pinned against a wall again like last time? What use would the elite of the South Australian police force be then?

He'd need her.

"What if Jake got to him?"

Nate sighed. "Sage, we've been over all this. Blade can handle himself. If he'd run across Browny, he'd have used... encouragement to get him to tell him where Lucky might be."

Sage hissed as the nail she'd been chewing began to bleed. "Then where is he, Nate?'

"He'll be here. And he'll have Lucky."

"How can you be so sure?"

"Because I know Blade. You need not only him, but Keyton. He'll be using every minute available to ensure you have him." Nate flicked a glance in her direction. "You need Keyton, right? The ritual won't work without him?"

"No." Sage started on another nail.

"Then that's what Blade's doing. We heard over the scanners that he got away. That's no small thing. He'll be there." Nate repeated his words. "He'll be there."

But Nate's jaw was set, and his eyes, which normally held a hint of easygoing amusement, were creased into narrow slits. He was just as worried as she was.

They stopped when they reached the main street, but they didn't drive down it. Partly because it was filled with half the residents of town, but mostly because they were stunned by what they were witnessing. They'd heard Taipan describe what was happening in the street, but it was another thing entirely seeing it.

Feeling it.

Anger, hatred, pure unadulterated evil permeated the area. The riot squad, their shields and batons drawn, were at either end of the street, blocking off the town, but not doing anything other than observing, and likely reporting, to someone. For now.

Bonfires had been lit, and people were throwing wood on them from the back of a Holden Ute. From the open bed at the rear of the vehicle, deck chairs were dragged out, cans of beer were yanked from open cartons, and unopened cartons were used as seats. Sparks shot up into the air as more and more stumps were thrown onto the already raging fires.

Sage opened her window. The stench of vomit and rotten eggs turned her stomach and she quickly closed it.

AC/DC's "Highway to Hell" was pumping through huge speakers on the back of a car at full volume, the vibrations pounding through Nate's 4WD and reverberating in Sage's chest. She usually loved AC/DC. Who didn't? But tonight, the lyrics carried a different meaning. The group of tradesmen in front of them, none of whom Sage recognized, shouted the words as though they were literal. And perhaps they were, Sage thought, taking it all in.

At first glance, it looked like any wild party. Perhaps a full-moon street party that, fueled by alcohol, had become unruly and out of control. But looking beneath the surface, at the details, that's what sent a chill down her spine.

The partiers were close to one another, too close, brushing up against each other, and the fights that broke out were seemingly random. Not aggression fueled by a wrong word taken as an insult. But rather people hurting each other for the sheer enjoyment of inflicting pain. Sage watched a guy smash his fist into someone's face and then turn and do the exact same thing to someone on his left. It didn't seem to matter who it was, as long as he was punching someone.

One man stabbed, for no apparent reason, the guy on his right in the stomach with a blade, and the guy who was stabbed, blood running down his legs, held up his blood-covered hand and laughed. Another man hefted a large chunk of wood overhead and brought it down on the skull of the man beside him, who crumpled to the ground, blood and brain matter oozing over his neck and onto his shirt.

And all the while, the music pounded and people danced and attacked each other. It was a quagmire of the most depraved, extreme violence imaginable. Untamed death danced wild and free. Was Jake in there too?

The group of people directly in their line of sight moved to the left. Behind where they'd been was a circle of naked men and women of all shapes and sizes, holding hands and chanting. Sage strained to hear the words over the heavy beat of the rap song that now blared out of the speakers, but whatever they were doing was causing the fire they circled around to emit a strange smoke that wound high in the sky, forming animal shapes and faces with horns and pointed tongues. The sight was as mesmerizing as it was terrifying.

"Let's go," Nate said, starting the engine. "It's too dangerous for you to be here."

"Wait," Sage said. "What if Ethan's in that crowd somewhere?"

Nate hesitated, his throat working as his hand clenched the steering wheel, clearly torn between wanting to get out and check and wanting to leave. "The guys are already out there," Nate said, referring to Taipan. "If Blade is there, they'll find him."

But what if they can't help him?

A child's scream rose above the thumping music, a scream of agony that turned into a chilling, girlish laugh.

A solidly built man with a shaved head walked past their vehicle. Sage guessed him to be somewhere in his mid-forties or even fifties. His eyes had that slightly unfocused, glazed look that she'd seen in Mark's at the cabin that night, the same look that she'd seen on Dougie and Jake. The same look Sage would no doubt find in the eyes of most of the crowd in the street tonight, were she close enough to see. The man paused, briefly turning in their direction, and through his unbuttoned flannel shirt something written in red, possibly blood, was visible across his chest. *I love Satan.*

"Idiot," Nate murmured, shaking his head. The irony of that statement was obviously lost on the shave-headed man. Love was the opposite of what

Satan represented. But the man's intention was clear, and that, coupled with the man's energy as he snarled through the windscreen at them, made Sage's stomach twist. She glared at him, a not-so-polite message to stay away loud in her mind. His eyes widened and his nostrils flared as though he'd actually heard her warning. He stumbled a bit, almost falling, before continuing his drunken ramble down the street. Whether it was in fact alcohol, or merely the energy he'd been possessed with, causing the stagger, Sage was unsure.

An old lady, wearing a blue floral dress, Ugg boots, and a navy cardigan came into view. She walked out from behind the butcher shop, through the thick wad of revelers, to the circle. She was carrying something brown and fluffy in her arms. Recognizing the woman and her Pekinese dog, Sage opened the door, but was immediately restrained by Nate's firm hand on her arm.

"What the hell do you think you're doing?"

"That's Louise Baker. Ken Baker from the hardware store's wife. Ken was killed a couple of days ago, remember?"

"Of course I remember Louise. I interviewed her about Ken's murder," Nate said. "But that's not what I meant, and you know it. You're not getting out, so close your door."

"But... I just want to talk to her. Find out what she's doing out here." Of course Sage knew what was happening to the town; she'd read Mary's account from a hundred years ago. But she wanted to speak to someone to get a personal take on the situation. Was this a seemingly random mob gone crazy, everyone out having a free-for-all, fueled by a dark energy that provoked anger, evil, and violence? Or did they believe they were doing something specific, working for some type of cause? Was it organized anarchy? And if so, was the leader Lucky? Louise might know where they could find him.

"Perhaps she's seen Ethan?" Sage suggested. "Or knows where Lucky is?"

"Sage," Nate said in that *don't argue with the cop* tone. He didn't release his grip on her arm until she'd shut the door.

"Damn it, Nate," Sage complained. Then her mouth dropped open in shock. "Oh my God! Did you just see that?" She blinked, then blinked again.

Louise Baker had thrown her beloved Scruffy onto the fire. The light was dim; perhaps Sage was mistaken? But the pained howls of the dog as it was consumed by the flames confirmed it.

Sage opened the door just in time to lose the contents of her stomach on the ground.

Dear God, was this what would be left of the town if she failed tonight? There were only a couple hours before midnight, and she still didn't know where Ethan was.

Still didn't have the grimoire, the amulet, or Lucky.

Sage's chances at succeeding with her inexperienced group of witches and without the things she needed were slim to none. At the rate things were going, the town would be devastated by the time the portal opened, much less when it closed.

"When the moon turns to blood, the doorway opens. A portal allows travel in both directions. For sixty minutes, no more, no less."

Sixty minutes the portal was open. She had sixty minutes to perform the ritual, the banishment rite that would send the entities infecting the town back to Hell.

If she failed, these crazed beings were what would be left of Cryton. And even if the townspeople survived the ritual, how long would they survive after? If they didn't kill each other, the government certainly would after seeing this.

And if she failed, the government men would be infected too. And they were heavily armed.

Sage dry-heaved again and leaned out the door, but there was nothing left in her besides bile.

Nate grabbed her shirt and hauled her roughly back into the car. "Goddamn it, Sage. Shut the door."

Sage glared at him, the way he kept barking at her beginning to grate on her nerves. She opened her mouth to tell him so, when something hit the roof of their car with a thud.

Instantly alert, Sage sat up straight.

There was another thud, then another. Sage peered out the window to see black objects slamming into the ground around them. Birds. Dead crows were falling from the sky to litter the ground.

"What the fuck?" Nate demanded, reversing the vehicle back the way they'd come. The Land Rover hit something solid. Sage looked over her shoulder, but was unable to see what they'd hit. The impact was as solid as if they'd hit a tree. Nate moved forward, then threw the vehicle into reverse. Again they hit an invisible wall, the tires spinning uselessly, unable to find traction.

All at once, they were swarmed by hooded figures in long black capes, pounding the vehicle with weapons and rocks. The 4WD jerked wildly and lowered several inches. They'd slashed the tires. Someone smashed her window in, and Sage covered her face as a spray of glass rained on her.

"Stay in here!" Nate had drawn his weapon and was out of the car before she could blink. "Freeze!" he ordered, aiming at two shadows directly in front of him. Without needing to shoot, he had one hooded figure over the bonnet of the car and cuffed, and sent another sprawling to the ground with an uppercut. Throwing the one from the bonnet to the ground alongside the other, Nate spun around to face not one, but five people in hooded capes. Sage saw Nate's feet kick, and watched with horror as she realized they were six inches off the ground. The hooded figures moved forward as a single unit, and while Nate was being held suspended in the air, one of them hit him on the back of the head. He slumped to the ground.

All of this took place in mere instants. She'd barely registered what was happening, when a hand with a rag was placed over her mouth and Sage tasted something bitter.

She tried to rip the hand away from her mouth and felt for her amulet, but of course it was gone. Sage tried to focus, to call upon the energy she'd used against the demon last week, but her head was spinning, her vision tunneling. And then the world faded to black.

———◆———

Sage blinked open eyes that were dry and gritty. She was no longer on the main street of town. There was no heavy beat of music pounding through her chest. She was in the forest, surrounded by gum trees and the whispers of voices she didn't recognize. The landscape looked somewhat familiar.

Was she in the forest behind Lucky's cabin? As she tried to get her bearings, the first thing that hit her was the stomach-turning scent of fresh blood. She tasted dirt on her tongue and gagged as something foul like rotting flesh rolled over her. The smell was thick and pungent and hung heavily in the air.

The second thing she became aware of was being surrounded by a circle of black flickering candles.

It was the blood moon and Sage was in a circle.

The wrong circle.

Panic flooded her body, and she tried to sit up, but her hands were tied behind her back, her feet tied at the ankles. It was a warm night, but where Sage was, the temperature had dropped to freezing, the chill penetrating to her bones.

Sage lifted her head. Seven hooded figures, cloaked from head to toe in black, stared back at her from outside the circle.

Seven. Was it simply a coincidence that there were exactly seven? They were speaking in low tones, but they silenced, as she recognized Lucky's voice.

"Behold, oh Dark Master," Lucky said from his position behind a lectern. "I have set at your feet the Angel of Light. Now, there is nothing standing in your way. Victory is yours. Ours."

Oh dear God!

If she died, the demon won. Sage fought against her bindings, lashing out and kicking. "Be still!" A hand slapped her face, sending her head backward. She hissed in pain as she hit the rock they'd placed under her neck. The way she'd been positioned, her skull rolled over the back of the rock, her neck offered upward as though a blade to the throat would be the method of her death.

"Oh almighty Dark Master Sytrolius," Lucky continued. "I invite you to join with us tonight, on this darkest of nights."

I can't be here.

Panic rose, threatened to consume her, and she struggled to control it. Whatever had been on the rag shoved in her mouth had affected her thoughts and sapped the strength in her muscles.

"At the conclusion of tonight's pact, the kingdom of the night will be ours," Lucky declared. Cheers rose up around her, and she cringed as someone spat on her face.

"The Dark Master is pleased." Another cheer went up.

"After the blood moon turns full, the Dark Master will bring forth his horned creatures of darkness. It is then that we will end our earthly suffering and become one with the darkness."

Black candles flickered, their flames casting an eerie glow around her. The flames had separated into two, appearing in the shape of wicked horns. She shivered and realized her shirt had been removed and a pentagram had been traced onto her naked chest in blood. On her stomach, written with something black, was the killer's signature: six, six, six, the numbers placed on top of each other and rotated by a third.

"Blood Fox, do you have an offering for the circle?" Lucky asked, summoning Dougie Roberts forward.

Sage flinched as something landed on her with a splat, her stomach roiling when she realized the black, bloodied mass was an animal of some kind, perhaps a cat, its head lolling back at an odd angle. *Where is Liquorice?* Sage choked back a sob.

Tears of frustration rolled from the corners of her eyes as Sage struggled furiously against the bindings.

What can I do?

Sage didn't have the angel amulet, the grimoire, or her seven. Where was Ethan? What had they done to Nate? She peered around in the darkness, but couldn't see him anywhere.

Sage lay in the center of the circle and squeezed her eyes shut. Around her, Lucky's minions chanted, their voices becoming clearer in their confidence. In the distance, dogs howled. A vortex of malevolent energy buffeted her bare skin, and Sage sensed the presence of the beast.

Foxes with yellow eyes appeared, prowling the circumference of the circle. No doubt waiting to gnaw on her lifeless body as soon as they got the chance. One crossed into the circle and approached her. It sniffed along her body to her face. She turned her head. Its cold, wet nose probed her neck, and she shuddered with disgust as its rough tongue dragged across her skin.

"Get away, Demon Fox," Sage hissed, meeting its eyes dead on, bracing herself for its retaliation. It growled, then continued its examination of her, and Sage felt its rough fur and teeth as it tested her flesh.

Now she knew what fur the evil teddy bear had been made from. Someone had skinned a demon fox.

The fox mouthed her calf, and she kicked at it with her bound legs. She connected with its snout, and it let out a low warning growl, baring its teeth, its fangs glistening in the moonlight.

"Be gone!" Sage demanded, attempting to summon strength, power, anything she could. But her words were just words, and the fox opened its jaws wide and latched onto her ankle. She screamed, the pain searing like fire up her leg. More than a flesh wound, the fox's bite marked her very soul.

"Silence, Sacrifice," Lucky said. "You're disrespecting the Dark Master with your sniveling. I have a little time to kill, so I'm going to enjoy you. Slowly."

Someone shoved something furry into her mouth and she gagged violently.

"Better." Lucky cleared his throat and continued to read from the ancient book he was holding. For a brief instant Sage thought he had her grimoire, but the words Lucky spoke were not from her book. They sounded like Bible passages, in reverse.

She closed her eyes, tried to block out the blinding pain from the bite on her leg, the hopelessness of her situation. Sage's hands were bound, but her fingers traced Ethan's leather band on her wrist, absorbing his strength. Where was he? Wordlessly, she cried out to him, forced the call to carry as far out into the night as she could. Prayed he could hear. Gave him strength, for wherever he was, he would likely need it. Nothing would stop him from getting to her if he were able.

Sage's eyes sprung open. Something hot and sticky was being poured across her skin.

Items were being placed around her, and something covered in feathers hit her stomach.

Lucky stepped forward, his knife glowing red in the crimson moonlight. An athame. The blade of the ceremonial knife glinted when a flash of lightning lit up the sky above them.

"It is time to have a little fun," Lucky declared. "Blood Fox, prepare the chalice so we may all enjoy sipping her blood."

"Get away from her!" Ethan's voice sliced through the air, and Sage literally sagged in relief. A surge of power replaced the sense of hopelessness she'd just been experiencing.

Ethan was here.

Somehow, his presence alone strengthened and healed something important inside her.

Standing over Sage, Lucky changed his grip on the knife, shifting it into a stabbing position. His eyes flashed a frightening scarlet, and his lips receded, showing teeth that were yellowed and rotting. His breath was vile, and with every exhale that washed over her, Sage's stomach heaved.

Lucky brought the knife down. But before he could drive it into her chest, he was lifted off the ground and thrown a surprising distance away to land at the base of a tree. She'd barely seen Ethan move. *Had* he moved? He must have, because she heard the sickening crunch of bones, and Dougie dropped the empty chalice and fell to the ground. With rapid-fire movements that were not entirely human, Ethan plowed through the hooded figures, systematically felling each one.

The fiery storm in the sky above her stopped swirling and the clouds jerked erratically, as though violently arrested. Ethan was immediately at her side. He quickly unbound her wrists and ankles.

"You've been bitten." His voice was thick with fury as his eyes traveled the length of her body.

His large hands were firm as they checked her for broken bones, or major injury. Seemingly satisfied there was nothing life-threatening, he whipped off his jacket and then his T-shirt, using it to wipe off the blood and stomach-turning black goo they'd used to mark her body. He tossed the soiled shirt away, then assisted her to her feet, testing her steadiness.

"Angel, can you walk?"

The jarring pain from the flesh wound on her calf muscle shot up her leg, but it was muted by the sensation of being held in Ethan's arms, against his chest. It was far more than comfort; something about Ethan's energy healed her.

Not dissimilar to how she'd healed him.

"We're out of time. You've got to get to the circle, and you've got to get there now." Ethan's urgent words shocked her back to the present moment with a powerful force. A crystalline energy mixed with the blood in her veins.

"Eth, you are doing something to me. Being near you is healing me. Giving me energy." Sage rubbed the unfamiliar bare place around her neck. She'd not taken the amulet off since she was three years old. She looked around.

"Where is Nate?" she asked.

"Nate?"

"He was knocked out at the same time I was. I woke up in the circle. I don't know where he is."

Ethan tensed. "I'll find him."

As sick as it made her feel, she clutched his arm. "You're leaving?" The words stuck in her throat. Of course Ethan needed to find Nate. Perhaps he was injured and lying somewhere hurt. But the selfish part inside of her insisted that they would all be more than just hurt if they didn't get to the circle. Now.

"I'll be there when you need me."

He covered her naked body with his leather jacket, and glanced at his watch. "Hurry. Go. They're all waiting for you."

"What about you?"

Lucky was beginning to moan. "I'll meet you there. With Lucky."

"Be careful," Sage said, knowing what Lucky was capable of. Ethan had snuck up from behind and caught Lucky off guard, while he was too eager to perform the sacrifice, but Lucky could summon the darkness like she could summon the light. He had access to a dark energy, an evil black magic that would be at its strongest right now.

Ethan's lips twitched before he kissed her once. Briefly, firmly, possessively. "No, Angel," he said. "*You* be careful."

He picked up a bag and handed it to her. "You'll need this." It was then that Sage recognized that the bag he'd been carrying was *her* bag. She peeked in to find the grimoire whole and well. And something even more precious to her. "My amulet!" She threw her arms around his neck and kissed him hard. "How did you find them?"

Ignoring her question, he lifted her hair and fastened the pendant securely around her neck. "Ethan, what happened?"

He silenced her with a finger across her lips. "No time to explain, you have to go." He gave her a little shove. She'd been hesitating, she knew. Being around Ethan was making her strong. Like a charger being plugged into a power source.

Ethan was the other half of her whole.

She was flooded with determination. And confidence.

"We're going to do this, aren't we?" Sage asked, adrenaline pumping through her veins.

"Hell yes, Angel."

Sage may have been filled with renewed determination, but she also was keenly aware this was still far from over.

The moon loomed full and red in the cloudless sky. She had to hurry. She took a step and turned around. Ethan was standing next to the circle, devastation all around him, moonlight glistening off his chest. He was a breathtakingly beautiful.

He raised one brow. "Angel?"

"And you said you couldn't protect me." She watched the beginning of a smile form at the corners of his lips, then she turned and ran. She didn't stop until she reached the circle.

The right circle this time.

Chapter Twenty-Nine

Sage gulped in air, her bare feet bruised and bleeding from her race over uneven ground. She'd made it, just barely.

"It's almost midnight," Pia whispered urgently. "Good luck."

"Thank you," Sage briefly embraced her friend, and took her place within the circle.

Sage glanced around at the small group of people who were risking their lives to help her. Only five of the seven she needed. Pia, Mark, Joyce, Pat, and Mona. Even if Sage had everything required for the ritual—the grimoire, her angel, Lucky, and a complete circle of protection—because her power was untried, Sage was going into this the clear underdog. There was no way to know what would transpire over the next sixty minutes. Or what would happen if they failed. Would they all die? Or perhaps worse, live their lives knowing they'd failed and could do nothing as they watched Sytrolius spread his evil through their world.

The unconditional loyalty and support of the people who chose to risk everything to be here with her was deeply humbling.

"I want you to know that whatever happens tonight, I appreciate you being here. No matter the outcome, know that I love you all very much." Sage met each pair of expectant eyes around her. Mark, with his ever-present camera at his feet. Pia looking at her with expectation, and Joyce, Pat, and Mona, dressed in white hooded cloaks, their eyes wide with... excitement.

"Let's do this." Sage inhaled deeply and a tingling warmth spread through her body. The grimoire was solid and heavy in her hands, but also as comforting as any plush teddy from her childhood. Softly, the primitive words chanted by those with her reached her ears.

Liquorice appeared from wherever cats go when they disappear, to rub his back against her leg. Relieved to see him, she briefly touched his head, silently acknowledging his support.

The blood moon was high, the sky tinted crimson.

"It's midnight," Pia called out, and Sage's heart began to pound.

Stay calm. You've got this.

Whatever happened, Sage knew she would have tried her best.

Sage called the start of the rite, at first stumbling on the words, before her voice grew stronger, clearer.

There was a shift in the air around them, and something warped in the atmosphere. The ancient rocks were as alive as any animal she'd ever seen, crouched in waiting. They glowed and hummed a musical vibrational frequency. Even without the light of the moon, she'd have been able to see them clearly, see the set of symbols engraved into their surfaces.

The energy in the circle crackled as her confidence grew.

She raised her arms in the air, bowed her head, and called for the assistance of her guides, her angels, and her ancestral spirits to join with her power. She called for Maeve, her mother, and all the seers who had stood here before her: Nan, Ada, Mary. All to join with her. Here in the circle.

She called for the energy of Earth, then opened to its flow.

Her body tingled, cool, then warm, as the power welled up. It rose from the ground through her bare feet, up through her body, then arrowed upward and outward, a spiraling cone rising deep into the night sky. The blood flowing through the vessels of her arms seemed to sparkle, as though infused with light from a higher dimension.

With outstretched arms, Sage reached out to the moon, the stars, the universe beyond and chanted the spiritual words.

The ancient rocks glowed brightly, illuminated from within by an otherworldly source. They vibrated to the tune of an ancient song, its gentle hum at once soothing and strengthening her. The rocks began to push up out of the ground, rising solid and strong. In divine perfection, they grew to form the mouth of the portal.

The prophecy was unfolding, just the way it had been foretold. The gateway between this world and another dimension was opening.

There was a vibrational frequency in the words she spoke, and it blended with the sacred song of the rocks and the chanting of the human circle around her. Energy as old as the earth itself, perhaps older, rose from the center of the rocks, blending with the torrent that came from above until it swirled in a sparkling vortex.

Sage felt seers from other times, ancient and future, watching. All intensely interested, immensely invested in the outcome. Instead of intimidating her, their witness gave her strength.

Sage's hair escaped from its ponytail and fanned out around her, blowing onto her face and into the sky. She braced herself, widened her stance, dug her toes into the sacred sand to find a more steady purchase, and ignored the pain still radiating from the bite on her leg.

Buoyed, lifted and carried by the intensity of the energy being collectively created, Sage's confidence grew.

Then something changed.

A low, rumbling growl of displeasure came from outside the vortex, and a series of explosions rocked the air, as though someone were throwing hand grenades at the circle. The vortex flexed but shouldered the impact.

A ferocious roar of pure hatred echoed in the atmosphere.

He had arrived.

His power hit fast and hard, penetrating the vortex with a shocking bolt of malevolence. The intrusion sickened her, his stench unimaginable, and her stomach roiled. His strike burned her, his touch unclean, as though he'd reached inside the circle and blackened an area of her soul.

They were only a circle of five, not seven. Were they strong enough to keep him out? This was what he'd waited a hundred years for. And he was determined to stop her.

Right now, Sage and her incomplete group were the only thing in his way.

Hurry, Ethan!

She had to trust he would come. And bring Lucky with him.

But how much time did they have left? And how long could she hold the beast back? Sage continued speaking the words she'd memorized.

The demon within the darkness was furious. Hissing, spitting, licking at the air with flames of fire.

"The entity is pissed off," Pia said.

"Yeah well, you get that with the bigger jobs," Sage replied.

An eerie disembodied growl rose outward from the surrounding forest. Despite the bravado in her words, the sound sent a chill racing through her body.

Dark clouds rolled in, covering the scarlet moon, and casting the circle in darkness. The temperature plummeted, ice washing over her skin. The trees shivered, and Sage felt their leaves cringe and curl.

The open space above them fractured, a black, hellish chill buffeting the circle in thick, pungent waves. Sage braced herself against the impact. A sinister wind swirled around them, then danced through the circle. Sage felt the protest of the ancient rocks, the change in their vibrational frequency as they buffered the malevolent force.

He was testing his power.

Her heart hammered in her chest. How could they hold the demon back without Ethan and Nate? How could they perform a ritual that required Lucky without Lucky? Sage's eyes briefly met Pia's wide ones. "Don't stop," Pia said urgently.

Sage continued reading from the grimoire; she hadn't stopped, but her concentration had faltered.

And that was the beast's intention.

Sage tried to shut him out, to focus on the words, but leaves and dirt particles lifted and swirled in the air, whipped about and stung her cheeks, forced her eyes shut. Haunting whispers, howls, and anguished cries from times gone by filtered through, filled her ears, sent shockwaves of horror and sadness ripping through her. These lost, tormented souls called out to her, in their desperation, their sorrow, and their grief. Screaming, tortured souls trapped in his omnipotent grip.

The beast fed on their pain, their suffering.

I'll set you free.

She knew he heard her vow, for the ground trembled and shook, cracks racing across the dirt, and for a heart-stopping moment, Sage thought the earth would open in a gaping chasm and swallow her and the circle whole.

But the ground steadied as she continued to speak the passages. She was now well into the chant, and unfamiliar voices from above joined in, the eternal nature of their power conjuring an otherworldly energy from times past.

It was almost time for the banishment rite.

Where are you, Ethan? Hurry!

Sage added as much of her energy as she could to attempt to make up for the shortfall in the circle of protection. A foul gust rushed over her and blew the candles out. Sage was only marginally aware of Pia moving in, relighting the candles. Pia didn't break the rhythm of her chant, quickly rejoining her hands with the others. Pia's face was creased in concentration, and Sage knew she was using everything she had inside her to make up the deficit as well.

Something lurking in the darkness of the gum trees let out a growl, low and deep. The threat in the sound was unmistakable. The growl was rising from somewhere near the molten core of the planet, and the beast's loathing for them was tangible.

Joyce gasped, and Pat screamed. Liquorice hissed, his back arched.

Sage held her balance, but understood their reaction. It was more than a sound. The growl was a *feeling*, a wicked, ungodly sensation that turned blood to ice, freezing the physical body with pure, unadulterated terror.

"Don't listen," Pia warned the others. "Pay him no attention. Focus only on our words. On adding our energy to Sage's."

Grateful for Pia, Sage noted what was happening in a removed sense. She was conscious of an expanded awareness far outside the circle. She felt the love of the light as well as the hatred from the darkness.

It was harder to focus on the ritual now that *he* was here. She fought his pull, his squalling storm of disgust and contempt.

His strength, his power, circled her, like a predator stalking her on the periphery of her vision. He tested her, pressed his energy against the bubble of light and protection being held around her, and she felt tendrils of evil seeping through the cracks.

The circle of protection was not complete, not strong enough. The entity would soon be at full strength, the most powerful he'd been for centuries.

What would happen then?

His laughter filled the air, echoing around them. An arrogant, sinister sound of lofty disdain.

Sage felt ridiculously inept. How could they outmatch a power so monstrous, so vast?

Fighting with everything she had, Sage concentrated on drawing as much energy through her as she could. She felt the strain on her body; would it injure the baby growing inside her?

She had to trust that the light would keep her safe.

They were already into the fateful hour past midnight; how much time did they have left?

Red moonlight, the color of fresh blood, bathed the area.

There was a sudden stillness. The quiet before the storm.

An attack was imminent. Surely.

A moment passed. Two.

A shocking growl of displeasure echoed in the air around them, the vibration shaking her body, as if she were standing right in front of a powerful speaker at a rock concert.

Ethan!

She faltered in her chant, as Ethan's name fell from her lips.

She knew he was there, that he was coming, before she turned to find him marching toward her. Like a boulder released from a mountaintop, anything in his way to her would be bowled over and flattened. Lucky stumbled behind him, half-walking, half being dragged. Nate walked beside Ethan. His shirt was covered with blood, but he was alive.

Her elation was visible; the energy that flowed through her brighter, more intense.

The beast paced.

Sage fought the instinct to warn Ethan away. To order him to dump Lucky in the center of the circle and leave. This was meant to be. *They* were meant to be, and they were doing this together. She now had everything she needed.

Ethan's sharp eyes swept the area. Cool, calculated, assessing. When his gaze captured hers, a tangible current flowed between them. An even stronger energetic bond formed. Connected them, like the positive and negative charge on two magnets. The space between them crackled with awareness.

"Sytrolius," Ethan called out. "It's over."

An angry spume of fire flamed upward from a place just beyond the circle. It raged in the sky above them, swirling black and red, and roaring like thunder.

Ethan dragged Lucky, kicking and fighting, into the circle. Lucky let out a bloodcurdling scream, as though the light of the circle burned his skin, insulted him. Ethan threw a book that looked similar to her grimoire on top of him. It landed with a thud before igniting into flames, and Lucky screamed again. In mere seconds, the book of evil was nothing but fine ash.

For all of Lucky's arrogance, his dedicated allegiance to the beast, Luke Keyton was just a sacrifice. A mere pawn in a preordained plot written centuries before his birth.

Perhaps they were all pawns in this ancient battle between good and evil, light and dark?

Lucky's black, soulless eyes turned to her, and instead of feeling scared, she felt sympathy for him. Just like his murder victims, Luke Keyton too was a victim. A demon's plaything. A wounded mouse kept alive by the wicked will of a playful cat. Now that the feline had had its fun, the body of the mouse was to be discarded without a second thought. Oblivious, or perhaps rejoicing in the suffering it had caused, the cat would begin the search for its next pleasure. Its next victim. A slow death was the entertainment.

If the demon succeeded, was allowed to enter their realm, humans would be mice. Possession and depraved acts of evil, the slow death they would suffer.

If Lucky's eyes were anything to go by, whatever was once human about Luke Keyton was long gone. Lucky's body was but a crumpled bag of empty flesh. A mouse who'd lain down in exhaustion.

The part of the demon that was inside Lucky was now inside the circle. The following rite would draw his demonic energy fully into the circle where Sage, the seer's daughter, would say the words that would send the demon back to Hell for the next hundred years.

With Nate joining the circle, and Ethan by her side, Sage put everything she could into the words that flowed out of her. The rite she recited was different now, more complex, because it had to draw the beast fully into the circle. She placed her palms on the grimoire. It was humming, just like the angel pendant around her neck, their vibrations acting as powerful amplifiers to the buzzing energy around her.

Pia moved forward with the tin, the grave dirt from Lance Virgil Keyton. She spoke a separate passage, and emptied the tin into the circle.

Sage closed her eyes. Focused.

"Sytrolius," Sage called out. "I command you inside the circle."

Out of the void crawled dark shadows. For a moment she thought they were demons, but then she recognized they were animals. Demonic wolves, with intelligent, red eyes.

They came out of that other dimension and entered the here and now. They skulked around the perimeter of the circle.

Had she made a mistake? She needed Sytrolius, the master demon, and his energy fully inside the circle. What were these animals?

The sound of a gun shattered her concentration, made her jump. One of the wolves yelped, then howled with pain.

"Eureka," Joyce said. "Direct hit! Come to Mumma, devil dogs."

Nate cursed and was on her in a heartbeat, smoothly divesting her of her gun.

"I got him," Joyce protested. "I can get more."

The sound of deep voices and heavy boots approached.

"Freeze!" a voice boomed out. "Put your hands in the air where we can see them."

Sage became distantly aware of uniforms in full protective gear surrounding them. The government had moved in, triggered by the gunshot. Liquorice was no longer at her legs; she could only hope he had taken himself off somewhere safe.

With the approach of the government troops and the distraction they presented, the circle of protection the seven had been holding was compromised and the energy Sage had summoned wavered. She used every ounce of concentration she had to rebuild its intensity. To tune out the chaos around them.

In the melee, she recognized the voices of Sam and Daniel and the barks of Max. Taipan, who'd been holding back the officers, were also here. Nate's voice rose above all others. "Hold your fire! Don't *anybody* fucking shoot!"

Sage prepared herself for a fight, digging in her heels and steeling her spine. She hadn't come this far to give up now. With Nate's and Ethan's attention diverted, Sage worried about the protection around the circle. Were the wolves waiting their opportunity to drag Lucky's body outside the circle?

The government officials didn't move in; they'd all frozen in position, staring in awe at the spiral of golden energy radiating upward from the circle. The devil-wolves weaved in between them, brushing up against their boots, but they paid them no attention.

Or perhaps they couldn't see them?

It didn't matter. Sage tuned out the distraction of the wolves and the government's presence, pushing through a sudden rush of exhaustion, and focused on drawing Sytrolius into the circle. The dark energy she was summoning closer battered her body.

Suddenly a connection to Sytrolius opened, making her wince at the depraved filth of his mind. Shuddering in disgust, she fought the impulse to break the connection, to build a wall against him. Instead, she drew the demon closer, into the light of the circle. He thrashed wildly and screamed in her mind. It was like dragging a kicking, spitting, wild beast against its will.

Sage held firm. Concentrated with everything she had. Summoned even more light to help her reach upward, into the universal consciousness. Her mouth fell open and she breathed in deeply as she touched the energy of the universe itself. The energy that had existed for eons, that had given birth to stars, planets, and every atom of her own insignificant self.

Sytrolius was in the circle now. But she was protected. Something else, something divine... and *more* than her, had taken over.

Sunlight rose up through her feet, flooded her whole body, then showered down in a sparkling waterfall upon her. The Earth energy grew, expanded, enveloping her body like a cocoon.

"I am Sage of Earth," she called out, beginning the final ritual. "I now release any and all spirits entrapped by the demonic entities of the prophecy. Go toward the light. Be cleansed with the love of everything holy and pure. Go forth. Go Home in peace. As I speak these words, so may it be."

The vortex of light had grown stronger, was now a giant cone of electromagnetic energy spearing high into the atmosphere.

Dark shadows appeared, writhing and shrieking, but they were no match for the vortex. Each demon howled as it was sucked upward.

Energy thrummed through Sage's veins; her palms pulsed to an ancient rhythm.

The image of the young woman who'd come back to Cryton for her grandmother's funeral appeared in her mind. So young, so naïve. So afraid.

Of life. Of discovering who she was. Of facing what grieved her.

She'd run away from Cryton. Fled to the city. The image of that woman, scared of a noise in the darkness, could have made her cringe. She could have been embarrassed by her weakness.

With the benefit of hindsight, Sage sent that frightened, confused girl her love. She'd thought the way to find happiness, the way to be strong, was by running away from everything that made her sad. But what she'd sought had been inside her all along. If she'd only known how to look. Problems were what brought out one's inner strength. You couldn't know how strong you were unless you knew weakness.

Just as you couldn't know light unless you knew darkness.

The stars above wouldn't twinkle with their diamond brilliance without the black curtain of the night sky.

The fiery mass that was the master demon resisted the vortex's pull and remained in the circle. Sage looked into the glowing eyes of the purest form of evil ever created.

"You don't have permission to be here. You have no right to be here on Earth." Sage spoke the words loud and clear.

His rage was black fire clashing with ice in a hissing, writhing mass of menace, a pit of starving vipers reduced to feeding upon themselves.

Sage spoke the final passage from the grimoire flawlessly. She didn't become attached to the words; she mentally stepped back, watched the confrontation without judgment. Hair whipped against her face; the wind, bitter cold, lashed against her skin.

She stood strong. Held firm against the hatred that spewed at her, ignored the blackened spittle that landed on her cheeks. Screams, the torturous cries of souls trapped in another world, ravaged her ears. Feeling their pain, she wished them peace.

She understood now that to have any real power, evil needed to be invited in; it needed permission. Like poison, it needed to be ingested.

Energy could not be destroyed, only transmuted. The ritual would send the demon's energy to a time and space where it wouldn't impact the lives of those in this dimension.

Sage became bathed in moonlight. Light-headed, she wondered at the strangeness of rays that were so golden coming from a moon the color of blood. Then her mind cleared, stabilized. She felt full. Alive.

Ready.

This is it.

The commotion around her silenced.

What would this look like to an outsider?

She had no time to contemplate the answer; the white light she'd summoned slammed down through her like a lightning bolt. She braced herself against the force.

She raised her arms. The heat seared her skin, and she fought the impulse to step backward, an instinctual response, like removing a hand from a hot stove. The energy soon balanced, reviving her. Her mind sharpened, focused, until it was clear as fine crystal.

She felt as if she'd stepped from a room of light into an even brighter, even clearer light. All sense of self dropped away, and she stood and faced evil with a sense of peace.

A sense of power and confidence.

Of knowing.

The demon, with fiery wings and a fleshy face, its skin stripped away, bared its blackened and missing teeth in a gruesome smile. Its eyes glowed red, but she saw a glimpse of wariness in them. The fire in his wings dimmed slightly as though to reflect the knock to his confidence.

She'd done it.

Everything she had been working for with Pia had paid off.

A huge dark shadow slithered up and out of Lucky's crumpled body, screeching as it was propelled upward to the light. "Virgil!" The name wrenched out of Lucky with a pained cry. Something murky, infinitely darker and shaped like devil horns, followed closely on its heels. Sytrolius.

With the loss of Sytrolius, Lucky's body burst into flames.

Sage's energy flagged. "I now declare the banishment ritual closed."

Her head fell backward, her neck not strong enough to hold it up. Her heart faltered in her chest and her knees gave way. She landed heavily on the ground.

She'd succeeded.

Watching the master demon being sucked into the light meant she'd fulfilled her role as the seer's daughter, as Mary had done before her, and banished the entity.

But was it enough?

They were safe for the next hundred years. Yet *only* a hundred years. When she thought of her future family, that amount of time no longer seemed very long.

With the exorcism of Lucky and the successful completion of the banishment rite, Sytrolius could no longer possess a human body on Earth for the time being, but he would try again.

For this to be truly over—*forever*—Sytrolius needed to be destroyed.

Should I ask Ethan about the cipher? Now, while there was still time?

No. There had to be another way. Sage sensed the entity hovering on the edge of her subconscious, restless. Savage.

The waves of violence that rolled over her were a bitter reminder that everything up to this point had been temporary. The many murders, the sacrifices and the suffering, the heinous acts of depravity, all would happen again.

A hundred years from now.

And a female of Sage's bloodline would face it next.

Sage needed to keep trying. She hadn't come this far to not at least try to destroy Sytrolius. She fought her watery limbs, struggled to stand.

But her bones were too weak, and her muscles felt shredded and useless.

Three divine beings of light appeared beside her: Nan, Maeve, and Ada. Sage reached for them, but couldn't touch them. They were there, but out of reach. But she sensed their powerful love, their concern for her. A brilliant white light appeared before her eyes, and she slammed her lids shut, lest it take her.

Was she dying?

She wasn't ready to leave yet. But she couldn't summon the energy to breathe, let alone stand.

The beings of light encircled her, their clear voices chanting in an ancient language she didn't understand. Warmth spread through Sage's body, and she knew that whatever her nan, her mother, and Ada were doing was healing her. Perhaps saving her very life.

Sage put her hand on her belly; if she didn't survive tonight, her daughter died as well. Panic ripped through her, but soothing words filled her mind, spoken in Nan's voice. She was going to be all right. She had to be for the baby.

She must have passed out because when she came to, Ethan had her wrapped in his arms, tremors of concern wracking his body. "You did it, baby." Her eyes wouldn't open, but she felt him. Felt his strong hands as they soothed her skin.

"I did." Sage's voice was raw and it hurt to speak. "But it's not over. I can still feel him," Sage said, referring to Sytrolius. She didn't know how much of the sixty minutes they had left, but was painfully aware of time ticking down.

"I feel him too," Ethan whispered. "I can't let this happen again. I won't," he said.

Sage's eyes sprang open. "What should we do?" She struggled to right herself, and although she felt stronger than she had moments ago, she was still extremely weak.

"Look at you," Ethan said, his voice rough and gravelly. "This could have killed you. You're not getting anywhere near the son of a bitch again. You've done more than I was comfortable with already."

Ethan picked up her boneless body and carried her away from the circle. His face was set in steely determination.

"This ends tonight."

"What are you doing?" she cried, panic clawing its way into her throat. But she knew. He was going to go ahead with the cipher.

Without her.

"Eth!" Sage half-screamed, half-sobbed. "Wait! Let's do this together. Let's try something. There must be an alternative."

"There isn't one." Ethan growled.

"We'll think of something. There has to be another way. Let's at least try." She started crawling back to the rocks. Strong hands grabbed her waist, pulled her back.

"Do you think I can allow him to hurt one of my own again?" Ethan's eyes were wild, desperate. "I won't leave this legacy to our children, Sage."

"And I won't risk losing you either." She clawed at his hands. "LET. ME. GO!"

"*I'm* the one who can end this," Ethan reminded her fiercely, and she felt his words like a slap in the face. "Not you."

Ethan stood, and she clutched at his leg, her fingers digging into the skin of his thigh.

"Don't you dare, Ethan Blade," Sage screamed. "Don't you fucking dare!" A shadow of concern flicked over his face. She must look like a wild woman, but she was in a damn near full-blown panic attack. She'd seen his death once before in the premonition; she couldn't survive it for real.

"Your part of this is done, Angel," Ethan said softly, kneeling next to her. "It's time now for me to end this forever."

"Give us a chance to try, Eth. Both of us. Aren't we worth it?"

His eyes softened. "You are worth everything."

He glanced at his watch. "I have four minutes."

Four minutes? Four minutes to decide the fate of future generations, possibly the entire world? It was not enough. She couldn't think clearly; her body and mind were shattered from the energy that had flooded through her. She began to keen.

"Let go," Ethan said. Sage realized her fingers were digging so tightly into his thigh they must be bruising him. She eased her grip, but still held on.

"Angel," Ethan spoke in a firm, reasonable tone. "I am the alchemist's son. I have the amulet, the wand, the cipher. Everything I need. What if the next ones to do this don't? Then this cycle goes on, and on and on. And what if next time, the demon wins? I have a duty to you and our daughter to end this."

Ethan knelt and touched her belly. "If there was another way I could be sure of, I'd take it. But this is the only way to end this. For you. For us. Forever."

He touched his lips briefly to hers. "Let me go, Angel."

God help her, there was a part of her that respected what he was about to do; there was even a traitorous little part deep inside her that rejoiced over her daughter and hers being protected from this.

But Ethan. *Her Ethan...*

Something thudded against her shoulder and landed on the ground. The impact hadn't hurt, but the object had come from the darkness above them. Immediately, Sage looked up, but the sky above was clear all the way up to the dark stormy clouds that covered the full moon. She then looked down at the object that had hit her.

It was the vile teddy bear.

And inscribed in blood on its belly were these words: *She's Mine.*

Sage's eyes locked onto Ethan's.

The decision had been made.

"He doesn't get to threaten my daughter." Ethan's words were bullets. There was no more discussion.

He had made up his mind.

A lump lodged in her throat. She wanted to beg him to stop. It was happening too fast. She couldn't breathe. She wanted to *think*. There had to be another way.

You promised, Ethan.

But she couldn't live with herself if they didn't do everything they could to stop this now. But oh, dear God, the price...

Nausea boiled up inside her, and her head spun.

To save her child, she was going to lose Ethan.

Was it even possible for her to choose?

She was aware of Ethan checking his watch. "Two minutes." He took her hand. "Angel?"

Ethan waited until her eyes locked with his. "I have to do this."

Sage's vision blurred, but still she saw him turn and head toward the circle. To face the demon, man to beast.

"I know," she whispered.

She didn't try to stop him. And hated herself to the very core of her being.

The roar of the sky was deafening, the most ferocious thunder Ethan had ever heard, rolling around the atmosphere in an angry growl. The government had moved in, but like Taipan, they were holding back, watching.

A part of Ethan's attention was on their every move, but his eyes were fixed on Sage. He worried about her, especially after she'd collapsed.

He glanced longingly at Sage. The vision of her battered, but beautiful, body sucked the air from his lungs. Ethan had to trust he'd see them again, Sage and the daughter he'd never get to hold in these arms. That in a life after this, they would be reunited and could watch future generations as they grew up and flourished.

And he would know he'd done the right thing.

He was doing the right thing, wasn't he?

Wasn't he?

He'd been too young to save his mother. Powerless to save his father. He had one shot at saving the woman he loved, at saving the family he'd never know....

Whatever it took. Whatever the cost. He'd take it.

Ethan swallowed his regret at the brief amount of time he'd had with Sage. Pushed aside his desperate need to hold his baby in his arms, to feel her soft, tender cheek against his. He'd never get to smell her hair, feel it tickle his nose as he inhaled, never see her first smile, never watch her first step.

Who would teach her to say Daddy?

But most of all, he'd miss telling her just how much he loved her. Someone else telling her *Daddy loved you* would not be the same as being able to show her himself.

Perhaps when she was old enough, she'd learn what he'd done, and maybe she'd understand the depth of his love.

The time he'd shared with Sage would never be enough, yet at the same time her love was far more than he'd ever expected. Far more than he deserved.

Ethan's gaze met Nate's and he hurried over.

"Take good care of her for me, mate," Ethan said, indicating Sage. "Our daughter too."

Nate's eyes glistened, and he slapped Ethan on the back, embracing him briefly. No words needed to be spoken. Nate would follow through. Ethan watched him go to Sage.

In his grasp, the wand sent vibrations through his hand and deep into his body. Something called to him, encouraging yet impatient. In ways he didn't understand, it summoned him forward, compelled him to respond.

The pendant—his amulet and talisman—was a solid, reassuring, weight around his neck. It hummed like a generator, and the low, steady vibrations soothed and comforted him. A warmth filled and surrounded his body, and he could almost imagine its energy covering him in a protective coat. A Kevlar vest of the supernatural kind.

Ethan closed his eyes, and took a moment to focus. He slipped into the state he used for work, unemotional and detached, and prepared himself to go through with the cipher.

With the heart of a warrior, the alchemist's son will enter via the flames to the fiery pit of Hell and stab the beast through the heart with a sword of light.

To achieve this, he must have made a choice. For only love as pure and as intense as the demon's hatred can void the curse. Not for just the next hundred years, but forever. His death will test the strength of his bond to her.

His wand, the sword of light, was firmly in his grip. When he located the beast on the other side, he was more than ready to stab the wand into the son of a bitch's heart.

The cipher said he must make a choice.

There was no choice in his mind.

He had no idea what he'd find on the other side, how the fight would play out, but he had to try. How would he ever live with himself if he didn't?

"Keep her there," Ethan mouthed to Nate. "No matter what." He maintained eye contact until Nate nodded.

Sage tried to stand, but her knees gave way. Nate lowered her back to the ground, held her tight as she cried and struggled. Ethan turned away so her distress didn't distract him.

The demon's threat to his daughter had steeled his mind. What he did now was bigger than him, bigger than his love for Sage. He must act for the greater good. To secure a better future for those to come. That was, after all, what he did every day in his job. He risked his life every single day for a greater good.

It was who he was.

Ethan thought of his unborn child. His daughter. In his mind's eye, he could see her, a tiny version of her mother. A miniature Sage. He thought of her life, of the children she would have.

He wouldn't fail them.

He had the power to end this. Here and now.

It was the greatest gift he could give her. He'd ensure the world Sage and his daughter lived in was free from the evil of Sytrolius forever.

Finish this once and for all.

The fateful moment was upon him. He was about to enter a world of darkness to save his world of light.

The demon growled, shaking the ground beneath his feet. He knew what Ethan was about to do, his rage turning the air thick as syrup.

The battle was about to begin.

Ethan looked at Sage. "I love you," he mouthed.

Turning from her, he recited the Latin verses of the cipher, and the center of the circle burst into flames. Ethan took a step forward.

"Ethan! No!" Sage screamed over the fire's roar.

He looked at her one last time. Her translucent green eyes glistened with tears. To him, she shone like a diamond, glowed like an angel. He imagined miniature stars twinkling like fairy dust on the golden strands of her hair.

His confidence faltered.

Dear God, I'm not strong enough to leave her.

A ragged noise, the cry of a wounded animal rose into the night, and he realized it came from him.

If he didn't act now, he never would.

He wouldn't say goodbye. Never that. Goodbye was far too final. There had to be a life after death. He held onto that. Had to.

"Thank you," he mouthed to Sage instead. "For everything. For the gift of you."

Sage kicked and lashed at Nate, who was doing his best to hold back her sudden burst of energy. The spiraling light from the center of the flames blinked off and on like a faulty globe. The final few seconds of the hour were upon them.

He turned from Sage. Holding her vision in his mind, he recited, in Latin, the final rite as he walked into the flames, into the dark depths of Hell to confront the demon.

Man to beast. The flames licked up his clothes, seared into his flesh. The pain was excruciating at first, then it was somehow muted by the energy that streamed outward from the amulet around his neck.

He closed his eyes, blocking out Sage's screams. Didn't want to take her sorrow with him to wherever he was going. He wanted his last memory on earth to be of his angel. Happy and at peace.

He was doing the right thing. *Dear God, tell me I'm doing the right thing.*

It was too late. The fire's bloody fingers consumed his body.

Sage's face floated up and danced in his mind's eye, soothing the sting of their goodbye, and Ethan left this earth to face off against the demon.

Chapter Thirty

Screams filled the air, wild and desperate.

Hers.

Ethan had stepped into the raging fire.

"Run!" Sage screamed, but her throat was raw. Ethan turned, facing her. His eyes found hers. Joined like a key in a lock. He was calm. At peace.

He smiled at her, softly, tenderly. The flames licked at his back, but he was still, at ease, as though he'd finally found the meaning of life.

Anguish rose in her throat and choked her. The heat was so intense, it singed her skin even from this distance.

The only man she'd ever loved had given his very life for her. *For us.* Sage placed a hand on her stomach.

No! Panic and desperation surged through her.

She fought Nate hard, with everything she had.

"Let me go," she spat, hating him. Hating everything that was stopping her from getting to the man she loved.

Nate didn't reply. Just held her while she struggled.

She kicked at Nate's shin. He cursed, but didn't release his grip. Damn him for being so strong. He took her abuse, weathered her bites, her scratches and kicks, without flinching.

"Pia!" Sage screamed. "Stop him."

Pia came to stand beside Nate. "It's what he wanted," she said.

"You knew?" Of course Pia knew. But… Sage whipped her head from side to side like an animal caught in a trap.

"Sage, calm down. You'll hurt yourself," Pia said.

Hurt herself? Sage couldn't care. Ethan was dying, and no one was going to save him.

Pia knelt beside her, took her hand in a steady grip. "Ethan's love for you is divine. Pure. The only thing that could defeat an evil so powerful, so depraved, is love in its highest form. Ethan's love for you is unselfish. He loves you more than he loves life itself. Plenty of people claim to have such a love; very few actually live it."

Sage could barely speak through the huge sobs tearing through her. "Let me go."

"He did it for you. For both of you."

She knew that. But it didn't do a damn thing to lessen the pain. The sky exploded above them as flames climbed Ethan's body, his hair aglow. He didn't flinch; his back was straight, his shoulders square. His eyes shone through the dark gloom of swirling smoke, full of love and devotion.

The round metal pendant hanging from a silver chain around Ethan's neck flashed a brilliant white light in the golden flames, then the light formed into a hazy, circular glow around his body.

Was the pendant protecting him somehow? Like her angel amulet had done for her?

The smell of burning flesh hung heavy in the air, but Sage could see the crystal wand, clutched tight in Ethan's grip, shining brightly. He raised it high in the air, then lowered his arm, placing it across his chest, the crystal like a shield covering his heart.

His expression was fierce, his jaw was etched in steely determination, and his eyes glistened with undying love.

Don't cry. This is for you. This is all for you. For her. His words pressed themselves into her mind.

"No," she sobbed uncontrollably.

I won't ever stop loving you. Not now. Not ever.

She didn't want to wait to see him then. She wanted him now! In *this* life. They still had so much left to do.

You and me. With the wand, Ethan traced the eternity symbol over his heart. The figure eight. The symbol of them eternally entwined.

She keened in agony as Ethan's body was consumed in a final whoosh. A match to gasoline.

She could no longer see his face, only the form of his body as flames licked at the chest that had lulled her to sleep with the rhythmic thump of his heart.

A heart that would no longer beat.

Your face will be the last thing I see when I leave this world.

The words formed in her mind. *See you on the other side.*

She stopped fighting. The light of the flames increased one final time, blinding her. The demon howled, hissed and spat.

Then came an explosion that shook the ground.

Sage was thrown back by the blast. The noise so ear-splittingly ferocious Sage believed it could only be caused by a bomb.

The government had bombed Cryton.

Ethan had given his life, but it was still too late.

They had failed after all.

Chapter Thirty-One

Early Hours of Monday Morning

When Sage woke, she was lying with her back against a tree, one leg twisted in the wiry limbs of a bush. She winced as she pulled it free, using the trunk behind her for balance as she drew herself to standing.

Everything around her, the trees, the bushes, the ground, had been blanketed in snow. Except...

The snow wasn't cold. It didn't melt when it touched her skin. It was... ash?

Whatever it was, it was still falling from the sky.

She blinked in confusion for a minute, while her mind came into focus. She remembered the fire, the blast.

Through fresh tears, Sage struggled to her feet, her ears ringing so loudly she couldn't hear. She'd thought the government had dropped a bomb. But as she looked at the shattered rocks of the circle, she knew now that it was the portal that had exploded.

Sage could only pray that it had not been all in vain. That Ethan had managed to make it through in time to destroy Sytrolius. She had to believe he'd succeeded. That his act of pure love was stronger than the demon's hatred.

Oh, Ethan!

She brought the leather band around her wrist to her lips. Tears fell unchecked down her face.

Everything around her was still.

All around her was devastation.

Armageddon.

A child's distant cry pierced the silence.

She imagined people beginning to walk around in bewilderment. Words reached Sage's ears. Disjointed sentences.

The bodies lying on the ground began to move, groan. One of the people rising from the devastation she hoped would be Pia, along with Joyce, Pat, and Mona. Mark, too, she hoped had survived, as well as Nate, Sam, Sean, Daniel... Max. *Liquorice!* Where was he?

Then she remembered their deception. Nate and Pia had not only allowed Ethan to do what he'd done, they'd stopped her from trying to change his mind.

Anger burned fierce within her, then drained away.

She couldn't even hold onto her rage. The emptiness within her couldn't hold it.

What did it matter now? What did *anything* matter now? It was too late. Her life was reduced to merely existing without Ethan.

She placed her hand on her belly. It was still flat, but would soon be swelling with proof of their love. It was a knife to her insides that Ethan would never see their daughter come into the world. Sage pictured his face as he'd looked at her that last time.

Captured the image. Froze it in her mind like a camera's still shot.

Picture—oh God, she didn't even have any pictures of Mummy and Daddy together to show their daughter.

She'd think of Ethan every day so his image didn't fade. She'd heard it did. She wanted his to be the last face she saw when she left this world as well.

Their love would last past this world and into the next.

Would survive beyond the grave.

"See you on the other side." Her whisper carried away in the breeze, and she collapsed.

———— • ————

"Sage. Sage. Wake up."

Go away.

"Sage." The annoying voice was becoming louder. More insistent. Someone was shaking her. *Nate.*

"Go away," she repeated, out loud this time. Her voice was barely a rasp, and her throat felt as though she'd swallowed razor blades.

"Sage," Nate said, hauling her to her feet.

Out of nowhere a surge of energy gave her life. She stiffened abruptly, anger a wildfire raging within her. "How could you do that to him? How could you let him die? *I hate you!*" She lashed out at Nate, pounded him hard on the chest.

He caught her fists in his hands, and she kicked at him. He grunted and whipped her into a restraining hold. "Damn it, Sage. Blade needs you."

Her mouth dropped open. She sucked in a breath. "How can you be so cruel?" Sage demanded, the pain in her chest crippling. Her knees wobbled. "I don't know you at all, do I?"

Nate relaxed his grip. His expression was grim, but determined. "I don't have time to explain. Do what you did with Max," Nate said. "Hurry." His grip tight on her arm, he half-dragged her behind him. Her mind slowly came to grips with what Nate was asking.

"Is he... is he alive?"

Impossible. She'd seen his body burning. No one could survive that.

But Nate wouldn't lie to her. Or would he? She never would have thought he'd stand there and watch his best friend burn to death either. Regardless of what Ethan had made him promise.

She shrugged out of Nate's grip. Determined to see for herself, and not wanting Nate's assistance, she ran past him.

She drew to an abrupt stop. There, in the circle, was Ethan's body.

She gasped. For a long moment she could only stare. Her Ethan.

Gone.

Was this Nate's idea of a cruel joke?

She made herself open her eyes. She made herself look. Hope swelled, then tentatively rose within her. Strangely, Ethan didn't appear burned, only coated in the same white ash that covered the town. The pendant that hung on a silver chain around his neck was strangely uncharred. As was the crystal wand still clutched in his hand. His arm rested diagonally across his chest, positioned in such a way that the crystal covered his heart.

Nate shoved her, and she stumbled forward. "Do it!" he demanded.

Could she? Could she do what she'd done with Max? She'd been unsure how she'd done it then, even more unsure she could do it now.

But she'd try. She'd do whatever it took.

Sage rushed to the circle, the soft ash still warm beneath her feet. She lowered herself to the ground, gently picked Ethan's head up and rested it on her lap.

Droplets of moisture landed on his face, smearing the ash. Her tears. Tenderly, she used his shirt to cleanse his face. Sage lowered her head, touched her lips to his forehead, to his cool lips.

And began.

She summoned the light, the Earth energy, with everything she had. With everything she was. She spoke passages from the grimoire, along with ancient words that she'd never heard spoken before. She opened her heart, her mind. Allowed herself to be a conduit for something far greater than she could have imagined. She filled herself with sparkling, crystalline light and radiated out love, allowing it to wash over the lifeless body of the man in her arms.

Her man.

The other half of her soul.

The crystal wand, still firmly clasped in Ethan's grip, seemed to react to her words. It began to glow and pulse to phrases she didn't consciously choose and knew she wouldn't remember later.

They had won. Ethan's sacrifice, his pure love for her, had defeated the master demon. Future generations would not have to face what they had.

They had won.

But without Ethan, *she* had lost.

"You will *not* leave me, Ethan Blade," Sage said fiercely. "You hear me? You come back to me right now."

Dawn's gray light turned into day. Sage was barely aware of the crowd of onlookers that had gathered around. She gave her focus to the most important thing she'd ever done in her whole life.

But it wasn't working.

His chest rose and fell once, twice, then stopped.

I won't give up.

I will stay here forever. I will never give up.

In desperation, Sage cried out for assistance, sent her prayer far into the universe. For a long moment, nothing happened. Then a strange calm washed over her. She felt the warmth of an unseen hand as it was placed over hers.

Nan.

Sage became aware of several other beings of light surrounding her, some she recognized: Mary, Ada, and her mother. But there were others as well. Someone with Ethan's features, only older, and another man, even older still, and others even more aged. Ethan's father? His grandfather? The generations of alchemists before him?

They circled around her, reached out with open palms. A powerful energy flooded through her hands and into Ethan's limp body. The rush was intense, like a bolt of lightning, or a jolt of electricity from a defibrillator.

Ethan's lids flickered, just enough for hope to steal the breath from her lungs.

"Eth?"

Had she done it?

A gentle breeze brushed her face, and she knew it was Nan. A kiss on her cheek to say goodbye.

And Ethan opened his eyes.

"Hi, Angel."

Chapter Thirty-Two

One Week Later

Sage looked around the bare shelves of Beyond the Grave and contemplated the future.

"I'm going to miss you, Sage," Mark said, sliding his voice recorder into a pocket in his black leather case. He'd come back to the shop to get some additional footage for his show. With the media coverage he'd received since the event, the next episode of *Debunking Reality* would be a blockbuster. Covering the battle with Sytrolius had given Mark instant, worldwide fame.

Debunking Reality already had a significant following, but signing with a major network would make him a household name. He also had plans to turn his footage into a feature-length documentary that would expose the government cover-up from a hundred years ago and the potential cover-up from today. as Along with the good—being overwhelmed by excitement and interest from everyone from fans to reporters—there came the bad. The threats from unknown sources high up trying to silence him.

Mark took it all in stride. Fame was a two-sided coin, and life had given Mark a thick skin. Sage knew, however, that his thick skin and polished veneer covered a man with a soft heart and a good soul.

He stepped forward and opened his arms, enveloping her in a hug.

She hugged him back, squeezing him with everything she had. "I'm going to miss you too."

Mark's phone, on silent, was flashing brightly with incoming calls. He glanced at the display. "How many times will the South Australia Police Commissioner call before he gives up?"

Sage shook her head and smiled. "I'm happy for you." She touched his arm. "Best of luck with your show."

Mark stilled, his smile dimming slightly. "This isn't goodbye."

Pia crossed the room. "We will see each other again," she said as she embraced Sage.

Nate's eyes followed Pia as she moved about the shop. Of course Pia could know things like that, but Sage didn't ask when or how their paths would cross again. She guessed Nate was wondering the same thing.

Sage would let fate run its course; she could do with a long dose of normal after these last few weeks.

So could Ethan.

As if on cue, the man himself appeared at the base of the stairs, his eyes immediately coming to rest on hers. A shiver of awareness rippled through her. He paused a moment, leant against the wall as his gaze briefly left hers to take in the proceedings in the room. He was wearing his favorite denim jeans, teamed with a fitted T-shirt that hugged his chest. His face looked thinner, slightly drawn from his recent ordeal, but his shoulders were square as he pushed off the wall and made his way to her. His steps faltered once, an outward sign of lingering pain, but he would continue to improve. To Sage, it didn't matter how long his recovery took.

He was alive.

"I woke up and you were gone," Ethan said, crushing her against him.

"Just saying goodbye to these guys."

Ethan's hand about her shoulders was strong but gentle. Possessive.

Nate had gone to Pia, helping her carry out boxes of crystals and other supplies.

Ethan stepped forward, holding out his hand to Mark. Mark took it, and as they locked grips, Ethan pulled him in briefly, giving him a manly slap on the back.

"All the best, mate," Ethan said.

"You too, DS," Mark replied, grinning. "Always entertaining to watch someone's skepticism get blown out of the water."

Ethan made a low sound in the back of his throat. "You want to hear me say you were right, that it?"

"Nah," Mark replied, lips twitching at the corners. "Don't need to hear what I already know. And now I get to show the world. What are you lovebirds going to do next?" Mark asked, looking between Ethan and Sage.

Ethan's grip tightened on her shoulder.

"We haven't had a chance to really discuss it yet," Sage said. "We—"

"I promised to take her to Mauritius." He turned to Sage. "We can discuss our future on the beach while we drink cocktails. Plan our wedding."

"So you're having the honeymoon before the wedding?" Pia smiled.

"Sure." Ethan shrugged. "Why not?"

Warmth filled Sage as she looked up at him, her mouth going dry at the intensity of his gaze. A look that told her drinking cocktails was the last thing he had on his mind while in Mauritius. It would certainly be the last thing on hers.

"Can you at least wait until you get there before you start?" Mark said in mock disgust, slinging his black bag over his shoulder. The rest of his crew were already outside in the van.

"Thank you, Mark." Sage smiled at him. "For everything. I look forward to watching your show."

"If you ever get bored of DS, come find me," Mark said, sending a grin Ethan's way.

Ethan glared, but there was no heat in it, no jealousy. The depth of Ethan's and Sage's love for each other would never be a question. Not now. Not ever.

Following everyone outside, Sage stood on the porch and locked the shop up for the last time. She left the key in the spot she'd arranged with the movers and thought of the girl she'd been before she'd returned for Nan's funeral. How she'd wasted so much precious time denying the part of herself that made her unique. All to feel accepted by society. To fit in.

We all are born with a special gift. Each one of us. Sage knew that now, with a certainty she felt to her very soul. It was, after all, why they were there in the first place. Whether it be the simple treasure of showing unconditional love to a being—animal or human—in a time of need, or something on a grander scale that contributes to many. One is not greater than the other.

We are all important. What we do in this life is felt by others, whether we put out love or hate. We are all in this together.

Something Sage had never understood before now.

What we do matters. We *matter.*

Sage looked back at her time in Cryton, at all the heartache of her childhood, at all the trials of these last weeks, and as scary as some of it had been, she wouldn't take any of it back.

It was the storms in life that shaped you. It was the wind pressing against the tree that made it strong.

A warm tingle rose up her arm, followed by a complete sense of peace and comfort. Sage would recognize that feeling anywhere.

Nan.

Sage was instantly overwhelmed by a powerful wave of pure love from the other side. "I thought you'd gone," Sage whispered, blinking furiously.

Liquorice brushed against her leg and began to purr.

You can sense her too, Sage spoke silently.

Sage didn't want Nan to leave. She wanted to hold onto Nan, this feeling. And then she realized. *The loved ones that crossed over never really leave us. They just aren't here, the way we are here.*

"Angel?" Ethan's deep voice filtered through to her. "I'm okay," she said, wiping her tears. She glanced at Pia.

Pia's eyes were wide, her blood red lips parted. She stepped forward, touching Sage's arm. "Your grandmother came back to tell you that what you did worked," Pia whispered. "The prophecy ended with Sytrolius's destruction, and the souls he'd stolen were all saved. Every single soul has been cleansed and is now safely in the light. She's proud of you. Ethan too."

Sage's legs wobbled, and instantly Ethan was at her side. She leaned into him and he supported her weight. Pia's words stole her breath, caused silent tears to roll down her cheeks. They'd won; there was no doubt now. Sage could now relax over future generations of Blades.

And then, just like that, the feeling of Nan was gone.

Instead of feeling bereft, Sage felt buoyed. *The other side is not as far away as we think it is.*

"We'd better hurry," Sage said, smiling up at Ethan. "I can hear the ice being stirred into my cocktail in Mauritius. Actually," she said, placing a hand on her still-flat stomach, "better make mine a mocktail."

Sage picked Liquorice up and walked down the steps with the man she loved. Her nan had always said she'd been given a gift. Yes, she'd been given the power to help defeat the demon. But Sage had also been given a greater gift than that.

The gift of true love.

Ethan assisted her into the warmth of his car. With one hand absently stroking Liquorice's soft black fur, Sage looked one last time back at the shop.

Thank you Nan, Sage whispered silently. *For everything.*

There'd be a time when Sage would see her again.

But not for many years.

Sage still had a lot of life to live before they met again, beyond the grave.

THE END

ABOUT THE AUTHOR

Athena Daniels is the award-winning author of the Beyond the Grave paranormal romance series and the romantic thriller *Desperate*. In 2016, Athena was nominated for Author of the Year and Best New Author in *AusRom Today's* Reader's Choice Awards.

Her novel *The Seer's Daughter* was the solo Medalist Winner in the Suspense/ Thriller category of the 2016 New Apple Annual Book Awards for Excellence in Independent Publishing.

The Seer's Daughter was a finalist in the 2016 Readers' Favorite® International Book Awards. *The Seer's Daughter* was also nominated for 2016 Book of the Year and 2016 Cover of the Year in *AusRom Today's* Reader's Choice Awards.

The Seer's Daughter was a Top Pick at *The Romance Reviews* and was featured in *AusRom Today's* January 2016 top-twenty list of "Lust-Have Sci-Fi, Paranormal, and Fantasy Novelists."

Athena has a natural curiosity about the "more" there is in life, and holds several qualifications in metaphysics and natural therapies. She is a neuro-linguistic programming (NLP) practitioner, life coach, and feng shui specialist.

athenadaniels.com

CPSIA information can be obtained
at www.ICGtesting.com
Printed in the USA
LVHW110130210519
618553LV00001B/124/P

9 780994 402936